Singapore of a Dutch-South African father and a mother, MARY NICHOLS came to England when three and has spent most of her life in different East Anglia. She has been a radiographer, school , editor for one of the John Lewis Partnership KIMB magazines and an information services manager 10|14 pen learning company, as well as a writer. From 04 ories and articles for a variety of newspapers and nes, she turned to writing novels. Mary writes cal romance for Mills & Boon as well as family She is also the author of *The Mother of Necton*, a aphy of her grandmother, who was a midwife and in a Norfolk village between the wars.

www.marynichols.co.uk

By Mary Nichols

Escape by Moonlight

MARY NICHOLS

Allison & Busby Limited
12 Fitzroy Mews
London W1T 6DW
www.allisonandbusby.com

First published in Great Britain by Allison & Busby in 2013.
This paperback edition published by Allison & Busby in 2014.

A CIP catalogue record for this book is available from
the British Library.

10 9 8 7 6 5 4 3 2 1

ISBN 978-0-7490-1313-4

Typeset in 10.5/16 pt Sabon by
Allison & Busby Ltd.

The paper used for this Allison & Busby publication
has been produced from trees that have been legally sourced
from well-managed and credibly certified forests.

Printed and bound by
CPI Group (UK) Ltd, Croydon, CR0 4YY

This one is for Polly and Dianne

Chapter One

Elizabeth propped her bicycle against the barn door and stood a moment to watch a buzzard circling above the meadows, searching for prey. She saw it plummet to earth and then rise clutching something in its talons before it flew off towards the line of trees higher up the slopes. She loved this little farm in the foothills of the Haute Savoie, home of her maternal grandparents. To her it was a place of holidays, a place where she was free to wander about the paths and meadows, to enjoy the shade of the woods, to cycle along its narrow paths, swim in the lakes, ice-cold though they were, and come back to huge delicious meals, cooked by Grandmère. In the summer everywhere was lush and green, the meadows where Grandpère's cattle and goats grazed were dotted with wild flowers. Higher up, above the forest, the peaks of the Alps poked upwards, bare rock in summer, covered in snow in winter.

The summer would come to an end soon, though it was taking its time this year, and she would go home to make up her mind what she was going to do with her life. Would Max ask her to marry him? Would she say yes? She was not altogether sure. She loved him, but was she ready to settle down to domestic life as the wife of a regular soldier? Wouldn't she rather have her own career, do something useful, learn to live a little first? And if there was a war, what then? Max had said war was incvitable, even after Chamberlain came back from Munich waving that piece of paper which he said meant 'peace in our time'. All it did, according to Max, was give the country time to step up its armaments, build more ships, aeroplanes and tanks, and train more troops in readiness. Would there be work for her to do in that event? After all, in the last war, women had done all sorts of jobs normally done by men, and done them well too.

Scattering the farmyard chickens, she turned towards the house. It was a squat two-storey building, half brick, half timber, with a steeply pitched, overhanging roof so the snow would run off it in winter. It was surrounded by a farmyard but there were a few flowers in a patch of garden on the roadside, and pelargoniums tumbled in profusion from its window boxes. It was not large, but roomy enough for her grandparents to have brought up three children: Pierre, who lived a few kilometres to the west of Annecy and had his own small vineyard; Annelise, Elizabeth's mother; and Justine, who had been born when her mother was in her forties and was only nine years older than Elizabeth. She taught at a school in Paris.

The kitchen was the largest room and the warmest – too warm in summer because the cooking and heating of water was done on an open range. A large table, flanked by two benches, stood in the middle of it covered with a red check cloth. It was laid with cutlery and dishes taken from the dresser that filled almost the whole of one wall. Grandmère, her face red from the fire, was standing at the range stirring something in a blackened pot that smelt delicious. She was a roly-poly of a woman, dressed in a long black skirt, a yellow blouse and a big white apron. Her long grey hair was pulled back into a bun.

'Where's Papie?' Elizabeth asked. Brought up by a French mother who had brought her and her siblings to visit her parents frequently as they grew up, she was completely bilingual.

'He went into Annecy to see the butcher. The old cow is past milking and will have to be slaughtered. He said he would be back in time for dinner.' To Marie Clavier the midday meal was always dinner, the evening meal supper.

Elizabeth busied herself fetching out the big round home-made loaf, glasses and wine in a jug which she put ready on the table. 'I saw a buzzard dive for a mouse just now. It always amazes me that they can see such a tiny creature from so high up.'

Her grandmother laughed. 'What is it they say, "eyes like a hawk"?'

They heard the noisy splutter of the ancient van her grandfather used to drive into town and two minutes later he came into the kitchen, followed by his black and white mongrel. 'It's all arranged,' he said, sitting in his rocking chair by the hearth to remove his boots. He wasn't a big man, but had a wiry strength that years of working a farm single-handed had bred in him. He had thin gingery hair and an untidy beard streaked with grey. 'Alphonse Montbaun will come for the cow at the end of the week. He'll cut it up and keep it in his deep freeze for us.'

'Will you buy another?' Elizabeth asked him. She had become inured to the idea of eating cattle she had seen munching grass on the slopes. Grandpère had called her soft when, as a small girl on her first visit, she had recoiled at the idea.

'I think I'll get a couple of heifers and introduce them to Alphonse's bull.' He came to the table and sat in an armchair at its head while his wife ladled the soup into bowls. 'When are you going home, young lady?' he asked.

Elizabeth laughed. 'Do you want to be rid of me, Papie?'

'You know I don't, but the rumours are flying. The German army is gathering on the Polish border and this time it won't be like Czechoslovakia; there'll be no appeasement. You'll be safer, at home.'

'*Sacredieu!*' the old lady said, crossing herself. 'You are never suggesting we are not safe here?'

'I don't know, do I? But we haven't got an English Channel between us and the Boche.'

'We've got the Maginot Line.'

'A fat lot of good that will do against aeroplanes and bombs.'

'Albert, you are frightening me. It was bad enough last time, I don't want to go through that again.'

'Perhaps you won't have to. If they come, our armies will drive them back again. That nice young man who came to stay earlier in the summer will see to that.' The 'nice young man' was Captain Max Coburn who had come to share a few days of his leave with Elizabeth. He had charmed her grandparents with his old-fashioned manners, his smart uniform, his blue eyes, golden hair and neatly clipped moustache. It had been a glorious few days; the weather had been perfect and she had taken him all round her favourite haunts: the glittering ice-cold lakes, the little hamlets with their agile goats and the canyon at the Devil's Bridge Gorge, not to mention the breathtaking scenery with Mont Blanc crowning it all. Not until his last day had either of them mentioned war.

'It's going to come, Liz,' he had said. 'Hitler will not be satisfied with Czechoslovakia; he wants the Danzig corridor and he'll go for Poland next. Britain and France will have to honour their commitment to help. Don't stay here too long.'

'Oh, Max, you can't think the Germans will come here, surely?'

'I don't know, but I would rather you were safe at home in England.'

'And you?'

'I'll go where I'm sent.'

11

'I hope you're wrong. I couldn't bear to think of you in the middle of the fighting and Papie and Mamie put in fear of their lives. They remember the last war so vividly. Perhaps I should try and persuade them to come home with me.'

'Yes, do that. I'm sure your parents would approve.'

'Mama has tried to get them to come to Nayton many times over the years but Papie would never leave the farm. He always said he wouldn't trust anyone else to look after his livestock: cows, goats, chickens and his beloved dog. And I think he is a little in awe of Papa, though he would never admit it.'

'Surely not? Lord de Lacey is the mildest of men and he adores your mother.' Her paternal grandfather had died when she was small and her father had inherited the baronetcy and Nayton Manor, her Norfolk home.

'I know.'

Everyone in the family knew how her father had met her mother; it was a tale Papa loved to tell. Already a widower, though childless, he had been a major in the British army in the Great War and had been taken prisoner and shipped off to Germany. He had jumped from the train on the way and made his escape. Annelise, who was working in the hospital at Châlons at the time to be near Jacques, her soldier fiancé, had found him wounded, hungry and thirsty in a ditch, too weak to move. She had fetched help and he had been carried on a stretcher to the hospital where she continued to look after him until he was strong enough to return to duty. He had not forgotten her and when the war ended in

November 1918, went to see her at her home in Dransville before going back to England. By then she had a small son, Jacques, whose father had been killed in the fighting.

They had fallen in love and, defying the conventions of the aristocracy and the ill-concealed disapproval of Papa's friends, were married in March 1919. He had adopted Jacques. Nine months later Elizabeth had been born, then Amy in August 1921, and finally young Edmund in 1927.

'I hope you are wrong. I hope you are all wrong,' she had told Max. 'I can't bear the thought of people being killed and maimed. Why can't governments settle their differences without going to war?'

He had no answer to that and the following day had left to rejoin his regiment, but he left her wondering about her grandparents. Would they come to England with her? 'My Channel crossing is booked for the ninth of September,' she told them as they ate their soup. 'I don't see any need to go before that.'

'Good, then we will have you for a little longer,' her grandmother said.

'I love being here, you know that, don't you? If I could, I'd live here all the time, except that I should miss Mama and Papa.'

'Of course you would. We love to have you, but they will want you home.'

'Come with me.'

'Me?'

'Both of you. Uncle Pierre will look after the farm for you.'

'He's got his own home and the vineyard to see to,' her

grandfather put in. 'And what would I do in England? I can't even speak the language.'

'You would soon learn and I'm sure you would find something to do. There is a farm on the estate.'

'Do you think I'd want to work like a labourer on someone else's property?' He was indignant. 'I've always had my own farm, handed down to me by my father. I won't leave that.'

'It was only an idea. If there's a war . . .'

'If there's a war, we'll carry on as we did before. It can't last. In any case, who'd want to trouble us here? We've got nothing.'

Alphonse Montbaun fetched the cow on the day the German army swept into Poland. The poor beast, aware that something dreadful was about to happen to her, was not at all keen to go into the truck Alphonse had brought to convey her to the slaughterhouse and it took a great deal of coaxing, pushing and pulling to get her into it. Her lowing struck at Elizabeth's heart and she wished it didn't have to happen. The cow was not the only one to be filled with dread of the future; everyone in the village, all of France, indeed the whole world, was in turmoil. And Elizabeth received a telegram from her father. 'Come home at once,' it said.

Nayton Halt was a typical country station which served the Norfolk village of Nayton and the estate of Lord de Lacey. It had an up line and a down line, two platforms, a waiting room, a ticket office and a house for the stationmaster. On the other side of the crossing gates was a signal box and a few yards beyond that a siding which had been used in the early days of the railways to transport goods from the estate to the main line. Now it was unused and overgrown.

'Lucy, the bell!' Her father always seemed to think it necessary to remind her of her duty as if she hadn't been doing the job ever since she was big enough and strong enough to manage the levers which held the gates open or closed.

'I heard it.' Lucy, who had been weeding the flower beds alongside the platform, took off her gardening gloves, threw them down on the border and went to shut the gates against the traffic on the lane just as a gig came bowling up.

Dressed in an impeccably cut country suit of houndstooth check cloth, the young man driving it was a toff, but a very pleasant toff in Lucy's eyes. He was tall and muscular without being heavy and had the unusual combination of curly fair hair and deep brown eyes. His mouth was firm and usually smiling. Or was it only when he encountered Lucy?

'Good afternoon, Lucy,' he called as he drew the horse to a stop in front of the closed gate. 'Beautiful day.'

'Yes, sir, it is.'

'Sir?' he queried with an amused smile which made her blush to the roots of her hair. 'How long have we known each other?'

'Twelve years, I suppose, considering it is that long since Pa first came here as stationmaster.' Stationmaster was a euphemism because he was also the porter, ticket collector and general dogsbody.

'Then why the formality?'

She was flustered. She always was when he was anywhere near and especially if he was looking at her like that, as if he could see right through the plain black skirt and flowered blouse she wore, right inside her, to the muscle and bone and the warm blood coursing through her veins and growing warmer under his scrutiny. She should not have feelings for this man; he was Lord de Lacey's son and lived at the big house and she was a stationmaster's daughter who lived in a two-up two-down beside the line, with its workaday kitchen, simply furnished parlour and narrow twisting stairs to its two bedrooms, all of which she was quite sure would fit easily into the smallest room at the Manor. It wasn't that she was cowed; she was simply overcome by an intense emotion she could not control. 'Mr de Lacey,' she said. 'I am on duty.'

'So you are.' He got down from the gig and walked to the gate, putting his hand on the top so close to hers it was almost touching. The contrast between that beautifully manicured hand and the workaday one with its nails ingrained with soil was marked and Lucy hastily took hers away. 'And so am I.'

'You? What duty do you have?'

'I have to meet my sister, Amy, off the train.'

'Oh, is that all?' She was dismissive.

'All? Why, my dear, it is a very onerous task, the horse has to be groomed and harnessed to the gig . . .'

'Which, I am quite sure, you do not do yourself.'

'No,' he admitted. 'But I have to see that it is done. Then

16

I have to change out of my riding clothes into something more fitting for driving and escorting a lady, put on a tie and comb my hair and remember to bring a parasol, for the sun is warm today and Amy is bound to have forgotten hers . . .'

'As you say, very onerous,' she said, knowing he was teasing her. 'But you could have sent Mr Bennett with the motor.'

'So I could, but then I would have been denied the wondrous sight of you.'

'You should not say such things, sir.'

'Why not? You are wondrous and I enjoy our little encounters.' He looked into her face, deciding the rosy blush suited her. 'Don't you?'

'Yes, but—'

'You see? And do you not agree it is a pity they do not happen more frequently?'

'What do you mean?'

'All duty must end sometime,' he said. 'Even for you, and you must have some free time.'

'Only if there are no trains or Pa is able to manage the gates as well as everything else.'

'What do you do with yourself then?'

'I read or sew or go shopping in Swaffham or Dereham. Now and again I go to Norwich if Pa wants something we can't get anywhere else.'

'And how do you go?'

'By train, of course.'

'Of course. Silly me. But do you never go for a walk?'

'Sometimes of a Sunday after church.' She wished he would stop quizzing her; he was making her nervous. 'What do you want to know all that for?'

He smiled. 'I was just thinking that if we were to meet when you are off duty, by chance of course, whether you would drop the formality and address me by my name.'

'Mr de Lacey.'

'I was thinking more on the lines of Jack.'

'On no, I couldn't do that.'

They had been hearing the train in the distance for a minute or so, but now its approach grew louder and a moment later it drew into the station and stopped with a hiss of steam, and then they could hear her father's voice loud above the bang and clatter of doors being opened and boxes of goods being manhandled into and out of the guard's van. 'Nayton Halt! Nayton Halt!'

Jack nipped nimbly through the little gate intended for pedestrians when the main gates were shut and set off up the slope of the platform, calling as he went, 'Think about it, because I shall see you again, you know, and we will talk some more.' At least that was what she thought he said; it was difficult to be sure when the train was letting off steam and coach doors were banging. His horse was nervous too and she went over to its head to calm it and also in an effort to calm herself.

'He is arrogant and self-opinionated and he thinks of me as someone to tease,' she told the beast. 'But I do not think he means to be unkind, do you?'

Her answer was a whicker of contentment. 'Yes, I knew

you would agree with me. But if he really knew what I thought of him, he would run a mile. He has only to smile at me and I shiver all over and that is foolish, when I know perfectly well he is only amusing himself.'

She turned her head towards the platform to see Miss Amy de Lacey emerge from one of the carriages. At eighteen, a year younger than Lucy, although you'd never know it to look at her, she was self-assured, had thick reddish hair, which defied all efforts to keep it confined, and a complexion that had the glow of youth made more brilliant by good food and expensive clothes. Before many more years had passed she would be a great beauty and break a dozen hearts.

After leaving finishing school in July, she had spent the summer holiday with friends in Devon, and that morning she had been driven to Liverpool Street station by her hosts' son, where they had been met by Annie, sent to accompany her the rest of the way home. Annie had been the girls' nursemaid when they were children and still kept a proprietorial eye on Amy.

Lucy knew Annie quite well. She was only a few years older than her charges and the fount of all knowledge as far as the doings at the big house were concerned. Not that Lucy would ever have repeated any of the gossip which was told to her with a great deal of hushed whispering even when there was no one within earshot, and entreaties to swear never to tell a soul. That was how Lucy had learnt that Jack had been Lady de Lacey's son before she married his lordship and that his lordship had adopted him. 'In spite of only being a stepson, he had high hopes of being the heir,' Annie had said. 'But when Edmund was born, it put an end to them. Not that he seems to mind, he is good-natured to the point of indolence.'

'Goodness what a mouthful!'

'That's what I heard His Lordship telling Her Ladyship.'

He was kissing his half-sister's cheek and laughing with her, and then taking the portmanteau from Annie, which just went to show that he was a true gentleman, for many in his position would not even think of helping a servant. And then they were coming down the platform towards her. She left the horse and returned to the crossing because the train was drawing out and the gates would have to be opened again. There was already a brewer's dray waiting on the other side.

'Lucy, how are you?' Amy asked, as they passed each other.

'Very well, thank you, Miss de Lacey. And you?'

'Glad to be home.'

Jack put her bag in the gig, helped her and the maid into their seats and then climbed up himself and picked up the reins. He winked at Lucy as he wheeled the horse about and set off back the way he had come.

Her day unaccountably brightened by the encounter, Lucy secured the gates and went back to see to the parcels, two crates of hens, a box of herrings and a large bundle of newspapers which had been disgorged from the guard's van. The carrier with his horse and cart would soon arrive to deliver the goods about the village. And then there were the takings from the ticket office to be totted up and matched against the tickets that had been issued, the weeding to finish, the flower tubs to water and the platform to sweep; and, in between, the dinner to cook and the washing to be mangled and put on the line. None of it, except perhaps adding up the money, needed much thought and she was free to allow her mind to wander. She had a recurring daydream, a fantasy in which Jack de Lacey held her in his arms and declared his undying love for her, and explained he was still unmarried at twenty-three because he had been waiting for her to grow up. She imagined being kissed by him, being held and caressed, and then the vision faded because she was not at all sure she should allow him to go any further, even in a dream.

'Haven't you finished that yet?' her father demanded, toiling up the platform pushing a trolley loaded with Miss de Lacey's luggage which would have to be sent up to the big house on the carrier's cart. He was thin as a rake and his uniform hung on him as if it were made for someone several sizes larger, which he had been before her mother left and he had never got around to admitting he had shrunk. Nor would he ever have admitted he was a changed man in other ways. He was irritable and never found anything to smile at and he was so demanding he made Lucy's life a misery. 'You've got your head in the clouds, as usual.'

'No, Pa, I was thinking about finishing the weeding. I need to keep on top of it.'

'Well, you can do it later. There isn't another train for an hour, so you can go indoors and get my dinner now.'

She rose, picked up her basket of weeds, and made her way along the platform to the house. If she were married to Jack de Lacey, there would be no getting of dinners, and even if there were, it would be a pleasure not a chore. For him she would cook beautiful meals and they would eat off the best china and drink wine from crystal glasses. She emptied the weeds onto the compost heap, left the basket, gloves and trowel in an outhouse and went indoors to cook stew and potatoes and jam suet pudding, in an effort to please her father and give him something that would put some weight on him.

Here, in this small cottage full of reminders of her mother, the dreams stopped; here was reality, the day-to-day grind of work in a house where love had died on the day her mother disappeared, perhaps even before that. Pa said she had upped and left them, but Lucy found that hard to believe. Her mother had been sweet and gentle and loving, even in the face of Pa's unkindness towards her. She had no idea what had caused her to leave and he wouldn't say. He wouldn't talk about his wife at all and he forbade Lucy to mention her name. 'She's gone,' he had said the evening Ma was no longer in the house to put her to bed. 'An' she ain't a-comin' back. And it's no good you snivellin',' he had added, when her lip trembled and tears filled her eyes. 'We shall just hev to rub along as best we may.' Over ten years ago that had been and never a word had they heard from her ma since. Sometimes Lucy thought she would leave home and try to trace her, but she had no idea where to start. Besides, her pa would never let her go.

*　*　*

'Well, how was your holiday?' Jack asked as they bowled along the familiar lanes, past farms and cottages.

'Fine. Lazy days walking and swimming and playing tennis.'

'Did you meet anyone new?' He turned in at the gates of Nayton Manor, past the hexagonal gatehouse and up the long curving drive lined with chestnut trees.

'One or two, no one special.'

'No young men to make your heart beat faster?'

'Course not. There was only James and he thinks he's so superior, always teasing me about my hair and tweaking it with his fingers. Belinda's all right, though.'

'And how was finishing school?'

'Boring.'

'Boring? How can learning to be a lady be boring?'

'You cannot learn to be a lady. Either you are one or you are not.'

'Mama might not agree with you.'

'Mama is different.'

He made no reply to that because both knew their mother was not of aristocratic birth. She was French, her father farmed a few acres in the Haute Savoie, and she had been brought up to do her share of the work, something that real ladies never did. And yet there was no one more ladylike, more diplomatic, or more beloved, especially by her husband. The children knew the tale of how they had met and married and as far as the girls, Elizabeth and Amy, were concerned it was a true love story, but Jack, who had never known his real father, tried to expunge

23

it from his memory. His shameful birth, his feeling that he did not belong, was a chip he carried on his shoulder, though to see him and hear him, you would never know it.

'I only went to please Papa, you know.'

'So you were telling the truth when you told Lucy you were glad to be home.'

'Of course I am.' She sighed. 'In some ways, I envy her.'

'Envy her?' He ignored the stifled choking sound Annie made. 'What is there to envy?'

'I envy her her freedom. She may work if she chooses to. She is not tied by convention.'

'My dear sis, it is not a question of choosing to work, it is a matter of having to and she is just as tied to convention as you are, surely you can see that? And in the fullness of time she will be expected to marry someone of her own kind, probably chosen for her by her father . . .' He paused a moment, thinking about that and suddenly felt very sorry for poor Lucy Storey.

'So will I, though that's not to say I will.'

He laughed. 'Not ever?'

'Oh, well perhaps one day, if I meet the right man, but not before I have done something with my life.'

'Such as?'

'Earning a living, doing something worthwhile.'

'Oh dear, not home five minutes and already I can see squalls on the horizon. You know Father will never allow it. And there is no need; everything you want you can have within reason.'

'Except my independence.'

24

'What can you do, anyway?'

'I don't know yet. A doctor perhaps, or a lawyer or a politician.'

He smiled. 'Oh, Amy dear, you will make Papa throw up his hands in horror at the thought. And you aren't brainy enough in any case.'

'Thanks for that, brother dear.' She sighed, realising he was probably right. 'But if there's a war . . .'

'And that will happen, you may depend on it, but I don't see how it will affect you.'

'Of course it will. I could work then, do something useful, perhaps in Papa's railway business.'

The first Lord de Lacey had been one of the first to recognise the revolution the railways would bring about, and besides involving himself in the construction of the railways, he had built up a large herd on the home farm, whose milk was sent in churns to London in the early hours of every morning, some of it destined to be canned. All these enterprises needed labourers and supporting industries like horsemen, farriers, harness-makers, basket-makers, shops, breweries and alehouses, carriers to take produce from the farms to the station and railwaymen to run the trains. His son and then his grandson, Amy's father, had carried on where he left off. When other aristocrats were having to sell their estates because they could not afford to keep them up, nor employ the army of servants needed to run them, he had prospered.

'Like Lucy?'

'No, silly, in the offices, like you do. Or you are supposed to do; I haven't seen much evidence of it. You'd rather live the idle life of a gentleman.'

'I haven't yet found my niche.'

'You are certainly taking your time about it.'

'Oh, don't let's quarrel about it. I have enough of that from Father and Mama. And you will need all your wits about you if you mean to go toe to toe with them over your plans.'

'I shan't go toe to toe, I shall be more subtle than that. I'll get Mama on my side.'

'She won't go against Father, you know that.'

'We'll see.'

She sat forward to have her first glimpse of the house through the trees. It was a magnificent building, its brick and stone weathered by three hundred years of wind and rain, its rows of windows gleaming in the afternoon sunshine. Whenever she came home from a journey, be it short or long, she breathed in the essence of it; it was almost like meeting a lover after a long absence. It was home and she could not imagine living anywhere else. If she married, she would have to leave it and go wherever her husband chose to live and he would have to be a very special man to persuade her to that.

He drew up at the front door, which was flung open almost before the wheels had stopped turning, and Annelise de Lacey ran down the front steps to greet her younger daughter, her arms wide, ready to embrace her as she stepped down onto the gravel. It was typical of their mother to forget or ignore her position as his lordship's wife and allow her exuberance and joy to show. Not for her the stiff hauteur of the born aristocrat.

'Amy, darling, let me look at you.' She held her at arm's length. 'Why, how grown up you look. Don't you think so, Jack?' At forty-four she was still beautiful, her figure only slightly thicker than it had been twenty-odd years before. Her lustrous hair, with no hint of grey in it, was wound in a heavy coil at the back of her neck.

'Oh, yes.' He grinned mischievously. 'Quite the lady.'

Annelise put her arm about Amy's shoulders and together they went indoors, followed by Annie, leaving Jack to drive the gig round the house to the stables. 'Did you have a good journey?'

'Yes, but the trains are as smutty as ever and I feel filthy. I'll have a bath and change before I do anything.'

'Of course. Papa is out riding with Edmund but they know what time the train was due in, so they will be back soon. Peters will take your portmanteau up. What have you done about your trunk?'

'Mr Storey is sending it up from the station on the carrier's cart.'

'Good. I'll have it taken up to your room as soon as it arrives.'

The hall was big and cool and smelt of polish and roses because a huge bowl of them stood on the table beside a silver tray. Amy breathed deeply, looking round at the portraits of earlier de Laceys that lined the walls and marched up the stairs to the top, where a gallery went round the upper level and where, as a child, she had peered through to look at the guests whenever her parents had company. 'Oh, it is so good to be home.'

She ran lightly up to her room and an hour later, bathed and dressed in a gown of blue silk, went downstairs again to be greeted in the small parlour by her father and her eleven-year-old brother, Edmund, still dressed in their riding clothes. She hugged Edmund, who bore it stoically, and went forward to be kissed by her father. He was a tall, well-built man who, at fifty-six, was still a handsome man. 'Well, Amy?' he said. 'Home for good, this time.'

'Yes, Papa.' She had meant what she said when she told Jack she wanted to earn her living, but she was not going to spoil her homecoming by saying anything too soon. She would bring up the subject in her own time. 'I am just going to explore everywhere before dinner, see what's new.'

'Oh, nothing is new. Everything is just as it was when you first went away, but off you go. You'll find Patch in his stable.'

Her father knew, as everyone else in the family knew, that her first port of call when she had been away was the stable to visit her horse and the first opportunity after that, she would be off riding him. But not today; it was already late and she must not keep dinner waiting

They dined *en famille* at seven o'clock. Everything operated like clockwork, as it had always done, and the conversation was lively. Amy recounted tales of her finishing school and her holiday and reiterated her pleasure at being home. She heard about Edmund's adventures at Gresham's, the boarding school he attended, and her parents' worries about the prospect of war.

'I've sent Lizzie a wire and told her to come home,' her father said. 'I don't suppose anything will happen immediately, but I would rather she was safely back here.'

'She hasn't got herself engaged yet, then?' Amy asked. 'I gather Max went out to spend some leave with her.'

'If she has, she's keeping it pretty quiet,' Jack said.

'There's plenty of time to think about things like that,' their mother put in. 'He's a soldier, who knows what will happen if there's a war . . .'

'Oh, don't,' Amy said. 'It doesn't bear thinking about. I saw hundreds and hundreds of children on Liverpool Street station when I came through. They were all labelled like parcels with gas masks in cardboard boxes hanging round their necks. Many of them were crying. And their mothers weren't allowed past the barriers and they were crying too. It brought home to me what going to war will mean.'

'Yes, I know.' her mother said. 'Mrs Hutchins came to see me today. She has been appointed welfare officer for the evacuees coming to this area. She asked me to give one or two of them a home.'

'You never said yes?' Jack queried in surprise.

'Of course I did. Poor things, dragged from their homes to live in strange places with strange people, you can't help feeling sorry for them. We've got plenty of room, the whole of the nursery suite. I've given instructions to Mrs Baxter to have the rooms made ready. They'll be here tomorrow.'

'I do hope they're house-trained,' Jack said.

Edmund stifled a giggle. He was allowed to have his meals with the rest of the family on sufferance and was expected to be seen and not heard. But it might be fun to have a pal or two he could boss around, at least until it was time to return to Gresham's. It was a great pity he would have to go back to school. It didn't seem fair when all the fun would be here at Nayton. The prospect of war didn't frighten him.

'I wonder how long it'll be before we start losing some of the staff,' Charles said, when they retired to the drawing room, leaving the servants to clear the table of the dinner things. The room was decorated in a delicate light green and cream, with a thick Brussels carpet whose rose pattern was echoed in the curtains at the long windows. It was furnished with two or three mahogany tables, a large glass-fronted cabinet containing a collection of porcelain figurines, two green-covered sofas, several armchairs and a grand piano. There were vases of flowers in the hearth, an ormolu clock on the marble mantel, flanked by two bronze sculptures of horses, a couple of busts and several papier mâché boxes with oriental designs on them, above which hung a heavy gilded mirror. The walls were covered in pictures, some very valuable, one or two painted by Jack who had discovered a talent for art at school. It was an elegant room, but it had a comfortable lived-in feel about it.

'I suppose some of the men will go,' Annelise said. 'But I don't know about the women.'

'Women did war work in the last war,' Amy said. 'They did all sorts of jobs normally done by men, driving buses and ambulances, working in factories, nursing. I want to do something like that.'

'Good heavens, child, why?' her father exclaimed. 'You do not need to . . .'

'I may not need to, but I want to. I want to be useful. I was never born to be an ornament.'

Charles smiled. 'And a very pretty ornament you are too.'

'You won't put me off by paying me compliments,' she said.

'You are too young, not yet nineteen.'

'Men died at nineteen in the last war and no doubt they will again.'

'You are not a man, Amy.'

Jack could see an argument developing and he did not want his sister calling on him for support; it might lead to questions about what he intended to do with his own life and he was not prepared to answer them, simply because he had no answers. His mother had had two miscarriages between Amy and Edmund, both boys, and by the time Edmund had come along Jack was thirteen and had become used to being considered Lord de Lacey's heir. It was his only ambition; he needed to be recognised as a gentleman, not the grandson of a French farmer. The fact that his mother had married an English nobleman did not mitigate his shameful origins and his feeling of inferiority. It was irrational, he knew. His mother adored him and Lord de Lacey treated him as if he were truly his son, except in the matter of the inheritance. He could hardly expect anything else, but it made him feel like a rudderless ship, tossed by every wave that came along. He excused himself and left them to it.

Stopping only to put on walking shoes and a hat, he left the house and set off through the wood which surrounded the estate. It had been planted by an earlier de Lacey to give the house some privacy and protect it from the prevailing north-east wind coming straight down from the Arctic. It was a mix of oak, ash and elm and a whole copse of sweet chestnuts, not to mention the ubiquitous elder. Its heavy scent filled his nostrils and reminded him of his childhood. He had always liked the woods, the darkness of them even when the sun was shining; their dank, peaty smell; the strange rustling sounds made by small animals and the chirrup of an occasional bird. It was here he used to hide from his tutor when he first arrived in Nayton, here he would talk to himself, a lonely little boy whose mother had suddenly found a new love.

Emerging onto a lane on the far side, he saw Bert Storey walking towards him, his dog at his heels. He was on his way to the Nayton Arms for his usual evening drink.

'Good evening, Mr Storey. Lovely evening, isn't it?'

'It'll rain come morning,' was the only response he got and that without a smile.

He was a miserable so-and-so, Jack decided, not like Lucy, who always seemed cheerful, no matter what. But that didn't mean Amy was right to envy her. Nothing could be worse than poverty and having to work all the hours there were to scrape a living. He was glad he was saved the necessity. And he could give Lucy a little pleasure if he chose. Making up his mind he strode off to the station.

* * *

Lucy was just opening the gates after a coal train had passed through when she saw Jack, walking towards her, his hat set at a jaunty angle, one hand in his pocket, the other twitching a stick he had cut for himself in the woods. Instead of turning to go back to the house, she waited for him to come to her. 'Good evening, Mr de Lacey.'

'Good evening, Lucy. Still on duty?'

'I have to look after the gates.'

'Day and night?'

'So long as there are trains. Of course there aren't so many between midnight and four in the morning when the milk train goes through.'

He wondered if her father ever considered opening and closing the gates himself, but then he supposed he would consider that beneath him. 'Surely you do not stay awake all night?'

'No, we leave the gates closed to road traffic and go to bed. If anyone comes along, they can open them, but usually one of us gets up to check they have been shut again. You must have done it yourself hundreds of times.'

'So I have.' He paused, thinking of her looking from her bedroom window in her nightdress to make sure he had fastened the gates properly. Next time he would look up and catch a glimpse of her. 'How long before the next train comes through?'

She laughed. 'Mr de Lacey, you know the timetable as well as I do. It's the ten-thirty to Norwich.'

'So you have over an hour before you are needed again.'

'I can always find something to keep me busy.'

'I am sure you can, but that's not what I meant. I am at a loose end. Take a stroll with me and you can tell me all about yourself.'

'You know all about me.'

'A feeble excuse if ever I heard one.' He paused to scrutinise her face. It was a lovely face, he realised and, in spite of her blushes, a serene kind of face. There was softness there and sweetness and he knew without being told that she was not given to selfish tantrums as so many of the young ladies of his acquaintance were. 'Don't you want to walk with me?'

'It's not fitting.'

'That's not an answer. I asked you what you wanted.'

'Pa—'

'Your father has gone to the Nayton Arms, I saw him not ten minutes ago. He won't be back until they throw him out at closing time.'

'H-how do you know that?' She was taken aback that her father's habits were known to the gentry. She knew he drank too much, probably to cheer himself up, but it made him even more morose and sometimes violent if she was so unwise as to provoke him.

'It is not a secret.' He wondered whether she knew that drinking in the Nayton Arms was not Bert Storey's only leisure activity and that there was a certain little widow whose company he enjoyed before he wended his way homeward. 'Come now, a gentle stroll. The woods are lovely at this time of the evening. I could show you a badger set.'

'You could?' Her eyes lit up.

'Yes. And if we are very, very quiet we might see them come out.'

It didn't sound as if he had any ulterior motive and to be in his company even for an hour was a treat not to be missed. She might find out if her idol was all she dreamt he was or if he had feet of clay. She was half afraid to say yes, in case she was disappointed, but on the other hand, if it should lead to her dreams coming true . . . No, that was foolish. He would not marry her when he could have the pick of any number of young ladies. But why was he bothering with her? To have his wicked way with her? She was not at all sure what that meant.

'Well?' he queried, looking into her eyes and seeing her doubts mirrored there. 'I am not going to eat you.' He smiled, looking her up and down; she was slim but she curved in all the right places and he felt his loins stir at the sight. 'Though I am quite sure you would taste delicious. It is only a few steps to see a badger set. Do you think I would harm a hair of your lovely head?'

'No, of course not,' she said. 'I'll fetch a shawl.' She sprinted up the slope of the platform and disappeared into the house, emerging several minutes later in a fresh cotton dress and a pink shawl.

Chapter Two

She fell into step beside him as they walked up the lane a little way, past a handful of cottages and a farmyard and through a gate in the wall of the estate. Now they were under the great vault of the trees, full of shadows brought about by the last of the sun playing through the branches. 'I've never been in here before,' she said, almost whispering in awe.

'You mean you have never trespassed to find chestnuts to roast for Christmas? I thought all the village children did that.'

'I never dared. Pa would have flayed me alive.'

'He is very strict, is he?'

'You could say so.'

'And you are not one to take risks?'

'I think I may be taking one right now.'

He gave a low chuckle. 'With me or with him?'

She looked sharply at him. 'You may laugh, but you have no notion . . .' She stopped; she could not tell him what her life was really like, he would not understand.

'Are you very unhappy?'

'I am not unhappy at all.'

'I am glad to hear it. I should hate to think that I made anyone as lovely as you sad.'

'Oh no, you would never do that.'

'How do you know? I am sometimes not a very nice person. I am lazy and inconsiderate and I take my pleasures where I can.'

'I do not believe that. You are putting yourself down. I know you to be a gentleman.'

He sighed. Was she really as innocent as she sounded? If she was, her nature belied her looks for she was sensuous and alluring and he was finding it very difficult to hold himself in check. But he would have to, because he was not a complete cad. 'Thank you for those kind words, Miss Storey.'

'Now who is being formal? This afternoon, you called me Lucy.'

'That was before I realised you were a true lady. But if you wish me to call you by your given name, you must use mine.'

'Jack,' she mused.

'Actually, it's Jacques.' He pronounced it the French way. 'But Jack will do very well. Jack of all trades, master of none, that's me.'

'I don't believe that. I am sure you are very clever. You have a loving family and a grand home and more money than you know what to do with. That goes a long way to being master of whatever you want.'

'True,' he said, then pointed. 'Look, there's the badger set. You can see the hole under that root and all the scuff marks around it. Let's sit here very quietly and perhaps they will come out.' He took off his jacket and spread it on the ground, then dropped down to sit on it, taking her hand and pulling her down beside him. He did not release her hand, but neither did he speak.

At first she shook with nerves, wondering what he would do, but when it became apparent he did not intend to do anything but watch for the nocturnal animals, she relaxed. They sat without moving, concentrating on the entrance to the set as darkness closed in around them. It was peaceful and she was not afraid while he was there holding her hand, but in the back of her mind there was a niggle of conscience which told her she should not be here with him, should not be entertaining unattainable dreams when she ought to be at home, mending her father's socks and listening for the bell. She jumped up in alarm. 'The gates. I forgot the train.' And she was off, crashing through the undergrowth back to the lane and the station.

He sighed and rose to follow. If the badgers were anywhere near they would not put in an appearance now and his main quarry had gone. And in a strange way, he was not sorry. He would see her again and it would be something to look forward to. He would lure her back with more badgers.

He caught her up as she emerged onto the lane. The

light on the top of the gates showed clearly that they had already been shut for the train. 'Pa!' she said, so out of breath she could hardly speak. 'He's back early. Don't come any further, he mustn't see you.'

'I could explain.'

'No. No. You would only make it worse. Go, please.'

'Oh, very well.'

She didn't wait to see if he went, but ran back to the station and through the pedestrian gate just as the train rattled through without stopping. She stepped back, feeling the rush of warm air on her face as it passed, trying to think of an excuse for not being at her post. The silence after it had gone was broken by the clatter of boots on the steps of the signal box as Frank Lambert came down to see to the gates.

Frank was in his thirties and had been working at Nayton Halt even longer than Pa. He was dark-haired and swarthy, his hands ingrained with the oil he used when operating the row of levers in the box. He was rough and uneducated and unmarried, which did not surprise her; he had no idea how to treat a lady. Not like Jack de Lacey who managed to make even her feel special. Frank lived with his widowed mother and worked long hours in his lonely signal box. What he did up there when there were no trains coming, she had no idea.

'Oh, it was you did the gates,' she said breathlessly. 'I thought Pa was back.'

'It was as well for you he i'n't,' he said, pushing his uniform cap to the back of his head. 'He'd hev skinned you alive. Negligence that's what it was. If I hadn't realised the gates hadn't been opened for the train, there would have been a very nasty accident and lives could have been lost. Yar Pa would ha' bin dismissed, like as not sent to jail for manslaughter and you'd be out on yar ear . . .' He paused to look at her. She was flushed and breathless and dressed very grandly for a weekday evening, but she was afraid, he could see it in her eyes and it excited him. 'What did you think you were playing at?'

What he had said was palpably true; there could have been a very nasty incident and it would have been entirely her fault. She should never have allowed soft words and flattery to lead her astray. Her remorse was genuine, but she was not ready to admit it to this man. 'It's none of your business.'

'Oh, indeed it is when you neglect your work. And if your Pa had come home and found you gone, what was I to say?'

'But he didn't. And what you don't know, can't hurt you.'

'I can see a lot from my box, you know.'

'I don't know what you mean.' She was very glad he could not possibly have seen through the trees.

'I reckon you do. What I am wondering is if I shouldn't tell your pa when he comes back.'

She gasped. 'There's nothing to tell.'

'Oh, then you'll not mind if I mention I saw you walking nice and cosy into Nayton woods with the young gentleman from the big house. A bit above yarself, i'n't you? Men of his kind want only one thing from mawthers like you.'

'That's a nasty thing to say!'

40

'But true. You stop and think about it. And if it hen't happened already, then I'd be doin' you a favour tellin' your pa and puttin' a stop to it.'

'Don't you dare!'

'Why shouldn't I?'

'Because Pa will beat me.'

'And you'd deserve it.'

'I've done nothing to be ashamed of. Don't say anything, please Frank.'

'Verra well. But you owe me.'

'I know and I'm beholden to you. I'll bring you a nice cup of tea, shall I?'

'Is that all my silence is worth, a cup o' tea?'

'What do you want then? I've got nothing.' Which was perfectly true; her father, though he received payment for her work, gave her no wages, deeming such a thing unnecessary when she was fed and housed and clothed by him, though most of her clothes were altered garments of her mother's. She had often wondered why her mother had not taken any of them with her, but Pa had said it was because he had bought them for her and that meant they belonged to him, not her.

'Your company now and again wouldn't go amiss,' he said.

'My company? What for?'

'Oh, come on gel, you i'n't that green. You know what I mean. Walk out with me.'

'When do I have time to go out walking?'

'If you can give y'self so freely to others, you can spare

41

some for me what's known you since you were a sprog.'

'I'll have to think about it.' She did not want an argument now; she was still full of the euphoria of meeting Jack de Lacey and he was spoiling it with his nasty innuendos. It would be easy to fob him off later, by telling him her father could not spare her.

'Just you do that.' He gave her another long, hard look and went back to his box, leaving her to see to the gates and light the lamps along each platform, which should have been done as soon as dusk fell, and then she went back to the house. She would stay up for half an hour to catch up on the mending she had meant to do earlier and then go to bed. She did not want to be up when her father came home, knowing her heightened colour and guilty conscience would almost certainly tell him she had been up to something. Besides, she wanted to lay in bed and go over every word Jack had said to her and try to relive the pressure of his hand holding hers. She did not give Frank Lambert another thought.

Jack walked slowly back to the house, his mind on the problem of getting Lucy out for longer than a snatched half-hour. She had looked dainty and fresh and so uncluttered he wanted to paint her, to try and capture that look on canvas. Would she sit for her portrait? Should he ask her father and put the stamp of respectability on it? But even as the thought crossed his mind he knew Bert Storey would never agree. He would see it as an insult to his daughter, a way of buying her, and no doubt he would imply that the young gentleman's motives were far from honourable. This led Jack to the vexed question of just how honourable he was, but he shrugged off answering it. Instead he told himself it was his artistic senses which had been aroused. She was a perfect subject with her bright eyes and that gentle expression. Serenity it was. He must capture that.

He drew railway engines all the time, both for work and pleasure, and he had painted his brother and sisters and his mother, even old Jones, the head gardener, hoeing the flower beds, and there were any number of attempts at painting horses, but Lucy would be his masterpiece. He bounded up the steps to the front door, and handed his hat to the footman on duty. 'Where is everyone?'

'I believe Lord and Lady de Lacey and Miss de Lacey are in the drawing room, Mr de Lacey,' the man said. 'Master Edmund has already retired.'

He put his head round the door of the drawing room, called goodnight and shut it again before anyone could ask him where he had been, then sprinted up to his room. It was an untidy room because he did not like the servants disturbing his things and the large table under the window was scattered with papers and books. He flicked the switch of the desk lamp, sat down and cleared a space by sweeping everything onto the floor, then he pulled out his sketch pad and flicked the pages over until he came to a blank sheet and began drawing.

He had not been working more than a few minutes when he screwed it up, threw it away and began again. He made several attempts before he realised he could not do it. The face was there all right, recognisably Lucy Storey, but the expression was wooden. The slightly quizzical look of amusement in the eyes, the quiet set of the mouth, the proud neck, all of which he held in his mind's eye, would not transfer themselves to paper. Angry with himself for being so taken up with her, he left the last effort lying there and went to bed.

She was a nobody, he told himself angrily, and he would do better to think of ways of finding himself a wife who would enhance his reputation. He did not need money, his allowance was more than adequate for his needs and he was paid a salary for the little work he did at the office. What he wanted was the status of a wife from the ranks of the aristocracy, a wife on equal social terms with his half-sisters, someone to make people forget the stock from which he had sprung. The trouble was that prospective parents-in-law were all too aware what his mother had been. He had never been very sure about his real father. He shook himself. He always felt guilty when his thoughts ran along those lines because he adored his mother and he could never tell her how dissatisfied he felt.

A servant brought him tea and shaving water at eight o'clock next morning and he dressed and went down to breakfast, determined to put Lucy Storey out of his mind.

Bernard Hodgkins had been instructed by his mother to look after his siblings and not let anyone separate them and on that Saturday afternoon, the second day of September 1939, he stood in the church hall at Nayton ready to defy the world. Twelve years old he was, and big for his age, and he was not going to be bulldozed into parting with Raymond or Cissie nor, if he could help it, his cousin Martin.

It had been a strange sort of day up to now. The week before, their mother had been dashing about trying to put together the clothes and toiletries that the evacuation people seemed to think were necessary. It had meant pawning their dad's overcoat and the counterpane off Mum's bed. Everything was second-hand but it was clean and mended and put into cardboard suitcases, also second-hand. At eight o'clock they had each been handed a case, a packet of sandwiches and their gas masks and taken to the school where, along with the rest of their schoolmates, they had a label pinned onto them and were herded onto buses and then a train. It was then Cissie had started to cry and she had been crying off and on ever since; her face was all swollen, her nose snotty and her eyes red.

All round him were other children from the same school, some were crying, some simply bewildered, some playing up, running up and down shouting and generally showing off. One by one they were inspected and carried off until Bernard began to wonder if they were going to be left behind. That was all right, he told himself, because then they could go back home.

The lady who had been there to greet them all and who had told them her name was Mrs Hutchins came towards the little group accompanied by a tubby woman in a black hat with a silk rose on the front and another lady who was dressed like a film star. She smiled at Bernard. 'What is your name, young man?' She even sounded like a film star, with a lilting accent that entranced him.

'I'm Bernie Hodgkins, missus. This here's my sister, Cissie, she's five and she's going to start school next term. That's my brother, Ray. He's ten.' He pointed at them one by one. 'And Martin's our cousin. He lives next door and he's ten, same as Ray. I'm twelve. Ma said we weren't to be split up. I'm to look after the others.'

'You address Lady de Lacey as "my lady",' the fat one said severely.

'It doesn't matter, Mrs Baxter,' the lovely lady said. Then to Bernard. 'Would you like to come home with me?'

'Only if the others come too.' It was said firmly enough to brook no argument.

The lady smiled. 'Of course. All four of you.'

'My lady . . .' the fat one protested.

'We can't separate them, Mrs Baxter, and we've plenty of room. I'll ask Annie if she'll take them under her wing. I'm sure she won't mind. Come along children, out to the car.'

'Oh, thank you, thank you, my lady,' Mrs Hutchins said and then to the children, 'You don't know what lucky children you are to be taken to such a lovely home. Mind and behave yourselves at the Manor. I shall soon learn about it if you don't.'

The children picked up their cases and trailed out behind the lovely lady and the fat one, leaving Mrs Hutchins to dash off to look after someone else. The boys cheered up at once when they saw how they were going to travel to their new home. They were going in a huge car with a uniformed chauffeur. Cissie had stopped crying but continued to sniff. Mrs Baxter gave a deep sigh and fished a handkerchief from her pocket. 'Here, wipe your nose and dry your eyes. There's nothing for you to cry about.'

'I expect you are missing your mama, aren't you, Cissie?' Lady de Lacey said as they squeezed in and moved off, and when the child nodded, added, 'Is Cissie your real name or does it stand for something else?'

'It's Cecily, mi–' Bernard hesitated.

'My lady,' Mrs Baxter finished for him.

'That's a very pretty name,' Lady de Lacey said, smiling at Cissie. 'I think I shall call you Cecily.'

It was only a couple of miles to Nayton Manor and they were soon stopping in front of a huge building with countless windows and ivy growing all over it. They tumbled out onto the gravel and stared up at it. 'It's a school,' Raymond said.

'No, it's not a school,' Mrs Baxter told him. 'It is Lord and Lady de Lacey's home and yours too, for the time being.'

They went inside, staring about them in awe. It was not what Bernard had expected at all. According to everyone he had spoken to when the subject of evacuation had been brought up, country people lived in hovels surrounded by pigs and mud. He hadn't seen a pig, nor a single speck of dirt. And this palace was certainly not a hovel.

A young woman in a plain grey dress with a white collar and cuffs arrived to conduct them to their rooms.

'I'm Annie,' she said, leading the way down a corridor and up two flights of stairs. 'You use the backstairs,' she told them as they were shown two large bedrooms. 'You don't go anywhere near the front of the house unless you're sent for. And you'll eat in the servants' hall.'

It was all very bewildering and Cissie began to cry again. Annie, whose heart was as soft as her voice was stern, scooped her up and sat on one of the beds with her on her lap. 'Don't cry, sweetheart. You'll have a lovely time here. Lady de Lacey is a nice lady and your mum and dad can come and see you whenever they want.'

'Tomorrow?' Cissie asked, looking a shade more cheerful.

'I don't know about tomorrow, but soon. Your big brother can write to them and tell them you have arrived safely. You can all write. I'll find pencils and paper for you. But I expect you are hungry, so I'll take you down for something to eat first.' She put Cissie from her lap and stood up. 'Come along, all of you.'

Bernard, scoffing sausages and mash in a huge room with a big table, could not believe living in the country would be like this. My, he was going to have such a lot to tell Ma when he wrote and she'd have to come and see for herself. All the same, he'd rather be at home.

After the milk train had gone through on Sunday morning a relief was sent from the railway company to undertake the duties of porter and ticket collector at Nayton Halt for the rest of the day and Lucy and her father were free to do as they wished. They were, like the servants at the Manor, encouraged to go to church, but after that, their time was their own. Bert Storey considered it his day off and would no more have thought of going to worship than growing wings and flying, but he did not stop Lucy from going, once she had done the chores. She was still expected to clean the house, cook his dinner, and sponge and press his uniform ready for Monday.

Her head still full of Jack de Lacey, she hurried through her work, put a stew in the oven to simmer gently, then changed into her best blue silk to go to church, a dress she had altered from one of her mother's. When she slipped it over her head and felt the soft material against her skin and the way the bodice nipped her waist in and the skirt draped itself over her hips, she was almost overcome with grief. Mama had been a good needlewoman and always dressed well. She could almost have been taken for a lady. In Lucy's eyes she had been one. She had been so gentle, so refined, so ready to listen to childish woes, losing her had been a blow she would never get over, made more difficult to bear because of the behaviour of her father.

He hated Lucy; it was as if he blamed her for his wife's disappearance and was determined to punish her. She was expected to work all her waking hours and she was allowed no friends of her own age. 'Heads full of nonsense,' he would say. 'Fripperies and enjoyin' theirselves is all they think of.' It was always his reply when she asked for time off or money to buy a little bit of ribbon to decorate a hat.

Today he looked her up and down and scowled. The girl

was becoming more and more like his wife and that worried him. Full of fancies, Maggie had been, too refined for her own good, teaching the child to ape her betters as well as filling her head with reading and writing and a whole load of romantic nonsense. How was he ever going to get her off his hands when she acted like she was one of those from the big house? What man who called himself a man would take her for a wife when she would show him up every time she opened her mouth? 'Where do you think you're off to looking like that?' he demanded.

'To church, Father.'

'If you think to tempt a fellow-me-lad with that finery, you're going to the wrong place. You'll not find a husband there.'

'I would not expect to, Father. I go to worship. Why don't you come too?' She knew perfectly well he would not; she was in no danger of having his company.

'I've got better things to do with my time. I'll see you at dinner.' He stomped off down the platform and up the lane towards the Nayton Arms, leaving her to perch a little pillbox hat on her hair and make her own way to church, glad the day was sunny because she only had one coat and it was old and worn and she did not want to cover her fine dress with it.

At the church gate she stepped aside to let Lord and Lady de Lacey, Amy, Jack and the evacuees pass. 'Good morning, My Lord, My Lady,' she said, but it was Jack she was most aware of. They nodded in acknowledgement and passed on towards the church porch and she fell in behind them.

Jack dropped back to speak to her. 'What did your father say?' His voice was low, almost conspiratorial.

'Nothing. He wasn't there. Frank Lambert had closed the gates for me.'

'So your father doesn't know?'

'That we went for a walk? No, he doesn't.'

'Good. I need to speak to you. There is something I want to ask you. Can you wait for me after church?'

Her heart began to pound and her breath fluttered in her throat, so that she had to swallow hard before she could answer and when she did speak it came out in a strangled squeak. 'Where?'

'In the woods by the gate we went through to see the badgers.' And then he was hurrying after the rest of his party and she followed more slowly and took her place at the back of the church.

It was as everyone gathered in the churchyard after the service that they learnt there had been no answer to the Allies' ultimatum to Germany to withdraw its troops from Poland and the country was at war. Everyone stood about discussing the implications, many remembering the Great War and all the young men who had been killed. There was a memorial in the churchyard with the names of local men on it, most of them known to the older members of the congregation.

Even the evacuees caught the sombre mood, although as far as they were concerned it was not destined to last. Bernard was anxious to explore the area and Edmund, whom he had met earlier that morning in the stable yard, had promised to show him round. The two boys were an unlikely pair, but both were self-assured in their own way, and ready for adventure.

'It can't happen again,' someone said. 'That last one was supposed to be the war to end all wars.'

'Well, that's not true now, is it?' someone else put in.

'God help us.'

The tension Lucy was feeling had nothing to do with the war, but everything to do with Jack de Lacey. She knew she was playing with fire. Frank Lambert, hateful though he was, had been right about that; men of his sort only wanted one thing from girls like her, lowly working girls with rough hands and hand-me-down finery. She ought not to go. But she knew she would.

Jack caught her up just as she reached the gate in the wall of the estate which, if she passed through it, would take her into the wood. 'Come,' he said, opening the gate and standing aside to allow her to pass. 'I will escort you home.'

'I . . .'

He smiled, sensing her hesitation. 'It is a short cut, you know, and cool in the trees.' She gave up even pretending to be reluctant and stepped from her world into his. He shut the gate behind them, then took her hand and tucked it into his arm. His hand, she noticed, was cool and firm. 'There, now we may be private.'

'Mr de Lacey!'

'Jack,' he corrected her. He turned and looked at her. She looked nothing like the girl in the railway company uniform who operated the crossing gate; she was hauntingly attractive in a dress the colour of an unclouded sky, which would not have been too commonplace for his younger sister. When he had seen her at the lychgate, all his good intentions had flown away on the wind and the words had come from him without conscious thought. 'You are looking very fetching today, Lucy. I am enchanted.'

'Thank you, kind sir.'

'So, you were not in trouble over coming out the other evening?'

'No, but if Frank had not opened the gates for the train, there could have been a dreadful accident and I feel so guilty over it. I should never have let you persuade me . . .'

'Oh, so it was my fault.'

'No, I never meant that . . .'

'You could have said no.' His voice was soft.

'I know.'

'But you didn't. You didn't say no today either.'

'I am not working today.'

He laughed suddenly. 'So it is only your sense of duty that holds you back.'

'Yes. No. Oh, you confuse me. I don't know why I went with you the other night, I don't know why I am here now, talking to you . . .'

'Oh, I am sure you do. Could it be that you like my company, just a little bit?'

She did not answer and he laughed again. 'Don't look so sorrowful about it. I enjoy your company too.'

'I must go home, I have to cook my father's dinner.'

'Oh, it's ages before the pub shuts and I want to talk to you.'

'What about?'

'I should like to paint you.'

'Paint me?'

'Yes. Paint a portrait. I can't stop thinking about the way your hair curls into your neck, the way you lift your chin, the way you stand, so proud and yet so soft, your expressive eyes. What colour are they?' He turned to take her face in his hands to study them. 'Grey sometimes, blue at others. Putting your likeness on canvas is the only way to cure my obsession.'

'Oh.' He wanted a cure, did he? He wanted to banish her from his mind. He knew, as she did in the very core of her, that what was happening between them was not real. But, oh, how she wanted it to go on. On and on and never stop. 'Is that what you wanted to ask me?'

'Yes. Will you sit for me?'

She pulled herself together. 'You are being foolish. You know it isn't possible and if Pa knew I was talking to you now, he would keep me in the house and never let me out again.'

'Why? Aren't I good enough to talk to a stationmaster's daughter?'

'You are a gentleman from the big house, rich and important, and you are only making fun of me.'

She had touched a raw nerve. Just how much of a gentleman was he? If his mother had not married Lord de Lacey, he could not claim to be anything more than she was. He had known poverty, when every penny counted, when his mother was dressed far more poorly than this girl who walked beside him now, and though it was so long ago it was only a distant memory, he didn't want to experience it again. But that was not to say he could not enjoy himself now and again with someone who made no demands on him, who looked up to him. He turned, picked up her hand and kissed the back of it. 'I am not making fun of you, Lucy, I am serious. I can draw and paint, you know, and you will make a splendid subject. If you are worried about it, I can ask your father's permission.'

'Oh no, don't do that. He will forbid it, I know he will.'

'Then we shall have to do it in secret.'

She knew her face was on fire. The touch of his lips on the back of her hand had set her pulses racing. She knew she was taking an enormous risk; she really did not know him at all and she also knew that gentlemen's sons were often not gentlemanly at all. She had heard tales from servants, and Annie in particular, that had made her insides curl up. And yet he sounded so sincere and it would be wonderful to have her portrait painted. 'How?' she asked.

'Come, I'll show you.' And he took her hand and led her deeper into the wood.

'Where are you taking me?' With her other hand she picked up her skirt in a bunch so that it would not become caught in the undergrowth. She had left home dressed neatly to go to church and, if she were honest, to impress him, but she had never expected this. She had gone mad. And so had he.

'Not far.'

They emerged into a small clearing and there before them were the ruins of a small cottage. Part of its roof had fallen in, revealing the bare timbers, its windows were broken and the door hung drunkenly on one hinge. Weeds grew up through the dirt floor and a small tree had seeded itself in the little thatch that remained on the roof.

She shuddered. 'What is it?'

'It once belonged to the gamekeeper, long before my time, but I used to play here as a child. It was my special place, somewhere to hide away from the world . . .'

'Why would you want to do that?'

'Perhaps I will tell you one day. Here is where I would like to paint you, here among the ruins.'

Her heart plummeted; to her a portrait meant sitting on a chair in a clean room with a classic column beside her or a plant on a stand, with painted blue sky behind her and perhaps a distant landscape, not among spiders and cobwebs and bats. 'It's horrible. I wouldn't want to come here alone. It gives me the shivers, as if there are ghosts . . .'

'Oh, foolish child, there are no such things as ghosts. And you won't have to come here alone. I will meet you on the edge of the wood and we'll come together. I will always be with you.' He stopped and turned towards her and smiled, lifting a tendril of hair from her cheek and tucking it behind her ear.

She tilted her head up to look at him. There was a bond between them, an invisible thread that stretched from him to her. Neither could put words to it, but each was aware of it. In him it manifested itself in a lustful desire, in her it was a great tenderness of feeling. He bent and very gently put his lips to hers, felt her start away from him and then relax.

He could take her now, here on this woodland floor in front of his playhouse, but something held him back. Maybe it was the thought that anticipation was more than half the pleasure and he wanted to make it last, maybe he was more of a gentleman than he had realised, though it hadn't stopped him enjoying other girls in the past and never giving them a second thought after the deed was done. Maybe it was too near his own doorstep and her father was of uncertain temper. Maybe it was her trusting nature. Whatever it was, he drew away. 'Now, my dear, I must see you safely on your way.'

And suddenly the spell was broken. She could have cried, though whether from disappointment or relief she could not have said. He took her hand as he led her back to the path where it forked, one way going back the way they had come, the other leading to the gate in the lane near the railway line. 'Next Sunday,' he said, as they emerged onto the lane. 'I will meet you in the same place as today and we will make a start on the picture, but do not wear that dress.'

'Why not? Don't you like it?'

'It is very fetching and suits you when you are trying to be the lady, but next week wear something plain, a blouse and skirt.' He smiled. 'Love among the ruins, where have I heard that phrase before?'

Love, he had said. She went home with a smile on her face. She did not see Frank Lambert.

* * *

Jack spent the afternoon riding round the estate on his bay mare. Nayton Manor had been his home since he was five years old and sometimes he forgot that it was not his birthright. Edmund would have it all. It wasn't Edmund's fault; it was just the way things were, and besides, his half-brother idolised him, so how could he be resentful? But he was. He might live like an aristocrat, but he could never be one. He was no grander than Lucy Storey, who at least knew where she stood. He smiled, thinking of her roundly curved body in that fetching blue dress. Next week he would paint her against the backdrop of the ruined keeper's cottage, not in that dress, but with next to nothing on and her hair wild and tangled. He would make her laugh and then perhaps she might let him kiss her and then . . . He savoured the idea of making love to her and wondered how she would react.

He emerged from the park and walked his horse along the riverbank, plodding along lost in contemplation, until he became aware of a fisherman sitting with his line in the water. He pulled up. The man was staring out across the river towards a distant mill, taking no notice of his jerking line. 'You've got a bite,' he said.

Startled, the man turned and looked up at him as if waking from a dream. 'You've got a bite,' Jack repeated, recognising the signalman, though he could not remember his name.

'So I hev.' The man jerked into life and began reeling in the fish. It was a sizeable one and Jack dismounted and watched while he landed it, took the hook from its mouth and tossed it into his keepnet.

'You've a good catch,' Jack said, looking down at the half-dozen fish that wriggled in the confines of the net. 'This must be a good spot.'

'So it is.' This said somewhat sourly.

'You work at Nayton Halt, don't you?'

'I do.'

'Good job, is it?'

'Good enough for me to take a wife. Miss Storey and me are going to be wed, so you just leave her be and stop fillin' her head with nonsense.'

Jack looked at the man with something akin to loathing. For one thing, he was unused to being addressed in that discourteous manner, and for another, he was suddenly faced with an image of Lucy in the arms of this uncouth man, and it sickened him. He could hardly believe she would have consented. But why would she not? They were on the same social level and sooner or later she would be expected to marry. 'Lucy Storey?' he queried, pretending not to understand.

'Yes. You know well enough who I mean. She's my girl, so you keep your sticky fingers off her.'

'I think, Mr Signalman, whatever your name is, you go too far. I will not be threatened. And if you wish to keep your job . . .'

Frank knew he had gone a step too far but he would not retract. 'I see you. I see you last week and I see you ag'in this morning, so I know what's going on. And you had best not threaten me either because I can take the matter to His Lordship.'

'Oh, this is ridiculous,' Jack said impatiently. 'What interest could I possibly have in Lucy Storey? She works on the railway just as you do . . .'

'Beneath you, is she? Same as me. Well, that's as maybe, but she won't be meeting you no more.'

'Do you know,' Jack said, remounting. 'I am entirely indifferent. Good day, to you.'

He rode home, furious with himself for minding so much. As long as they did the jobs they were paid for, what the lower orders did was no concern of his. They could marry and have hordes of children for all he cared. It did not matter one jot to him what Lucy Storey did with her life. But she would have made a splendid model. He pulled up so suddenly the mare reared a little and whinnied. 'Sorry, old girl,' he said and walked her on, still musing on Lucy, remembering her bright eyes and ready smile, her look of innocence which belied the invitation in her eyes, a temptation as old as time. Was he going to let that man, any man, dictate to him whom he saw?

He approached the house from the rear and stopped when he came within sight of it. The sun was shining on its myriad of windows, making them dazzle like so many mirrors against the green of the ivy which clung to its red-brick walls. He remembered when he first arrived, how overawed he had been, how miserable and unsettled, having to learn to speak English when all he wanted was to go back to Dransville and have his mother to himself again and be spoilt by his grandmother. Time had dimmed that memory and he hardly ever thought about it now, but today his sensitivity to things past had been heightened by a few words exchanged with a simple country girl and a nobody of a railway employee.

He trotted round to the stables, left the horse with a stable boy, and went into the house by a side door, through a corridor carpeted with a red Turkey runner, to the front hall, and thence up to his room to change for dinner. A servant had filled his bath and laid out his evening clothes, but before changing he went over to the table where his sketchbook had been left open. His last effort to draw Lucy looked up at him from the page. He ripped it out, screwed it in a ball and flung it into the waste-paper basket. What did it matter whether he painted her or not? It would not make one iota of difference to his future.

His mother and sister were already in the drawing room when he went down, both beautifully gowned; his mother in dark-green taffeta that enhanced the richness of her hair, while fire-headed Amy was in blue with her cream shoulders peeping above the boat-shaped neckline. They knew exactly how to behave in society, with whom it was permissible to speak and what should be avoided at all costs. They would most decidedly disapprove of dalliance with a stationmaster's daughter, especially one from Nayton Halt, and they would deprecate a slanging match with a signalman as beneath his dignity, which it was and he wished now he had never spoken to the fellow.

'Good evening, Mama.' He bent to kiss his mother's cheek. 'Amy.'

'Where have you been all afternoon?' Amy asked him.

61

'I decided to go for a ride. Have I missed anything?'

'No. I wish you'd said, I'd have come with you.'

'I didn't go far.' He was saved having to elaborate by the arrival of his father and Edmund, followed almost immediately by the butler who announced that dinner was served. They trooped into the dining room, Lord and Lady de Lacey side by side, followed by Jack, with Amy bringing up the rear with Edmund.

No one, looking at them, would guess the momentous news that had burst upon them that morning, though the conversation inevitably turned to it and what it would mean. Charles and Annelise could call on their memories of the Great War, but even they agreed this one wouldn't be like that. 'I certainly hope and pray not,' Annelise said. 'The carnage was dreadful. All those young men . . .' She stopped, remembering Jacques, to whom she had been engaged, whose legacy had been the handsome son who sat next to her. 'But it can't happen again, can it?'

'Of course not, my dear,' Charles said. 'But I hope Lizzie got my wire. I want her home.'

'So do I, but she is booked to come on the ninth in any case and I can't think anything will happen before then, if at all. Savoie is a peaceful place. It always has been.'

'Of course, my love. I was simply being cautious.'

Chapter Three

'That's it, then,' Albert said, switching off the wireless to save the accumulators. It was early evening and listeners had just been given the news that France had followed Britain's lead and declared war. 'Time you packed your bags, Lisabette.'

'I'll go on the ninth, like I said. Hitler's not going to panic me into doing anything I don't want to do. He's busy in the east, he's not going to come here in the next few days, is he?'

Albert laughed. 'No, of course not. Do you want to come into Annecy with me tomorrow? I'm going to look at some cattle. We could call on Pierre.'

'Yes, I'd like that. I can say goodbye to Uncle Pierre and Aunt Jeanne and collect some wine to take back with me.'

They set off next morning in the van which coughed and spluttered its way up and down the hills and had them in Annecy just after midday. Known to almost everyone, Grandpère was in his element in the market and spent time examining cows before deciding to bid for two heifers that took his fancy. He managed to get them at a good price, probably because some of the sellers were panicking over the war news. Having paid for them and arranged for them to be delivered, they returned to the van to drive to Pierre's vineyard just outside the town.

It was only a small independent vineyard but its grapes produced good wine and Pierre had done well for himself. Albert was justly proud of his son's achievements, as he was of Annelise who, in spite of the disgrace of having a child out of wedlock, had managed to bag herself an English lord. And there was Justine, his youngest, teaching in a school in Paris and living in her own apartment on the rue de la Pompe. He fervently hoped and prayed this war would not upset their lives too much.

Pierre, at forty-eight, was a younger version of his father, not tall but immensely strong. His wife was blond and tiny, seemingly fragile, but she had borne two boys, Henri and Philippe, now in their twenties, who helped run the vineyard. They were all there when Albert and Elizabeth arrived, sitting round the table enjoying a late lunch of soup and crusty bread. Room was made for them at the table and more bowls fetched.

'What do you think of the news, eh?' Pierre asked his father, after Elizabeth had been hugged and kissed and Albert had explained what they had been doing in Annecy.

The old man shrugged. 'What is there to think?'

'It'll be over by Christmas,' Philippe said.

'They said that last time and we had four years of it.' Albert paused before continuing. 'How's the grape coming on?'

'Not bad, not bad at all,' Pierre told him. 'We should begin harvesting next month.'

'If Hitler lets you.'

'I doubt he'll stop us. There will always be a need for good wine.'

'If the boys get called up, you'll be short-handed.'

'I could stay and help,' Elizabeth said.

'You, Lisabette, are going home at the end of the week,' her grandfather said firmly.

'Have you enjoyed your stay?' Jeanne asked her.

'Very much. I always do. Dransville is my second home. I wonder if I'll be able to come next year?'

'Let's drink to that,' Pierre said, raising his glass. 'To next year and may there be peace again.'

'To peace.' Their voices rose together.

Elizabeth, loaded with a basket containing six bottles of the best wine for her parents, said goodbye to everyone and settled in the van beside her grandfather for the journey home. They were both thoughtful and didn't talk much, and Elizabeth had no idea anything was wrong until Grandpère suddenly said he didn't feel well. He had hardly uttered the words before he slumped across the steering wheel and the little van careered all over the road.

Elizabeth tried to grab the wheel but his whole weight was resting on it and she couldn't steer. He still had his foot on the accelerator. She reached over and switched off the engine, but that made little difference on the steep downward slope. They tore down the hill while she wrestled with the steering wheel and tried to slow the van down with the handbrake. There was a bend in the road at the bottom of the hill and they failed to negotiate it. The van went over the side of the road, tumbled down the hillside and came to rest on its side against the stump of a tree.

Elizabeth, who had been knocked unconscious, came to her senses while the wheels were still turning. The bottles had broken and the smell of wine filled the little vehicle. Trying not to panic, she attempted to move. A pain shot across her shoulder and made her pause. 'Papie' she said, feeling his throat for a pulse. Thank God, he wasn't dead. 'Papie, wake up. We've got to get out.' He did not stir. She had to get help. Struggling with the pain in her shoulder and the strange upside-downness of everything, it seemed a lifetime before she could get the door open and then she saw several people scrambling down to reach them. 'It's all right, miss. We'll get you out. Don't try and move.'

'I never counted the windows before now,' Annelise said to Charles at breakfast. He was getting ready to catch the train to London and the War Office where he hoped he would be given something useful to do for the war effort. 'Do you know how many there are?'

Everyone had been ordered to black out all their windows after dark, so that not a chink of light could be seen from the air, and that caused problems at Nayton Manor. There were so many and most of them large. It would take miles of blackout material.

'I have no idea, a hundred, I should think.'

'We can't make blackout curtains for all of them, Charles. I suggest we close off part of the house and lock the doors. We don't use all the rooms, and if we lose staff it will be a job to keep them clean and heated in any case.'

'Good idea. I leave it to you.'

The post arrived while they had been talking, brought on a silver salver by a servant. Among the letters was one from Elizabeth. Annelise picked it up and slit it open.

'Oh, my goodness, Lizzie is in hospital,' she said. 'She and Pa had an accident in the van.'

'Is she badly hurt? Let me see.' Charles abandoned his own post and held out his hand for the letter but she hung onto it. 'Let me finish it first. My father had a stroke while at the wheel and the van overturned. He's in the same hospital but out of danger. Lizzie broke her left upper arm, and she has a few cuts, nothing to worry about, so she says. I ought to go out and see for myself.'

'That won't be easy,' he said. 'There are restrictions on travel now, especially to France, considering all the boats are filled with troops being sent out there. How is your mother coping?'

Annelise went on reading. 'She's staying with Pierre and Jeanne while Father is in hospital and Alphonse Montbaun is looking after the farm.' She looked up as he stood up and moved towards the door. 'Where are you going?'

'To see if I can get through to Pierre,' he called over his shoulder.

She followed him into the hall where the telephone

67

stood on a small table and watched as he picked it up and asked to be put through to Annecy. The lines were all busy and they were advised to try again later.

'Put the call through as soon as you get a free line,' he told the operator. 'And then ring me back. It's urgent.'

Three hours later the telephone rang and Annelise ran and snatched it up. A few seconds later she heard her brother's voice. 'Pierre, is that you? What happened? How is Lizzie? And Papa? Shall we come?'

She listened as he explained what had happened, that their father's stroke meant he was unable to move or speak properly, but the doctors hoped he would make at least a partial recovery. Elizabeth had her arm in plaster and a lot of cuts and bruises, but she was young and strong and there would be no lasting damage.

'She won't be coming home at the end of the week, then?' Annelise said, knowing the answer.

'No, but there's no need to panic. The war hasn't got going yet and we're safe enough here. As soon as she's discharged, we'll send her home. Don't worry.'

Annelise put the phone back on its hook and turned to Charles who had abandoned his trip to London and followed her into the hall. 'She's OK, but Pa is partially paralysed. Pierre seems to think he'll recover. I hope and pray he does. He'll hate not being able to work the farm. I wish we could persuade them to come here, at least for the duration.'

'They would be very welcome, I've told them so many times. But, you know, your father would be like a fish out of water. He wouldn't be happy.'

She sighed. 'I suppose you are right.'

'I'll ring Max. Chances are he'll be sent to France with his regiment. He might be able to get a spot of leave to go and see Lizzie.' He picked up the telephone and booked another call. But he didn't manage to speak to Max. Captain Coburn had already left for France.

Max and his company had arrived in France as part of the British Expeditionary Force and been deployed alongside the French troops who had advanced five miles into Germany with the intention of cutting off Saarbrucken and forcing the Germans to transfer troops from the Polish front to defend it. The Germans simply retreated as far as the Siegfried Line and sat tight. An assault on that formidable line of defence was considered out of the question by the French command. British troops had to content themselves with training and exercises and digging defences along the Belgian border to fill the gap between the English Channel and the most northerly point of the Maginot Line, while the quartermasters of the various regiments sent urgent messages back home for more weapons and equipment.

'How is this helping the Poles?' Lieutenant Greenford grumbled to Max, the day after Russia invaded Poland and the country was being slowly squeezed to death by two powerful armies, one from the west and one from the east. Ill-equipped and unprepared for the onslaught, they were fighting bravely, but fighting a losing battle 'We should be attacking not hanging about waiting.'

'It all takes time,' he said. 'Be patient.'

He was reading a letter from Lord de Lacey and it was taking all his attention. Lizzie had not gone home. Lizzie was hurt and in hospital in Annecy. In spite of assurances that her injuries were not serious and she would come home as soon as she was discharged, they were worried about her. His lordship did not know how Max was fixed but if he could get some leave and go and see her, it might set her mother's mind at rest.

Nothing much was happening on the front, a few patrols, a skirmish or two, but that was all. Max lost no time in applying for leave.

Elizabeth, her arm in plaster, was sitting beside her grandfather's bed. Her grandmother sat on the other side, holding his hand, talking to him, trying to get a response from him. 'Albert, can you hear me?' she was saying. 'Squeeze my hand.'

Always so active and cheerful, Grandmère was suddenly looking old and worn. It was the first time Elizabeth had thought of either of them as mortal and it shocked her. She had always taken them for granted, but seeing her grandmother bowed down with worry tugged at her heart. She ought to do more to help.

'You are going to get better, do you hear me?' the old lady said, leaning over him.

His face was all lopsided, but his right eye flickered open and then shut again. He muttered something incomprehensible.

'I can't understand what he's saying.' She appealed to Elizabeth.

'I can't either. Perhaps we should let him rest.'

'Van.' The word came out quite clearly.

'Oh, you are worried about that old van,' his wife said. 'It's been taken to the garage. I don't know if it can be mended. It's not important.' She stood up and bent over to kiss his cheek. 'Go to sleep. I'll come back again later.'

'Fancy worrying about the van,' Grandmère said, as she and Elizabeth walked down the ward. 'It was falling to bits anyway. I've been saying for ages he ought to get the brakes fixed.'

'It wouldn't have made any difference, Mamie. He would still have had his stroke.'

'I don't know what's to become of us now. Without the farm we'd starve, and I can't manage it on my own. It isn't fair to ask Pierre, he's got his own business to worry about.'

'I'll stay and help you. My arm will mend and there's nothing else wrong with me.'

'You, *ma chère*? You must go home to England.'

'There's no must about it. You need me and I'm staying.'

'But if the Germans come . . .'

'So what can they do to us? An old man, an old lady and a girl. They won't be interested in us. And if things get too uncomfortable we can always hop over the border into Switzerland.'

'You make it sound so simple. There's a mountain to climb, you know.'

'I know, but it won't come to that. Papie will get well enough to potter about and tell me what to do, and with a

71

little help from our friends in the village, we'll manage very well.'

The old lady sighed. 'I don't know what your father will say.'

'He can't say much. I'm old enough to know my own mind. If Papie gets well enough to cope without my help, then I'll think about going home.'

They emerged from the hospital and caught a bus to her uncle's vineyard and Elizabeth repeated her arguments for his benefit. He seemed relieved. 'I'll do what I can to help,' he said. 'But knowing you are with Maman will be a great weight off my mind.'

It was settled to everyone's satisfaction. Elizabeth and the old lady would stay with Pierre and Jeanne until Elizabeth's plaster was taken off and then they would take Grandpère home to Dransville and look after him there. 'He will get better all the quicker at home where he can see what's happening on the farm,' Elizabeth said. Already she was marshalling her arguments ready for a letter to her parents. And there was Max too. He had been anxious for her to return home. What would he think about her decision?

She learnt what he thought about it the very next day when he turned up unannounced. She was sitting at the table in Pierre's living room with Grandmère at her side, filling in a form to claim insurance for the van. They were hoping the money would be enough to buy another one which Elizabeth could drive.

When Jeanne ushered him in, Elizabeth jumped up and

ran into his arms. 'Max! How did you get here? Oh, it is so good to see you.'

He hugged and kissed her. 'I came by train,' he said, putting his cap on the table beside the forms. 'I went to the hospital but they said you had discharged yourself. Was that wise?'

'Why not? I'm not ill. I don't need nursing.' She sat on the sofa and pulled him down beside her. Her grandmother tactfully left the room. 'I'm just awkward while I have to wear this plaster. What are you doing here?'

'I had a letter from His Lordship.'

'Oh. And he told you to make me go home?'

'No, not at all, but he is worried about you. I bagged a bit of leave to see for myself.'

'As you see, there is nothing wrong with me that won't heal.'

'How is your grandfather?'

She gave him the latest news and told him about her decision to stay in France, a decision he strongly deprecated. 'You should have gone home a month ago,' he said. 'Then you wouldn't have been here to break your arm.'

She laughed. 'I could break it just as easily in Nayton or anywhere else and Grandpère would still have had a stroke, and if I had not been with him, it might have been fatal. My grandparents need me and I'm staying.'

'But there's a war on.'

'So there is. It makes no difference.'

'If I ask you to marry me, will that make a difference?'

'Oh, Max.' She paused to digest this. It wasn't how she

had hoped and expected he would propose. 'That sounds a bit like bribery, not a declaration of love, not romantic at all.'

'I'm sorry but I'm worried about you. I want you to be safe.'

'I will be as safe here as anywhere else.'

'So you won't marry me?'

'Not as things are. I can't believe the Germans will conquer France, but in the unlikely event that they do, I stand a better chance of remaining unnoticed as a Frenchwoman than the wife of an English officer.'

'I didn't mean I wanted to marry you here and now. Surely you would rather be married from Nayton Manor with all your friends and relations about you?'

'Yes, I would, which is why I want to wait until Grandpère recovers enough to look after the farm again and I can go home. And,' she added with heavy emphasis and a winning smile meant to disarm him, 'until the man I love tells me he loves me too and asks me properly.'

'Oh, you are impossible. What am I to tell your father?'

'Whatever you like. I have already written to tell him my decision.'

'He won't like it.'

'No, but I have a feeling Mama will approve.'

On Sunday morning, mindful of what Jack had said, Lucy dressed in a printed cotton skirt and a white blouse with a gathered neckline and small puffed sleeves, but the day was not so warm as the previous Sunday and so she added a warm shawl the colour of port wine which had been her mother's.

She pulled it up over her head as she entered the church and took her place. The organist was playing quietly while the congregation waited for Lord de Lacey and his family to arrive. She looked about her at the flowers, the polished cross on the altar, the de Lacey family banner hanging from one of the oak beams, the embroidered hassock at her feet, and a kind of peace stole over her.

Jack, coming up the aisle in the wake of his parents, saw her out of the corner of his eye and was struck by her serenity. He had decided not to keep their tryst, but now he changed his mind again. He gave her a wink which made the colour flare in her face.

The parson seemed to go on interminably, but at last the service was over and they emerged onto the church path to be greeted by the Reverend Royston with a handshake. Jack spoke to him briefly and hurried away. Lucy slipped past unnoticed and made for the door in the estate wall that led into the woods. She did not see Frank Lambert, who was standing behind one of the larger gravestones, emerge from his hiding place and follow.

There was a moment when she thought she was lost; all the paths through the wood looked the same and there was a lot of dense undergrowth, which stung her face as she pushed past it. But there it was, at last, the clearing and the ruins of the cottage, looking as though it had grown out of the earth like that, all broken and twisted. The sight of it sent shivers through her, more even than the week before because today there was no sun to cast its beams through the branches and brighten the scene.

But Jack was there before her, sitting on a fallen tree trunk, tending a small fire. His horse was tethered nearby. He rose and took both her hands in his and stood leaning back to look at her. 'My lovely girl. You came, then?'

'Yes, but I wasn't sure you would.'

'How could I stay away? I have thought of nothing else since I parted with you last week.'

'The painting?'

He laughed and his laugh crinkled up his eyes and made her want to laugh too. 'Oh, certainly the painting. Now come and sit here beside the fire.' He led her to the place where he had been sitting and watched her seat herself self-consciously. 'I want to paint you as a gypsy, watching the pot over the fire.'

'I'm not one of those.'

'I know, but we could pretend.' He smiled. 'Life is like that, isn't it? Half the time we are pretending, sometimes we even deceive ourselves. We pretend to be someone we are not, we pretend to like people we hate because it is polite to do so, we flatter people because we do not want to hurt their feelings or because we want something from them . . .'

'Is that what you are doing now?'

'No, it is not,' he said sharply. Then more softly, 'No, my dear. I am being honest with you. I will always be straight with you.'

'Why?' she demanded, disconcerting him.

'Oh, I don't know. I suppose because I know you are honest and straightforward yourself, a child of nature, at home in the woods . . .'

'No, I am not. They give me the shivers.'

'Why? There is nothing to be afraid of, no lions or wolves, just little animals like badgers and squirrels and mice, and birds. When I was little, I used to run away from my tutor and hide here. I considered the wild creatures were my friends.'

'Were you a lonely child?' She was interested enough to relax.

'I suppose I was. I didn't fit, you see.'

'What do you mean?'

'Perhaps one day I will tell you.' His mood had been slightly sombre, but now he brightened. 'Let's make a start, shall we? Do you think you could slip your blouse off one shoulder?' He reached forward to do it for her and she started back. He smiled. 'Only a little bit, nothing improper, and there is no one to see you but me and I am an artist. I am allowed a little licence.'

She took a deep breath and slipped the blouse down a little way. 'Is that enough?'

'Yes, I think so. Now let down your hair . . .'

'Oh, I couldn't do that. I'd never get it up again.'

'But whoever heard of a gypsy with a head full of pins? Go on, take it down. It is such lovely hair. I want to run my fingers through it. I want to paint it, rippling like silk over your bare shoulder. Please.' He reached up and drew out a hairpin and when she made no protest, pulled out another and then another until her hair was free. It was the colour of dark honey, much longer and thicker than he had imagined it would be; it fell around her face and shoulders like a curtain and he picked up a handful and buried his face in it. She was sat unmoving, unable to do anything. All her dreams were coming true. He must love her. She did not doubt she loved him.

He brushed the hair away from her face and kissed her. And then he paused to lean back and look at her and saw the tears glistening on her lashes and the love in her eyes and he could not do it. Smiling, he touched her cheek with his finger. 'Now, I have you in the right mood, my dear, I will begin.' And to her consternation he got up, went to his saddlebag and produced a sketch pad and crayons. 'Sit quite still.'

She did not need to be told; she had been turned to stone. She had been ready to give herself to him and he had rejected her. Was that all she was to him, a model for his painting? Why, in heaven's name did she think she was anything else? He did not speak and neither did she, not for a very long time. She could hear the birds twittering in the trees, the scratching sound his crayons made, the croak of a frog and the scampering of a small animal across the floor of the cottage behind her, even her own ragged breathing, but they were sounds from far off, all but obliterated by the crying inside her. He had been right about pretending and self-deception and she was a silly fool.

He looked up at last and smiled; it was as if nothing had happened. 'Are you getting stiff?'

'Yes, a bit.'

'Stand up and walk about. I think I've done enough for the moment. I can work on it at home.'

'Can I see it?'

'No. It is not fit to be seen yet. When it is finished, you shall be the first to see it.' He put his materials back in the saddlebag and came back to her, leading his horse. She had replaced her blouse and was busy searching the ground for her hairpins. 'I can't put it up without them,' she said.

'Then leave it down.'

'Pa will flay me when he sees it.' She found one or two, wound her hair in a thick coil and endeavoured to secure it behind her head. Then she put her shawl up to cover it. 'If I can get indoors without anyone seeing me, I can see to it.'

'I'll walk you as far as the gate.'

They set off along the path which was more clearly defined than the one she had used to find the place and she realised she had probably taken the wrong one. It seemed strange to her that in a small village where she knew every turn in the road, every building, there could be somewhere like this, a wood, and not a particularly large one, in which it would be easy to become hopelessly lost.

'Can you come again next Sunday?' he asked. 'We'll meet here and work some more on the picture.'

'If you like.'

'I do like.'

She could see the wall through the trees, the wall that divided her make-believe life from her real life. 'You needn't come any further. I can find my own way from here.'

'Very well.' He reached out and kissed her very gently. 'Goodbye for now, my gentle Lucy.'

She ran from him, struggled a few moments with the door and then next moment was on the lane and hurrying towards the station and home where she hurried up to her room to pin her hair up properly.

Frank Lambert propped his fishing rod against the wall of the Nayton Arms and went inside. The bar parlour was crowded with working men, enjoying an hour or two of leisure, while their womenfolk cooked the Sunday dinner. For some, whose employment warranted a good wage, there might be a roast, for others a mutton stew or perhaps a poached rabbit. No one in the bar parlour of the Nayton Arms that Sunday was talking about their dinner; they were all discussing what the war might mean and some of the younger men were talking of joining up and seeing something of the world.

Frank was not interested in anything like that. He would go on as he always had, looking after the signal box and doing a bit of fishing and shooting. Most of the time he went alone, being of a solitary disposition, but his widowed mother, who had given birth to him when she thought her time for child bearing had long passed, was getting old and complained frequently that she was not long for this world and if he didn't want to end up alone for the rest of his life he ought to do something about finding a wife. 'And one who's capable of looking after me when I can't get about anymore,' she had added. 'You don't want to see me in the workhouse, do you?'

He had thought about it long and hard and had come to the conclusion he could do no better than Lucy Storey. She was robust and healthy and wasn't afraid of hard work. She made his loins churn whenever she was near and he was convinced she would, given a little persuasion, come to think the same way about him. Her only fault, that he could see, was a certain independence, a flash of spirit and a light in her eye which attracted other members of the male sex beside himself, men like that bastard, Jack de Lacey. But as long as she remained faithful, he might even be proud to own a wife that other men coveted. They would soon learn he was not to be trifled with and so would she.

He found Bert sitting at a table in a corner, almost hidden from the crowd in the main part of the room, where he was enjoying a tankard of ale and the company of Molly Parsons. When Bert was with that buxom lady, he was usually affable and he could hardly deny Frank a pleasure he so patently enjoyed himself. Besides, Frank had once done him a huge favour and he could always call it in, but not in front of Molly.

'Hallo Frank, what brings you here? Nothing wrong is there?'

'No, naught wrong at all,' Frank said, wondering what Bert would say if he told him that he had seen Lucy and Jack de Lacey going arm in arm into Nayton wood for a second time in a week. But that titbit of information could keep until it served a useful purpose. 'I was goin' fishin' '

'Good luck to you, then. Want a tankard of ale afore you go?'

'I'll get it,' he said quickly and then to Molly, 'What are you drinkin' Mrs Parsons?'

'I'll have a gin and orange, Frank. And you can call me Molly.'

As she was no older than he was, married and widowed all in one year, he could see no reason why he should not, though Bert looked none too pleased. 'Right you are, Molly, a gin it shall be. And another beer for you, Bert?'

'So, if there's nothing wrong, what can I do for you Frank?' Bert asked, when the drinks had been fetched and Frank had seated himself opposite them.

'I've been thinkin' it's time I took a wife.'

Bert chuckled. 'So wha's put that notion into yar head?'

'Me ma. She says it's about time I took the plunge. She i'n't gettin' any younger and so I thought . . .' He paused and grinned. 'I was thinkin' of your Lucy.'

'My Lucy! Well, I'm blessed. What does she say about it?'

'I hen't asked her yet.'

'What are yer waiting for?'

'I wanted to ask you if you'd put the word in. I've a good job and when Ma don't need me no more, I can move on, make me way, find an assistant stationmaster's job . . .'

'You don't have to tell me that, bor, tell Lucy.' Bert slapped the younger man on the shoulder. 'But do you think you can handle her? She's not exactly biddable. And she do have some fancy ways her mother taught her.'

Frank didn't say the fancy ways were a large part of Lucy's attractions. For a man with ambition, they would be an asset. 'Oh, I don't give no mind to that,' he said. 'It mek her different from all the others.'

'Then you'd best put yar toe in the water and see how warm 'tis, don't you think?'

'Right you are.' He stood up. 'I'll call when I come back from me fishin'. You'll be home by then.'

'What's the matter with you, bor? You don' need me. Strike while the iron's hot. Go now and tell her not to expect me home for dinner. You can have my share with her.'

Frank grinned. 'Ta. I'll tek me rods home ag'in and tell Ma, then I'll go right over there.'

'She won't have him,' Molly said as Frank disappeared. 'I reckon she'll be lookin' higher than a signalman.'

'And where would she find such a one in a place like Nayton?' he asked. 'She don't know anyone else.' He grinned and put his arm about her shoulders, pulling her to him so that he could give her a smacking kiss on the cheek. 'Besides, once she's out of the house, you can move in.'

'Not without we go to the parson first, Bert Storey. I ha' got my reputation to think of.' A statement which made him roar with laughter. 'I mean it.'

'Hev you forget I've got a wife?'

'Do you know where she is?'

'No, haven't heard hide nor hair on her since she left. Might be dead for all I know.'

'She's bin gone more'n seven year, you can have her declared dead, then you'd be free.'

'Tha's a thought.'

'Why'd she leave in the first place?'

'I threw her out. She'd been out with someone else – couldn't hev that, could I?'

'That's grounds for divorce.'

'Maybe but that costs money.'

'Then let's assume she's dead. She i'n't a-goin' to come back and contradict you, is she?'

He laughed again. 'No. So, it's the parson as soon as Lucy's matched.'

'I still say she'll kick against it.'

'She can kick all she likes, I can kick harder.' He stood up and pulled her to her feet. 'And seeings I'm not expected back for me dinner, we've the whole day to ourselves, so come on, let's be off enjoying ourselves.'

Lucy was stirring the stew when she heard footsteps approaching the door. Thinking it was her father, she stuck a fork in the potatoes to see if they were cooked and turned towards the table to check that everything was ready. He hated to be kept waiting, even a minute, and had been known to tip a saucepan full of hot food all over her, if he was drunk, which he was more often than not on a Sunday.

She was taken by surprise when, instead of the door being flung open, someone rapped on it. Wiping her hands on her pinafore, she went to open it. 'Frank, what are you doing here?'

'I've a message from yer pa. He said not to expect him home for his dinner.'

'Thank you for telling me. Did he say why?'

'No. But he did say I was to stay and partake with you.'

This was so out of character that she simply stared at him. It wasn't that Pa was not coming home for his dinner, but that he was giving it away. It would have been more like him to send a message that she was to keep it hot, as had happened on more than one occasion before.

'Well, aren't you going to ask me in?' he demanded, removing his cap. 'I can't verra well eat it on the step, can I?'

She stood aside to admit him. He was newly shaved, she noticed, and had slicked his hair back with oil. 'Why did he say that? What happened? Where is he?'

He grinned and stepped inside. 'Oh, he's got other fish to fry, m'dear, so he give me permission to call on you . . .'

'What do you mean?' She indicated a chair at the table, but made no move to dish up the food.

'Why, to come courtin'.' He was grinning more than ever now.

'Me?' She laughed. 'You must have misunderstood. He'd never say that.'

'Why not? I'n't I good enough for you?'

'No, that wasn't what I meant,' she said hastily. 'He would never let me go. He needs me.'

'Not anymore he don't. He's got pretty widow Parsons in his arms this verra minute an' she's expectin' to move in here right soon.'

She could hardly credit what he was saying. Pa with another woman? 'I don't believe that – he'd have said.'

'I don't like being called a liar, Lucy Storey.'

'I wasn't calling you a liar, Frank, I just thought you must be mistaken, that's all.'

'There's no mistake, everyone in the village knows about it – bin goin' on for years, it hev.'

'Years?' she queried.

'A man needs his comforts.' He looked sideways at her, knowing he had shocked her into silence. 'Hen't I just come from takin' a drink with them in the Nayton Arms. Gave us his blessing, your Pa did, told me to come right away and sample your cooking.'

'Then you better had,' she snapped, her mind in a whirl. She wasn't sure which was worse, the revelation about Pa and Mrs Parsons or the thought of marrying Frank Lambert. Pa couldn't force her, but he could make her life a misery if she refused. Oh, how she longed to run to Jack, but she knew she could not do that. She dished up two plates of food and slapped them down on the table, before sitting down opposite him. He began to wolf his down, but she had no appetite and sat looking at the food growing cold on her plate and said nothing, waiting for him to finish.

'My, that was good,' he said, sitting back and smiling at her. 'A good cook as well as a beauty, I'm a lucky man.'

'You take too much for granted, Frank Lambert. Pa giving you permission to eat his dinner don't mean I'm yours for the asking.'

'No, s'pose not,' he admitted. 'You want me to court you proper. Well, I can do that. Get those dishes washed and we'll go for a walk.'

'I don't want to go for a walk. I'm tired.'

'Not too tired to skulk in the woods with that bastard, Jack de Lacey, are you? I'm as good as he is, any day of the week.'

'You're . . .' She had been going to say 'not fit to lick his boots' but realised that would be foolish. Instead she added, '. . . mistaken.'

'I saw you, with my own eyes, dressed fit to kill. How long afore he had that off you, eh? How long afore you were lying on yer back lookin' up at the trees.' He had been tormenting himself with visions of her naked, squirming under the fellow from the big house, and far from putting him off it had excited him to such a pitch he could hardly contain himself. She became aware of it and was suddenly afraid.

'You're disgusting!' she said, rattling the crockery as she gathered it together to wash up. 'And you know it isn't true. I would never do such a thing.' He had spoilt what had been a simple, innocent pleasure, made it dirty and shameful, and she would not forgive him for it.

'And right glad I am to hear it, but it's got to stop, you must see that. Mister High and Mighty de Lacey i'n't interested in the likes of you, bar the enjoyment he'd get from couplin' with you, that is. He'll never wed you, if that's what you've got in mind. You should stick to your own. I've got a lot to offer: a cottage what'll be mine one day, a good job and a chance to better m'self. We'd do right fine together. It'd be better'n sharin' this kitchen with another woman.'

'You'd rather have me sharing one with your mother,' she snapped. 'What's the difference?' His revelation about her father was making her feel very insecure and ill-used, as if everyone was plotting to destroy her happiness. Two hours before she had been almost content; two hours before, no doubt about her future had entered her head. She was nearly nineteen, enjoying her burgeoning womanhood in the company of someone who made her feel special, who called her beautiful. And now, here she was being importuned by this awkward, rough man who had no more idea of how to treat a woman than fly. And apparently with the full connivance of her father.

'Ma's gettin' on, you wouldn't have to share it long. On the other hand, Molly Parsons i'n't much older than you.'

'I'll believe it when Pa tells me so himself. Now, please leave. I have work to do.' She spoke firmly, but it crossed her mind that he might not go, that he might force himself on her. He was standing halfway between the table and the door, looking at her with his head on one side as if considering it. She prepared herself to fight him off. If she made enough noise, the relief stationmaster would come rushing to see what the rumpus was about and he must know that.

'Verra well,' he said slowly. 'You ask him and when I come callin' ag'in, I'm hopin' you'll have given the matter of walkin' out with me proper consideration. It were offered in good faith.'

'I'll think about it,' she said, more to get rid of him than because she meant it.

He picked up his cap and turned to go. 'I'll see you tomorrow.'

That was inevitable, she knew, they both worked at the station and there was no avoiding each other. 'It's a big step to take,' she said. 'So don't expect me to make up my mind in a hurry.'

'Oh, I'm in no hurry, but I reckon your pa is.' And with that he ducked his head below the lintel and strode off down the platform, nodding a cheerful good afternoon to the relief stationmaster as he passed him.

Lucy sat down at the cluttered table and put her head in her hands. Her whole day had been spoilt. Was her father really thinking of bringing another woman into their home, a home where every stick of furniture, every ornament, every rag rug must remind him of the wife he had lost? Did that count for nothing? Lucy had meticulously taken care of her mother's things, kept the house spotless, just as she had liked it, not only because it comforted her to do it, but because she believed that was what her father wanted.

Oh, how she wished she could go back to Jack. It wasn't his money or position which attracted her, at least not altogether; it was his gentleness, his consideration, his engaging smile. He was clean and smelt fresh and when he touched her, ever so briefly, she felt the warmth coursing through her. He made her feel important to him; he didn't need her for a skivvy, he had servants for that. Until a week ago, her dreams had been just dreams, but since he had taken her into the woods and showed her that ruined cottage, her dreams had taken on a different quality. They were becoming almost real. How could she even think of Frank Lambert, after that?

Slowly she stood up, finished the washing up and put the flat iron on the stove to heat ready to press her father's uniform. She would give him no cause for complaint, no reason to hasten a decision to marry her off.

Chapter Four

Before the war was a month old, Poland had succumbed and Germany and Russia carved the country up between them which meant Hitler could turn his attention elsewhere and everyone was wondering how soon it would be before the French army and the British Expeditionary Force would be in action. But nothing happened; at least, it wasn't happening on land. At sea it was a different matter. The first casualties of the war had occurred with the sinking of the passenger liner, *SS Athenia*, in the North Atlantic only hours after war was declared. She was hit by a torpedo and over a hundred people died. A fortnight later, the aircraft carrier *Courageous* was sunk with the loss of over five hundred of her crew, and U-boats even penetrated Scapa Flow where most of the British fleet was based and sank the *Royal Oak* with over eight hundred men losing their lives. Besides the U-boats there was the menace of surface vessels preying on naval and merchant ships bringing much needed supplies. If anything could persuade Annelise against going to France, that was it.

It didn't stop her worrying about Elizabeth and her parents. Elizabeth was being foolish, but she was very proud of her and perhaps she was right and she was just as safe in Dransville as she would be in England. All this bother about blackout curtains and gas masks and ration books and listening for air-raid sirens made it sound as if everyone in Britain was going to be in the front line. A quiet Alpine village might be more peaceful, which was the argument she used to console herself.

Charles, too old for active service, had volunteered for work at the War Office but they hadn't yet found anything for him to do. Amy had got her wish and was in Norwich, training to be a nurse. Only Jack seemed unconcerned but Jack, being Jack, was deeper and more thoughtful than he seemed on the surface and she did not doubt he would become as unsettled as everyone else and volunteer for something. Thank goodness Edmund was too young for anything like that, although they had a cadet force at Gresham's which he had joined and said was great fun.

To stop herself from brooding over Elizabeth and to feel she was doing something to help the war effort, Annelise had joined the Women's Voluntary Service, so here she was in a dark-green uniform and an unbecoming hat, trying to organise donated clothes for the benefit of the evacuees, many of whom were poorly clad. Seeing what Bernard and his siblings had in their cardboard cases had dismayed her and she had immediately searched through Jack's and Edmund's cast-off clothes to pass down to them. And she had set to work on some outgrown dresses of Amy's and made new ones for Cicely. Mrs Hodgkins had come once to see the children but she found the train fare a bit of a problem. Annelise had not offered her money, knowing the woman would view it as an insult. But she didn't object to the clothes when Annelise explained they had been outgrown and she would have given them away anyway.

When the expected bombing raids on London had not materialised, many of the evacuees had gone home, but Mrs Hodgkins was pregnant again and the pregnancy was not going well, so she had decided to leave the children at Nayton. 'They've settled in so well,' she had told Annelise. 'And the country air is good for them. It would be a pity to uproot them again. We'll wait until after the baby is born, if that's all right with you.'

Annelise had assured her that she was glad to have them and they weren't any trouble at all. This was an exaggeration because Bernard was constantly in trouble for one thing and another. As so many evacuees had gone home, those that remained had been integrated with the village children and he didn't seem able to get on with them.

'Your Bernard's been fighting again,' Mrs Hutchins told her as they worked in the clothes store at the village hall. 'He gave Tom Byers a black eye yesterday and Mrs Byers is complaining bitterly.'

It was strange how the boy had suddenly become 'your Bernard'. He was as mischievous as a cartload of monkeys, but he looked out for the younger ones and she liked him for it. 'I'll have a word with him.'

'Thank you. We've all got to learn to get along with each other now, old and young, whatever our background.'

'Quite.' Annelise was unsure if that was a veiled reference to her own lowly background or not; it was funny how stick-in-the-mud some people still were over rank.

Bernard was unrepentant when she tackled him at teatime. The children had been practising putting their gas masks on in class and sitting in them for several minutes. The older boys had taken this as a signal to play up and torment the younger ones and Tom Byers was one of the worst. 'He frightened Cissie,' he told her. 'Puttin' his face right up close to hers, wavin' 'is arms about and makin' 'orrible noises. I couldn't let 'im get away with that, now could I?'

'It's bad enough the country is at war without you fighting the village children,' she said, trying to sound stern. 'Try and settle your differences peaceably.'

'I ain't havin' Cissie frightened, not nohow,' he insisted. 'Anyway I already got the cane for it.'

She let him go.

He wandered off alone, smarting under a sense of injustice. Most of his London pals had gone home again but Ma had explained why they had to stay, which he didn't think was fair. He'd have made his own way back, if it hadn't been for Cissie. He couldn't take her and he couldn't leave her behind, so he had to make the best of it. He wouldn't have minded if he'd had Edmund to mess about with but Edmund was too grand for the village school and had gone back to Gresham's. Bernard missed him; he was good fun and he knew all sorts of interesting places in the woods, places to have hideouts and make dens or climb trees; places where they could get through the fence onto the railway line and put ha'pennies on the line for the trains to run over and then they came off bigger than pennies.

Their special place was an old tumbledown cottage in the wood which he had been told was where the gamekeeper once lived. Bernard didn't know what a gamekeeper was and had to have it explained to him. They had brought food and built a fire and cooked potatoes on it. Now the leaves on the trees were changing colour and the ground beneath his feet was littered with the prickly chestnuts. He kicked at them savagely. And then he stopped.

There was someone sitting on a log he and Edmund had dragged to the front of the cottage to use as a seat. It was the girl he had seen at the station when they first arrived. He had seen her in church too. What was she doing there? He hid behind a bush and watched her, just sitting there, staring into space. And then someone else arrived, a man in a railway uniform. Bernard waited developments.

'What are you doing here, Frank Lambert?' she demanded, jumping to her feet.

'Looking out for you, my lovely,' he said, advancing towards her.

She backed away. 'I do not need you to look out for me.'

'I'm thinkin' you do. You might get lost. It's dark in the trees and there are paths everywhere, some plainer than others, but you know it's not always the easiest which is best, the right one . . .'

'I won't get lost and you are talking in riddles.'

'He'll not come, you know.'

'Who?'

'Mr High and Mighty de Lacey, that's who. I told him you and me was to be wed. You know, he didn't seem that interested.'

'I wouldn't marry you if you were the last man on earth, Frank Lambert.'

'No? I reckon I c'n change yar mind. Yar pa seems to think I've bin too soft with you. Tek off them there clothes.'

'Certainly not!'

'You tek 'em off fast enough for de Lacey.'

'He's painting my picture.'

Frank laughed. 'Tha's a good one, that is. Painting yar picture and what else I wonder?'

'Nothin' else. Go away, Frank, he'll be here soon.'

'Good, then I'll hev it out with him.' He stepped forward and took her shoulder in a grip that made her cry out.

'You're hurting me.'

His answer was to rip her blouse from her, exposing her bra and a wide expanse of creamy flesh. Watched by the astonished Bernard, he took a step closer. She tried to step sideways and in doing so stumbled over a log and then they were both sprawling on the floor. 'I'll hev you yet,' he grunted, while she squirmed beneath him. 'I hev yar pa's permission.'

His hands seemed to be everywhere, all over her breasts, up her skirt between her thighs, holding her down. He loosened his hold slightly to undo his trousers and she tried to roll away from him, but he was at her again, slamming his big hand over her mouth when she opened her mouth to scream. 'Won't do you no good. A right good doin' you've been asking for and a right good doin' you're a-goin' to get.'

She struggled, trying to free her arms, but he pinned them to her sides. She thrashed her head from side to side until at last her mouth was free and she gulped in mouthfuls of clean air and then she started to scream.

Bernard, eyes agog, wondered what was going to happen next and whether he ought to make a noise and let them know they weren't alone, but before he could make up his mind, Jack de Lacey came running up, dropping an easel and a large flat case on the way, and pulled the railwayman off her, then punched him so hard he fell flat on his back.

'Jack, you've knocked him out,' she said, sitting up.

'Serve him right.' He touched the fallen man with his toe. 'Get up, you miserable brute. Get up.'

Frank scrambled to his feet, rubbing his chin. 'You leave my girl alone,' he said.

'Your girl?' Jack queried. 'I think not. Lucy, are you this man's girl?'

'Never in a million years.'

Frank turned to her. 'You'll change your mind about that. I could ruin you and your pa if I'd a mind to. He's beholden to me in a big way, he is.'

'Clear off!' Jack said, raising his fist again.

Frank disappeared in the direction of the railway line and Jack bent to help Lucy to her feet. She was shaking. He held her in his arms. 'It's all right, sweetheart, he can't hurt you, I'll see to that.'

'What did he mean about Pa?'

'Goodness knows. It doesn't matter. Do you feel up to sitting for me today?'

'I ought to go home and change.'

'You look perfect as you are.' He stroked the exposed flesh and cupped her breast in his hand. 'I'll paint you like that, all wild and unkempt.'

'No, Jack, please don't. Someone might see it.' She pulled her bra strap up again and straightened her blouse.

'You're upset, I can understand that.' He pushed her hair back from her face and kissed her gently. 'Not all men are like that fellow, you know. I would never hurt you or do anything you didn't want me to, I promise.'

'Oh, Jack, I wish . . .'

'What do you wish?'

'Never mind. It doesn't matter. I'll go home, if you don't mind.'

'I'll see you safely back to the station. He might be hanging around still.' He picked up his scattered belongings and took her arm.

Bernard watched them go and then emerged from his

hiding place. What a turn-up for the books! My, wouldn't he have a tale to tell Edmund when he came home for the Christmas holidays.

Lucy went indoors and up to her room where she stripped off her torn blouse and sat on the edge of the bed, gazing at herself in the mirror. There was a row of finger-shaped bruises coming up on her shoulder which were tender to touch. She considered telling her father what Frank had done, but dismissed the idea. He would almost certainly want to know what she was doing in Nayton woods and how could she tell him?

She had been so happy, snatching a half-hour here and a half-hour there to sit for Jack. She had even consented to take off her blouse and bra and drape a colourful shawl over her shoulder to cover her breasts. It was all very tasteful, so he told her, nothing to be ashamed of, and if his fingers stroked her bare flesh while he was getting the pose right, that hadn't mattered. It had given her a lovely tingling feeling and she would sit there, dreaming that he would finish the picture and then he would become famous and he would say it was all down to her and tell her he loved her. Frank had spoilt it all; she dare not go there again. The picture would never be finished. She had not felt so miserable since her mother left. She curled up on the bed and let the tears flow. She cried for broken dreams, for a mother she had loved but who had not cared enough for her, for a life of drudgery with a father she could not please.

She sat up when she heard the back door bang and knew her father was back from the Nayton Arms and early too. She scrubbed at her eyes, scrambled into a clean bra and blouse and made her way downstairs. 'You're home early, Pa.' She hoped her voice didn't sound too watery.

'Yes, well I've got something to say to you.'

Had Frank told him about Jack? She held her breath, waiting. He took off his jacket and cap, hung them on the hook behind the door, then sat in the chair by the hearth in his shirtsleeves. 'When are you going to wed Frank?'

That wasn't what she had been expecting at all. 'I'm not. I don't like him.'

'You'll not do any better.'

'How do you know I won't? I'm only nineteen, too young to marry.'

'There's plenty wed at your age. I've looked after you all your life when many a man would have thrown you out alonga your ma, but I took pity on you, but that's it. I want you off my hands.'

'Pa!'

'And you can stop callin' me Pa. I i'n't your pa.'

'Wh . . . what do you mean?'

'Don't you understand plain English, gel? I said I i'n't your pa. You're not my child. I can't have children, not since I was wounded in the last war. I thought I might tek to you but I couldn't. I wouldn't throw you out while you was growin' up, but enough is enough. I want to wed again m'self . . .'

Lucy's legs refused to support her and she sank into a

chair by the kitchen table. 'It isn't true, it can't be true. Mum wouldn't. She wasn't like that. And you can't marry again, you've got a wife.'

'The law says if she's been gone more'n seven year and no one's seen hide nor hair of her in that time, I can have her declared dead.'

'But what if she comes back?'

'It'll be too late.'

'I wish I knew where she was. I'd go and find her. Haven't you any idea where she might have gone?'

'No, and d'you think she'd want you? She could have took you with her but she didn't, did she?'

This was a truth that hurt. 'Are you turning me out?'

'I'm tellin' you to marry Frank Lambert. He's right keen to have you. You'll be all right with him. His mother's cottage will come to him and he's got a safe job. They won't call him up.'

'I don't care if they do. I am not marrying him and you can't make me.'

'No, but he can make it so you dussn't say no.'

Frank had already tried that, but she decided not to tell him so because he would want to know how she had escaped and she wouldn't tell him about Jack.

She stood up wearily. 'I'd better dish up your dinner.'

He ate it and left again, no doubt to tell his new lady-love that he had broken the news. He had not returned by the time she went to bed. She had been miserable enough before he came home, but now she was in the depths of despair. She crossed to the window. From where she stood she could see the crossing gate and the signal box and, across the line, the dark outline of Nayton wood. Beyond it, though she could not see through the trees, was Nayton Manor. Jack would be there, perhaps with his family, perhaps alone in his room touching up the painting that would not now be finished. She must let him know she couldn't meet him again and, more importantly, she must decide what she was going to do.

Jack sat at the table in his room, studying the portrait. It was coming along better now. Lucy's soft, dreamy expression was there in the mouth and eyes and her lovely figure, with the shawl carelessly thrown over her shoulder, hiding very little, hinted at pleasures to come. He had been looking forward to today's session, hoping that he might persuade her to allow more than a few chaste kisses, but that miserable cur, Frank Lambert, had spoilt it. For two pins he'd have beaten the living daylights out of him when all the man had been doing was something Jack himself had in mind, though not so brutally. But it was funny how rescuing her had changed how he felt about her. He found himself being touchingly protective, wanting to cherish her, to make her feel safe. He was becoming too soft for his own good.

He was unsettled, fidgety, and it was all to do with the war. Many of the young men in the village had already enlisted in one or other of the armed forces. Amy had overcome their father's objections and was training to be a nurse and Elizabeth appeared to be running the farm in Dransville single-handedly. He ought to be doing his bit. Working in the drawing office of the de Lacey engineering factory, even though it was working flat out making engine parts, was boring and not enough. He'd be called up sooner or later anyway, so he might as well volunteer. If he did that, he could put Lucy from his mind. He looked at the picture and sighed. Pity, but there it was.

He was walking to the station early the following morning, intending to put in a token appearance at the office and then go to the recruiting office. He expected to see Lucy on the platform or manning the gates when he would tell her of his intention to join up and not finish the portrait. He was forming the words in his head, something about winter setting in and it being too cold now, when he met her hurrying towards him. She was wrapped up in a plain wool coat with a headscarf covering her hair. Her head was hunched in her shoulders, her eyes were looking at the ground.

'Lucy, where are you off to at this time of the morning?' he asked. 'The eight o'clock train is due any minute. I thought I'd see you at the station.'

She looked up startled. 'Oh, it's you.' Her eyes were swollen and red from weeping.

'What's the matter?' He stopped in front of her, making her stop too. 'Has Lambert been bothering you again?'

'No.'

'What then?'

'Don't ask me, Jack, please. I was going to the cottage to

leave a note to tell you I wouldn't be able to see you again.' Tears were very near the surface and she choked them back.

The fact that he had come to the same conclusion went out of his head in the face of her distress. He took her arm and guided her off the road into the shelter of the trees. 'Why? Has your father found out and forbidden it?'

'No, it's not that. I've got to go away.'

'Go away? Why? Where to? When?'

She sniffed and tried to smile. 'Questions, questions . . .'

'I want answers. Something is very wrong, that's obvious. Come on, Lucy, out with it. You can tell me. I won't breathe a word to a soul, but I might be able to help.'

'You can't.'

'I'm not letting you go until you tell me.' He took her shoulders in his hands and noticed her wince. 'Are you hurt?' He undid the top button of her coat and pushed her blouse off her shoulder. 'You're black and blue. Is that why you've been crying?'

'No, course not. What's a bruise now and again? I've had plenty of those.'

Did she mean her father? He pulled her clothes back in place and buttoned the coat again. 'But it is something to do with Frank Lambert?'

'Pa says I've got to marry him.'

'Of course you haven't got to marry him, that's nonsense. You don't have to marry anyone you don't want to.'

'Pa wants to marry again and he says there's no room for two women in the house.'

'God! I can't believe any man would do that to his own daughter. Whatever is he thinking of?'

'He says . . .' She stopped and gulped. 'No, I can't tell you . . .'

'Go on. You've got this far.'

'He says I'm not his daughter.'

He whistled. 'Do you believe that?'

'I don't know what to believe. He told me he couldn't have children on account of his war wound and Mum had been unfaithful to him, but he decided to bring me up anyway. Now he's turned on me.' The tears, so near the surface, spilt over and ran down her cheeks. 'If only I could find my mother . . .'

'You mean she's alive? I always assumed . . .'

'She left when I was nine. He says he doesn't know where she went and he's going to have her declared dead so he can marry again.'

'Oh, my poor, poor darling.' He took her into his arms and held her close. 'We'll think of something. You're not marrying that lout just to please your father.'

'But it's nothing to do with you.'

'Did you think I would abandon you, just because—' He stopped. He knew exactly what it was like to be a bastard; it coloured a lot of what he did, how he felt, and his heart went out to her, making him feel more protective than ever. 'Where were you planning on going?'

'I don't know. I'll have to find a job.'

'On the railways?'

'I thought of that but it would be easy for Pa or Frank

to find me if I did that. I could work in a factory, but then I'd have to find somewhere to live as well and I haven't got any money. Oh, Jack, it's all such a muddle. Perhaps I'd be better marrying Frank . . .'

'Over my dead body!'

'What can you do?'

'Quite a lot. I can find you a job and somewhere to live. Leave it to me.'

'Could you?' Her eyes brightened through her tears. 'Would you?'

'Yes. Can you bear to stay at home until I've arranged it?'

'Yes. Pa thinks I'll give in.'

'Then let him think it. I was going into Norwich today. I'll scout around while I'm there and let you know. Come, let's go back to the station. I don't want to miss my train.'

'You go. I'll follow when the train's gone and shut the gates again.'

'Cheer up, all is not lost.' He dropped a kiss on her forehead and left her.

It wasn't until he was sitting on the train and it was drawing away from Nayton, that he asked himself why he was bothering with her and the answer was that he didn't know, except he felt sorry for her. He was a bastard himself but he had been fortunate that his mother had married Lord de Lacey and he had enjoyed a privileged upbringing. How much worse it must be for Lucy Storey living with that sour old man, knowing her mother had abandoned her. He'd get her a job and find her some clean lodgings. He brightened suddenly. He'd be able to finish the portrait after all, indoors where it was warm.

On the surface, Dransville was as peaceful as ever. Everyone was trying to carry on with their usual occupations, looking after their livestock, making butter and cheese as they always had and, notwithstanding they were at war, the people at the local hotels were getting ready for the winter season and the visitors they hoped would still come to take advantage of the skiing.

Elizabeth had fully recovered and was learning a lot about the work on the farm. She found herself milking cows and goats, making butter and cheese, collecting eggs, getting in hay for the winter feed, mending hinges, replacing windows, clearing out gutters, digging up potatoes and cutting cabbages. She had even overcome her squeamishness enough to wring the neck of a chicken now and again for Grandmère to cook for dinner. And she had shot a rabbit with Grandpère's shotgun which had made a tasty meal. She had learnt to shoot on her father's estate and realised if food became scarce it was a skill which might come in useful.

Grandpère was recovering slowly but he couldn't walk properly and his speech, though still slurred, was improving. She would wheel him out to the yard in a bath chair so that he could see what was going on and make sure she did things the way he liked, but when the weather became very cold, he preferred to stay in the warmth of the kitchen. If it wasn't for the ever-present shadow of the war and everybody making their own guesses about when and where something would start to happen, Elizabeth would have been as happy as a sandboy.

Russia had invaded Finland but that was too far away to bother them and Hitler seemed reluctant to attack the west. The weather wasn't in his favour. By early December it was already exceptionally cold. Everywhere was frozen, even the canals and rivers, which hampered the movement of supplies and equipment on both sides. The ground was frozen so hard the troops found it impossible to dig the trenches and defensive works on the border with Belgium which had been ongoing ever since the BEF arrived in France. Everyone was fed up with the situation and called it the Bore War, but some, who had been in France since September, were cheered by the news that they would be granted leave to spend Christmas with their families. Max decided to go to Dransville.

He found Elizabeth in the cowshed, her head in the flank of a cow, her fingers skilfully easing the milk into a pail. 'Your grandmother said I'd find you here.'

The sound of his voice made her whirl round on her stool. 'Max!' She abandoned the cow to stand up and hug him. 'What are you doing here?'

'I had a spot of leave and thought I'd spend Christmas with you. That's if you'll have me.'

'Of course we'll have you. It's a wonderful surprise.' A swish of the cow's tail reminded her she had an unfinished job to do. 'I must finish the milking. Go indoors and I'll be with you in two shakes.'

'I'll stay and watch.' He released her reluctantly and she went back to the cow. He stood leaning against the byre door, smiling at the sight of her. She was dressed in a simple gathered skirt, a blouse and cardigan, topped by a sacking apron; her lovely hair was hidden beneath a headscarf. Her feet were encased in rubber boots. 'Very rural, you look.'

She laughed. 'If I'd known you were coming, I'd have dressed up.'

'I didn't know myself until yesterday. I caught the first train out of Paris this morning.'

'You must be hungry.'

'Hungry for the sight of you.'

'Give over.' She laughed as she emptied the milk into a churn and took the pail out to the trough to wash it before taking it indoors to be properly scrubbed. Then she took his arm and led him into the kitchen.

It was warm inside. Grandmère was busy cooking. Food was already becoming scarce, but they were almost self-sufficient on the farm and there would be no problem with the Christmas dinner. There was a stuffed goose on a shelf in the larder ready to be put into the oven first thing the next morning.

'What news of the war?' Albert asked from his chair by the hearth after Max had taken off his cap and greatcoat and taken a seat opposite him.

'No news at all. A few skirmishes, a few patrols to see what the other side is up to, but that's all. The French troops are calling it La Drôle de Guerre.'

'Hitler's afraid to take us on,' the old man said. The arrival of Max and someone different to talk to seemed to stimulate him to speak more clearly.

'Seems like it,' Max said. 'But the weather isn't helping him. Nor us either, come to that. It's why some of us have been granted leave.'

Elizabeth perched herself on the arm of Max's chair. 'Why didn't you go home to England?'

'What for?' He put his arm about her waist. 'You're here and that's where I want to be. My sister is busy looking after her own family and, besides, if I went back to Scotland, half my leave would have been spent travelling.'

'We're glad to have you,' Grandmère said. 'Justine is coming later today and Pierre and Jeanne and the boys tomorrow, so we'll have a good party and forget the war for a little while.'

'Wish we could,' Albert put in. 'We don't know how long Henri and Philippe will avoid call-up, and if they have to go, how's Pierre going to manage? I can't help him.'

'We'll cross that bridge when we come to it,' Elizabeth said. 'Perhaps the war will end sooner than we think.'

'Have you thought any more about going home, Liz?' Max asked her.

'I won't go while I'm needed here. And I can't see there's any danger staying. Hitler seems to think he can win the war at sea and Haute Savoie is a long way from the sea.'

Max laughed at her naivety, but he wouldn't disillusion her. 'At least while I'm in France I'll be closer to you, though if anything bad happened I'm not sure what I could do.'

The conversation was being conducted in French and though Max's accent was most decidedly English, he was able to hold his end up much better than he had on his previous visit. 'Your French has improved no end,' Elizabeth said. 'Have you been taking lessons?'

He laughed. 'I've been working alongside French troops for three months, some of it's bound to have rubbed off. I only hope I haven't learnt bad habits.'

The back door opened, letting in an icy blast and a woman in her thirties. She was slim and chic. Her dark hair, topped by a fetching felt hat with a feather across its brim, was coiled into a roll down the back of her head.

'Justine!' The old lady darted forward to embrace her. 'Take off your coat and hat and come and warm yourself by the fire. You are just in time for supper.'

Justine put a small suitcase down and bent to kiss her father's cheek. 'How are you, Papa?'

'Good,' he said. 'Good.'

She turned to hug Elizabeth. 'Hallo, Lisabette. You have been doing sterling work on the farm, I hear, looking after everything.'

'Who told you that?'

'Maman writes letters and so does Pierre. I know all about it.' She turned to Max who had stood up on her entrance. 'You must be Max.'

'Oh, let me introduce you,' Elizabeth said. 'Justine, this is Captain Max Coburn, a very good friend of mine who is spending his Christmas leave with us. Max, Ma'amselle Justine Clavier, my mother's younger sister. She teaches English in a school in Paris.'

They shook hands and both said 'How do you do' in English.

'Max speaks good French,' Grandmère said, letting them know that she wanted to be in on the conversation. 'Lisabette, lay the table, this chicken is ready to carve.'

'What's happening in Paris?' Elizabeth asked Justine as they sat down to eat.

'Nothing much. There's a shortage of petrol and coal and it's a job to keep warm, most of the young men have disappeared into the army, but everyone else is trying to carry on as usual. The great and the good spend their time giving charity balls in aid of the troops, and Coco Chanel has set her seamstresses to making gloves and pullovers for the army.' She laughed. 'She has put her label on them, so I bet a lot of them will never be worn but stashed away as souvenirs.'

'The young men are going from the farms too,' Elizabeth said. 'I'm not the only woman trying to cope without them. Mama says the same thing is happening in England. She says Jack has volunteered for the air force, though he hasn't been sent for yet. Amy is training to be a nurse. I didn't think she'd be any good at it, she hasn't seen much of life and I thought she would be too squeamish, but she says she likes it.'

'You were squeamish once,' her grandmother reminded her. 'You soon learn to get over it when you have to.'

Elizabeth laughed. 'So I was.' She turned to Max. 'I

can wring a chicken's neck and shoot a rabbit and skin it. I helped pluck the Christmas goose and watched Grandmère draw it. It's stuffed ready for the oven tomorrow.'

'I shall enjoy it all the more knowing you had a hand in its preparation,' Max said.

No one sitting down to the gargantuan meal the following day would have guessed there was a war on and many people were suffering shortages of food and fuel, and if any of them thought it might be the last good Christmas dinner they had for some time, they did not voice it.

Afterwards Max and Elizabeth wrapped themselves in warm coats, boots and gloves and went for a walk, Pierre and the boys went out cutting logs for firewood, while Jeanne and Justine washed up and her grandparents snoozed by the fire.

It had been snowing and the hills were white with it. The skiers were out, expert and beginners, whooshing down the slopes enjoying a holiday that might very well be the last for a long time.

'I still think you should change your mind and go home,' Max said. 'This Phoney War won't last, you know. Hitler won't be content to sit on his gains. Either we'll have to take the initiative and attack him or he'll come to us. The trouble is that the French seem content to fight a defensive war. We'll never win that way.'

'Max, let's not talk about it.' She took his arm in both her hands and put her head on his shoulder. 'It's lovely to have you here. You'll come as often as you can, won't you?

It's surely easier than having to go all the way to England to see me when you get leave.'

He laughed. 'There is that.'

They stopped in the shelter of a hut where he took her into his arms and kissed her. She clung to him. 'I wish you didn't have to go back so soon.'

'So do I. It's been a grand leave, something to remember when I'm cold and dirty and hungry.'

'I'll miss you. Take care of yourself, won't you?'

'Of course. I mean to see this war out and ask you to marry me properly and I hope you are going to say yes.' He put his finger over her lips when she opened her mouth to answer him. 'Not now. Save it. It has to be special.'

'Oh, Max.' She reached up and pulled his head down to kiss him back.

He left next morning to travel back to Paris with Justine.

Chapter Five

May 1940

The troops were exhausted. They had known the attack was coming and thought they were ready, but the truth was they were beaten, beaten by a ruthless enemy who had overrun Denmark, forced Norway to capitulate and advanced rapidly across Holland and Belgium and were knocking at the doors of France, all in the space of a few weeks. The long hard winter was behind them and the spring well advanced when the so-called Bore War ended, cataclysmically for the Allies. The Netherlands and Belgium had tried to hold onto their neutrality but the German troops had ignored that and continued their relentless advance to the French border. The population of France waited for its army and the BEF to bring them to a halt.

The attack, when it came, was in the Ardennes, south of where it had been expected. Supported by bombers,

German Panzers crossed the Meuse at Sedan and were on French soil. In spite of patchy opposition, some so weak as to be almost non-existent, some ferociously determined, the invaders had turned north towards the Channel to encircle the Allied armies. Max and his men found themselves fighting a rearguard action as they were forced to withdraw inside a tighter and tighter perimeter. His orders were to hold off the enemy as long as possible in order for the troops behind him to be evacuated by sea.

The noise was deafening as shells rained down on them from enemy positions, throwing up clouds of earth and debris, and they were constantly dive bombed by screaming Stukas. Max had lost half his men and the others, though fighting bravely, had almost lost hope. Holed up in a barn, they watched the road ahead of them, sniping at anything that moved, wondering how long it would be before they were given the order to withdraw and could make their way to the coast where they had been told there were ships waiting to take them off.

But the order never came.

'We're beaten,' Grandpère said. 'Better go while you can, Lisabette. Go over the border to Switzerland. You can get home from there.'

'I'm not leaving you. And how do you know we're beaten? That's defeatist talk. And even if we are beaten, you still need me.' They were sitting round the kitchen table after listening to the wireless while they ate their supper. The plentiful food of Christmas was a dream that had passed, leaving the stark reality of rationing and shortages. If her grandparents were to survive, she had to do all she could to help them. She was more use here than in England.

'You are as stubborn as your mother,' Grandmère said. 'She wouldn't listen either. She insisted on going to the front to be near Jacques and look what happened.'

Elizabeth smiled. 'What did happen?'

'She got herself pregnant, didn't she? Came home as big as a mountain and Jacques dead. She wouldn't have the baby adopted . . .'

'I should think not. I wouldn't either, especially if I loved the man who gave him to me. Were you angry with her?'

'I suppose I was to start with. It was a disgrace and I felt everyone was pointing at us, but when little Jacques was born, of course we loved him. And Annelise was lucky, she met your father again and he gave her a second chance.'

'They have been very happy together. I hope Max and I—'

'*Sacredieu*, you are not *enceinte*, are you?'

'No, Mamie, I'm not. But one day we plan to marry, when this war is over.'

'You'll have a long wait then,' the old man put in.

'You, Papie, are a pessimist.' Elizabeth paused, as her thoughts went to wondering what had happened to Max. Had he got safely away with all the others at Dunkirk? It had been a massive undertaking and seemed to turn a defeat into a triumph, but was Max with them? She told herself over and over again he was a survivor, but she wished she could have some news. She had heard nothing from him for over a month and that had told her very little except that he was well. Letters from home were taking a long time to reach her too; she had no idea how everyone was coping. She had written to say she was safe and well, but she had no way of knowing if the letter had reached its destination. That was the worst part of the separation, not knowing. They had to rely on rumour fed by thousands of fleeing refugees and the heavily censored wireless for news. They listened to the BBC and knew Churchill was now prime minister and making stirring speeches aimed at boosting everyone's morale, but of her own family she knew nothing.

Men were tearing up the wrought iron gates at Nayton Manor. They were watched by Bernard on his way home from school. 'Everyone has to give up their metal to help the war effort,' one of the workmen told him. 'To make aeroplanes and guns.'

Bernard knew about that because he had heard it on the wireless. According to the news London parks were losing all their railings and housewives were giving up their saucepans. At school they had been urged to collect scrap metal from neighbours and bring it all to school. What they collected would be melted down and go towards making a Spitfire. Bernard had liked the idea of that: doing something to aid the war effort. He had fetched a wheelbarrow from the gardener's shed and gone round the village begging for metal. He had acquired several old saucepans, a colander, some cutlery, tins that had once held peas and carrots, a few battered garden implements and sundry unidentifiable bits of tools, which had taken the whole of one Saturday to collect. Proud of himself he had wheeled it to the field at the back of the school and added it to the growing heap.

'Well done,' Jack had said when he told him he thought there was enough there for at least one Spitfire. 'We'll soon have old Jerry beaten.' Jack was in the air force and flying Spitfires, but he came home now and then on leave. Bernard wondered what had happened to the portrait he had been painting of the railway-crossing girl. She had disappeared before Christmas and there was a new woman operating the crossing gates since Mr Storey had married again.

He had told Edmund about the picture and Edmund had sneaked into Jack's room to look for it, but he couldn't find it. According to Edmund, he must have misunderstood what was going on; Jack wouldn't look twice at the likes of a railway worker. They had had a fight over it, but had made it up when Edmund had conceded that if Jack had come across a girl being attacked, of course he would wade in to help, but that didn't mean there was any more to it than that. Bernard didn't believe him but, for the sake of peace, had agreed he was probably right.

He wished he could go home. He had a new brother now, called Joe. Ma had brought him down to visit them, but she still wouldn't take them home. He had only one more year at school after this one and then he'd leave and find a job and he'd go home whether she wanted him to or not. Cissie wouldn't mind, not now. Cissie had grown so fond of Annie that she had stopped fretting for her mother. He wasn't sure if that was a good thing or not. As for Raymond and Martin, they had become real Norfolk dumplings, were even beginning to sound like them, calling each other 'bor' and dragging out their vowels. He wondered if they would ever settle back in London among grimy streets and back-to-back houses.

He watched the men loading the gates onto a lorry and turned to go up the drive to the house. Lady de Lacey, in her WVS uniform, was cycling towards him. She went everywhere on her bicycle now they couldn't get petrol for the big car.

She dismounted when she saw him. 'Have you got homework to do, Bernard?'

'Yes, My Lady.' The polite address tripped easily off his tongue now, though he didn't see that she was any different from any other woman except, of course, she was rich. 'It don't seem right, do it, takin' the gates away?'

'No, but we must all make sacrifices if we are to win the war.'

'As soon as I'm old enough I'm going to join up.'

She smiled at him. 'I hope the war is over long before that happens.'

'Jack likes it. He said it was great fun.'

She chuckled. 'He would say that. Now run along and do your homework before you go out again.'

Annelise remounted and went on her way to her WVS meeting at the village hall, musing about Jack. He did seem to be enjoying life but, as far as she knew, he hadn't seen any action yet and she hoped he never would, but that hope was fast dwindling. Since the horror of Dunkirk, the Germans had continued their relentless advance; according to the news, the heavy guns could be heard in Paris. How long her countrymen could hold out, she did not know. She feared not long and then the beautiful city of her homeland, the scene of her idyllic honeymoon, would become just another conquest for the barbarian. And then what? Lizzie and her parents were constantly in her thoughts. How they were coping, she had no idea; there had been no letter for months. Lizzie probably didn't even know that Max was missing.

She cycled along Nayton's country lanes savouring the warmth of the afternoon sun, her nostrils full of the scent of the cow parsley growing in the verges, half listening to a noisy blackbird calling from the hedgerow. It was so peaceful, it was difficult to believe that everyone was gearing themselves up to resist an invasion. Charles had been worrying the War Office to give him something useful to do but all that happened was that he was given command of the Nayton Local Defence Volunteers. With their armbands and tin hats, all the uniform they had so far, they drilled with brooms for rifles and listened to lectures. According to Charles, they were grittily determined to hold off any Jerry who had the temerity to invade their homeland. It was too amateurish for words.

She dismounted at the station and wheeled her cycle through the pedestrian gate and across the tracks, saying good afternoon to Mrs Storey who was on her knees weeding the patch of station garden. 'It's a beautiful afternoon, isn't it?'

'For them as hev time to enjoy it, mayhap.'

'Yes, it must be hard work keeping the station tidy, but I must say you make a very good job of it. The flowers are lovely. Lucy used to keep it nice too. How is she getting on in her new job?' Lucy's sudden disappearance had been the gossip of the village for a while. Had she done something wrong and been dismissed? Had she got herself pregnant and gone away to have the baby in secret? Had she quarrelled with her new stepmother? Mr Storey had been unforthcoming but according to Mrs Storey she had left for a better job.

'Don' know. She don' keep in touch.'

'I'm sorry to hear that, but perhaps you'll hear from her soon.' She remounted and went on her way as a train drew into the station behind her. There was something strange about that girl's disappearance, but it was none of her business and she put it from her mind.

Lucy left the doctor's surgery and made for home. What he had told her had been no surprise; she knew what was wrong with her. No, not wrong, she corrected herself, she wasn't ill and having Jack's baby was not wrong; she didn't care what anyone said. She hoped Jack would be pleased about it.

He had been as good as his word and found her a job in an engineering factory making aeroplane parts and a

121

little two-up two-down terrace cottage in Waterloo Road. 'Better than a miserable room with a landlady breathing down your neck all the time,' he had told her. 'You can please yourself what you do and I can visit you if I want.'

'And will you want to?'

'Of course. We can finish the portrait.'

'But I don't think I can afford the rent, it's more than for one room, isn't it?'

'Don't worry about that. I'll take care of it.'

'But you can't do that. It's not right.'

'Of course it's right. I've got plenty of money and nothing to spend it on but pleasure and if it is my pleasure to help you, what's wrong with that?'

She had not continued to argue; it was nice to have someone who cared enough to want to look after her. She would find some way to repay him.

The house was supposed to be furnished but had only the bare necessities and he had taken her on a shopping spree to add a few things of her own to make it more homely. He had even bought her some clothes because, remembering how her father had said her mother's clothes belonged to him, she had brought only the minimum with her. She liked to imagine it was like being married, except Jack was not there all the time. His family at Nayton Manor claimed him, but he had dropped in sometimes on a Saturday or a Sunday and had his tea with her. Then he had joined the Royal Air Force and disappeared for weeks to do his training. When he came on leave it was a joyful reunion, so joyful she had thrown herself into his arms, kissed him exuberantly and allowed him to stay the night.

He was a thoughtful and tender-hearted lover and she gave herself to him willingly and lovingly and if the result was a new, smaller edition of Jack de Lacey, well, that was all right by her. She had never been so happy in her life. The only drawback was the lack of a wedding ring, and though she told herself she didn't care whether they were married or not, she did wonder what her neighbours and workmates might think, so she bought herself a cheap ring in Woolworths.

She'd have to keep working until the last minute, but as the factory needed every hand it could get with so many of the men leaving for the forces, she didn't think they'd get rid of her until she was too big to sit comfortably at her workbench. One thing she had not done and never would do, was contact the man she had called Pa for so long. Nor would she write to Jack to tell him her news; she would wait until he came to her. She wanted to see his face when she told him.

He came a week after the news had broken about Dunkirk. He looked haggard and exhausted, too tired even to talk or eat. She didn't bother him but let him sleep the clock round, and it was not until the following morning when she put a huge breakfast in front of him and he had demolished it, he came alive again. 'Thanks for understanding, Lucy,' he said, taking her hand and putting it against his cheek. 'I needed to sleep. I couldn't go home like that, they'd have quizzed me about what was wrong and I couldn't tell them. They'd have been too upset.'

'You don't have to tell me either, if you don't want to, but perhaps it'd be better out than in.'

He was silent for some moments, then went on. 'It was awful. We were sent to Dunkirk to keep Jerry from bombing our troops on the beach. There were thousands and thousands of them in long lines waiting for anything afloat to come and take them off, and there wasn't a scrap of cover except a few dunes. The Stukas came screaming in and mowed them down. And even the men who reached the ships weren't safe. Many were sunk, even the hospital ship with its red cross. When I flew low, I could see the sea and beach were full of debris and dead bodies. I never learnt to hate before but seeing the merciless way the men were strafed, and not being able to do much but chase the buggers off, made me furious. I went after them and I might have downed one. One! That was all I could do. And I kept thinking of Max and wondering if he was down there in the middle of it all . . .'

'I'm sorry, Jack.' She put his head against her stomach and stood there holding him, looking over his tousled head at the portrait which took pride of place over the mantel. He had continued to work on it in fits and starts and had finished it on his last leave. She didn't know anything about art or the value of pictures, but she valued it because he had painted it and it flattered her, or so she thought, though he said it was a good likeness. His shoulders began to shake and she realised he was sobbing. She said nothing and in a little while he lifted his head.

'Let's go to bed. I need you.'

It was afterwards, when they were lying side by side on their backs, happily satiated and he was almost asleep again, that she broached the subject uppermost in her mind. 'Jack, I've got something to tell you.'

Alerted by her tone he opened his eyes and turned his head towards her. 'Out with it, then.'

'I'm pregnant.'

'The devil you are!'

'It's what happens, you know, when you . . . you do what we just did.'

'I do know that, Lucy.'

'I hoped you'd be pleased.'

'Pleased isn't exactly the word I'd have used.'

She was disappointed by his reaction; his face hadn't lit up with pleasure as she had hoped it would. Perhaps he was too tired to take it in. 'You're not angry, are you?'

'Angry?' He laughed. 'What have I got to be angry about? It's my own fault. What are you going to do about it?'

'What am *I* going to do?' she squeaked. 'It isn't up to me on my own, is it?'

'No, of course not.' He backtracked hurriedly. 'So what are *we* going to do?'

'I'm not going to some backstreet abortionist, if that's what you're thinking,' she said. 'I heard the girls at the factory talking about it. One of them had been. It was awful. In any case, I can't kill my baby, not nohow. He's yours too, part of you.'

He turned on his side to face her. 'I know.'

'You couldn't kill him either, could you?'

125

'No.'

'Then you're going to be a father.'

'When?'

'In the New Year, so they tell me. I'll work as long as I can, but after that . . .'

'Sweetheart,' he said firmly. 'You and our baby will not suffer because of my carelessness. You will be looked after, as long as you need it, I promise you.'

'I hoped you'd say that. A girl on her own without a man—'

'You've got me. But if someone should come along who wants to marry you and you want to marry him, we'll think again.'

He couldn't understand why she burst into tears and put it down to her condition making her weepy. He comforted her as best he could and a little later left for Nayton.

Lucy had certainly given him something to think about. Why he hadn't been more careful, he couldn't say, but it was done now and he was going to be a father of a little bastard. He knew what that was like, to grow up not knowing the man who had conceived you, knowing you were different in some way from all the other boys and that it was something to be ashamed of. Poor little beggar! At least he could make sure neither Lucy nor the child suffered materially. Should he give her a lump sum or a regular allowance? Should it be hers to do with as she liked or put in trust for the child? Should he stop seeing her? After all, why did he keep seeing her?

The original offer to help her after that brute of a father had as good as turned her out had been made on the spur of the moment and it had tickled his fancy to set her up as his mistress, though the word had never been mentioned by either of them. But he found himself looking forward to his visits, to the restful atmosphere she created, to her obvious adoration. Was he prepared to give that up?

He still hadn't made up his mind about it when he left the train at Nayton Halt. Bert Storey was trundling a barrow loaded with punnets of strawberries down the platform and his wife was standing by the gates ready to open them when the train had gone. He wondered what they would say if they knew, but it wasn't up to him to tell them and he didn't think Lucy would. He bade them good-day and carried on his way. It was good to be home, and now he felt rested, he needn't go into details of the horrors he had seen or the constant fear which every one of his pals felt but disguised with bonhomie and foolishness. No doubt his father would want to discuss the situation with him and ask him what he thought about Lizzie still being in France. And what could he say about that? It was up to Lizzie.

Grandpère had been right. France was defeated. On the day Italy entered the war as an ally of Germany, the French government had fled to Tours leaving Paris an open city. The Germans had marched in unopposed and now a Swastika was flying from the Eiffel Tower. The roads were clogged with refugees, trying to escape. They drove cars which had to be abandoned when they ran out of petrol; they harnessed horses to carts and loaded them with their possessions; they took bicycles and handcarts, anything which would carry what they considered essentials. Some, who had come from farms, were driving livestock, some of which died on the way and were abandoned on the roadside along with broken-down, petrol-less cars. Their presence prevented the remnants of the French army from regrouping. 'Half the time, they don't know where they are going,' Pierre told Elizabeth and his parents one day when he arrived on a visit to the farm. The streets of Annecy and the railway station were clogged with refugees, hoping to get into Switzerland. 'As for the trains . . .' He shrugged. 'Lisabette is better staying here.'

On 16th June Paul Reynaud resigned as prime minister and Philippe Pétain took over. Almost his first act was to broadcast to the French people to explain why an armistice was necessary to save the country more bloodshed, a sentiment which those who remembered the carnage of the Great War agreed with.

'I have this evening approached the enemy to ask if he is ready to try to find, between soldiers, with the struggle over and in honour, the means to put an end to the hostilities,' he said.

The little group around the wireless set in the farmhouse kitchen looked at each other in silence. Albert reached out with his good right hand and switched it off; they needed to save the accumulators and they had heard enough. They might not call a negotiated armistice a defeat, but in the days that followed and the terms made known, it became apparent that defeat it was.

The German army was to occupy three-fifths of the country, the remaining two-fifths in the south being ruled by Pétain's government from the town of Vichy. They would be allowed to maintain a small force to keep law and order, but all French warships must be laid up. Any French nationals caught fighting for Britain would be shot and French soldiers who had been taken prisoner would remain in German camps. British nationals must report to their local police station every day.

Albert looked at Elizabeth and smiled wearily. 'Do you still say you are staying here?'

'Yes, but if anyone asks, I'm French. I don't trust them not to round up all the British citizens and throw them in jail. I'll be Uncle Pierre's child, if he agrees.'

They laughed. 'I don't know what Jeanne will say to that,' Grandmère said.

Elizabeth took the replacement van into Annecy the next day to ask Jeanne and found herself witnessing the exodus of refugees. There was no panic; they seemed dazed, and shuffled along one behind the other in a kind of torpor. Luckily she was not travelling in their direct line and was able to find a way through them to the road leading to the vineyard.

Pierre and Jeanne readily agreed to acquire a daughter and they spent a little time discussing when and where she had been born and decided she had been privately educated in Switzerland; it was too easy for those in authority to check French schools. 'You'll need an identity card,' Pierre said. 'How are we going to get that?'

'I'll say I've lost it and get issued with a new one in the name of Lisabette Clavier.'

The boys, who had pleaded the necessity of working in the vineyard to avoid national service, laughed when they were told. 'We've got a grown-up sister, would you believe,' Philippe said, hugging her. 'We shall have to take good care of her.'

'I can take care of myself,' she said. 'And I'd better be off or I won't be back before dark.'

Two weeks later, she was sitting at the supper table with her grandparents eating a rabbit stew, when the back door opened and Justine came in. She was accompanied by a man in a heavy overcoat with a black hat pulled down over his eyes. He was bent and frail but he straightened up when he came into the kitchen.

'Max!' Elizabeth squealed, rushing to take his hand and pull him forward. 'How did you get here?'

'It's a long story,' he said. His voice and his whole demeanour betrayed immense weariness. He sank into a chair.

Elizabeth turned to Justine, who had been hugged by her mother and was being bombarded with questions. She, too, looked tired and not her usual chic self. 'Maman, let me gather myself, then I'll tell you everything.'

'Are you hungry?'

'Yes, but more thirsty than anything.'

Grandmère poured them coffee and heated up the stew again. 'Eat and drink and go to bed. We'll talk tomorrow. You aren't in any trouble, are you?'

Justine laughed. 'No, Maman. I have permission to visit my parents.'

'And Captain Coburn?'

'I don't know anything about a Captain Coburn. This is my French soldier boyfriend, Antoine Descourt, who was wounded in the throat and cannot speak properly.' She laughed. 'His French accent is atrocious and I couldn't risk it.'

That statement brought home to Elizabeth more than anything what had happened up to that point and what life in France was going to be like in the future. A small shudder of apprehension passed through her but was quickly suppressed.

Grandmère was as good as her word and refrained from asking questions. She was just thankful to have her daughter safely under her roof. Justine did not say anything about staying or leaving, until she and Elizabeth were in bed. Max was occupying the spare room, so she took the second bed in Elizabeth's room.

'What's it like in Paris now?' Elizabeth asked.

'Kind of peaceful if you discount the German flags flying from all the government buildings and their troops swaggering about, laughing and joking, filling the cafés and eating all our food. Half the population has fled and those that are left are going to work and trying to pretend everything is normal. How can it be normal? There are so many new regulations, it's difficult to keep up with them, and everyone is fearful of what is going to happen next.'

'How did you meet up with Max? He looks ghastly.'

'He turned up on my doorstep early one morning before anyone was about. He was on the point of collapse, so I dragged him in and put him to bed and when he woke I fed him. I couldn't let him go out again, he'd have been picked up straight away, so I had to think of something.'

'How did he get to you? Where had he come from?'

'No doubt he'll tell you, though he might spare you the horror. I certainly don't want it spoken of in front of Maman and Papa.'

'Go on.'

'He and the men he had with him were holed up in a barn on the Belgium border, trying to hold the Boche up so the evacuation could go ahead . . .'

'You mean Dunkirk?'

'Yes. They were overrun and had to surrender. He said they were marched for days without food or water, and when they complained about this they were all herded into a shed on someone's farm and shot. He was saved because the man beside him fell against him and took him down with him. The bullet intended for him grazed his leg. He was afraid the officer would go round finishing everyone off with a pistol, but luckily he didn't. Max played dead until they'd gone.

'He wasn't sure if there were any British troops left in France and he hadn't known there'd been an armistice, so he dragged himself back. God knows how he made it, but there he was in the middle of Paris, hungry, thirsty and exhausted with a nasty gash in his leg. He'd put a field dressing on it, but that was filthy.'

'And you looked after him. Thank you, Justine.'

'I didn't have much choice, did I?' she said with a chuckle. 'But I was glad to do it. De Gaulle says we must fight on and if helping people in danger is the only way we can do it, so be it. I'd do it for anyone in a similar situation.' General De Gaulle had escaped to England and was urging everyone not to give up, that they should continue the fight in whatever way they could, wherever they were. 'Whatever happens,' he had said in a broadcast to the French people from London, 'the flame of French resistance must not and shall not die.'

'What happens now?'

'I'm going to see Max safely over the Swiss border so he can make his way home, then I'm off back to Paris.'

'You're not staying here in the *Zone Libre*, then?'

'Free, you call it?' Justine laughed again. 'It might not be quite so manacled as the occupied zone, but believe me, it's far from free. Pétain is pulling the wool over your eyes if you believe that.'

'No, I don't believe it.'

'You could go back with Max.'

'No, I'm staying put, but I'll go as far as the border with you and see Max safely over. Do you think he's up to the climb?'

'He says he is. We'll see how he is in the morning. Let's go to sleep.'

It was a long while before Elizabeth slept. She had been shocked by Max's appearance and the dreadful story of prisoners being shot. It was something she had never thought of, let alone considered possible. How thankful she was that Max had escaped and that he had thought of Justine. She would send him home with loving messages to her family.

Max came out to the yard next morning just as she was driving the cows in to be milked. He looked better after a good night's sleep. He kissed her lightly and then stood leaning against the cowshed door while she did the milking.

'I gather from Justine you've had a pretty bad time of it,' she said, her head in the side of one of the cows, her hands moving rhythmically on the udders.

'Yes, though others have fared worse. They shot my men in cold blood, every single one of them. What am I to tell their families? How am I to explain how I survived and they didn't?'

'I don't know, Max, but I suppose the truth is always best. It was a fluke that you survived, not anything to be ashamed of. You were wounded, after all.'

'A mere flea bite.'

'That's not what Justine says. She told me you had walked all the way to Paris with a festering leg.'

He laughed. '"Hobbled" would be a more accurate word, but I didn't have any choice. It is the duty of every man to escape and I could not think of any other way to do it. A few people I met gave me food and drink but none wanted to risk harbouring me. In any case I was bent on finding our own lines. I had no idea France had fallen. It was a shock to find all those Nazi flags flying in Paris. Thank goodness for Justine's courage. She risked her life to help me.'

'She says she is going to take you over the border into Switzerland.'

'Yes.'

'It will be patrolled by the Vichy police. Whether they'll turn a blind eye is debatable.'

'We aren't going to risk it. Justine says she knows a route we can use; she used to climb there when she was a young girl. It's hard going but safer.'

'Will you manage it?'

'I'll have to, won't I? Come too.'

She could not deny she was tempted. To be safe at home with Mama and Papa and Amy and the boys seemed like a distant dream. She sighed and put it from her. 'No, my duty is here, just as it's yours to go back, but I'll come to the border with you.'

Justine was right; it was a hard climb once they left the meadows behind, plodded through the forest and then out onto the peaks. Justine went ahead, leaving Max and Elizabeth to walk together. Occasionally he stumbled and she put out a hand to steady him. She was glad it was summer and the snow gone; she doubted if he could have managed it in winter.

'You know where to go when you get over the border?' she asked him.

'Yes, Justine has given me instructions.' He paused. 'We might not see each other again for a very long time.'

'Oh, you never know. The war might be over in no time.'

They had been plodding steadily upwards, but now the slope flattened out and then they were looking down, and below them a mountain path snaked through the hills. Justine stopped and pointed. 'Switzerland, Max.'

Max and Elizabeth stood close together, his arm about her, apparently watching the path. A few goats had strayed onto it and above them a buzzard hovered. She looked up into his face. 'You'll be all right?'

'Of course. All I have to do is scramble down there and walk along the path until I come to the road, and strike out along that until I come to Les Crosets where I tell them who I am. Simple.' He paused, then added quietly, 'Come with me, Liz.'

'No. My grandparents need me. I'll be all right. We're in the unoccupied zone, after all. Don't worry about me.'

Justine had gone a little way from them and was examining the path through binoculars, leaving them a little privacy to say goodbye, but she was on her way back to them. Elizabeth turned to put her arms about his waist and looked up into his face. 'Take care of yourself, Max. I'll be thinking of you. If you can, let us know you've got safely back. Give my parents my letter and assure them I am fit and well and they are not to worry about me.'

'I'll try. Now I must go.' He hugged her close and she clung to him. It seemed so final, that goodbye, as if they would never see each other again, a possibility neither of them wanted to face. They stood together, two figures moulded together on what seemed the top of the world. He kissed her, softly at first and then more fervently, then slowly put her from him. 'Goodbye, sweetheart. God keep you safe until we meet again.' He turned from her to Justine who had rejoined them. 'Thank you for all you've done, Justine. I shan't forget it.' He kissed her cheek and then he was stumbling away from them towards the distant path. They watched him for several minutes then Justine took Elizabeth's arm. 'Come, Lisabette, we can do no more for him and we must get back.'

Reluctantly Elizabeth turned her back on the man making his way down the hill towards freedom and allowed Justine to lead her back to the farm, her vision blurred by tears.

The next day Justine insisted on returning to Paris in spite of the entreaties of her mother to stay. 'I may have lost half my pupils,' she told them. 'But the other half need educating and I can't leave my job without notice. Besides, my permit was only for four days and if I overstay they'll come looking for me. I don't intend to get into trouble if I can help it.'

Her job wasn't the only reason, she later confided when Elizabeth was driving her to the railway station in Annecy. 'If I can help one man escape, I can help more. There must be dozens of our soldiers, French and British, hiding up, trying to keep out of the hands of the Boche. It will be my way of continuing the fight.'

'Send them to me. I'll get them over the border.'

'I hoped you'd say that. Not a word to Maman, though, not until it becomes necessary.'

'Did you tell Max?'

'Yes. How the word will get about I don't know, but he seems to think it will. In the meantime I intend to be a good teacher, looking after my pupils, minding my own business and doing everything our conquerors expect of us. I will give them no cause for complaint.'

Compared to the suffocating crowds on the southbound trains, those going north were practically empty. They said their goodbyes, then Elizabeth drove back to Dransville. The little van was almost out of petrol and she didn't know when they would be able to get any more. But she had been uplifted by Justine's visit and the short but sweet reunion with Max. If there were more men like him on the run, then she would do all she could to help them. She started to sing: 'We'll meet again, don't know where, don't know when, but I know we'll meet again some sunny day . . .' She had to stop because her tears were choking her.

Chapter Six

The Battle for France was over, the Battle for Britain had yet to begin. Everywhere defences were being strengthened, pillboxes built, beaches mined, sandbags put up over doors and windows, blackout enforced to the point of being silly and often dangerous. Anyone who showed a chink of light from a window after dark was liable to have an air-raid warden knock on their door and tell them curtly, 'Put that light out.' Even lighting a cigarette out of doors was supposed to help guide the enemy. And the number of pedestrians hurt by cars and buses with their headlights blacked out was worrying. Rules were relaxed to allow headlights to have narrow slits so drivers could see and be seen. The faint blue light allowed in the trains after dark turned everyone's features a ghostly hue and was useless for reading purposes.

Factories were working round the clock producing guns,

aeroplanes, tanks and ammunition which were transported in long freight trains. Shipyards were turning out ships as fast as they could, but the shipping losses continued and the country was also desperately short of aeroplanes. Jack, circling above the fields of southern England, smiled to himself to think of the piles of metal in Nayton school playground, duplicated at almost every school in the country. It was next to useless and the whole idea had been a propaganda exercise. It was annoying to think that Nayton Manor had lost its intricate wrought iron gates. It would cost the earth to have them replaced.

His father had been philosophical about it, shrugging his shoulders and saying, 'It's war, Jack. Can't be helped.' And then he'd gone off to train his part-time troops, now called the Home Guard. They had recently been issued with uniforms and rifles and spent their time tramping over the fields and flinging themselves down to fire at unseen targets. They dug defensive ditches and practised throwing grenades at imaginary tanks. They ranged in age from the very young to the very old, those not physically fit enough for the armed forces and those, like Frank Lambert, who were in reserved occupations. Bernard who wanted desperately to join them, was allowed to call himself a messenger, though they wouldn't give him a uniform or a rifle. He donned his Boy Scout uniform and made himself an armband. They took themselves very seriously, which amused Jack.

'You won't laugh if we're invaded,' his father had told him. 'I doubt the RAF would be able to stop it.'

'We'd have a damn good try.'

Since the evacuation of Dunkirk, the Luftwaffe had concentrated on attacking shipping in the Channel and occasional bombing sorties over the mainland to test the country's defences. Jack was well aware that he and his fellow pilots were a large part of that defence. It was their job to shoot down the bombers before they could reach their targets without being shot down themselves. This task was made doubly difficult when the airfields of southern England became the enemy's main target.

Only the day before they had been scrambled to intercept a raid of hundreds of German bombers, supported by fighters. The trepidation he had felt, the nerves which stirred his stomach into knots before take-off, disappeared as soon as he was airborne and had a job to do. He had climbed and swirled about the cloudless sky, leaving vapour trails and puffs of smoke as he dived in, guns blazing, to claim a Messerschmitt. Jubilant, he had returned to base to find a scene of such devastation it sobered him at once. The administration buildings were badly damaged and still smoking. One of the gun emplacements had had a direct hit and was nothing but a hole in the ground and shattered metal. He only just managed to avoid a huge crater in the runway as he came down to land.

Luckily most of the aircraft had been airborne at the time of the raid, but those left on the ground would never fly again and there had been casualties among the ground crew and WAAFs who worked in the offices, stores and in the operations room. He had gone to a makeshift hut to be debriefed and then taken what rest he could before the enemy returned, which they did to every airfield they could reach, over and over again. This was air warfare with a vengeance. Over that beautiful summer he lost several good friends. How he managed to survive himself was down to luck, he supposed. Every spare minute off the base was precious. Depending how long he had he would go with his pals to the pub or home for a few days, and occasionally he would go and see Lucy.

She was always pleased to see him and she had a sort of sixth sense about whether he wanted to talk or not. If his head was full of what he had been doing and he needed to talk, she let him ramble on without interrupting. If he wanted to be quiet, she sat beside him, her head on his shoulder, in a sort of silent companionship that didn't need words. Sometimes they went to bed. By September, her pregnancy was beginning to show and he would lie and stroke her firm round stomach and feel the baby kick. He was still unsure how he felt about fatherhood and had certainly said nothing to his family about it. They did not know about Lucy.

Sometimes when he and Amy were at home at the same time, she teased him about girlfriends, but he would answer vaguely that he had hundreds of them and which one did she mean? Sometimes, in his more serious moments, he told her that he didn't think it was right to commit oneself to anyone when life was so precarious. Besides, he thought telling anyone about his relationship with Lucy would spoil it, make it cheap and nasty, when it was nothing of the sort. Lucy understood that. He would return to the station refreshed and ready for the next battle.

The time had come when they were almost beaten. The shortage of aircraft was critical and the shortage of men to fly them even more so. Pilots were grey with fatigue and ground crews were working against the clock to have the aircraft ready to take off as soon as another alert was sounded. One warm day, early in September, those of his squadron on call were sitting outside the assembly hut on deckchairs, reading or catching up on lost sleep, waiting for the telephone to ring and their squadron leader to shout 'Scramble!'. It was eerily quiet. The sun shone and there wasn't a cloud in the sky. Where was Jerry? It was perfect weather for bombing. They found out the next day. The Luftwaffe turned on London.

It was a beautiful afternoon, the sky was blue and the trees in London parks afforded a welcome shade from the unseasonably high temperature. There were people about, civilians as well as those in uniform of one sort or another, going about their business, among them Captain Max Coburn, newly arrived in England, making his way to Liverpool Street station to catch a train to report to his regimental headquarters in Norwich after an extensive debriefing by Intelligence. He didn't pay any particular attention to the siren, presuming it presaged a raid on the airfields close to the capital and so he continued on his way to the underground.

It was then he became aware of the drone of aircraft and people in the street running for shelter, many of them pushing past him to go down into the safety of the underground. The noise made him stop and look up at the sky. There were so many aircraft he gave up trying to count them and it was obvious they were making for the docks. As he stood there he saw the bombs falling, and even though he was some distance away, he could hear the dull thud of explosions and saw the huge clouds of smoke and, very soon, flames reaching high into the sky. He forgot about his own safety, as he watched.

'I should take shelter, if I were you, sir,' he was advised by a man in a navy uniform wearing a tin hat and an armband both inscribed with the letters ARP. 'No sense in taking unnecessary risks.'

The voice brought him out of his reverie and he hastened to the shelter pointed out to him, where he settled down with others to wait for the all-clear, while he mused on how he had arrived where he was.

He had made his way into Switzerland after leaving Lizzie and Justine, though by the time he had found someone to help him, he was dropping with exhaustion. The long walk dragging himself from the Belgium border to Paris with a painful gash in his leg had taken its toll and finding his way over the mountains had nearly finished him. Justine knew how bad it was, though he had kept it from Lizzie. He thanked God for Justine because, without her, he would have died. He had been at his last gasp when he knocked on her door. She had fetched a sympathetic doctor, let him rest and fed him with her own rations. He had known he could not stay with her; it was far too risky and so, as soon as he felt he could walk, she had obtained *cartes de travail* for them both and they had taken a train to Annecy where they took a cab to Dransville. 'I can get you across the border into Switzerland from there,' she had told him. 'After that it will be up to you.'

The Swiss authorities had been suspicious at first and it was not until after a prolonged interrogation and several telephone calls to England that they accepted that he was who he said he was. They sent him to hospital in Geneva where he stayed a month having his wound cleaned and dressed and being given physiotherapy to strengthen the damaged muscle. Then they arranged for him to go on a passenger flight to Lisbon where he reported to the British Embassy. After interminable red tape and waiting about, he had been flown back to England, arriving in September just as the Battle of Britain was ending.

It wasn't until everyone started to leave the shelter he realised the all-clear had sounded. He emerged to stand with everyone else looking towards the river. Above the rooftops, the sky was red with flames. In the street around them fire engines, their bells clanging, raced past, followed by ambulances.

'They've got the docks,' a woman said.

'Poor devils,' someone else murmured, referring to the people who lived and worked in the dock areas. It was the most closely inhabited area of London, much of it overcrowded slums. The old terraces of back-to-back dwellings would burn like tinder. Drawn, he did not know why, Max walked down towards the river. As he approached he was aware of smoke and a smell of burning and other smells: beer, glue, melting tar, syrup. Grey dust filled the air and covered everything and he could feel the heat. Breathing was difficult. He stopped a warden cycling towards him. 'Is there anything I can do to help?'

'No, Captain, unless you're a doctor.'

'No, 'fraid not.'

'Then I'd say get the hell out of here, the fires are spreading and we've enough on our plates without spectators.'

Duly chastened Max went back to Liverpool Street station. There was pandemonium there as people trying to get onto trains merged with people coming up from sheltering in the underground which was strictly against regulations. There were one or two disused stations and tunnels which had been designated air-raid shelters but there were not enough of them, and in any case, people seeking shelter dived into the first place they came to.

He had a long wait for a train, and before one came the siren went again and the bombers returned in even greater numbers. If the curving ribbon of the Thames had not been landmark enough, the fires acted as a beacon. Max refused to join the exodus going below ground and continued to sit on a bench on the platform and from his seat was only too aware of what was happening. He could hear the drone of aeroplanes even if he could not see them, wave after wave of them. He could hear the rumble and thud of explosions, could feel the ground move beneath his feet, and by walking down to the end of the platform to the open air, he could see the whole horizon towards the east was a glaring orange, licked with blue and red. Searchlight beams tried to pick out the bombers for the ack-ack guns, whose firing was reassuring if not particularly accurate. He went back to his bench to wait for the train.

It did not arrive until after the all-clear had sounded and then it travelled to Norwich at the pace of a snail, stopping frequently in sidings. He arrived at barracks late the following morning, red-eyed from lack of sleep but, like the rest of his countrymen, he was not cowed. If anything he was more angry and more determined than ever to exact revenge. 'Just you wait, Adolf Hitler, just you wait,' he murmured as he fell into bed. 'You are going to be sorry for this night's work.'

The bombing of London after that was relentless. Night after night until Christmas the raiders came, with only one free night owing to fog. The docks suffered terribly, but so did the rest of London. Railways and mainline stations were hit, so that travellers coming in from the country found their journey ending in the suburbs and they had to find their own way into the city. The population was getting used to going into the shelters for the night and emerging in the morning, not knowing what faced them: destroyed or damaged houses and businesses, roads torn up, vehicles mangled, broken glass, dust and rubble everywhere, burst water and gas mains. If, when they returned to their homes, they found only a few broken windows and some plaster down from the ceiling, they offered up a little prayer of thanks. But it wasn't only Londoners who suffered. The centre of Coventry and its fine cathedral were reduced to rubble, Liverpool, Bristol, Southampton and many large towns, including Norwich, were hit.

Lucy, getting very close to her time, had only one more week to work and then she would be reliant on the allowance Jack paid into her bank account every month. He had been surprised when she told him she had never had a bank account, had never had the need of one since her pa never gave her more than a few shillings a week pocket money. 'No good putting that in the bank was it?' she had said cheerfully.

'No, but I think I can do better than that. We'll open an account for you and get you a chequebook, then you can draw out what you need.'

The chequebook had remained unused because, while Jack paid her rent, she managed quite well on her wages, but she supposed she would have to get used to using it. Her whole life was geared to her coming baby and Jack's infrequent visits. He didn't get much leave and what he did have she had to share with his family at Nayton Manor. She understood that and supposed she ought to be grateful that he came at all. Her dream that he would marry her and they would be a proper family, was just that – a dream. He was far and away above her. But even so, her life was a hundred times better than it would have been with Frank Lambert and she was content.

She was waiting for a bus to take her home after her shift one evening about a week before Christmas when she found herself standing in the queue next to Amy de Lacey.

She turned her coat collar up, tied her headscarf tighter over her hair and pretended to be studying her feet on the slushy pavement. All in vain.

'Lucy? It is Lucy Storey, isn't it?'

Lucy lifted her head. Amy was in nurse's uniform, grey dress and navy-blue cloak with a red lining. She was regarding Lucy with her head cocked on one side. Lucy's pride came to her rescue. 'Why, Miss de Lacey, I didn't realise it was you. How are you? How is everyone at the Manor?'

'Everyone is fine as far as I know. I'm going home for Christmas. With a bit of luck Jack will get leave too, though we won't see Lizzie.'

'Is she still in France?'

'Yes, and likely to be for the duration. But what about you? Are you going home for Christmas?'

'My home is here in Norwich.'

'Yes, quite.' She looked down at Lucy's swollen belly. 'I understand.'

Lucy gave her a quirky smile. 'I doubt it. Please don't tell my father you have seen me.'

'No, of course not, if you don't want me to. Wouldn't dream of it. How are you managing?'

'I'm managing very well, thank you. I have   ' she paused searching for the word '. . . a protector.'

'Good. If you need any help at all, you can reach me at the Norfolk and Norwich hospital. Don't be afraid to ask.'

'Thank you.'

A bus drew up and the queue began to shuffle forward. 'This is my bus,' Amy said. 'You catching this one too?'

'No, the next one.'

'Cheerio, then. Have a happy Christmas.'

'Same to you.'

Amy climbed aboard the bus, leaving Lucy to stand about in the cold for the next half-hour. If it hadn't been for Miss de Lacey she would be sitting comfortably in that bus on her way home instead of having to wait half an hour for the next one. But she really did not want to be questioned.

'You'll never guess who I saw in Norwich last week,' Amy said during dinner on Christmas Eve. All the family except Elizabeth was there: her father and mother, Edmund, and even Jack, looking older all of a sudden, but splendidly fit.

The conversation had been lively while everyone caught up with what the others had been doing and discussed the progress of the war, the latest casualties and the war in North Africa where the Allies were having some success. It was when the subject of the war dwindled to a halt Amy remembered seeing Lucy.

'No, but no doubt you are about to tell us,' her father said.

'Lucy Storey. You remember, the girl who used to open the crossing gates.'

'Oh, so that's where she's got to,' Annelise said. 'We wondered. She disappeared so suddenly.'

'I'm not surprised,' Amy said. 'She's as big as a bus.'

'You mean she's pregnant?'

'Yes. I asked her how she was managing and she said she had a protector.' She looked sharply at Jack who seemed to be choking on his pudding.

'Protector?' her mother queried. 'You don't mean she's fallen into the hands of a pimp? I would never have believed that of her.'

'I expect she meant her baby's father was looking after her,' Jack said, regaining his composure.

'I hope that is the case,' Annelise said, then to Amy, 'Did she say who that was?'

'No, my bus came and I left her. In any case I don't think she would have told me, she seemed reluctant to talk.'

'Who can blame her?' Jack said. 'Everyone condemning her and looking at her in disgust. It might not have been her fault.'

'No, of course not,' Amy agreed. 'After all, it takes two.'

'Do you think her father threw her out?' Charles put in, glancing at Edmund who was busy eating his pudding and pretending not to listen.

'No, she begged me not to tell him, so I assume he doesn't know about it. Don't any of you say anything.'

'We wouldn't dream of it,' Annelise said. 'It's none of our business.'

'Quite,' Jack said. 'Let's talk about something else.'

Edmund had been listening to the exchange with curiosity, though endeavouring not to show it. He had discovered about making babies the year before from a school friend and imparted his knowledge to Bernard, who had known about it for ages and laughed at him for his ignorance. 'If you lived in London like I do, where the walls are thin and women have babies all the time, you'd have found out too.

You'd have to go about with eyes and ears shut not to.' And he had proceeded to fill in the details to Edmund's shock and disgust. Now, dinner over, he couldn't wait to find Bernard and tell him this latest titbit.

Bernard's mother had come to Nayton for Christmas, bringing baby Joe with her. Mr Hodgkins was in the army in North Africa – Mrs Hodgkins hadn't heard from him for some time. Annelise had suggested they might like to take their meals together in the nursery dining room so they could be private together. She had had a fire lit in what had once been the nursemaid's quarters so they would be snug and warm. Edmund had to wait until their meal was over and Mrs Hodgkins was busy seeing to the baby to draw his friend away.

They went to the billiard room, but Jack and his father were in there playing snooker, so they hurriedly retreated to Edmund's bedroom where Edmund repeated the dinner conversation almost word for word. 'What d'you think of that?' he finished.

'It's either your brother or the signalman.'

'What is?'

'The baby's father, of course. After what I saw at the gamekeeper's cottage, I don't think it's the signalman, unless he tried to rape her again.'

'Rape – what's that?'

'You don't know nothin', do you? It's when a man forces himself on a woman when she don' want 'im to. I told you about it. It's against the law.'

'That so? Jack wouldn't do that.'

'I didn't say he would. He's sweet on her and she disappeared right after that signalman tried to rape her and he rescued her. I saw them talking together on my way to school the day after it happened. I don' reckon she'd say no to 'im.'

'I don't believe it. He wouldn't.'

Bernard shrugged. 'Up to you. You could ask him.'

'No fear. And you're not to say anything either.'

'Course I won't.'

But Edmund was intrigued. His conviction that Jack would have nothing to do with anyone like Lucy was wavering. His brother had certainly reacted strangely to Amy's story. But he kept that feeling to himself; somehow it felt like a betrayal, but he would keep his eyes and ears open for more clues.

Everyone went to church the following morning, including Mrs Hodgkins and her children, and afterwards they came back to have Christmas dinner together. There was a goose Charles had been given by one of the tenant farmers, plenty of vegetables and a huge Christmas pudding, the ingredients for which had been hoarded by Mrs Baxter for months. In the afternoon there were presents for everyone and parlour games and much noisy hilarity, which Eileen Hodgkins found bewildering.

It had been an awkward sort of reunion. The children had learnt all sorts of things that worried their mother: daily baths, different tastes in food, fussiness about their clothes, especially Cissie who insisted on being called Cecily.

They spoke differently, were polite and seemed far more knowledgeable than she was. The next day she went back home to a war-torn London feeling sad and inadequate and wondering how it was all going to end.

'I've scrounged some petrol for my car,' Jack said to Amy when it was her turn to leave. 'I'll take you back to Norwich, if you like.'

'But isn't it out of your way?'

'Not much and I don't mind. There's been so much going on over Christmas we've hardly had a chance to talk.'

'OK.'

They had been journeying in silence for half an hour, before she said. 'You've got something on your mind.'

'I was wondering about Lucy. Lucy Storey, you know.'

Amy laughed. 'Now, I wonder why that should be?'

'It can't be easy for her.'

'No, but I hope that protector of hers is really looking after her.'

'I'm sure he is.'

She turned to look at him. 'Stop beating about the bush, Jack.'

'It's not what you think.'

'What do I think?'

'You probably think it's sordid and disgusting.'

'And it isn't?'

'No. If I tell you, you won't breathe a word to Ma and Pa, will you?'

'Course not. What do you take me for?'

He kept his eyes on the road as he told her about rescuing her from Lambert and her pa throwing her out because he wanted to marry again and telling her he wasn't her real father.

'Do you think that's true?' she asked.

'Don't know, do I? Bert Storey must think it is. She was so distressed . . .'

'But why turn to you? Had you . . . ?'

'No, I hadn't.' His answer was swift. 'But I'd been painting her portrait. It was good too. I was hoping to exhibit it, but the war came and everything else . . .'

'So Frank Lambert is the father?'

'No, he is not. I am. It happened later, after I'd helped her find a job and a home in Norwich. Sometimes I needed a little consolation.'

'Oh, I see, and she provided it.'

'Yes.'

She chuckled. 'So my big brother is going to be a daddy. But how do you think you are going to keep that from Mama and Papa? Are you going to marry her?'

'That's not on the cards. Life's too short and we'd both be sorry in the end.'

'Then why bother telling me about it?'

'I don't know. I wanted to tell someone. I thought you'd understand.'

'Oh, I understand all right.'

He decided to ignore the tartness in her tone. 'Because she lives alone and it's her first, she's booked into the Norfolk and Norwich for the birth and I was wondering . . .'

'If I'd look out for her?'

'Would you?'

'Of course I will. I feel nothing but sympathy for her.'

He smiled. 'Lucy, being Lucy, wouldn't want your sympathy. She'd positively hate it.'

'No, I already gathered that. Are you going to see her now?'

'Yes, just to make sure she's all right.'

'Jack, you are the most mixed-up individual I have ever encountered. You pretend to be hard, but underneath you are as soft as butter. But if you'll take a spot of advice from your little sister, who really knows nothing at all, you won't string her along . . .'

'You are right,' he said. 'You really know nothing at all.'

'Point taken.'

Since she had finished her job, Lucy had nothing to do but wait and knit and sew baby clothes. She had always been used to hard work, to having her days filled, and this sudden inactivity was both boring and unsettling. Boring because she was idle and clumsy, unsettling because she was more than a little frightened at the prospect of becoming a mother. Would she be a good mother? Would she love the little one as she ought? She was reminded of her own mother. Girls naturally turned to their mums when they became mothers themselves, but where was hers? She had been thinking of her a lot lately, wondering where she was and if she would like the idea of being a granny.

Mum hadn't had a family of her own, or so she had said. Nor had she said why she had come to marry Bert Storey.

They were poles apart. Her mother was gentle, well educated, well spoken, always smartly dressed. She had tried to bring Lucy up in the same vein. Her father – no, not her father, if what he had told her was true – was rough and ready, coarsely spoken and a great drinker. He had a kind of inverted snobbery and decried those of higher rank. So why had he chosen her mother for a wife? If he knew Jack de Lacey was the father of her child, he would explode with hatred, so he must never know. She prayed Amy de Lacey would keep her secret.

She was just going to scramble some dried egg for her tea when Jack arrived. He had a way of turning up just when the loneliness was getting the better of her. She ran into his arms. He kissed her and then she burst into tears.

'What's this?' he said, leaning back and taking her chin in his hands. 'Not pleased to see me?'

'Oh, I am, I am. I've been so lonely.'

'Don't you talk to the neighbours?'

'Not much. Only to pass the time of day. I'm so glad you've come.' She sniffed and blew her nose on the handkerchief he offered. 'There! I'm better now. Do you want some scrambled egg?'

'Yes, if you're having some too.'

'How long can you stay?'

'Until tomorrow. I'll have to be away soon after breakfast. Are you all right? Apart from being lonely, I mean.'

'Yes. I'm told at the clinic everything is as it should be and it won't be long.' She tried to laugh. 'After that I'll be too busy to be lonely.' She put the powdered egg in a saucepan, and mixed in some milk and a tiny knob of butter from her ration and set it on the stove, stirring it all the time otherwise it would go lumpy. 'Make some toast, Jack.'

He did so willingly. Cooking was something he never had to do at home, nor any menial task about the house, and would have laughed if anyone had suggested it, but here with Lucy it seemed a natural thing to do. He poked the fire into a blaze and stuck a round of bread on a toasting fork. 'I could ask my sister to look in on you, keep you company now and again, if you'd like that.'

'She told you she had seen me?'

'Yes.' He pretended to concentrate on holding the bread to the heat.

'So she knows about us.'

'I told her. I thought it would be nice for you to have someone to turn to when I'm not here.' He turned the bread over to toast the other side.

'She said she wouldn't tell Pa and his new wife.'

'Then I'm sure she won't. In any case, she's back in Norwich now.' He paused and began on the next slice of bread. 'What do you say?'

'I'll get in touch with her, if I need anything. But I'm all right, just big and awkward and tired.' She buttered the finished toast, scraping it on thinly. 'I'll be glad when it's all over.'

It was all over before he left the following day, much later than he intended. They had hardly settled in bed with his arm about her and her head fitting snugly into his shoulder when she suddenly stirred and groaned. 'Oh, Jack, I've got a pain.'

158

'How much of a pain?'

'A lot. God, it's coming. The baby's coming.'

He scrambled out of bed and dressed hurriedly, helped her to dress, bundled her in his car and drove to the Norfolk and Norwich hospital, frightened to death by her groans of agony, though she did her best to stifle them. She was put in a wheelchair and taken from him, leaving him to pace up and down the corridor all night. The nurses brought him cups of tea and advised him to sit down, but he couldn't. He was wound up like a coiled spring; it was worse than going on ops. He had never expected that. Did all prospective fathers feel this gut-wrenching apprehension?

Amy came to him in the early hours. 'I asked the midwifery section to let me know when Lucy came in,' she said. 'I didn't expect it to be tonight.'

'Neither did I! Amy, does it always take this long?'

'It's hardly started. Why don't you go and rest somewhere?'

'I can't. I keep thinking of all the things that could go wrong. If anything happens to Lucy, what will I do? It doesn't bear thinking of and yet I can't stop thinking of it.'

'You're really rather fond of her, aren't you?'

'She's the mother of my child. Or will be. All being well. But what if it isn't? What will I do? I don't know anything about babies.'

'You are being a pessimist. Of course nothing bad will happen. Lucy is young and healthy. Stop worrying.'

A midwife came to them at six o'clock. She was smiling.

'Lieutenant Storey,' she said, addressing Jack. 'You have a fine son. Seven and a half pounds.'

He had been persuaded to sit in the waiting room, but jumped up as soon as he saw her approaching. He hardly registered the name she had given him. 'And Lucy?'

'Your wife is fine. You can come and see her now.'

He followed her in a daze and into the delivery ward. Lucy was sitting up in bed with the baby in a shawl in her arms. She was smiling and crying at the same time. She held out her free hand to him. 'Jack, come and see him. He's beautiful.'

He took her hand and sat on the edge of the bed and looked at the new life he and Lucy had created. There was a huge lump in his throat. He hadn't expected to feel so moved. He reached out and touched the baby's cheek with the back of his finger. 'What are we going to call him?'

'Not Jack.'

'No, better not Jack.'

'Have you got a second name?'

'Pierre Albert, after my uncle and grandfather.'

'That's French, isn't it?'

'Yes, English translation Peter Albert.'

'I'm certainly not calling him Albert, that's my fa— his name. But Peter is nice.'

'Peter, it shall be.'

'You've got to report back on duty, haven't you?'

'Afraid so.'

'You had better go, then.'

'I don't want to, I want to get to know this little chap.' He

160

reached out and took the baby from her, holding him in his arms and gazing down at him, holding out a finger for the little one to clutch. He did not speak. He was overwhelmed. After a minute or two, he handed him back. 'Look after him, sweetheart, and take care of yourself. I'll come back as soon as I can.' He stood up and turned towards the door just as Amy came in.

'Can I see my nephew?' She came forward and stood by the bed. 'Off you go, brother dear. We'll be fine.'

He left them and walked out to where he had left his car. He didn't have enough petrol to take him back to Biggin Hill and so he drove it to a garage and asked them to lay it up somewhere for the duration, then he took a train to Liverpool Street.

He had plenty of time to think on the journey. His thoughts were a mass of contradictions. Where was the happy-go-lucky, somewhat indolent young man he had been at the start of the war? Where was his ambition to marry someone with breeding who was prepared to overlook his lack of it and give him *entrée* into the world of the aristocrat in the same way that his mother had done? Where was that man? Was he still around? Could anyone resembling that man survive amid the mayhem of war? More to the point, did he want to? But it was hard to let go.

Chapter Seven

After reporting to Norwich, Max had been given fourteen days leave and had taken a train to Nayton to deliver news of Elizabeth and hand over her letter and snapshots. Lord and Lady de Lacey had quizzed him almost as hard as his army interrogators, but he knew they were anxious and he had done his best to reassure them. He had gone from there to finish his leave with his sister in Scotland, going for walks, amusing his nephew and niece and trying to pretend all was well, though the anger never left him. And then it was back to the war and waiting for something to happen. When it did, the nature of it took him by surprise.

He was told to present himself at the Inter-Services Research Bureau in Orchard Park, not far from Baker Street, where he was to report to Major Lewis Gielgud. 'He's heard about your escape from France and he's keen to learn about it from your own lips,' his commanding officer told him. Max had already been thoroughly debriefed at the War Office and he didn't see what more he could tell. Major Gielgud was the brother of the famous actor and he guessed they were going to use it in a propaganda film or something of the sort. He didn't like that idea. He hadn't done anything out of the ordinary. In fact he still felt guilty for surviving when his men had not.

On arrival, a doorman took him by lift to a second-floor flat where he was ushered into a room and asked to wait. He looked about him. There was a desk and chair, a couple of armchairs and a cupboard. There was an ashtray on the desk. He sat down and lit a cigarette. He had smoked half of it when Major Gielgud entered the room; he stubbed it out and stood up.

'At ease, Captain. Sit down again, there's a good fellow.'

Max sat.

The major perched himself on the edge of the desk. 'Do you know why we have asked you here?'

'I was told you wanted to know about my escape from France.'

'That's right. You will forgive me if I ask seemingly foolish questions but I need to know every tiny detail.'

'You doubt I did it?'

'Good heavens, no! But it's only through chaps like you, who've been through it, that we can learn what life is like over there and perhaps help others. So, let me have your account, especially the difficulties you encountered.'

Max went over it all again. Major Gielgud listened

attentively, now and again interrupting with a question. One of the most difficult to answer was, 'How did you find the mood of the French?'

'I didn't come into contact with many – Justine was anxious about my English accent – but to me they seemed resigned, almost apathetic, but she assured me there were others with the spirit to resist. She said she would help anyone trying to escape and there were others who would do so too.'

'That is heartening. And the people in the village? Dransville, you said?'

'Yes. I only met the grandparents of my girlfriend. She is staying with them.'

'She is French?'

'No, English. The daughter of Lord de Lacey. Her mother is French.'

'Didn't she want to come home with you?'

'No, she felt her grandparents needed her. Her grandfather has had a stroke and can't manage their farm.'

'Isn't she afraid?'

Max laughed. 'She doesn't see the need to be afraid, since the village is in the *Zone Libre*, but she has taken the precaution of pretending to be French, the daughter of her uncle. She is completely bilingual, of course. Whether that will be enough to protect her, I have no idea.'

'She sounds like a spirited young lady.'

'Oh, she's definitely that.'

'And Mademoiselle Justine Clavier seems to me to be another spirited lady. Courageous too, don't you think?'

'Very.' He paused. 'What's this all about, Major?'

Gielgud smiled. 'You have no doubt gathered that I do not ask out of idle curiosity. Our work is very hush-hush, but I think you can help us in a practical way.'

'Anything.'

'How's your French?'

'Reasonably good, but my French friends laugh at my accent.'

'We can work on that. Would you be prepared to go back?'

'Go back?' Max queried. 'You mean back to France?'

'Yes. There will inevitably be downed airmen, escaped POWs, Frenchmen needing to join the Free French, and we are trying to organise escape routes, safe houses, and recruit people like Mademoiselle Clavier who can be trusted to help, that sort of thing. And sabotage, of course.'

'I see.'

'Do you want time to consider?'

'No.' He didn't need to think about it; he wanted revenge for what the Huns had done to his men. He had written a personal letter to their next of kin, emphasising the bravery and devotion to duty each had shown. It had been a harrowing task and left him feeling close to tears and very angry. 'If it helps, I'll do what I can.'

'You will be required to sign the Official Secrets Act and you will not utter a word of what you are being trained to do to anyone, anyone at all, not even your nearest and dearest.'

'My nearest and dearest is in France.'

'Have you any way of communicating with her?'

'No, none at all.' Max brightened at the prospect of letting Lizzie know that he might be seeing her again sooner than they thought, but he was soon disabused of that idea.

'Good. You will not on any account attempt it. I'm going to hand you over to someone else to complete the formalities and then you will be one of us and under our direction. You will return to your unit until you are sent for, probably in two or three weeks. Your commanding officer will be informed. No one else. Security is of the utmost importance.'

'I understand. How will I be sent back and when?'

'No idea. You've some intensive training to get through before that happens and there will have to be reports on your suitability, both mental and physical, and only if you pass all the tests will you be sent out and then it might be by sea or air. Now I will introduce you to Miss Atkins. She will ask you some more questions and will fill you in on the next step.'

Miss Atkins was in a smart civilian suit so he had no idea what rank she held, if she had one at all, but she had seemed very contained, charming but contained. She managed, without in any way appearing to interrogate him, to find out all about him from the cradle to his service with the BEF and escape over the mountains of Haute Savoie. At the end of the interview, conducted in French throughout, he left with his head buzzing, knowing his life had taken a dramatic turn. He was going back to France, back to a country occupied by the enemy, to be an undercover agent, and for that he would be trained. Miss Atkins' last words had been: 'I should practise your French, Captain. The more fluent you are the better. If we can't eradicate your accent, we can give you a cover story to account for it.'

Arriving at Liverpool Street station to wait for a train to take him back to Britannia Barracks, he sat on a bench and imagined himself in France, concocting conversations with himself in French. When the train came in, it brought Jack de Lacey with it.

'Hallo, Max,' he greeted him cheerfully. Jack was always cheerful. 'I haven't seen you since you got back. Mother told me all about it. It was a damned gutsy thing, getting yourself out of France under the noses of the Boche.'

'I had help. Justine and Lizzie were the gutsy ones, not me.' After the warnings about security he had just had he wasn't disposed to talk about it. 'How are you?'

'Tickety-boo. I'm just going back from leave. What about you? Not been invalided out, I see.'

'No. I'm fully fit.'

'Have you heard anything of Lizzie since?'

'No, have you?'

'No. It's a bugger, isn't it, not knowing?'

'Yes.'

'At least, she's saved the blitz,' Jack said, 'I shouldn't think they're being bombed in Haute Savoie.'

'No, there is that. What are you doing these days?'

'Flying Spitfires, trying to stop the bombers, but once they reach London . . .' He shrugged. 'We can't go in after them for fear of our own guns and the barrage balloons but you can see the fires for miles and I keep thinking of all the poor devils on the ground having to put up with it night after night. I get so ruddy angry. I want to hit back.'

'Me too.'

'Are you due to go abroad again soon?'

'Probably. Waiting for orders.'

'Well, good luck to you.'

'You too.' They shook hands and parted.

Max boarded the train and found a corner seat, where he sat down to muse on his meeting with Jack. Aware of the strictures he was under for secrecy, he had been wary of answering Jack's questions. It was symptomatic of what his life was going to be like in the future. Secrecy and lies, playing a part, pretending to be something he was not. It was bad enough in England, it would be a hundred times worse when he went to France. One false move, one cover story demolished through carelessness could cost him his life and that of everyone else involved. He had to learn to be a disseminator and think on his feet.

It went against the grain to lie. His parents had brought him up to be strictly honest in all his dealings. At school he had had the reputation of being a goody-goody, especially after his parents had died, one after the other, in the space of a year. His mother was already terminally ill when his father had been killed in France in the last days of the Great War, the war, so they said, to end all wars. He had only been ten at the time and doing his best to be brave. His mother's death had been slow and painful. Her last words to him had been, 'Be good, Max; work hard, always be truthful and honest and make me proud of you. And look after Sylvia for me.'

He had promised to do so and, always aware of that promise, had grown up a rather serious young man. He and his sister had lived with their Aunt Gladys in Edinburgh, who was very strict and not given to shows of emotion. He felt she had taken the orphans in out of duty, not love. When he won a scholarship to St Andrews he had left home and, after graduating, had looked about for a way of earning a living, as far away from Edinburgh as possible. His father had been in the Royal Norfolk Regiment and so to Norfolk he had gone and joined the regular army. It was a life he liked. He was fed and housed and could be his own man. For the first time in his life he had learnt to enjoy himself. One of his teachers had been Elizabeth de Lacey.

He had been staying on one of his leaves with James Davenport, a friend from college, at his home in Devon. The Davenports were a gregarious family and had a huge number of social contacts. James had been convinced he would instantly fall in love with his sister, Belinda, but his eye had lighted on Lizzie who was also staying with them, part of a noisy house party of young people. By the time the party broke up, they had agreed to correspond and everything went on from there. He had been invited to stay at Nayton Manor with her family and found himself welcomed and made a fuss of by her delightful mother. Everyone was so open and affectionate, so different from his own childhood, and he had been warmed by it. Had he not already been in love with Lizzie, he would have fallen for her then. She was caring, loving and fun to be with. She made him laugh. If the war had not come they would have been arranging a wedding by now. Instead she was in France and he was in England, waiting to be called back to Baker Street. He was full of a mixture of trepidation and excitement.

He had no idea where he would be sent to in France and had been told he was not to contact Lizzie and that would be hard, but at least he would be nearer to her, and when the Allies turned this war around and invaded the Continent, he would be there, ready to whisk her away. It was, as far as he was concerned, the light at the end of the tunnel.

Jack was not due back at base until the following morning and decided to have a night on the town. In spite of the air raids, London was trying to carry on as normal. The cinemas, theatres, concert halls and nightclubs were all functioning. In fact they were busier and noisier than usual as people tried to forget the war for a few hours. He went to the cinema. The air-raid siren sounded just as the film was finishing and he joined the exodus leaving the building for the shelters.

'Jack de Lacey, by all that's wonderful!'

He swung round to face Belinda Davenport. She was elegantly dressed as always, fur coat, felt hat with a sweeping feather, silk stockings and smart high-heeled shoes. 'Belinda, how are you?'

'The better for seeing you.' She linked her arm in his. 'My date stood me up and I had to sit through that awful film alone.'

'Perhaps he couldn't help it. In wartime these things happen.'

'True, but it doesn't matter, I'd just as soon have you for an escort. You aren't in any hurry to go somewhere, are you?'

'Only to the shelter.'

'Oh, I can't be bothered with that. It's dreadful with everyone sitting about eating, drinking and knitting and trying to organise sing-songs to drown out the noise of the bombs. And they smell disgusting. I'd rather be out in the fresh air.'

'We can't stay on the streets, Belinda. I didn't come through the Battle of Britain to be killed by a bomb.'

'No, I suppose not. I'm staying at Daddy's pied-à-terre. There's a shelter in the basement for the residents. Let's go there. It's only round the corner.' She took his hand and began to run as the drone of aeroplanes could be heard approaching. Everyone else was running. He went, willy-nilly.

They dived into the block of flats just as the first bombs began to fall. 'Down here,' she said, leading the way to the boiler room in the basement, where two or three people were already making themselves comfortable and were bringing out hip flasks of spirits and thermos flasks of tea. Jack and Belinda sat side by side on an old sofa which the caretaker had brought down along with some armchairs and a coffee table or two. There were magazines scattered about and a few books. It was unlike any public shelter he had been in.

'Well now, tell me what you've been up to?' she said in a low voice so the others could not listen in, though they didn't appear interested. 'What are you flying?'

'How do you know I'm a flyer? I might be ground crew.'

'Not you, my sweet, you'd never stay on the ground if there was a little adventure to be had in the air.'

He grinned ruefully. 'You know me so well.'

'Of course I do. We've known each other all our lives. Played together as children, didn't we, you, Amy and Lizzie and me and James. How are they all? How are your parents?'

'Ma and Pa are well, still at Nayton Manor of course . . .'

'Ah, Nayton Manor, lovely old house, that. I don't suppose they have to put up with this.' She jerked her head towards the ceiling. Above them there was a deafening noise, screeching whistles and earth-moving thuds. They flinched now and again, but then relaxed as they realised that one wasn't for them.

'No. It's fairly quiet there, apart from nearby aerodromes, that is.'

'You're not stationed at one of those?'

'No, Biggin Hill.'

'That took a pasting, didn't it?'

'Yes, pretty bad. But not as bad as London. The change of target let us off the hook.'

'And Lizzie and Amy, what are they doing?'

'Amy's training to be a nurse at the Norfolk and Norwich. She was home for Christmas. Lizzie's in France, staying with our grandparents.'

'Good heavens, what's she doing there?'

'She was on holiday there when war broke out and couldn't get home.'

'That's rotten luck.'

'Yes. What about you?'

'Me? Oh, I'm surviving the best I can. My parents are both busy helping the war effort in their own way and James is in the army. I've just been to register for war work.'

'You?' He laughed at the idea of Belinda Davenport doing work of any kind, let alone war work, but all women between the ages of twenty and twenty-one had been instructed to register.

'Yes, me, and it's not funny. Seems I have to go into one of the services, the land army or a factory. I think I fancy the Wrens. Nice uniform and all those handsome sailors to look after.'

'You'd enhance any uniform.'

'Thank you, kind sir.'

The raid didn't seem to be easing at all. The noise outside was enough to drown any conversation and they gave up talking. She kicked off her shoes and pulled her legs up on the sofa beside her before snuggling down and putting her head on his shoulder. His arm went about her and thus they sat for hours, listening and wondering how much longer the raid would go on and if they would be lucky enough to survive it. Some of the bombs were dropping very close, making the ground shake.

He must have dozed because he woke when she sat

up and began putting on her shoes. 'All-clear's gone,' she said. 'I'm going upstairs to make a cup of coffee. Coming?'

He straightened his tie and stood up to sling his haversack over his shoulder. 'Thanks. I could do with a drink.'

They climbed the stairs to the third floor because the lift wasn't working and she let them into the flat. The blackout hadn't been drawn and the drawing room was lit up like day. They both crossed to the window. The whole of London seemed to be on fire. The red glow in the sky was like a vast red sunset, flickering and glowing in the smoke-laden air, outlining the stark ruins of buildings. Below them, in the street, fire appliances and ambulances rushed to the scene, bells clanging loudly. People emerging from the shelters stood about staring at it, as if unable to believe what their eyes were telling them.

'My God!' Jack said. 'Talk about the Great Fire of London, it couldn't have been any worse than this. If it wasn't so terrible, it would be awesome, don't you think?'

'Yes.' She drew the heavy curtains and went to switch on the light. Nothing happened. 'Damn! The electricity is off again.' She flung the curtains back again so they could see by the light from outside. 'Can't make that coffee, I'm afraid.'

'Never mind, it doesn't matter.'

'There's some whisky somewhere.'

'Better still.'

They sat side by side on the sofa drinking her father's whisky. 'This damn war is upsetting everyone's lives, isn't it?' she said. 'Everything is changing: death and destruction everywhere, shortages of everything, people being bombed out, women doing hard manual work, the lives we used to live, gone for ever.'

'Oh, I don't know, when it's all over, we'll go back to normal.'

'The eternal optimist, aren't you? That's what I remember most about you, you were always so cheerful, even when you broke your arm falling out of that tree, do you remember?'

He laughed. 'Yes. Damned painful it was too.'

'But you didn't let on.'

'No point, it wouldn't have mended any quicker if I'd made a fuss.'

'Do you never get afraid?'

'Course I do. I'd be a liar if I said I didn't. You?'

'While I'm at home in Devon it's not so bad, but here, in London . . . Yes, I'm terrified.'

'Why did you come up?'

'James had a spot of leave and I fancied some shopping, so we had a couple of days together before he went back to his unit. Besides, I wanted to see what it's really like. I couldn't believe it was as bad as they say.' She shuddered. 'If anything, it's worse.'

'So you're going back home?'

'Tomorrow.' She laughed. 'Unless I can persuade you to stay.'

'Sorry, I've got to report for duty in the morning.'

'Then we've got the rest of tonight together. Let's make

the most of it, shall we?' She put her glass on a table, took his from him and set it beside the other, then turned and, taking his face in both her hands, put her lips to his. 'You will stay, won't you?' she murmured.

He chuckled. 'I'd have to be made of stone to resist an invitation like that.'

'And you're not made of stone.'

'No; flesh and blood and all five senses which, at this moment, are reeling.' He gathered her in his arms and kissed her back and then he began slowly to undress her and then himself while the fires of London lit their bodies in a rosy glow.

Elizabeth came out of the farmhouse and looked up at the mountains, white with snow, wondering how long it would be before it disappeared. They might be living in the unoccupied zone, but you would never know it because German soldiers on leave came for the skiing and had as good as taken over the hotels. She could see them now, going up in the ski lift and hurtling down the slopes, shouting and laughing and enjoying themselves. Some of them were arrogant and noisy, others were no more than boys drafted into the army to serve their Fuehrer. She avoided them when she could, but it served her purpose to be seen on the slopes herself occasionally, enjoying the exercise after doing her chores on the farm, and sometimes she was obliged to speak to them.

The heavy snow made it difficult to guide people over the border as they had done with Max and several men afterwards. Justine had sent them down to her. Apparently there was a network of people in the know and they brought the men to Justine to be sent on. They were not all Englishmen either; there were Canadians, Poles and French. Some were airmen who had been shot down and been helped by sympathetic French families, a few had escaped from prisoner of war camps, some were Frenchmen eager to join the Free French under General de Gaulle in Algeria.

Justine did not always come herself because the story of the boyfriend could not be used too often and she had to think of other reasons for travelling with the men, especially if they could not speak French. And she had to maintain her job as a teacher. Sometimes she dressed as a nurse, saying she was escorting the men to a hospital in the *Zone Libre*, but she still had to be very careful. Elizabeth would hide the escapees at the farm with the full connivance of her grandparents who liked the idea of pulling the wool over the eyes of the Vichy authorities.

When the snow came, the crossing had become too difficult on foot, and in any case, the tracks they made were too obvious from the air. The route had to be abandoned until the snow melted. Justine was trying to find an alternative via Marseilles and the Pyrenees into Spain, but it was a long haul and needed several safe houses on the way. In the meantime, Allied airmen were being looked after in sympathetic houses all over the region, which was marginally safer than the occupied zone. Pierre had two, Alphonse Montbaun had three hiding in his slaughterhouse and Elizabeth was looking after one, trying to keep him from going out and being seen by the German skiers and those French people sympathetic to the new regime. He had been with her for some time and was growing impatient.

It was also difficult feeding them. They obviously had no ration cards and were dependent on the local inhabitants to share what food they had, which was difficult with rations being as skimpy as they were; the bread ration had recently been cut to three hundred grams a day. Philippe and Henri had burgled the *maire*'s office from where the ration cards were distributed each month and stolen a whole batch of them. There had been a hue and cry over it, but they hadn't been caught and now the cards were being used judicially with false names on them. Every time Elizabeth used one, usually in Annecy but sometimes in other places where she wasn't known, she was a mass of nerves, expecting a heavy hand on her shoulder at any minute. And what worried her more than being caught using a stolen card, was that she might be forced into telling where she had obtained it. So far, she had been lucky.

She turned from the slopes and made her way into the cowshed where the animals were housed for the winter. Even feeding them had become difficult and fodder was rationed for them as food was for humans. What galled her more than anything was that much of the milk, butter and cheese they produced went to feed the German army.

Flight Lieutenant John Sandford emerged from a pile of straw when he saw her. He used his hands to brush down the rough clothes of a French farm worker he had been given. 'Any news?' he asked. He was young, no older than she was, touchingly grateful for what she did for him. But that didn't stop him being impatient.

'No, sorry.'

'I've been thinking I might make a run for it.'

'If you do, I shall shoot you myself.'

He looked shocked. 'You wouldn't?'

'I would. I couldn't risk you being picked up and talking. There are dozens, no hundreds, of people risking their lives to help people like you escape and one man recaptured means everyone connected with him is in danger.' She had to sound as if she meant it in order to drive her point home, and saw him struggling with himself. She smiled. 'I'll get you away as soon as I can. Believe me, I don't want you here any longer than can be helped.'

'I'm a risk.'

'You are a bigger one on the loose.'

'Point taken. Can I help with the milking?'

'Do you know how?'

'Yes, I was brought up on a farm.'

'Then I'll be glad of your help. There's a pail over there.' She nodded towards it.

He picked it up, found a stool and settled down beside one of the cows.

'Have you got a family?' she asked him, watching his deft fingers extracting the milk.

'Mother, father, two sisters and a young brother. They probably don't even know I'm alive. I can't think what they are going through.'

'No, it's hard to be separated from loved ones.' She fetched another stool and began on the cow next in line. There wasn't anything like as much milk as the animal should have produced, but it was hardly surprising given they, like the civilian population, didn't have enough to eat.

'Are you? Separated from a loved one, I mean.'

She hesitated. The less the escapees knew about the people who helped them the better. 'He's in the army,' she said without specifying which army. 'I haven't heard from him for ages.'

'I'm sorry.'

'Don't be. We all have to learn to cope, don't we?'

When the milking was done she took him across the yard to the kitchen to share the family breakfast, after which he would try and occupy himself about the farmyard, always alert for unexpected visitors when he would disappear into the straw of the barn again. He did this when they heard the sound of a pony and trap coming up the road towards them. Elizabeth went to the gate to forestall anyone from coming in. But she need not have worried; it was Justine.

'Alphonse lent me his trap,' she said, jumping down and hugging Elizabeth. 'I've come to take your airman away.'

'Good, he's getting impatient.'

Justine left the pony and trap with John to look after, then followed Elizabeth into the kitchen where her arrival set both her parents smiling and her mother busying herself finding her something to eat and drink. 'How is it in Paris?' she asked her.

'If you ignore the German troops, the swastikas on all

the buildings and German notices everywhere, Paris is the same as ever,' Justine said guardedly.

'Do you get enough to eat?'

'Yes, Maman, I eat well.'

'And the Boche do not trouble you?'

'No, Maman, I am left to get on with my work at the school.'

'Good.'

It was only when she and Elizabeth were alone, that she told her the true state of affairs. 'Shortages of food are taking their toll, especially among the poor. Some of my pupils are becoming truly undernourished and I can't do much to help them, I'm hungry myself. The rich are thriving on the black market, of course. There are long queues outside all the shops the minute they open but most of the time they have very little to sell. And what there is the Boche take and they don't queue. It's not only those who are billeted in Paris, but others come and spend their leave there, filling the cafés and theatres. I have to bite my tongue not to tell them what I think.'

'It's the same here. They've as good as taken over the hotels for the skiing. It's why I've been on hot coals over Lieutenant Sandford. He's been threatening to go off alone.'

'I'll take him off your hands tomorrow.'

'How did you get leave?'

'I discovered that my headmaster, Monsieur Chalfont, is a *resistant*. He allows an undercover newspaper to be duplicated on the office Roneo. I saw someone doing it one evening when I stayed late marking books; it's called *France*

Vivra. He'd be in real trouble if the police found out, but now he knows what I'm doing, we can help each other. I drop copies in shops and cafés and into people's shopping bags. We have to counteract the lies Vichy puts out about the war. Giles covers for me while I'm away. The story this time is that I have to visit my sick parents.'

'How risky is it?'

'You have to be careful, of course, and can be asked for your identity papers at any time, so it's not a good idea to be seen out and about with our men on the run, especially after curfew. But I'm becoming adept at knowing if I'm being followed and I always ask the men to follow a few yards behind when I'm leading them anywhere, then if either of us is stopped, it doesn't implicate the other. They understand that. At the station I buy the tickets but I don't keep them on me but hand each man his own, then it's up to them how they deal with a search. Remember that, Lizzie, if you ever have to escort anyone. Having more than one ticket is asking to be arrested.'

'I will, but we don't need tickets to take them over the mountain and, so far, that's all I've done. Can't even do that until the snow melts.'

'I know, but I'm going to take the lieutenant to a safe house in Lyon. Someone else will take him on to Marseilles and he'll be passed on from there over the border into Spain. Spain's not the best way out because so many there are pro-German, but it's better than staying in France.'

'The longer the line the more danger there is of being caught.'

'I know, but each section is run separately and, apart from the organisers who are responsible for communications, they don't know the people in the next one.'

'You do?'

'I've helped organise it, but I'm not going to tell you how. Best not to know.'

'I understand, but things are not so bad in the *Zone Libre* unless some busybody decides to spill the beans. Vichy are nothing but lapdogs of the Germans and delight in following up information and throwing their own countrymen in jail.'

'How many people know you are not Pierre's daughter?'

'Almost everybody in Dransville, I expect, but unless they are asked the specific question, I'm safe enough.'

'If you'd rather not . . . ?' Her voice faded on a question.

'I'll do what I can. Goodness it's little enough and it makes me feel as though I'm helping the war effort.'

'London is getting involved, sending agents in to help us. It remains to be seen how much help they are, but at least it shows willing and they're sending wireless operators so we can ask for supplies to be dropped.'

'How do you know that?'

Justine tapped her nose. 'Best not to know.'

Elizabeth accepted that. Just lately life had become one of secrecy and lies. 'I wonder how they are getting on at home. According to the wireless, London is being flattened, and not only London but all the big cities, and morale is so low the people are ready to surrender, not that I believe everything Vichy Radio says – they only broadcast what they're told.'

'Nayton isn't near any big cities, is it?'

'No. Norwich is the nearest, but I'm thinking of Max and Jack. They are serving somewhere, but I don't know where. I assume Max got back safely and his leg healed properly. I wish I could have news of them. Mama must be worrying about Papie and Mamie.'

'If you write a note, just a few words, I'll give it to Flight Lieutenant Sandford when I hand him over. Don't write anything incriminating and use tissue paper so it can easily be destroyed if he gets stopped.'

The next day, Elizabeth said goodbye to the lieutenant, who hugged her and promised to see her parents as soon as he could. The note he carried was written on toilet paper and simply said: 'All well and enjoying my holiday. See you when I get back. Love to all. L.' It could have been written by anyone anywhere, but those at home would know she was safe.

Chapter Eight

The news of the war was dismal, the bombers had come back to Britain after a short respite; Hitler's forces had occupied Yugoslavia and were heading for Greece; Rommel had taken the offensive in North Africa and allied losses at sea were horrendous. But the long, cold winter was at an end and there were signs of spring in the countryside; green buds on the trees, primroses in the woods. The arrival of John Sandford at Nayton one Saturday afternoon at the end of April, bringing with him a tiny scrap of paper, cheered Annelise more than anything else could have done.

She invited him to share their luncheon and bombarded him with questions. How was it in France? How was Lizzie? Was she well and did she have enough to eat? And the old couple, how were they faring, especially her father who had had a stroke? When he had answered as best he could, she asked about him, about himself and how he had managed to get out of France.

'I'm not allowed to say, Lady de Lacey. I really should not have come to see you, but I promised your daughter I would deliver her note.'

'Thank you for that. But she has written so little.'

'She dare not risk any more. She did not want me to be carrying evidence that I had been helped if I were picked up.'

'Does that mean she is in danger?'

'She is very careful and Dransville is remote.'

'How did you come to be there?'

'I was taken there from Paris by Miss Clavier.'

'Justine! She is my young sister. How is she?'

'She told me to tell you she is well. I did not realise Elizabeth was not Pierre Clavier's daughter until she gave me her note and told me the address to come to.'

'It all sounds very clandestine.'

'Yes. I'm sorry. Please, do not ask me any more, I should not have told you that much.'

'We understand,' Charles said, laying his hand on his wife's arm to restrain her. 'We are grateful you have taken the trouble to come and see us.'

The meal over, John rose to go. 'I must get back. I believe there is a train at two-thirty.'

'Yes, I'll have Bennett run you to the station in the pony and trap.' Charles laughed. 'Bennett is our chauffeur but since we cannot get petrol for the car, he has had to turn his hand to four legs instead of an engine. I imagine it must be the same in France.'

'Yes. I saw a van in an outhouse at the farm, but Elizabeth said they could not get the petrol to use it. When I was there, nearly two months ago now, there was a lot of snow and the people were using snowshoes and skis.'

Their goodbyes said and an invitation given to call again when he could, Charles took him out to the stables where the pony was harnessed by a middle-aged man who spoke in monosyllables in a broad Norfolk accent. In no time he was bowling along the country lanes, listening to the steady clop of the horse's hooves, musing on the meeting with Lord and Lady de Lacey.

It was a pity he hadn't been able to tell them more, but he had been thoroughly debriefed when he finally arrived back in England and warned he would be in trouble if he divulged anything of the escape route. The debriefing had been done at the War Office and had been more like an interrogation than a friendly chat. But they had seemed satisfied and sent him back to his unit where he was given leave. His first port of call had been his home near Hereford and then Nayton. And now it was back to business, knocking the hell out of the Hun. And he was going to do it in one of the new Lancaster bombers.

The trap stopped at the crossing gates. He jumped down, thanked his driver and went up onto the platform where a woman in a turban and a flowered apron was sweeping. He bade her good afternoon and received a grunt in reply, probably because she had a half-smoked cigarette in her mouth. He sat on a bench to wait for the train. The pony and trap had turned round and gone back the way it had come.

The woman carried her broom into the waiting-room-cum-ticket-office and he heard her say something and then a man's voice shouting. 'God woman, you're worse than our Lucy and she was bad enough. Why does it take you all morning to do a simple job? I'd ha' done it quicker meself.'

'Then why the hell, don't you? I didn't marry you to be your dogsbody . . .'

There was more of the same as they both became heated. He couldn't see the man but he assumed he was the stationmaster. 'And for God's sake take off that pinny. You shouldn't be seen by the public wearing it. You look like a slut.'

'You didn't say that a few months ago, you were glad enough to share my bed. Now you've married me, you think you can boss me about. Well, you're wrong. I'm not your precious Maggie, Bert Storey. I'm not surprised she left you . . .'

John heard the sound of a slap and her cry and wondered whether to go and intervene, but was stopped by the arrival of the train and a man in railway uniform came out of the waiting room to see to it. 'Nayton Halt!' he shouted, but no one got out. He took some parcels and crates from the guard, piled them on the platform and prepared to send the train on its way. John climbed aboard and shuffled along the corridor until he found a vacant seat. He saw the platform buildings, the crossing gate and the signal box slide past him as they left Nayton behind.

'We must let Max and Jack know about Lizzie,' Annelise said to Charles as soon as their visitor had gone. 'Do you know where Max is?'

'Last I heard he was up in Scotland somewhere, don't know the address.'

'Try Britannia Barracks. If he's been posted, they are bound to know where.'

But those at Britannia Barracks could not, or would not, tell him. 'If you write to him here, I'll see that it's forwarded,' he was told by the CO.

It was easier getting hold of Jack. A message left at his station to ring home had him on the end of the telephone that evening.

'What's up, Mama? Why the mysterious message? Somebody ill?'

'No. Good news. We've heard from Lizzie. She's well.'

'That *is* good news, but how did you hear?'

'A young flier who'd been shot down was helped to escape by Justine and Lizzie and she gave him a note to bring to us. He was here this afternoon.'

'What did she say? What's it like out there?'

'She didn't say a lot. I'll read it to you. "All well and enjoying my holiday. See you when I get back. Love to all. L."'

'That all?'

'Yes. It was apparently too risky to say any more. We're trying to get hold of Max but no luck so far. I believe he's in Scotland.'

'What's he doing there?'

'I've no idea. The CO at Norwich said he'd forward a letter if we sent it to him, so that's what we'll do. He'll be relieved to know Lizzie is OK.'

'Yes.'

'When is your next leave?'

'It depends on what's going on. In a few weeks, perhaps. I'll let you know.'

Max was not in Scotland, he was back in London. He had had a long wait after that first interview while Intelligence checked him out, looking for any signs that he might have Nazi sympathies, ensuring themselves of his complete loyalty and trustworthiness. He had obviously passed that test because he had been sent to the Western Highlands for physical training under the instruction of Captains Eric Sykes and William Fairbairn, which had honed him down to twelve stone of bone and muscle, sharp as the knife he had been issued with and hard as the bullets he put into his colt pistol. The knife, double-bladed with a very sharp point and a heavy grip, he kept in his left-hand trouser pocket. The gun was in a special holster sewn into his right trouser leg. Both could be withdrawn and used in a matter of seconds. He could kill accurately with either, or his bare hands if necessary. He had learnt to kill silently in a dozen different ways, a skill he found hard to come to terms with, but he knew any squeamishness would mean being sent back to his unit as unsuitable.

Long marches with heavy equipment, running, jumping, scrambling over obstacle courses, swimming and wrestling had all played a part. He thought he had been fit before but it was nothing to his fitness when he finished that part of his training. But that was only the beginning; there was the mental side to deal with and that, he knew, was going to be harder.

'So far so good,' was the comment of Major Buckmaster, who had recently been appointed to take over the running of the French section of SOE, the Special Operations Executive, when he reported back to Baker Street. The major had Captain Sykes' report in front of him. 'Still want to carry on?'

'Yes, sir.'

'Good. What have you told your family? You have a married sister, I believe?'

'Yes, but as far as she knows I'm still with the Norfolks.'

'And your girlfriend's family?'

'Same for them.'

'I have had a message from your colonel that they are trying to contact you. Have you any idea why?'

'No. Perhaps to invite me to stay. They do sometimes.'

'Ring them, but I want to know what it's about. You can do it from here.' He indicated a telephone on the desk, got up and left the room.

Max felt sure someone was listening in as he dialled the number. Annelise answered it. 'Lady de Lacey, it's Max here.'

'Oh, good, they've found you. We've heard from Lizzie.'

'You have? How?'

'She sent a note by an airman she and Justine helped to escape.'

'What did it say?'

Annelise read the short message. 'That's all, but I am so

relieved. I am sure if my parents had been ill or anything she would have found some way of saying so.'

'Thank you for telling me. It's a weight off my mind too. I'm afraid I can't talk now but I'll be in touch.'

'You know you are welcome to stay any time you have leave, if you can't get home.'

'Yes, I do. Thank you.'

'Bye, then. Take care.'

'I will.' He rang off.

Major Buckmaster returned immediately, confirming Max's suspicion that he had been listening on an extension. 'You heard that, sir?'

'Yes. Sorry and all that, but we have to be careful.'

'It doesn't affect what I'm doing, does it?'

'I wouldn't think so. I'm going to pass you for the next stage.' He handed him a travel warrant and instructions to report to Ringway, Manchester, for parachute training.

Two days later, Annelise and Charles had a visit from Maurice Buckmaster and though he appeared friendly and unconcerned they knew they were being investigated, along with poor John Sandford who had only been trying to help them. They were warned not to tell anyone they had heard from Elizabeth and certainly not to say how she had helped Lieutenant Sandford escape. Doing so could put the lives of their daughter and sister and everyone else connected to them in danger. 'The penalty for careless talk will be your swift arrest and incarceration for the duration,' he warned them.

'We've already told our son,' Charles said. 'He's a flight lieutenant in the air force.'

'That's a pity. Let us hope he has not told anyone else.'

Jack was next to receive a visit from the major. Ordered to report to the station commander's office, he was given the same lecture and the same warning which he received light-heartedly. 'I told my sister, Amy, and my girlfriend,' he said. 'Are you proposing to have me locked up for that?' He laughed. 'I thought we were short of pilots.'

'Tell me about your sister and your girlfriend.'

Jack, suddenly realising that this was serious, sketched in a few details and apparently satisfied the major. 'I am sure Sandford was only trying to set my mother's mind at rest,' he said. 'We have all been worried about Lizzie and with good reason if what Sandford says is true about her helping escapees. But then, that's the sort of thing she would do.'

'I assume she is bilingual.'

'Yes, we all are. My mother is French and I was born in Dransville.'

'Really?' Buckmaster sounded more than usually interested.

'Yes, which is why I have as strong a reason as anyone to beat the Boche.'

'Glad to hear it.' The other sounded relieved and stood to leave. 'But take my warning to heart, will you, Flight Lieutenant?' And then he was gone, leaving Jack wondering just what outfit he belonged to. He'd said the

War Office, but there was more to it than that. And who had put him onto Lieutenant Sandford's indiscretion?

May passed with its worst ever bombing of London; Crete was abandoned and shipping losses were the highest ever, though there was one bright note when Allied ships hounded and sank the German battleship, *Bismarck*. In June Hitler invaded Russia, making the Soviet Union an unexpected ally, and for a little while the beleaguered cities of Britain were given a respite from the bombing.

Jack had some leave due and decided it was time he saw Lucy and his son again. Peter was growing fast; he had four teeth and was able to sit up in his pram. Lucy swore he looked like Jack and would grow into a big strong man just like his father. 'I talk to him all the time about you,' she said. They had been walking in the park, Jack and Lucy and Peter in his pram, just like a normal, happy family, and had returned home in time for tea. 'I don't want him to grow up thinking he has no daddy.'

'That would never do,' Jack said, laughing and picking Peter up to throw him up and catch him, which made the child giggle.

'Time he was in bed.' Lucy took the baby from him and carried him upstairs to the back bedroom followed by Jack.

'Lucy, what do you do when I'm not around?' he asked, as he watched her.

'I look after Peter and the house and go shopping – queueing takes ages – and I do washing and ironing and gardening, all sorts of things.'

'Don't you go out enjoying yourself? Don't you meet other people, have a good gossip . . . ?'

'What on earth have I got to gossip about? I am polite to my neighbours and sometimes I meet friends I knew from work and we go to a café and have that awful Camp coffee. God knows what it's made of, it certainly isn't coffee.'

'So you don't talk about the family, about me and what I tell you?'

She tucked Peter in and kissed him before turning to Jack. 'What are you getting at, Jack? The neighbours see you come and go, so no doubt they think you are my husband. I haven't told them any different. What do you expect me to do, go about shouting that I'm not married and my child is a bastard? I don't care for myself, but I do care for Peter's sake.'

'I didn't mean that.' When she talked like that it made him feel guilty. He ought to offer her marriage, but it wasn't what he wanted. He was seriously considering proposing to Belinda. On the other hand, he loved his little son. He hadn't realised how much of an emotional pull being a father would be. 'I meant about Ma and Pa and Lizzie.'

'Miss Elizabeth? I hardly know her. She's still in France, isn't she?'

'Yes, but that's the trouble. She could be in danger if we talk about what she's doing.'

'Helping people escape, you mean?'

'Yes. I've had a visit from some high-up in the War Office warning me about careless talk . . .' He paused. 'Lucy, promise me you'll not speak of it to anyone, anyone at all.'

'Not even Amy?'

'I'll tell Amy the same thing as I've told you. It's between ourselves. I wouldn't forgive myself if anything happened to Lizzie.'

'Nor me. Anyway, I've no one to tell.'

He left her the following day, musing on the kind of life she led. She must feel lonely, isolated, but she never complained. Her whole life was wrapped up in her child. But that child would grow up and would not always be dependent on her, so what then? Would he be stifled by his mother's love and his father's lack of it? No, not lack, because he did love the boy. But how would that manifest itself in the years to come? It was a question he could not answer and because he could not answer it, he pushed it to one side. Decisions like that could be left until after the war was over.

Amy was well into her training and fast learning not to become emotionally involved with her patients' troubles. 'Be efficient, be sympathetic,' Sister Tutor had told the class. 'But do not weep or turn away. You will perhaps find yourself looking after wounded soldiers when you qualify and they don't want to see tears, they want someone who is positive and cheerful. The same goes for bomb victims, especially the children.'

She knew it would be hard; she had already seen poorly children on the wards and it had almost broken her heart, but she stiffened her spine and they saw only a pretty, smiling nurse who would make them all better. Her time off was precious for recharging her batteries and if she did not have time to go home to Nayton she would go and see Lucy and they would take young Peter out in his pram and enjoy a meal together afterwards. She loved her nephew and was very fond of Lucy and disgusted with her brother for not making an honest woman of the girl. And she hated keeping secrets from her parents. She resolved to have it out with Jack.

She did not see him again until the beginning of September, when they were both together at Nayton for a few days' leave. The weather was glorious and the harvest in full swing. The reapers and binders were working all the daylight hours there were and the air was full of a hot, oily, dusty smell. The children were on holiday and both Edmund and Bernard, armed with stout sticks, were determined to catch the rabbits that fled from the last few yards of standing corn. Amy and Jack had been for a walk and were standing leaning over the field gate watching them. She was in a printed cotton frock and he had left off his jacket and tie and rolled up his sleeves.

'Peaceful, isn't it?' she said. 'You'd never believe there was a war on.'

'Not here, no. Plenty of places where you can't get away from it, though. We're lucky we have this to come back to.'

'But it's not going to be the same is it? Not after the war, I mean.'

'No, I suppose not. There are bound to be changes.'

'I shan't come out, for a start. There's no point, when I've been working in the big wide world for ages. It's an anachronism. Class distinction and all that will disappear ...'

'Not altogether.'

197

'Perhaps not, but it will be replaced by something more equitable, based on worth – and I don't mean wealth. I mean our worth as individuals.'

'That's very profound, little sister. What's brought that on?'

'I was thinking of Lucy.'

'What about her?'

'She needs you, Jack, and so does little Peter. You ought to tell Mama and Papa about her and marry her. The way you treat her is awful.'

'Has she complained of my treatment of her?'

'No, she never complains. She accepts the way you are because she doesn't think she is worth anything better. But she is, you know. She's worth a hundred Belinda Davenports.'

'What do you know about Belinda Davenport?' he asked sharply.

'She's my friend, she writes to me, you know.'

'Oh.' He took a moment to digest this information. 'So you know she's got a job at the Admiralty and lives in her family's London apartment?'

'Yes, her father wangled it. And I know you've been seeing her.'

'Nothing wrong in that, is there? I can easily get up from Biggin Hill if I'm not on standby.'

'I bet you haven't told her about Lucy and Peter, have you?'

'Of course not.'

'And Lucy doesn't know about Belinda?'

'Don't be daft!'

'You know, if anything happened to you, and I pray it does not, Lucy would be in poor straits. She's not your next of kin and there'd be no war widow's pension for her.'

'I give her a more than adequate allowance.'

'No doubt that would stop if you haven't made proper provision. Mama and Papa would help her, but how can they, if they don't know about her and the baby?'

'Amy, stop lecturing me. I'm not in the mood for it. And if you say one word to Belinda, I'll never speak to you again.'

'Course I won't. What do you take me for?'

He sighed and turned from the gate to go back to the Manor. Amy walked beside him, not speaking. She had had her say and made him feel thoroughly uncomfortable.

'I've been thinking,' he said, a few minutes later. 'We ought to try and find Lucy's mother for her. It would be wonderful if they could be reunited.'

'I thought she was dead. According to Bert Storey, she is.'

'Well, he would say that, wouldn't he? He wanted to marry his buxom widow. According to Lucy her mother just upped and left.'

'Really? You mean Bert Storey is a bigamist?'

'It wouldn't surprise me.'

'Well, I'll be blowed! What hidden stories there are in our quiet village. But do you think Lucy would like us interfering?'

'I'm sure she would be glad. At least that way she would have someone to turn to.'

'Oh, I see. You are trying to abrogate your responsibilities.'

'Not at all. It would please Lucy.'

'Supposing her mother doesn't want to know. After all, she abandoned her.'

'I think it would help Lucy to come to terms with it, if she knew the truth.'

'How would we go about finding out?'

'I've no idea. I'll have to think about it. You could try asking about Mrs Storey in the village, discreetly, of course.'

'I'm not at home any more often than you are, Jack. When am I going to have the time? Why not tell Mama and Papa about Lucy and get them to help? I'm sure Papa would know how to go about it.'

'Do you never give up?' He swished angrily at a tall clump of cow parsley with a stick he had cut from the hedge. Its petals flew about scattering strong-smelling pollen.

'All right, I'll say no more. I'll leave it to your conscience.'

The trouble was his conscience was bothering him. He enjoyed going out with Belinda, she was light-hearted and fun and she had no hang-ups over their relationship. He could easily imagine himself married to her, idly enjoying the social whirl: parties, tennis, yachting, shooting game, all the things the upper crust had taken for granted before the war. She wouldn't even bat an eyelid if he occasionally strayed, so long as he did it discreetly. She would probably do the same. What she would say if she learnt about Lucy and Peter was another matter.

Lucy was a different case altogether. She was loyal, serene, and hard-working. Her very devotion flattered him, but it was more than that. When he was exhausted, stressed by the work he did, miserable after watching a pal spiral down and crash in a ball of flame, it was to Lucy he went for solace. Belinda would be hopeless in that kind of situation. Two women and he needed them both.

Bernard and Edmund raced home in glee. They each had a dead rabbit suspended on a stick by its hind legs, which they intended to give to Mrs Baxter to cook for dinner. Jack and Amy were both on leave and there would be extra people to feed.

'Do you reckon your brother knows what happened to that girl?' Bernard asked, when he caught sight of Jack and Amy walking ahead of them.

'What girl?'

'The one who used to open the railway gates.'

'Lucy Storey? Why would he?'

'You know why. I told you. I reckon the baby's been born by now.'

'So?'

'I just wondered. I bet your sister knows.'

'Well, I'm not going to ask her, if that's what you're thinking. Anyway, if you're so keen to know what happened to her, why don't you ask Frank Lambert?'

'He wouldn't know; she wouldn't have told him what she was going to do. Anyway, I don't trust him, nor Mr Storey, come to that.'

'Why not?'

'I don't know. I just don't. Did you ever find that picture?'

'No. If you ask me it never existed.'

'Oh, yes it did. I saw it. It was this big.' Bernard spread his arms wide, dropping the rabbit. He bent to pick it up. It was still warm and soft to the touch, though its head was a bloody mess where he had hit it. 'If it's not in the house, then Lucy must have it and that means your brother gave it to her.'

'Why are you so interested in her?'

'It's a mystery, that's why. I like solving mysteries. I think I'll be a detective when I leave school.'

School was a sore subject with him. The head had been to see Lady de Lacey, and after they had been talking for some time, he had been sent for and told he should not be leaving school at fourteen, but sit the entrance exam for the Grammar School in Swaffham. 'Miss Graham thinks you have great potential,' her ladyship had said. 'I know you did not sit the scholarship when you were eleven, but it's not too late to transfer.'

He had been torn between his desire to be a grown man, earn his own living and help his ma, and his growing taste for learning. He was always top of the class and he loved to read, which was something he had never done at home. Books cost money and they had never had enough for luxuries like that. Nor had he ever been in a library until he came to Nayton. The fact that Edmund obviously knew so much more than he did was an added incentive.

'Me ma couldn't afford it,' he had told them.

'You wouldn't have to pay if you passed the scholarship,' Miss Graham had said. 'It wouldn't cost anything except for your uniform.'

'Shall we ask what your mother thinks?' Lady de Lacey had suggested.

The upshot of that was that Ma came down and talked to Lord and Lady de Lacey and instead of leaving school and going home, he was going to Swaffham Grammar School the following term. Lord de Lacey was going to pay whatever was necessary, and for a tutor to give him extra lessons so he could catch up with those who had gone to the grammar school the previous year. 'It's no big deal,' had been Edmund's comment when he told him. 'I'm going to university when I'm eighteen. You could come too.'

That was so far beyond him he didn't even consider it, but the idea of doing something more interesting than labouring on the docks, appealed to him.

'You mean like Sherlock Holmes?' queried Edmund as they slowed down behind the couple ahead of them.

'Something like that. I could catch spies and get a medal and go to Buckingham Palace and have it pinned on by the king.'

Edmund laughed.

'Well, why not?' Bernard demanded.

'There aren't any spies round here.'

'How do you know? Anyone could be a spy, ordinary people like Frank Lambert and Mr Storey.'

'All right, then,' Edmund said, still laughing. 'You prove it and I'll believe you.'

Chapter Nine

Max followed two other would-be agents, Etienne Ambrose and Anne Barnard, over to where a tethered balloon strained at its moorings. He was a bundle of nerves, unsure whether he had the guts to do it. It was all very well to jump from the tower in the hangar where their descent was controlled by a fan and they were not subject to the vagaries of wind and weather, but jumping from a balloon cage a great deal further from the ground was another matter. Neither of the others was showing any sign of nerves so he gritted his teeth and followed them into the cage where they sat round a hole in the floor and fastened their static lines ready for the off. They had been kept apart from the usual intake of trainees and their period of training was shorter, intended to give them the confidence to jump safely and no more. He did not doubt the instructor knew they were destined for something special, but no one mentioned it.

The dispatcher closed the gate, the mooring lines were released and the balloon began to ascend. Above him the late autumn sky was marred only by a few vapour trails left by aircraft. Below him through the hole in the floor, he could see the airfield with its runway and hangars and tiny dots that were the people on the ground. At eight hundred feet, the dispatcher sent them out. 'Number One, go!' Etienne disappeared through the hole. 'Number Two, go!' Max didn't have time to think, let alone hesitate, and he was in the air and his parachute had opened above him and he was drifting down, trying to remember his drill. He heard one of the ground staff with a megaphone shouting at him to keep his ruddy feet together, and then he was on the ground, rolling as he had been taught. He sat up and began gathering in his parachute just as Anne landed not far away. All three safely down. They were all laughing with the sudden release of tension.

The next day they jumped from a Whitley bomber and two days later made a night jump because they would undoubtedly be landing in the dark. It was the scariest thing he had ever done, but he was rapidly learning that every day brought a new challenge, a new fear to conquer and he knew there was more to come. The clandestine part had yet to be mastered.

After passing out, all three reported back to Orchard Park, where Major Buckmaster interviewed them one by one. He had the reports from their instructors in front of him. Max, trying to read his upside down, managed to decipher: 'A dependable man, a little staid, not given to high jinks, but not without humour. Hides his feelings well.'

'Something distracting you, Captain?' the major enquired mildly.

'No, sir. I was wondering . . .'

'About your report? It is perfectly satisfactory, no black marks, so I'm passing you for the last part of your training. Present yourself to the officer in charge at Beaulieu tomorrow. There you will take on your new identity and learn to convince whoever asks you that you are who you say you are. Miss Atkins will give you a travel warrant.'

'No leave, sir?'

'Not yet. Later perhaps. Off you go and good luck.'

At Beaulieu, he was soon practising how to survive in a hostile environment without being detected, and resisting interrogation if captured. Giving in meant the lives of everyone with whom he was connected would be in danger. It was one of the reasons why the people in each group, called a circuit, never knew those in other groups. The circuit he was going to set up would be referred to as 'Oberon'.

The time for action was getting very close and as each day passed, so the tension built up. Until it was time to go, he had to get used to his new identity. Using the name Justine had invented for him, he was Antoine Descourt, born of a Canadian father and a French mother. His parents had brought him to France at the end of the Great War when he was ten and both had died in the flu epidemic shortly afterwards. He had been brought up by his mother's sister, but she had fled to Algeria when war was declared in 1939 and so he had no immediate relatives in France. He memorised his fictitious birthdate, his parents' names and ages and anything else he might be asked so that he could answer without hesitation. All conversations were now held in French and his fluency had come on by leaps and bounds. The slight accent he still retained was accounted for by his early years in Canada.

His new alter ego earned his living as a travelling salesman, dealing in paint and wallpaper. He would be given money, brochures, colour charts and business cards, but his samples would have to be purchased in France. He was learning how to deceive, how to make himself look insignificant, wearing an ill-fitting suit and down-at-heel shoes. He could be stopped at any time and asked for his papers and interrogated, and though his interrogators at Beaulieu were English, they made it as uncomfortably realistic as possible.

'It's important to hold out for at least forty-eight hours,' he was told. 'News of your arrest will have gone round the network and that will give everyone time to get rid of incriminating evidence, close down letter boxes and safe houses and disappear.'

When he was as ready as he would ever be, he was given a few days' leave which he spent with his sister, days in which he began to live another lie, one for the benefit of those at home. 'The regiment will probably go abroad,' he told her. 'So you mustn't worry if the mail is held up. You'll learn soon enough if anything happens to me.'

Leave over, he found himself standing on the grass of the airfield adjacent to Newmarket racecourse, looking at the black-painted Lysander which was to take him to France. He was going in alone and being dropped on a field in the grounds of a chateau belonging to Count François Mollet, who was a patriot and prepared to turn a blind eye to the sudden activity on the far side of his estate.

'You will be met by someone from the Prosper circuit and taken to a safe house,' Buckmaster had told him. 'After that initial contact you will have no communication with them except in the direst emergency. As soon as it is safe to do so, you are to approach Ma'amselle Clavier for help.'

'Justine?' he queried.

'Yes. You said you thought she would be willing . . .'

'So I did, but this is altogether more chancy than simply helping one or two people on their way to a neutral country.'

'We know that. If she is reluctant you are on no account to coerce her. You can use Prosper's wireless operator to report your arrival and if all goes well, we'll send you your own operator.'

'And if it doesn't?'

'You will be recalled until we can put something else in place.'

'Ready?' Vera Atkins stood beside him to see him off. She had conducted his last interview, had inspected all his clothes to make sure there were no telltale English labels in them, had asked him one more time if he was sure he wanted to go and, on being answered in the affirmative, had given him a packet of Gauloise cigarettes, a recent French newspaper and a suicide pill. He could not imagine a situation in which he might want to use that, but it certainly brought home to him the risks he was taking.

'Yes.'

'Then good luck.' She offered her hand, he shook it and then hefting up his equipment, he strode over and climbed into the aeroplane behind the pilot. The engines, which had been idling, sprang into life and the aircraft began to move. A minute later they were in the air. This was what all the training had been about. It all seemed surreal and he found it difficult to believe it was really going to happen, that very soon he would be on French soil, to all intents and purposes Antoine Descourt.

As the Lysander flew steadily on its way, he had time to reflect on all he had learnt since that day, months ago now, when he had been interviewed by Major Gielgud. His life seemed to have taken on a different meaning, geared to what he was being trained to do. Cool, in command of himself, lying to order, he felt his personality was already subtly changing. He was not the same man who had fought at Dunkirk, nothing like the shy young man who had courted Elizabeth de Lacey. He wondered if she would notice the difference when they were eventually reunited. Would she still love him and want to marry him? It was a pity he could not tell her what he was doing.

The Lysander began to buck about as the pilot dodged

the anti-aircraft guns over the coast of France and a few minutes later it straightened out and began to lose height. 'Two minutes to go,' the pilot shouted back at him.

Elizabeth stood at the door of the farmhouse and looked up at the mountain slopes. 'It will snow before long,' she said.

'I know.' Justine was standing beside her. Both women were much thinner than they had been, particularly Justine who was always on the move and never had enough to eat. 'We had better make this the last crossing this year.'

'Perhaps there won't be any more wanting to go.'

'Don't you believe it. British aircraft are being shot down all the time and whoever picks the crew up, somehow or other finds me.'

'Do you wish you weren't doing it?' Recently there had been a German decree that any man caught giving aid to Allied airmen would be shot without trial and women would be sent to a labour camp in Germany. Justine risked that with every man she helped.

'Sometimes, when I'm extra stressed, but then I think where would the poor men go, if I didn't help them?' She laughed suddenly. 'It's my contribution to the war effort, sending them back to fly again and no doubt getting shot down again.'

'So you'll take the next one down to Lyon?'

'Yes.'

'I'll take Roger and Andrew over the border tomorrow. Will you stay?'

Roger Wainbridge was an army captain who had been in a prisoner of war camp ever since Dunkirk and had managed to escape in a rubbish truck. He had learnt about Justine from another escapee who had been recaptured after being on the run for weeks and who had been caught as Justine led him from her apartment to the train station. The information he brought back with him was useful to others planning an escape and that included Roger. He was a handsome self-assured man who had been unbearably thin when he arrived, but had soon put on a little weight.

Andrew Lawton was a pilot who had baled out when his Mosquito had been crippled by flak. He had been caught stealing food by a farmer in the Ardennes who had passed him onto an agricultural salesman who had taken him to a large villa near Versailles. The people there had hidden him and fetched Justine.

'No, I must go back on the early morning train. You'll be all right on your own, won't you?'

'Yes, I'm used to it now and the gendarmerie seem not to be interested. Papie provides them with eggs and butter.'

'All the same, be careful.'

'I will. But I'm more worried about the risks you are taking.'

Elizabeth had lost count of the number of men she and Justine had helped, Justine particularly because she passed some on to others besides Elizabeth. Nor did she know how many of them had actually made it back home, but she was sure the powers in London must know what they were doing by now. She wondered if news of it ever got back to Nayton. She could not imagine that quiet village and its inhabitants ever changing. Sometimes she was terribly homesick and wished she could correspond with her parents. And Max, of course. Where was he?

The news that came over Vichy Radio told them nothing except how well the Germans were doing. Papie tuned into the BBC Overseas Service and she heard its reports of what was happening, which she trusted to be more accurate. The RAF were bombing Germany continually, something she knew by the number of bombers shot down, something the Vichy Radio reported with satisfaction. There was fierce fighting in Russia where Leningrad was under siege, but Malta had been relieved, which was a blessing. Besides the news the BBC broadcast personal messages to friends and relatives in France, some of them so strange only those in the know could understand. She listened avidly but none seemed to be for her.

'I think I'll give Roger or Andrew a note for my folks,' she told Justine. 'Maybe they didn't get the last one. I could ask them to let me know how they are through the BBC.'

'I don't think you should compromise the boys or yourself, Lisabette.'

'I won't hand it over until we reach the border.'

Elizabeth roused her charges long before daybreak because she wanted to cover the first, most dangerous part of the walk in the dark. It was all very well to tell Justine the gendarmerie turned a blind eye, but there were others who saw no reason to help the Allies and would turn them in if they saw them. They ate breakfast in the farmhouse kitchen with Justine who was leaving at the same time to take a bus to Annecy and catch a train back to Paris.

It was a journey she had done dozens of times, often in disguise because she did not want her frequent trips to Dransville to be noticed and questioned. Today she was wrapped in an unbecoming black overcoat, green with age, which came down to her ankles, and a black cloche hat that covered her hair. She wore down-at-heel flat shoes and no make-up. A basket containing a loaf of bread, a dozen eggs and some cheese hung on her arm. Anyone less like the usual chic Parisienne would be hard to imagine.

On leaving the station in Paris, she shuffled along, pretending to search for cigarette ends in the gutter, until she came to her own home, when she looked about her carefully and then darted up the steps and in at the front door. Racing upstairs to her first floor apartment, she let herself in, breathing relief. An arm went round her and a large hand came over her mouth and a male voice said. 'Don't scream. It's only me.'

He dropped his hand and she swivelled round to face Max, dressed in an ill-fitting civilian suit and a black beret.

'Max! What in God's name are you doing here?' She was shaking with shock. Her life was so geared to secrecy, to never knowing when a heavy hand would land on her shoulder, that finding someone in her flat had frightened her to death, making her heart beat uncomfortably fast.

'Waiting for you.'

'Why? How did you get here? How did you get in?'

He laughed. 'One of the things I've learnt recently is how to pick a lock. I daren't wait outside, I didn't know how long you'd be. I was just beginning to think I'd have to go away again.' This was said in perfect French which made her doubt her own ears. But it was undoubtedly Max.

'You scared me to death.'

'Sorry about that. Is it safe to talk here?'

'Yes. Let me get this coat and hat off and make some coffee – if you can call it coffee, God knows what it's made of – and then you'd better tell me why you're here. Didn't you make it home after all?'

'Oh, yes, I've been home, but I decided I'd be more useful in France.'

They sat over ersatz coffee and then over wine and omelettes, made with eggs she had brought from Dransville, while he explained what he had been instructed to do. 'I'm expected to set up a new circuit in the Ardennes area,' he told her. 'That means recruiting *resistants* and after that to arrange for supplies of money, arms and explosives to be dropped to them and organise the sabotage of enemy installations and communications.' He paused. 'I've been told to ask you if you would be willing to help with recruiting and act as a courier until they send me one from London. You don't have to, of course, it's entirely voluntary.' He paused. 'To tell the truth, I am not sure I should ask. It's more than a bit risky.'

'A bit risky,' she laughed. 'That's an understatement,

and it's a bit different from guiding airmen over the pass at Dransville.'

'Are you still doing that?'

'Yes, I've just left numbers twenty and twenty-one with Lisabette. What she's going to say to all this, I don't know.'

'She is not to know.'

'Not to know? You mean the fact that you are in France masquerading as a paint salesman is to be kept from her?'

'Yes. It's all to do with security. She would be compromised if the Germans found out about the connection.'

'And I wouldn't be, I suppose?'

'I know it's asking a lot. In fact, I think I'll radio London to say you can't do it.'

'You will do no such thing.'

'You mean you want to?'

'Of course I want to. Where are you staying?'

'I was going to book into a *pension*.'

'I shouldn't. They're full of Germans. You'd better stay here, at least until we can find you a safe house.'

'That's hardly respectable.'

'Who cares? Besides, you aren't the first man I've had staying here and I don't suppose you'll be the last. I'm getting quite a reputation.'

'Don't you mind?'

'No.' She shrugged expressively. 'The people I care about and who care for me know the truth. Besides, we need to decide how you're going to fulfil your brief. I'll make up the spare bed. Tomorrow I must report for duty at the school, but I think I'll talk to Giles Chalfont, my principal, about it. He's involved with the Resistance.'

'You mean he belongs to one of the circuits?'

'No, I don't think so, it's just a group of people anxious to make things difficult for the Boche, mostly by printing and distributing an underground newspaper. They may make your first recruits. We'll need to have a meeting to thrash out the details.'

'I've got a rendezvous with a wireless operator tomorrow.'

'Right. You keep that and I'll meet you back here after school is out. We'll go on from there.'

'If you're sure . . .'

'I'm sure. I imagine you had no sleep last night, so I'll make up your bed.'

She left the room and he sat in contemplation. Everything had gone like clockwork so far, but he was not such a fool as to suppose it would always be plain sailing. Justine was a marvel, a real heroine, the way she coped. She made him feel safe and he supposed that was the same for all her escapees, but at what cost to herself? He had really frightened her, hiding behind the door of the flat like that. It was symptomatic of the high tension under which she lived and operated. But he was glad he had found her and even more glad that they would be working together.

Annelise picked the post up from the doormat. Gone were the days when a footman brought it to her on a silver salver. They didn't have any footmen now; there was only Peters, the butler who was too old for military service, Mrs Baxter, housekeeper-cum-cook, and a couple of daily women coming in from the village to do the cleaning and laundry. Annelise found herself doing much of the housework herself. She didn't mind that half as much as her well-to-do friends who complained bitterly about the difficulty of hiring and retaining staff, as if they couldn't live without them. The last letter she had had from Lady Davenport was full of it. But the letter she had in her hand was not from Serena Davenport, nor anyone whose handwriting she recognised.

She slit it open and another envelope tumbled out and the writing on that she did recognise. 'Charles! Charles!' she shouted, running along the hall and into the library where he was working on some accounts. She waved the letter at him. 'This is from Lizzie.'

He looked up at her excited flushed face. 'How did it get here?'

'In another envelope.'

'Well, open it. See what she says.'

Her hands shook so much she could hardly obey. He rose and took it from her, drew out the single sheet and started to read aloud.

'Dear Mama and Papa, I hope you receive this because I want you to know I think of you all the time and wonder how you are. I can only imagine what wartime life must be like for you and hope it is not too bad. We get so little news here, and very little of it can be trusted. We are safe and well here on the farm and not troubled too much by the Germans, though they come for the

skiing in winter and walking in summer. I am supposed to be Uncle Pierre's daughter. Isn't that funny? We decided it would be safer.'

Charles turned the paper over and continued.

'Since Vichy is only allowed a small army to keep order, Henri and Philippe have not been called up and still work at the vineyard. The wine was good this year, most of it bought by the Germans. Papie is well in himself, though he cannot do much since his stroke and spends his time telling me what to do. I have become a very efficient farmer. Mamie is her usual placid self. They both send their love and say you are not to worry about them. We are better off in the Zone Libre than in occupied France, but Justine manages to visit now and again. She, too, is well.

'You cannot answer this letter, I know, but I would love to hear that you have received it and are well. Can you get a message to me through the BBC? We tune in to it every day. All my love, your dutiful daughter, Lizzie.'

He stopped reading and looked at his wife who had flopped into a chair with tears running down her face. He smiled. 'Don't cry, sweetheart, this is good news, isn't it? She doesn't sound at all troubled.'

'No, thank God.' She mopped at her eyes with a handkerchief. 'She must have helped another airman escape, don't you think? How else did this get here?' She looked in the envelope in which the letter had come but it was empty. 'There's no note.'

'No, but you remember what Major Buckmaster said when we got the last one. We tell no one.'

'We can't not tell Amy and Jack. And Max too.'

'No, but we'll wait until we see them face-to-face. Amy is due home next week and Jack will get leave, but as for Max, I don't know. Do you suppose he's still in Scotland?'

'We could write care of Britannia Barracks like we did before.'

'I don't think we can, sweetheart. I'm sure Major Buckmaster would say putting pen to paper is too much of a risk. You never know who might see it.'

'You are probably right', she agreed. 'Do you think we could get a message to Lizzie through the BBC?'

'I don't know,' he said, carefully folding the letter and returning it to its envelope. 'I'll have to take advice about what is permitted.'

Charles took the train to London the next day and went to the War Office where he asked to speak to Major Buckmaster, which caused a little consternation. After a long wait while someone went off to find out where the major was, a rendezvous was arranged in Marietta's restaurant in Mayfair the following lunchtime. Charles was more than ever convinced the major was involved in some secret work.

Buckmaster was already there when Charles arrived, having stayed at the Ritz the previous night. They greeted each other warily. The major ordered drinks for them both and they sat in red leather chairs in a secluded corner to talk.

'How can I help you, My Lord?' he asked, when they had been served.

'You had better see this,' Charles said, pushing Elizabeth's letter across the table to him.

'Thank you for showing it to me,' the major said, after reading it. 'How did it come to you?'

'I imagine through another escapee. It was in a second envelope posted in London with no indication of who had sent it.'

'But it is your daughter's handwriting?'

'Oh, no doubt of it. I want to do as she asks and send her a message via the BBC. I thought perhaps you would know how to go about it.'

Buckmaster smiled. 'I think it can be arranged. What do you want to say?'

'I just want Lizzie to know we have the letter and are well. I imagine there are rules about what can be said.'

'Yes, indeed. We have to vet everything. Have you thought of the wording?'

'How about: "Papa and Mama will save some of Mrs Baxter's Christmas pudding for Lizzie."?'

'Who is Mrs Baxter?'

'Our cook. She is famous in the family for her puddings.'

'Then that will do very well.'

'Is she as safe as she would have us believe? After all, if she is ferrying men over the border . . .' He paused, watching Buckmaster's lean face, but it was inscrutable.

'She is in the unoccupied zone and so long as she keeps her head down, she should be all right.'

'And Justine? My wife is concerned for her. She lives and teaches in Paris.'

He tapped the letter. 'Your daughter says she is well.'

There was something about the way the major said this that alerted Charles to undercurrents. Buckmaster knew more than he was saying. 'Do you think she is safe?'

'I have no reason to think she is not.'

Charles smiled. 'But you would hear if she were not, wouldn't you?'

'What makes you say that?'

'Let's not beat about the bush, Major. You would know, wouldn't you?'

Buckmaster shrugged. 'I cannot tell you anything, My Lord.'

'No, I suppose not. I wish I could have a useful job to do, but no one seems to want me. Could you use me?'

The major smiled. 'It's a thought. Are you as fluent in French as your son and daughters?'

'Almost, not quite. My wife tells me I have an English upper-class accent, but I can read and write it well.'

'There might be a job in the communications room. I'll let you know. In the meantime, I'll arrange to have a BBC message sent.'

'Thank you.'

They rose to go and came face-to-face with Jack and Belinda Davenport, who were being shown to a table.

'Pa!' Jack exclaimed, in the way he had as a small boy

when caught out in some mischief. 'What are you doing here?' Then to Buckmaster, as if remembering his manners. 'Good afternoon, sir.'

The major smiled. 'Flight Lieutenant.' He offered Charles his hand. 'I'll be in touch.' And with that he left them.

'Pa, what are you up to?' Jack asked.

'Nothing, trying to get myself involved, but no one will have me.'

'I imagine that will please Mama.'

'Hallo, Belinda,' Charles said, turning to the girl who was looking very attractive and efficient in WRNS uniform. 'Nice to see you again.'

'Nice to see you,' she said. 'Jack and I were going to have lunch. Will you join us?'

'Thank you, but no. I'll leave you to it.' Then to Jack. 'When are you coming home again?'

'I've only got a twenty-four-hour pass this time, not long enough to come home. Are you staying in town? We could meet this evening.' He ignored the black looks from Belinda who was expecting to be taken to the theatre.

'No, I'm going back to Nayton on the four o'clock train. I'd better go or I'll miss it.'

Jack turned to Belinda. 'I'll see my father into a taxi and come back. Order for both of us, will you? Whatever the waiter suggests.'

He followed his father up the stairs to the ground floor. 'Come on, Pa, what's going on? The major is the one who warned us about talking. Is he at it again?'

'No, I went to ask him if he could get a BBC message to Lizzie.'

'You've heard from her again?'

'Yes, but keep it under your hat. She's well and so is everyone else.'

'Good. What message have you asked for?'

Charles smiled and told him. 'She'll know it's meant for her, mentioning Mrs Baxter.' He saw a cruising taxi and held up his hand to stop it. 'Come home when you can, Jack. Your mother misses you.'

'I will, I promise.' He saw the older man into the vehicle, then turned and went back to Belinda. She was studying a very truncated menu and smoking a cigarette in a long holder. He sat down as the hovering waiter came for their order.

It seemed all wrong somehow. Apart from the fact she was in a smart uniform, Belinda's life had hardly changed in spite of the war. She still had everything she wanted; money could still buy food and alcohol, good clothes and visits to the theatre and dances. Lizzie was stuck in France and even if she was well, it couldn't be easy for her. As for Lucy . . . Lucy was coping, just. He hadn't been to see her since the summer; he really must make an effort to go next time he had leave.

'What are you thinking about?' Belinda broke in on his thoughts. 'You're miles away.'

He forced himself to pay attention. 'I was wondering what to order.'

'It shouldn't take long. Woolton Pie or fish cakes.'

He laughed. 'Woolton Pie it shall be, but I bet it isn't as good as Mrs Baxter's.'

Mrs Baxter's Christmas pudding. If he started lobbying now, could he get home for Christmas?

'I saw Jack in London,' Charles told Annelise after he had recounted his interview with Maurice Buckmaster. 'He was with Belinda Davenport. They were having lunch in Marietta's. I didn't know he was seeing her.'

'Serena Davenport told me. She is hoping they will make a match of it.'

'He could do worse, I suppose. Wonder why he didn't say anything to us?'

'I don't think he is in any hurry to commit himself. Perhaps he thinks that with the war and everything, now is not the time to get married.'

'Perhaps.'

'Did he say when he was coming home on leave?'

'No. I don't think he knows.'

'Perhaps he'll come for Christmas. That would be lovely. Mrs Baxter is already saving the ingredients for a pudding.'

He laughed. 'We must remember to save some for Lizzie.'

Elizabeth sat with her ear close to the speaker, listening to the bizarre messages being broadcast, as she had done every day since she had sent that letter. She had seen Andrew over the border and given him her letter because Roger had suddenly changed his mind and told her he wanted to stay in France. 'I can do more good here,' he had said when she protested.

'Doing what?'

'I can help you.'

She laughed. 'We've only got half the herd we had before the war. There's hardly enough work for my grandparents and me.'

'But that's not all you do, is it? The farm is only a cover.'

'For what?'

'Work with the Resistance.'

'What makes you think I do that?'

'Oh, come on, Lisabette, it's plain you've got a well-organised escape route going here. There must be days when you don't feel like climbing that mountain, when you'd rather be doing something else. Besides, in winter when there's snow on the ground, the men will have to be taken south to Spain. I could do that, save Ma'amselle Clavier the trip.'

'You would never make it. Your French is terrible.'

'But my German is good. I was talking to that fellow, Hans, the other day and he didn't comment on my accent.'

'You were talking to Leutnant Shermann?' She was dismayed and angry. Hans, who was stationed at the Mairie as some sort of liaison between the Vichy government and the Germans in the north, often came to the farm to buy butter, cheese and eggs. He was young and apparently guileless, but she was always careful to treat him civilly but not to encourage him to stay longer than he needed to make his purchases. She had no idea he and Roger had met. 'Roger, how could you? You could have had us all shot.'

'I told him I came from Alsace Lorraine and my parents had brought me up to think of myself as German. He accepted that and told me about his family in Cologne. He's worried about them being bombed.'

'You'll have to leave. I'll take you over the pass tomorrow.'

'No. I'm staying. I can help organise the *resistants*. They are a raggle-taggle mob with no clear direction. If they are to do any good at all, they must be properly organised and commanded.'

'What makes you think they want you to command them?'

'Henri and Philippe both agreed they did. They said they wished you were not involved and if I could relieve you, so much the better. They are concerned for their little sister.'

With her ear close to the mesh of the wireless speaker, she smiled at the memory of that deception and almost missed the announcement. 'Papa and Mama will save some of Mrs Baxter's Christmas pudding for Lizzie.' Only when it was repeated did she realise it was for her.

'They got it!' she squealed, turning to her grandparents. The old man was sitting by the fire smoking a pipe containing some horrible concoction that was certainly not tobacco and her grandmother was stirring leek soup over the fire. 'Papie, Mamie, it worked. They got my letter and they're OK.'

The old lady crossed herself. 'God be praised. Now, better call that young man in for his supper. It's a good thing we have him for the milking since you have taken to gluing yourself to the wireless set.'

Elizabeth called Roger, who had just finished scouring out the milking pans. He washed and dried his hands and joined them at the table. 'I'm going into Annecy tomorrow,' he said.

Elizabeth was appalled. 'What for?'

'To see Henri and Philippe, get things moving.'

'And how do you propose to go?'

'I'll borrow Monsieur's bicycle.'

'You can't go alone. You've got no papers. If you're stopped . . .'

'I'm a German soldier on leave. I left my papers in my room.'

'What's your name, then, and where is this room?'

'My name is Leutnant Otto Bergman and I'm billeted at the Dransville Mairie.'

'You're mad.'

'No more insane than you are.'

'I'd better come with you.'

And so they set out early next morning. It was a cold, bright day. There had been a scattering of snow on the tops during the night and she knew it would soon be too late to use the pass, so how was she to get him safely away? He was becoming a liability.

Henri and Philippe didn't agree with her when she tackled them about it. They thought he could be useful, someone who could liaise between the *resistants* and London, arrange for arms, ammunition and explosives to be dropped. They would never beat the Boche unless they were armed.

'And how do you propose to contact London?' she demanded with some asperity.

'Justine can do it,' Roger said. 'She is in touch with them all the time.'

'No, she isn't. She would have said.'

'I bet she is. You ask her.'

'I can't do that until she comes again and I have no idea when that will be.'

'Then I'll go to her,' Roger said.

'Without papers?' The whole idea was ridiculous and she was inclined to treat it as a joke, wishful thinking on his part.

'I'll get them,' Roger said. 'I'll ask Hans. He'll do it for a consideration. He's desperately anxious to get his parents and young sister out of Cologne.'

'I haven't any spare cash and neither have my grandparents.'

'We'll find it,' Henri said, leaving the room and returning with a cash box which he unlocked. It was crammed with paper money. 'We might as well spend it,' he said. 'It will be worthless before long, I don't doubt.' He handed a bundle to Roger who stuffed it into his jacket pocket, then Roger and Elizabeth took their leave and returned to Dransville the way they had come in almost total silence.

'You're angry with me, aren't you?' he said as they propped their bicycles in the shed beside the byre.

'You don't seem to understand the risks.'

'Oh, yes I do. But don't you see, we have to take risks or we can't win? You have been taking them for over a year now, haven't you? You must have thought they were worth taking.'

'That's different. I belong here, you don't.'

'This is not just about Dransville. It's bigger, wider, more important than that. It's global. The free world must win or God knows what will happen to this planet of ours.'

It was the first time he had spoken seriously about the situation they were in and it gave her a new insight into his character. Under all his brashness and light-hearted refusal to admit the risks and the danger, she sensed a vulnerable man, a man who had been hurt and would do anything to hide it. She wondered if it had been a woman. Or was it something else? She knew he would not tell her if she asked and so she accepted him as he was, courageous to the point of being foolhardy. 'And what do you think Justine will say, when she has taken the risk to bring you here to safety and you refuse to go?'

'She will understand.'

'Then what?'

'When I've contacted London and enlisted their help, I'll come back here.'

'Very well, if you must, you must.' It was said with a heavy sigh. 'But if Justine can't help, then promise me you'll leave for the border. We can use the pass for a few more days.'

'I promise,' he said solemnly and then laughed. 'If

Ma'amselle Clavier doesn't know how to contact London then I'll have to go there myself and arrange things. But I will be back, my lovely Lisabette, either way, I will be back.'

When the knock came on the door, Justine ushered Max into a cupboard among the brooms and mops and suitcases and shut the door on him. Then she carried their coffee cups and wine glasses into the kitchen and went to answer the knock, opening the door a crack, no more.

The man on the landing was in a German captain's uniform which made her catch her breath, but then he grinned. 'Hallo, Justine.'

'What in heaven's name are you doing back here?' She put her head out in the corridor and looked both ways. Luckily there was no one about. 'Come in quickly. I hope you weren't followed.'

'No, I was very careful.'

She led the way into the sitting room. 'Sit down. You had better have a good reason for turning up here again.'

He sat down on the sofa, though she continued to stand. 'Oh, a very good one. I want you to contact London for me.'

'Whatever makes you think I can do that?'

'A hunch, that's all. I decided to stay and help the Resistance and to do that we need supplies which London can send us.'

'Who is "we"?'

'Your brother Pierre, your nephews, Henri and Philippe, your niece, Lisabette. There are others, I am told.'

'Did you make your way here alone?'

'Yes. I've got papers. I was asked for them several times on the way here, but they passed muster every time.'

'Where did you get them?'

'A German Leutnant got them for me. I bribed him with money Henri gave me.' He pulled them from his pocket and gave them to her.

'My God, they're identity documents for Hauptmann Otto Bergman.'

'Nothing but the best,' he said blithely. 'I had to be a captain, a private would be liable to be ordered about.'

'And can this German lieutenant be trusted?'

'He is very anxious to get his family out of Cologne, so I promised him more money. That's one of the things I want you to do. Get London to send cash. And guns. We can't fight without weapons.'

She handed his papers back and went to let Max out of the cupboard. 'Did you hear all that?' she asked him.

'Yes.'

'Who's he?' Roger demanded.

'Antoine Descourt,' Max said.

'Why were you hiding in the cupboard? Are you another of her escapees?'

Max looked at Justine, who gave him a slight nod. 'You could say that,' he said.

'Sit down,' Justine said, addressing Roger. 'I'll make some more coffee and see if I can rustle up something to eat. No doubt you are hungry.'

'Lisabette gave me a good breakfast, but that was hours and hours ago.'

'Lisabette?' Max queried, careful to keep his voice neutral.

'Yes, Justine's niece. Do you know her?'

'I've heard Justine speak of her.'

'Lovely girl,' Roger went on. 'Brave too.'

'Brave?'

'Taking in escapees and guiding them over the pass under the noses of the Boche, but you knew that, didn't you?'

'No, should I?'

'They are taken to her by Justine, just as she took me.'

Max managed a laugh. 'Some things are best not to know.'

'Quite. I don't blame you for being wary, but you have nothing to fear from me.'

Justine left them, put the kettle on the stove in the kitchen and then hurried into the spare room and removed all evidence of Max's stay, taking his clothes and toiletries into her own room, then she made up the bed afresh and went back and made some coffee and sandwiches, filling them with thin slices of sausage that were more breadcrumbs than meat. The men were still talking warily when she took the loaded tray into the sitting room.

'You English?' Roger asked Max.

'French Canadian. I was part of de Gaulle's army and was captured in North Africa. I managed to escape and found Justine. Now you tell me your story.'

Roger complied and as each appeared to believe the other, the tension in the room relaxed and they sat eating sandwiches, drinking bitter ersatz coffee and talking about the war. But when the conversation dried up, Roger returned to the reason for his visit. 'Are you going to contact London for me?' he asked Justine.

'Contrary to what you believe, Roger, I have no idea how to do it, but I will try to find out. I need to be careful so it might take some time. You can stay here for the time being, but for God's sake don't dare put your nose out of the door.'

'What about Antoine?'

'Never mind about Antoine,' she said, giving Max a warning look. 'What he does shouldn't concern you.'

He grinned and tapped his nose. 'Oh, I see how the land lies. You are old friends and Monsieur Antoine Descourt is in no hurry to cross the border.'

'I'll go when Justine decides to take me,' Max said stiffly.

The food consumed, Justine took Roger to the spare bedroom. 'You slept here before,' she said. 'I didn't expect you to be doing it again.'

'I didn't expect to either, but when I saw how brave and clever Lisabette was, I decided I must do my bit to help. She's a marvel, isn't she, the way she manages the farm and gets up to milk the cows after being up all night taking people to the crossing? She shouldn't have to do that. It's too risky.'

The enthusiastic way he spoke made her look closely at him. How sincere was he? It was difficult to tell. 'It's her choice,' she said.

'When are you going back to Dransville?' he asked.

'I don't know. We live each day as it comes. Are you anxious to return?'

'Yes, but not to escape. There's work to do there.'

'You're mad and I shouldn't encourage you, but I can't turn you away; you'd be a liability if you were caught. I've got to think of a way out. You stay here in this room until I do. Is that understood?'

He gave her a mock salute. 'Perfectly, Ma'amselle, but don't be too long.'

'Oh, I won't be any longer than I can help, you can be sure of that.' She went to the door, removed the key from the lock and fitted it back on the outside.

'Are you locking me in?'

'I'm afraid so. For everyone's sake. Goodnight. Sleep well.'

She left, locked the door, put the key in her skirt pocket and went back to Max. He was sitting on the sofa staring into the flames of a meagre fire, a glass of red wine at his elbow, deep in thought. She poured herself a glass of wine and sat beside him.

'What are we going to do about him?' he asked in an undertone.

'I don't know. What do you suggest? He's too cocky for my liking. He thinks that German uniform will protect him.'

'Perhaps it will. Perhaps it's genuine. We've only his word that he is who he says he is. He might be playing a double game. Supposing he's an infiltrator, supposing he decided he hadn't learnt enough just being taken to Dransville and dreamt up this way of learning more . . .' He gave a brittle laugh. 'I've learnt to mistrust everyone, Justine, to look for hidden motives in everyone's behaviour.'

'Even mine?' she queried.

'Good God, no!' He put his hand over hers. 'I trust you with my life, as you trust me. There's no way I'd betray you. But he might.'

'That's why I can't turn him out.' She was very conscious of the warmth of his hand. In the three weeks they had been working together and, to all intents and purposes, living together, it was the first time he had touched her in that way. It made her realise the way her feelings were going and it shocked her. 'But you must maintain your cover, don't let it slip, not even with me.'

'I'll get a message through to London tomorrow, get them to check him out. They'll tell us what to do about him.'

Etienne had been dropped to be his wireless operator and he had regular schedules for contacting London. His was the most dangerous job of all and he flitted about from one place to another in the suburbs of Paris, living in safe houses and *pensions*, one step ahead of the German detector vans. They met only when Max had something to transmit or was expecting instructions from London. The other agent was Anne Barnard who had joined them as a courier. Like Etienne, she was here, there and everywhere.

The circuit was growing all the time. Justine's principal, Giles Chalfont, had turned out to be a real find. He was thin as a rake, with keen blue eyes and an aura of calmness which was just what was needed to restrain the more hot-headed of the group. He had been instrumental in recruiting and vetting volunteers and they were planning sabotage on an ammunition train and for that they were expecting a drop of explosives, guns, ammunition and money. They could do without the added complication of Roger Wainbridge, if that was his real name. Perhaps it really was Otto Bergman.

'You'd better go to bed,' he said. 'I'll doss down on the sofa. I'll be gone at first light.'

Chapter Ten

'Lucy, tell me about your mother,' Amy said. It was the week before Christmas and she had gone to spend a few off-duty hours with Lucy and Peter. The little one was pulling himself up on his feet now, shuffling round the furniture; it would not be long before he walked. He was a lovable little lad, chubby with good health and a smile to melt the hardest heart. He recognised her now and always held up his arms to her when she arrived. Now she was sitting on the sofa with him on her lap, determined to solve the riddle of Lucy's missing mother. The girl was lonely, feeling the stigma of having a child out of wedlock, and she was wary of making friends in case the truth came out. It was sad that Jack saw so little of her and their son; as far as Amy knew he had not followed her advice and told their parents. It would soon be Christmas and after that

Peter's first birthday; surely he would find some way of commemorating that?

'My mother, why?' She had covered the kitchen table with an old folded blanket and was busy ironing Peter's playsuits and the sheets from his cot.

'I wondered if she could be found. Wouldn't you like to be reunited with her?'

'Yes, but she wouldn't want to know me.'

'Why not?'

'Because of . . . Oh, you know.'

'Peter, you mean? I'm sure no loving mother would hold that against you.'

'How do I know she is a loving mother, she left me behind, didn't she?'

Amy detected a degree of bitterness in her tone. 'Maybe she couldn't help it. Maybe she was prevented somehow. Maybe she thought you would be better off with Mr Storey. You'll never know if you don't try to find her.'

'He's had her declared dead.'

'I know, but that doesn't mean she *is* dead, does it?'

'I suppose not, but it would mean he's a bigamist.'

'That's his problem, not yours. So, tell me about her.'

'I thought she was lovely, she smelt of lavender. She said it was her favourite perfume. When she put me to bed she would cuddle me and tell me stories about a big house and happy children who had all sorts of exciting adventures, climbing trees, going boating, swimming in the river, holidays by the sea.'

'A real house? Real children?'

238

'I don't know. She didn't say. She could have been making it up. She often said I'd grow up to be a real lady. I didn't know what she meant, but after she left, Pa would complain she had filled my head with nonsense and said the sooner I forgot the stories the better.'

'Did something happen to make her leave?'

'I don't know. I know they quarrelled a lot and it frightened me, especially when Pa got angry. He shouted at her and once I saw him hit her. Then one day she disappeared while I was at school. I was eight years old. Pa said she wasn't coming back. He said she was no better than she should be . . .'

'Do you believe that?'

'I didn't understand what he meant at the time, except I guessed it was nasty.'

'Do you think he really knows where she is?'

Amy watched as Lucy switched off the iron, climbed on a chair to take the plug out of the light socket and replace the bulb. 'I don't know,' she said clambering down off the chair and switching on the light. 'If he does, then he shouldn't have had her declared dead, should he?'

'No, he shouldn't. Do you think he'd lie about that?'

Lucy shrugged. 'I don't know.'

'Wouldn't you like to know the truth?'

'I've thought about it a lot. When I suggested to Pa that we ought to try and find her, he got very angry. In any case, I've no idea how to go about it.' She picked Peter off Amy's lap. 'It's time he was in bed.'

It was almost as if she didn't want to talk about it, but Amy, having begun the conversation, was disinclined to let it drop. She followed Lucy up the stairs to the little back room and watched her as she put the child in his cot and tucked him up.

'Do you know your mother's maiden name or where they were married?' Amy persisted.

'No. We lived in a place called Eccles. I had to learn the address when I started school in case I got lost and needed to ask the way, but that doesn't mean she was married there.'

'What was the address? Do you still remember it?'

Lucy laughed. 'When you learn things as a child, they stick, don't they? It was number two Station Road, Eccles.' She kissed Peter. 'Now you be a good boy and go to sleep. It will soon be Christmas and then you'll have lots of presents.'

Amy was reminded of the wooden truck full of coloured bricks she had bought for him as she kissed him too and followed Lucy downstairs. She would bring it on Christmas Day after she came off duty. She would be working the early shift and there wouldn't be time to go home. It would be the first time she had ever been away from home at Christmas and she would miss the fun at Nayton Manor. But with Lizzie still in France, Jack liable to be on duty and her father once more in uniform and in London, working at the War Office, it wouldn't be the same. Nothing was the same anymore.

'Eccles. Where is that?'

'I've no idea. I know we seemed a long time getting to Nayton when we moved, but I was only five or six, so it probably seemed longer than it was. We travelled on the removal van – Mum sat next to the driver with me on her lap. Pa was in the back. At least I imagine he was because he was with us when we arrived.'

'Do you think you were born there?'

'I don't know.'

'It will be on your birth certificate, surely?'

'I haven't got it. I left in a hurry and didn't think of it. I can't ever remember seeing it. Why are you asking all these questions?'

'I'd like to have a shot at tracing your mother. Would you agree?'

'Finding out where she came from isn't going to help with where she's gone, is it?'

'It might. She might have decided to go back to her family.'

'She always said she didn't have anyone.'

'It's worth trying to find out, don't you think?'

Lucy put the kettle on to make a cup of tea and began making sandwiches, filling them with a couple of rashers of bacon she had put into the frying pan on the gas stove. 'You could try,' she said, slowly. 'But if you find her and she doesn't want to know, that's it. I shan't try again. I know when I'm not wanted.'

Amy hurried over to her and put her arm round the girl's shoulders and hugged her. 'I want you and so does Jack.' She paused. 'What are you going to do at Christmas?'

'I'll be here, where else?'

'I'll come in the afternoon, if you like. I leave off at midday.'

'Yes, I'd like that, and you never know, Jack might get leave.'

'No, you never know,' Amy agreed.

According to the station medic Jack had done more than his fair share of operations and he needed a rest if he were not to become a liability. He protested but not very forcefully; he was undoubtedly tired and the loss of one of his oldest friends the week before had hit him hard. Coming down after chasing bombers and fighter escorts all over the sky, to find an empty place at the table, brought home to him his own vulnerability. He was already defying the odds. He took the chit he was given to his CO who said he wasn't surprised. 'Take fourteen days' leave as of now,' he said.

Tucking his travel warrant into his breast pocket, he waited until he was out of earshot before yelling, 'Whoopee!' Two whole weeks, two whole weeks in which to recharge his batteries and have a bit of fun. He hurried to his room to throw a few clothes into a kitbag. He would arrange to meet Belinda, take her out to dinner and perhaps to a dance, and propose and when she said yes, they could go to Nayton together to tell his parents, possibly for Christmas, and then . . .' He stopped suddenly and sat heavily on the bed, a pair of socks in his hand.

Lucy. The mother of his son. Peter. His secret family. He could not, in all conscience, propose to Belinda until he had resolved his relationship with Lucy. And what was Belinda going to say when he told her? She might have no more to do with him. On the other hand, she might tell him she didn't care as long as he didn't see Lucy again. Would that be pretence on her part? If it was the truth, what did it say for her feelings towards him, that she didn't love him enough to be jealous? And how could he promise not to see Lucy again? He ought to see her more often; his conscience was already troubled about that. What a dilemma to be in! He was too tired, too uncertain, to do anything about it. He'd go home to Nayton. Perhaps a solution would come to him while he was there.

He finished packing, cadged a lift into London and caught a train to Norwich, intending to pick up a connection to Nayton, but when he left the train his steps took him out to the bus stop for Waterloo Road.

Lucy was giving Peter his dinner, coaxing him to eat a little more of the stew and potatoes she had mashed up for him. 'Come on, Peter, have just one more spoonful. Look, Mummy will have one to show you how good it is.' She popped the spoon into her own mouth. 'Yum, yum, that's good.' She filled the spoon again and offered it to him. He opened his mouth and in it went. 'One more,' she said, 'then you can have some apples and custard. You like custard, don't you?'

She was so engrossed in her child she did not hear the back door open, but Peter, who was facing the door, saw him and pointed, saying something in his baby language.

Lucy twisted round, dropped the spoon on the table, flew across the room and flung herself into Jack's arms. 'You came. I knew you would. I told Amy you would.'

He kissed her and smiled. 'Someone's pleased to see me, at any rate.' He went over and picked Peter out of his high chair. 'And how's my little man?'

'Give Daddy a kiss,' Lucy told the child.

He planted a wet kiss on Jack's cheek. Jack laughed and sat down at the table with Peter on his lap. 'Do you know who I am?' he asked him.

'Of course he does,' Lucy said. 'He kisses your photo every night when I put him to bed and I talk about you all the time.'

'Oh, and what do you tell him? That he has a father who neglects him shamefully?'

'Don't be silly, you don't neglect him. You can't help it if there's a war on and you can't get to see us as often as you'd like. I understand that.'

Her understanding made him feel ten times worse. He could have come before now, he could have used a forty-eight-hour pass to come to Norwich instead of staying with Belinda. 'I've been taken off flying and given two weeks' leave,' he said. 'I'll have to spend some of it at home, but for the rest, I'm all yours.'

'Oh, Jack, we'll have the most wonderful Christmas. Amy's going to come for dinner. Have you had anything to eat today?'

'I had breakfast and I bought a bun at the station café, but it was so dry I fed it to the pigeons.'

'I'll heat this stew up again and make some dumplings. And there's stewed apples and custard, will that do?'

'Lovely,' he said, momentarily thinking of the dinner he could have been having with Belinda, but then dismissed the thought as unworthy. He picked up the small dish of fruit and custard she had already served up for Peter and began feeding it to him.

They ate their meal after Peter had been put to bed, and then sat together on the sofa facing a fire made of logs which she had acquired from a man with a horse and cart who came round selling them. They had a mug of cocoa each on an occasional table in front of them. He put his arm about her and she tucked her feet under her and nuzzled her head against his chest. 'This is lovely,' she said.

'It's always great to come home to you,' he said, and meant it. 'You make me feel cosy and relaxed, as if none of the world's ills can touch us.'

'Good, that's how I want it to be. Always. You see, I love you very much.'

'Oh, Lucy,' he said, choked. 'I don't deserve you.'

'Don't be silly, of course you do. You gave me a life when I didn't have one.'

'You call this a life?'

'Oh, yes, yes I do. It's a hundred times better than the one I had before. I can please myself what I do and I've got Peter. And you. And Amy and a few friends from work.' She paused. 'Amy said she was going to try and trace my mother.'

'Is that what you want?'

245

She shrugged. 'It would be nice to know.'

'Does Amy know how to go about it?'

'I told her the address we lived at before we moved to Nayton. She said she would start there.'

'I didn't know you knew it.'

'I didn't either until she asked me and I remembered. I'm not getting my expectations up because I have no idea how long we lived there and where we were before. Railwaymen get moved about a lot if they want advancement.' She stopped suddenly. 'I wonder if it's such a good idea.'

'Of course it is. Whatever the outcome, it's best to know, don't you think? Your mother might be sad that she lost touch with you.'

'And when she discovers she's a grandmother?'

'All the better.'

She scrambled from his embrace and took the empty mugs to the kitchen to wash them up. She didn't want to talk about her situation as an unmarried mother. Her dream of being married to Jack was just that; she was deluding herself if she thought any different. She turned as he followed her and put his arms about her from behind, nuzzling his face in the hair at the back of her neck. 'Let's go to bed.'

Bernard moved stealthily through the undergrowth in the wood, trying not to step on twigs which would betray his presence. It was a game he played a lot at weekends and holidays when he had nothing much to do but mooch round the village with his hands in his pockets. Sometimes he enrolled Ray and Martin to be the criminals he was tracking, but they soon became bored with it and went off to play something else. He had taken to tracking real people. Sometimes it was the Reverend Royston as he went about the village visiting people but he never seemed to do anything interesting; sometimes it was Bennett the chauffeur, or Mr Jones, the gardener, or Mrs Hutchins, who was responsible for the welfare of the evacuees. More often it was Frank Lambert or Bert Storey. He knew everyone's habits and where they were most likely to be at any given time of day, but he was no nearer uncovering any spies.

One thing he had discovered was that Bert and Frank, though appearing to be good friends and colleagues, really didn't like each other, and Mrs Storey was always rowing with her husband; he often heard them shouting at each other when he was stalking round the station. The outcome was that Mr Storey would go to the Nayton Arms and stay there until closing time, while she went off to meet Mr Lambert, sometimes in his signal box, which would have meant instant dismissal if they had been caught, sometimes in the cottage in the wood. It amused Bernard to think that it seemed to be a trysting place for lovers.

On this occasion he crept up to the cottage and squatted below the window out of sight. The glass in it was broken and he could hear their conversation quite clearly.

'He's getting worse and worse,' she said. 'It was the biggest mistake of my life, marrying him.'

'I could have told you that if you'd asked me,' Frank said.

'Well, I didn't, did I? I thought you were his friend.'

'He's no friend of mine.'

'Why? Because of Lucy?'

'No.' He laughed. 'Nothing to do with Lucy.'

'So you're not still carrying a torch for her?'

'Don't be daft. I never was. It was Ma's idea for me to marry her, not mine. Anyway, she's gone now.'

'True. Do you know where she is?'

'No idea. Don't care either.'

'She wasn't his daughter, he told me that. He said she belonged to his wife by another man and that's why he got rid of her.'

'Got rid of who?' The voice was sharp.

Bernard, ears strained to catch every word, crept even closer and risked peeping over the window sill. They were sitting side by side on the floor, propped against the wall, Frank's arm about her, a blanket over their legs. He ducked down again when Mrs Storey stirred in his arms.

'Lucy,' she said. 'Who did you think I meant?'

'Maggie, his first wife.'

'What about her?

'Nothing. Did he tell you what happened?

'Only that she was playing fast and loose and so he threw her out. He said he hadn't seen hide nor hair of her since the day she left. He had her declared dead. Seems you can do that if someone's been gone a long time.'

'Do you think she is? Dead, I mean.'

'Dunno, do I? But if she were alive and we could prove

it, then he'd be a bigamist and I'd be free of him.'

'Why bother with all that? Why not just leave him?'

'To do what?'

'Move in with me.'

'And your ma.' She laughed. 'No, thank you. But if you should hear one day that I've taken the carving knife to him, don't be surprised.'

'For God's sake, Molly, don't do that. You'll probably come off worse. He's got a vicious temper.'

'Don't I know it.'

Bernard could hear movement and realised they were standing up ready to leave. He scuttled round the back of the cottage and hid in some bushes until they had gone, then he rushed back home to write it all down in his notebook before he forgot it. He'd show it to Edmund who was home for the Christmas holidays and had gone out riding with his mother. Bernard could have gone too, but he had never been comfortable on a horse, not even Amy's Patch which was getting old now and as docile as anything.

'I wonder if Bert Storey knows what's going on?' Edmund said when they were alone in Edmund's room later that evening.

'Don't know, do I? But I'm not going to tell him; he's a nasty piece of work and you never know what he might do.'

'Bernie, you've got your head full of murder and spies and goodness knows what, making a mountain out of a molehill.'

'She did threaten to kill her husband.'

'Oh, that's just talk. I should keep mum about it if I were you.'

Bernard was disappointed. He thought Edmund would be all for reporting the conversation, but perhaps his friend was right; he didn't have enough to go on yet. He'd keep watching.

Jack arrived home on New Year's Eve, no nearer a solution to his dilemma. When he was with Belinda, she was the one he wanted; when he was with Lucy, he knew he could never give her up. Amy had asked him why he was so keen on Belinda and all he could think of to say was, 'She's fun to be with, she's a looker and always well dressed, in spite of the war, and she's one of our kind.' He had been walking Amy back to the nurse's home after their little Christmas Day party, which he had to admit he had enjoyed. Where Lucy managed to get so much to eat, he had no idea, but they had stuffed themselves on a chicken, a little bit of sausage meat and vegetables, followed by a tiny fruit cake and half a dozen home-made mince pies. They weren't the rich-filled crumbly pastry he remembered having at home before the war but he did not doubt even Mrs Baxter had had to make do.

'What is our kind, Jack?'

'Oh, you know, upper crust, moneyed, well educated. She knows how to behave in Society.'

Amy gave a snort of derision. 'She certainly knows how to throw her orders about and complain if things are not to her liking. As for being well educated, just because she went to Roedean and a finishing school doesn't mean she's educated. I bet if Lucy had had her opportunities, she'd be educated and well dressed too and she'd know how to behave in Society. Those things can all be acquired, Jack, patience and a loving nature cannot. Look at Mama, you'd never know she wasn't upper crust, would you?'

'No, of course not.'

'Did Lucy ever tell you about her mother?'

'No, she always shied away from it.'

'Do you remember her?'

'Only vaguely. She often opened the crossing gates for us. I remember she had a nice smile, a bit like Lucy . . .'

'Lucy's been hurt, Jack, more than we can ever know. Please, please, don't hurt her any further.'

'My, she has got under your skin, hasn't she?'

She had laughed. 'And she's under yours too, isn't she? Admit it.'

He had refused to answer, but in his heart he knew she was right. Lucy was part of him, part of the man he had become since the start of this terrible war. The trouble was that he was reluctant to give up his youthful dream of finding his place in society. And what would his parents think if they ever learnt about him and Lucy and little Peter, who according to both Lucy and Amy, was his spitting image? Amy thought they ought to know, but he could never find the right words to tell them.

His mother, looking a little greyer and thinner, was overjoyed to see him and he was fussed over and fed. It was only after she was satisfied he was no longer hungry that she asked him for all his news. He could have mentioned Lucy then, but just as he was forming the words, she went on, 'Papa said he saw you in London with Belinda Davenport. Are you going to make a match of it?'

'I don't know,' he said. 'It's not a good time to think of marriage, is it? You never know . . .'

'Don't talk like that, Jack. The worst danger is over now, don't you think? The raids are not so bad as they were, and with the Americans in the war now, it will soon be over.' The Japanese had attacked American shipping in Pearl Harbour in the early part of December with the result that America had abandoned its neutrality and was now part of a global war. What difference it was going to make had yet to be seen, but no one doubted it would be significant.

'I hope so, Mama,' he said, not wishing to disillusion her, though he could not see an early end to the conflict, what with the fighting in North Africa and Russia and the shipping losses as bad as ever.

'Serena Davenport seems to think you are seriously courting Belinda.'

'I take her out now and again when I've got a few hours off, that's all.'

'You are being very cagey.'

'No, I'm not, I'm telling it as it is. Now what news have you got? What's Pa doing in London? I never thought they'd let him back into uniform; he's too old.'

'Apparently not. He's working in Intelligence. I don't know any details, it's all very hush-hush. Anyway, he's coming home this evening for a few days' leave, you can talk to him yourself.'

Jack spent the afternoon wandering about the estate. The nearby airfield had been enlarged, taking in some acres of the estate, and there was a gun emplacement on the edge of it. It looked as though the war had come to Nayton. He wandered through the wood, picking up a pocketful of sweet chestnuts as he went, until he came to the gamekeeper's cottage. For a few minutes he was a small child again, trying to come to terms with a new environment and the need to learn a different language, and the misery he had felt then came rushing back to him. He had resented his mother's husband and had not been prepared to like him, but soon realised Maman was obviously very happy and the aura of contentment about the place had eventually overcome his resistance, especially as his new Papa took the trouble to get to know him and include him in everything that was going on. He had gradually come to realise that Lord de Lacey was a very important man, that he was rich and respected and he decided he wanted to be like him.

That ambition had coloured his growing up until he met Lucy. How she had come to entwine herself about his heart he could not explain. He sat on the tree trunk outside the dilapidated cottage and mused on his encounters with her. He could almost see her sitting there while he painted her, her honey-coloured hair strewn about her white shoulders, barely covering her breasts. There had been no thought of loving her then, only of sexual gratification. It had taken Frank Lambert's attack to make him realise that he couldn't do it, not then, not until . . . He smiled to himself, remembering that first time, so sweet, so right. Did he love her now? Of course he did, in a way, but was it enough?

He heard someone walking on the fallen leaves and Bernard came strolling along the path. He stopped suddenly when he saw Jack.

'Hallo, young man,' Jack said. 'What are you up to?'

'Nothing. I'm not doing anything wrong.'

'I didn't say you were.' He indicated a place on the log beside him. 'Come and sit down. Tell me about school. Getting on all right there, are you?'

'It's all right.'

'What do you want to be when you leave?'

'A detective.'

'The police force, very commendable. But why?'

'I like solving mysteries.'

'And have you found any mysteries to solve?'

'No, not really except...' He hesitated. 'It's about Mr Storey. I reckon he's hiding something.'

'What makes you say that?'

For answer Bernard took a scruffy notebook from his jacket pocket and thumbed through the pages, then he handed it to Jack. 'I wrote it down.'

Jack read it through. 'Is this *exactly* what was said?'

'Yes. Eddie said it didn't mean anything.'

'I'm inclined to agree with him. Where were they when they were talking? How did you manage to overhear it so clearly?'

'They were in there.' The boy jerked his head in the

254

direction of the cottage behind them. 'Go in there regular, they do.'

Jack was intrigued. 'Oh, I see. Have you discovered anything else?'

'No, but I'm still on the case.'

Jack laughed. 'You keep on it. You never know what you might uncover. And if you do find something interesting, you let me know, OK?'

'OK.'

Jack stood up. 'I think we had better be going back to the house. It's nearly dinner time.'

His father had arrived by the time the gong went for dinner and because there were so few people in the house, and it made it easier for Mrs Baxter, the children all ate with them. It was not until Jack and Charles went to the billiard room afterwards that the conversation turned to what Charles was doing in London.

'You managed to find a niche for yourself after all,' Jack said, placing the coloured balls on the table. 'Mama said you were in Intelligence.'

'Sort of.'

'Can't you tell me?'

'I shouldn't, but I know it won't go any further. I'm working in the communications room of MI6, taking messages from our agents in France and relaying them to the appropriate people for action. Sometimes I'm asked to devise questions to decide whether someone is genuine or not.'

'Fascinating. What's happening out there? Anything

about Dransville? Is Lizzie still helping people over the border?'

'It seems so. And Justine is very involved with the Resistance. Max is with her.'

'Max?' Jack queried in surprise. 'My God! What does Lizzie think about that?'

'Lizzie doesn't know. He's not working anywhere near her and it's safer for her not to know.'

'I thought Max was a bit cagey when I bumped into him in London. Well, well, well.'

'Not a word to anyone, Jack, or you'll have me shot.'

'Of course not. I wouldn't mind having a go at that myself.'

'Don't be an idiot, Jack. You've got a job to do and it's an important one.'

'I need a change.'

'But not that. The chances of survival are pretty slim and if anything happened to you it would devastate your mother, what with Lizzie and Justine being out there. Besides, I doubt they'd let you go. Good pilots are pretty thin on the ground.'

'Yes, I suppose you're right. Do you get news of Lizzie?'

'No, she's not part of the set-up and radio communication has to be kept to a minimum. I can't ask personal questions. Dransville is in the unoccupied zone, so I am assuming she has sense enough to keep her head down. I think if anything did happen to her, then Justine or Max would find a way of letting us know. At least, working where I do, I get to know the news.'

'Does Mama know about this?'

'No, and don't you tell her. I should not have told you.'

'I'm glad you did.'

They turned as Annelise came into the room; if either of them looked guilty she didn't seem to notice it. 'Come into the drawing room. Big Ben will be striking the new year soon. Let's raise a glass to that.'

Obediently they followed her, listened to the wireless as the clock struck midnight and then toasted the new year. 'To 1942, may it see the end of this terrible bloodshed. And may Lizzie come home safe and sound.'

Neither man attempted to disillusion her.

Chapter Eleven

Roger, still dressed as a German captain, took the two airmen from Justine's apartment, for all the world as if he had just arrested them. From her drawing room window, Justine and Max watched them marching down the slushy street towards the Metro. 'He's got nerve, I'll give him that,' Max said.

'You're still not sure of him are you?'

'I can't make up my mind. He's either a very brave man or a stupid one, unless of course, he knows he has nothing to fear from the Boche.'

'London said he was OK. He answered all their questions correctly.'

'But that doesn't necessarily mean they trust him wholeheartedly; he has to prove himself.' Major Buckmaster had instructed him to give Captain Wainbridge some of the money they had provided him with and they would send more with the next drop, and to tell him to go ahead with organising resistance in Haute Savoie. This was all supposedly done through Justine and her mysterious contact, not Max who still maintained his alias. 'No doubt they'll keep a close watch on what he's up to.'

'Giles has told Jeanne Clements to follow him as far as the Gare de Lyon,' she said. 'If he communicates with anyone on the way or they get on a different train, she will know.' Jeanne taught mathematics at the same school as Justine and was one of the early recruits, helping to duplicate and distribute *France Vivra*.

'Then he doesn't trust him either.'

'He's just being extra cautious.'

'And if the man's an infiltrator?'

She shrugged. 'We'd have to deal with him.'

'Kill him, you mean?'

'We wouldn't have any choice, would we?'

He laughed. 'God, you're getting hard, Justine.'

'We have to protect the circuit. At least he'll be out of the way when London sends the stuff you asked for.'

All they were waiting for was the BBC message to say the drop was on as arranged. They locked the door and drew the curtains and then settled down beside the wireless set and tuned it in, waiting for the personal messages.

After listening to several bizarre messages which could have no meaning except to the recipients, they heard the one meant for them. 'The dog is out of the kennel and running after the bone.' It was repeated and they looked at each other and grasped hands. 'We're on,' he said. 'Better get a move on.' They had to be off the city streets before curfew or they would be picked up.

Justine retuned the wireless to Radio Paris and switched it off. Then they donned coats and hats and left the building, arm in arm, to all intents and purposes a couple out for a stroll, so absorbed in each other's company they took no notice of others in the street: men and women hurrying home from work, playing children and scavenging dogs, and German soldiers, some on patrol, others out for a good time. Walking unhurriedly, they left the centre of the city and made for a house in the suburbs where Giles was waiting for them with a borrowed van. They climbed in and were driven along country roads to Count Mollet's estate. So far the count had escaped the attentions of the German occupiers and the Vichy police, but for how much longer, they could only guess. Here they were joined by a dozen others. No one spoke.

They had barely lit the flares to mark the drop before they heard the drone of an aircraft. This was the most dangerous time, when anything could go wrong, and they waited, with hearts in mouths, while the noise grew louder and they thought the whole German army couldn't fail to hear it. The aircraft flew low and then they saw the parachutes leave it and the sky was filled with billowing silk, floating dark against the lighter sky. The Lysander climbed, banked and disappeared. It was only seconds but it seemed an age before the canisters hit the ground.

The watchers ran forward to extinguish the flares, then began gathering everything up and loading it into the van. Everyone except Giles, Max and Justine disappeared into the darkness as silently as they had arrived. Max and Justine squeezed in the front of the vehicle beside Giles. Then they were off again, bumping over the rough ground towards the chateau where there was an underground wine cellar. Part of it had been sealed off from the house and could only be approached through a secret entrance in the grounds. It held some of the count's best wine, hidden from the occupiers, but was also ideal for storing the arms, ammunition and explosives until such time as it was needed. Here the supplies were unloaded and checked to make sure it was all there, then they left, making sure the entrance was secure and well hidden.

'So far, so good,' Max said, as they drove back to Paris, arriving just before dawn. Here they parted, Max to rendezvous with Etienne to report the successful drop and Justine to go home to snatch a quick breakfast before going to school, leaving Giles to take the van back to its owner before going to school himself. Here they learnt from Jeanne that Roger had done nothing out of the ordinary on his way to the railway station with the escapees and they had all boarded the train without incident.

The snow lay thick on the mountain and was piled up either side of the road through the village, which was busy with skiers, almost all of them German soldiers on leave. They filled the hotels and crowded on the ski lift to hurtle down the piste, calling out to each other and laughing when they came a cropper. The villagers tolerated them because they brought much needed revenue. Some made friends of them, accepting the extra food or cigarettes they were offered.

Elizabeth did not go out of her way to avoid them, nor did she encourage them, but she was always wary when they came to the farmhouse door for milk or eggs. Hans Shermann often came, enquiring if she had heard from Roger, but she could truthfully say she had not. He was a worried man, she could see that. He had helped Roger with a uniform and identity papers and was beginning to regret it. 'I hope he hasn't been picked up,' he had said, only the day before. 'If he talks, I'm done for.'

'He won't,' she had said, crossing her fingers behind her back.

She was just settling down to have supper with her grandparents two evenings later, when the dog started barking. Albert hastily switched off the wireless which was tuned to the BBC and they sat motionless, hearts beating erratically, waiting for a knock on the door. They heard a voice calling to the noisy dog and then silence, followed by a low voice singing in English. 'Run rabbit, run rabbit, run, run, run . . .'

Elizabeth rushed to open the door and pulled Roger inside. 'For God's sake, man, you'll have us all shot.'

'That's a fine greeting for a chap who's braved hell and high water to get back to the woman of his dreams.'

'Don't talk nonsense. Come and sit down and tell us what's been happening. Did you find Justine? Is she well?'

'Justine is in perfect health. They seem to lead a charmed life.'

'They? Who's they?'

'Oh, sorry, I appear to have spoken out of turn. You don't know?'

'No, we don't,' she said. 'But now you've started, you had better tell the rest.'

'She's living with a man called Antoine Descourt. He says he's a paint and wallpaper salesman, but I think it's more to do with the Resistance than anything, though he denies it, of course. Doesn't trust me.'

'Antoine!' Elizabeth gasped. 'Are you sure that's his name?'

'Yes, do you know him?'

She stilled her fast-beating heart with an effort. 'I thought I'd heard Justine mention someone of that name. What do you know about him?'

Roger shrugged. 'Not much. He's a big man, good-looking too, speaks French with an accent which he says comes from being brought up in French Canada.' He was speaking in English which frustrated Grandmère.

'I wish you would speak French,' she complained. 'What's he saying about Justine?'

Elizabeth translated for her.

'I don't believe it,' Grandmère said. 'She would have told us.'

'Maybe she will when she comes home next time,' Elizabeth soothed her. 'Do you think you can find Roger something to eat?'

'Yes, and I suppose he'll want a bed too.'

Roger caught the gist of that and smiled disarmingly at the old lady. 'If you can manage it, Madame Clavier, I would appreciate it.'

The old lady set about preparing a meal while Elizabeth continued to question Roger. 'Did you manage to contact London?'

'Justine did or she knew someone who did, I didn't question her too closely and she was certainly not disposed to tell me. They gave her a lot of damn fool questions for me to answer, but I suppose they had to be sure I was who I said I was. I seem to have satisfied them because I've been given the go-ahead to form a resistance group here in Haute Savoie. I need to see Henri and Philippe and Alphonse to make a start.'

'Not in that uniform. Hans Shermann has been worrying himself sick about it. He's on tenterhooks you'll be arrested with it and his part will come to light, and it worries me too. You had better be a farm worker. Dutch perhaps, you'll never pass for French. We'll find some other clothes for you.'

'That's OK by me, but I'll need different papers. Hans will get them for me.'

'Roger, it's unfair to involve him, he's hardly more than a boy and he's scared stiff. If he's questioned—'

'People have to grow up quickly in this war, Lisabette, and he knows what he's risking and why. I've brought him some money, quite a lot in fact, that should stiffen his spine.'

'You are heartless.'

'No, my dear Lisabette, I am all heart and most of it is yours.'

'What on earth do you mean by that?'

'Exactly what I say. At any other time, in different circumstances, I would be wining and dining you, buying you chocolates and flowers and going down on one knee to propose, with a diamond ring in my hand.'

She laughed. 'You do talk nonsense, Roger.' She paused. 'Hadn't you better have a different name. Roger sounds awfully British.'

'OK, you choose one.'

'Dirk.' It was the first name to come into her head. 'Dirk Van something or other. Vanveldt, that will do.'

'Right, from now on, I'm Dirk Vanveldt.'

They sat down to leak and potato soup, but it was clear that, for all his bonhomie, Roger was dead tired and he excused himself as soon as the meal was finished and went to bed.

'Antoine Descourt,' Grandpère said slowly after he had gone. 'Isn't that the name Justine gave Max?'

'Yes,' Elizabeth agreed. 'But it doesn't mean it is Max. Justine may simply have used the name again for someone else. Why would Max come back after getting safely away?'

'Why would Roger stay when he had a chance to escape?' her grandmother countered. 'The world's gone mad.'

'You are right there,' Elizabeth said, laughing. 'And if Max were in France, I'm sure he would have found some way of letting me know.'

All the same she couldn't help wondering. Was Antoine

Descourt simply a name Justine plucked out of the air, or was he a real person whose identity she had conveniently borrowed for Max? Or was it really Max? Could it be? But if it were, why had he come back? Justine's visits were few and far between, especially since using the crossing into Switzerland was inadvisable during the winter, which was why Roger had taken the last two men to Lyon to be passed on. Moving from the occupied to the unoccupied zone was becoming increasingly risky too; the trains were stopped for hours while everyone's papers were scrutinised. The least thing out of order and the culprit was hauled off for questioning. She was unlikely to see Justine for some time. Nor dare she write; letters were censored. Not knowing was tying her up in knots, especially as Roger had hinted Justine and Antoine were living together. They wouldn't do that, would they? No, she decided, Antoine Descourt couldn't possibly be Max.

The men and women, all wearing dark clothes, all armed, some carrying packs of explosives and detonators, made their way in ones and twos across the field to the railway line. They had chosen a spot where the line went through a wood, away from habitation. While the rest lay on the ground under cover of the trees, rifles at the ready, Max and Giles crept forward to lay the charges. Wanting to make sure they had the whole train and not just the engine, they put them at intervals along fifty yards of track. They had just set the last one, when they heard the sound of the train. 'Good timing,' Max said as they ran back to the shelter of the trees and flung themselves face down on the ground, covering their heads with their arms.

The explosions, following one another at intervals, almost burst their eardrums so close were they and fragments of red-hot metal were flung high in the sky and rained down on them, catching light to the nearest trees. 'Let's get out of here,' Max said, scrambling to his feet and beckoning everyone away. They would learn the extent of the damage the following morning when, no doubt, the Vichy police and their German masters would initiate a full-scale search for the culprits. There would be reprisals, but no one wanted to think about that.

Justine was waiting by the roadside with Giles's van. 'My, that was a mighty big bang,' she said. 'I should think it could be heard all the way to Paris.'

'Get in,' Giles said, as others of the party joined them. 'The sooner we are out of here, the better.'

They all crammed in the back, squeezed up against each other as the overloaded van stuttered its way back to Paris. Justine was in danger of having her head cracked against the sides every time they went round a bend and Max put his arm about her so that her head was protected by his chest. She could hear his heart beating hard and fast and knew he was not as cool as he appeared to be. She would have liked to think it was because of her nearness, but thought it was more likely to be reaction from a successful sabotage operation with all its attendant risks. And those were not over yet; they had to beat the roadblocks which would undoubtedly be set up in the wake of the explosion.

She put her hand up to clasp his. He did not take it away.

Giles stopped every now and then to let someone off, so that by the time they reached the outskirts of Paris, there was only Max and Justine left. They had not moved, but were still sitting on the floor of the van, leaning against the side, arms about each other.

At the junction of rue de la Reine and avenue Versailles, Giles pulled up. It was just beginning to get light, but the curfew had not yet been lifted. 'I should take a stroll in the Bois de Boulogne until there are more people on the streets,' he called over his shoulder. 'I shan't expect you in school until this afternoon, Justine.' He paused. 'The road is clear. Go now.'

They tumbled out and ran, hand in hand, up the road to the park where they stopped and turned to each other, breathless and laughing. Suddenly their merriment ceased and they stood looking at each other. Without a word, Max held out his arms and she went into them. They stood for several moments, locked in an embrace that spoke volumes, though neither said a word. When she tipped her face up to his, he bent to kiss her. It was more than a gentle kiss of brotherly affection, much more; it was the kiss of a man in the throes of passion. She felt her insides flare up in response.

'Let's go home,' he murmured when at last he raised his head. 'I want to make love to you.'

They turned and still with their arms about each other walked through the park to the Port Dauphine and out onto Avenue Foch. By this time the streets were becoming busy with people going to work, children going to school and shopkeepers opening their shutters, though there was little in their windows to sell. No one paid any attention to a lovesick couple who looked as though they had been out enjoying themselves all night and didn't want it to end.

Once safely in the apartment, he turned to her, took both her hands in his and held her from him. 'Yes?' he queried.

'Yes,' she said, then led the way to her bedroom.

It was some time later before either spoke and then he said, 'I suppose it had to happen.'

'Yes.'

'No regrets?'

'No. And you?'

'None.' He paused. 'What are we going to tell Lizzie?'

'Oh, God, I'd forgotten all about Lizzie,' she said.

'She'll have to be told.'

'Told what? That you so far forgot yourself as to make love to her aunt?'

'Correction. Fall in love with her.'

'Have you?'

'Have I what?'

'Fallen in love with me? It's not just some passing fancy?'

'You should know me better than that.'

'Yes, I suppose I do.'

'What about you?'

'My love for you has been growing ever since you turned up on my doorstep nearly two years ago, filthy, unshaven and wounded.'

He chuckled. 'That was just pity.'

'If it was, it changed when you came back into my life a second time. It was like being given another chance at happiness and I wanted to seize it while I could.'

'So, is that what we tell Lizzie?'

'We can't tell her anything now. You've been expressly ordered not to contact her.'

'I know. It will have to wait.' He reached for her again.

'No, Max, I have to get ready for school and don't you have a rendezvous with Etienne?'

He sighed dramatically. 'Oh, well, back to the war.'

They dressed, made some of the dreadful coffee which was all that was to be had these days, found a crust of bread and some jam her mother had given her the last time she was home, and after consuming it in silence, she kissed him and left the apartment, leaving him to follow a few minutes later.

The streets of Paris were alive with armed troops, searching for the perpetrators of the latest outrage. Hundreds of tons of guns and ammunition, not to mention fifty German lives, all gone up in smoke, and not only that, the track was unusable and would have to be re-laid. Someone was harbouring the guilty ones and they would winkle them out if they had to arrest the whole population to do it. Justine was unsure how best to behave as she set off to walk to school: curious or indifferent, unconcerned or frightened? Many of the people being questioned were looking terrified, though she knew they were innocent. Others blustered and threatened to report their rough treatment to superiors, which only made the soldiers laugh.

She would have liked to go back home and tell Max not to venture out, but she dare not draw attention to herself by turning back. She walked purposefully, but unhurriedly, along the street, though her instinct was to run for her life. She looked up as two men, one a German sergeant, the other a Vichy policeman, stood and blocked her path. 'Papers,' the policeman demanded, holding out his hand.

She opened her handbag and handed them to him, forgetting about the pistol she had put in there the evening before. The soldier who, until then, had only been overseeing his colleague, grabbed her bag and turned the contents out on the pavement. 'Ah, what have we here?' he said, retrieving the pistol, her purse and her door keys from handkerchief, powder compact, lipstick and a couple of safety pins, which he kicked to one side. 'I think, Ma'amselle, you had better come with us.' He indicated a police van parked along the road.

'What for? I've done nothing wrong.'

'It is a crime for civilians to carry a gun.'

'I've only got it to protect myself from terrorists. They are everywhere these days. Nowhere is safe.'

It was true about the so-called terrorists, gun-happy patriots who took every opportunity to shoot senior members of the occupying forces or those they considered collaborators. Justine had no reason to fear them, but many Parisians did. They wanted only to be left in peace, and though not actively collaborating with the occupying forces, were certainly accommodating. Life was easier that way.

'Nevertheless, you will come with us,' the policeman said, pushing her towards the van where several other people were being hustled inside.

They were taken to the headquarters of the Sûreté Nationale on the rue des Saussaies where they were herded inside. Here they were separated and Justine found herself in an office with a German major, who sat at a desk signing papers. The badge on his cap, lying on the desk, indicated he belonged to the Gestapo. She made herself stay calm, though her heart was beating like a piston engine. She stood in the middle of the room, flanked by her escorts who each held an arm as if they expected her to bolt. Where was there to bolt to? After several minutes in which she tried not to shift impatiently from foot to foot, he looked up and barked, 'Name?'

She felt like saying he knew her name since he had her identity documents, but decided not to antagonise him. 'Justine Clavier.'

'Age?'

'Thirty-two.'

'Address?'

She told him because there was no point in lying about it; they would soon find out the truth. She hoped fervently if the police went there, Max had gone.

'You know it is against the law for a French civilian to carry arms?'

'No, is it?' she queried innocently. 'I didn't know.'

'Ignorance is no excuse. Where did you get it?'

That posed a problem. Max had given it to her; it was

part of a drop from London, though it was of French manufacture. 'I bought it in a junk shop.'

'Which junk shop?'

'I don't know its name.'

'Where is this junk shop?'

'I can't remember. It was ages ago.'

'Did you also buy ammunition?'

'It wouldn't be much good without it, would it?'

'How much have you got?'

'Not much, a few bullets.'

'And do you know how to use it?'

'I was shown, but I've never tried. I don't think I could.'

'Paris is full of hotheads who claim never to have used a gun and wouldn't know how to, but they somehow manage it when the opportunity arises.'

'Opportunity?' she queried, still acting the innocent. 'You mean in self-defence?'

'No, I mean to shoot German soldiers.' He thumped his fist on the desk, making the papers on it jump and his hitherto mild interrogation changed up a gear. 'This cannot and will not be allowed to go on,' he shouted. 'Anyone carrying a firearm, however innocent they claim to be, will be shot.'

'Without a trial?'

'You think you deserve a trial?' He left his desk and began circling round her. 'Do you know what I think? I think you belong to one of these crackpot organisations who think it is clever to resist the lawful government of the country and blow up railways. It is not clever, it is foolhardy and futile.'

He signalled to her escort. 'Take her home.' Her relief at this was soon squashed when he added. 'Search the place, I want evidence and when you've got it, bring her back.'

She was marched out of the building and pushed into the back of a car, an escort either side of her, which took her to the rue de la Pompe where it stopped outside her door. She prayed fervently that Max was not there and he had left nothing incriminating behind. But even if the apartment was empty, they would keep watch for anyone returning. Her heart was beating so loudly she felt sure her captors could hear it, as they hustled her up the stairs and unlocked the door with her key.

She hadn't had time to tidy the apartment before she left and she remembered there were used plates and coffee cups in the sink, evidence that more than one person had been in occupation the night before, and the bed had not been made. Now it was pristine. The bed was made, the cushions on the sofa plumped up, the fire cleaned out and ready to relight, and the washing-up was done. There was no evidence of Max's occupation; everything belonging to him had gone. It left her feeling strangely at odds with herself. Had he already regretted the time they had spent in bed together and it was his way of ending an affair before it had really begun? No, she told herself; he was too honourable to leave like that. She preferred to think he knew she had been arrested and was, in his usual meticulous way, making everything right for her.

The searchers were thorough. They pulled all the covers off the bed and turned the mattress over; they emptied every cupboard in the kitchen and pulled every book from the bookcase in the drawing room, piling some of them up to take away. 'Banned,' they said before turning their attention to her desk. She held her breath. Had she left anything in there to connect her with *France Vivra*? Or notes about BBC news they meant to copy and print? Her diary was in there but she had been very careful not to put anything in it about her clandestine activities and appeared unconcerned when they added it to the books, along with her small portable typewriter.

'What are these?' the sergeant demanded in guttural French, pulling out a pile of school exercise books.

'My pupils' exercises. I am a teacher.'

He thumbed through them. 'They are in English.'

'Yes, I taught English before the war. The lessons have been discontinued since Marshal Pétain took over the government.'

'You are an Anglophile?'

'No, simply a linguist. I also teach French and Italian.'

'*Deutsch?*'

'Sadly, no. It was not taught at the school I attended.' She did have a smattering of German but decided not to admit it.

The books were added to the pile to be confiscated.

Then, with a cry of triumph, they produced a bottle of ink she had bought for the school's Roneo machine. 'What's this?'

'Ink, by the look of it.'

'Yes, ink for a duplicating machine, no?'

'Yes, it says so on the bottle.'

'Where have you hidden the machine?'

'I don't posses one.'

'Then what is this doing here?'

'I told you, I am a teacher. We have a machine at school and I sometimes need to copy lessons for my pupils and I provide my own ink. There's nothing wrong in that, is there?' It was taking all her self-control to keep answering their questions, while all the time she was listening for Max returning. She prayed he wouldn't come, though there was no one she needed more at that moment.

Having turned the apartment upside down, they turned their attention to the rubbish bin. And here they found a page of *France Vivra* she had used to wrap some fish bones she had boiled up to make soup. It had not been a good copy, the ink had smudged and it had been rejected. 'What's this?' the senior of the two demanded, holding it up between finger and thumb.

'It looks like a sheet of newspaper.'

'An illegal one. What were you doing with it?'

'Someone put it in my shopping basket when I wasn't looking. I don't know who.' She pretended to laugh. 'You can see what I think of it, only fit to wrap fish bones.'

He folded it inside a clean piece of paper and added it to the items they were taking away, then they picked them up and escorted her back to the car.

They didn't take her back to rue des Saussaies, but to the Prison du Cherche-Midi, where she was locked in a tiny cell. It had a bed with planks instead of springs topped with a straw mattress and a filthy blanket, a small table on which stood a cracked enamel bowl and beside it water in a chipped jug. In the corner was a slop bucket with an ill-fitting lid. Daylight penetrated through a fanlight high up on one wall and there was a naked electric light bulb dangling from the middle of the ceiling. The walls had been whitewashed, but they were filthy.

'May I have pen and paper to write to my principal to tell him why I am not in school?' she asked the Frenchwoman who had taken over from her escorts and was obviously in charge of the female prisoners.

'Not necessary. He will hear soon enough.' And with that she left, banging the door shut and turning the key in the lock.

As soon as she heard the footsteps of her gaoler receding, Justine collapsed onto the bed, every jangling nerve and sinew suddenly released of tension. The almost inevitable had happened and she had been arrested. Everyone had been told what to expect if one of their number was picked up. As soon as the news was passed round, all evidence of involvement with the Resistance would magically disappear and people like Max, his wireless operator and courier would scuttle under cover into safe houses and everyone else in the circuit would go about their normal business. She hoped they managed to do that. But the reality was hard to come to terms with, especially now, when she and Max had only just discovered their love for each other. She had to keep him safe, safe from the attentions of the Gestapo, safe to carry on with the work they were doing, safe to be reunited with her at some time in the future. She prayed for it, prayed, too, that he would do nothing impetuous to try and free her and put himself and the whole circuit in danger. She was on her own and had only her own inner resources to call on, because this was not the end, far from it. She would be in for more interrogation and she had to hold out as long as possible to give everyone else a chance to escape.

Max had left the apartment building just in time to see Justine being hustled towards the police van by a French gendarme and a German sergeant. He hesitated only a second while he debated whether to run after them and protest her innocence, but then his meticulous training came to the fore and he had turned and gone back into the apartment. He had removed all trace of his own presence, the used cups and wine glasses, the ashtray with its cigarette stubs. He went through Justine's clothes and papers to make sure there was nothing suspicious to be found and took the scruffy black coat and hat she sometimes used for a disguise, and put them with all his own clothes into a kitbag, topped it with his colour charts and, throwing it over his shoulder, once again left the building. He was stopped once, but his forged papers and colour charts stood up to the test and he was allowed to go.

He had worked methodically, trying to keep a cool head, trying not to think of what Justine might be going through, but as he walked down the street, he felt as though he were abandoning her to her fate, a terrible fate if her captors took it into their heads that she was part of a resistance movement. He could not leave her to suffer that. Was there any way he could effect her release? Even if it meant his own life was forfeit? Love and duty were certainly in conflict now and he was being torn apart.

He went to his rendezvous with Etienne at an apartment overlooking the Montparnasse cemetery where Etienne set up his radio and reported what had happened to London and asked for instructions. As soon as the transmission was acknowledged, he pulled in the aerial and packed everything into its suitcase. He had to move quickly before the detector vans fixed his position. 'Cheerio for now,' he said. 'I'll be at the Chateau Mollet, if you want me.' And with that he and his incriminating equipment were gone.

Max looked round checking everything was as it should be and left too. He had to alert Giles at the school.

'I know about it,' Giles said, when he found him tidying his office, picking up papers and books strewn about the floor. 'A Vichy policeman and a German sergeant were here half an hour ago. You only just missed them.'

'Did they find anything?'

'They were very interested in the Roneo machine and wanted to know what it was used for. Luckily there was nothing to connect it with *France Vivra* and they seemed to accept that it was only used for schoolwork, but they warned me I needed a permit to own one and took it away until such time as I was provided with one.'

'And Justine?'

'They asked a lot of questions about her and I gathered from that she had been arrested.' He grinned. 'I said: "So that's why she didn't turn up for work today." Then I grumbled about being left short-handed and having to teach her class myself. They asked if I knew she carried a pistol in her handbag and I denied all knowledge of the contents of her bag.'

'Will they let her go?'

'I doubt it. They'll have her for the gun if nothing else. But if that is all they can find, the circuit should be safe.'

'I wish I'd never given her that damned pistol. It's all my fault. I dragged her into this . . .'

'She was already in it, before you came,' Giles said. 'She spent hours typing out BBC news and de Gaulle's speeches, helping with the duplication and distribution, beside taking escapees down to Dransville. It was her choice.'

'Dransville,' Max said suddenly. 'Do you think they will hear what's happened?'

Giles shrugged. 'No reason why they should. The only person who could possibly tell them is Roger and he wasn't here.'

'He knew I'd given Justine the gun, though. If he—'

'Hold on, my friend, let's just wait and see, shall we? We'll lie low for a bit until we know.'

'If they force her to talk . . .' Max stopped with a shudder; that didn't bear thinking about. How strong would Justine be in the face of torture? 'I've alerted London and asked for instructions. Maybe we could find some way of getting her out.'

'Antoine, she knew what she was risking, we all do. I know how you feel about her—'

'You do?' he asked in surprise.

Giles laughed. 'All but a blind man could see it. But you mustn't let it come between you and your duty. We keep our heads down and do nothing. While she's in Cherche-Midi, we can't attempt an escape without risking goodness knows how many lives. We'll have to wait until she's moved.' He paused. 'Where are you going to stay? You can't go back to Justine's apartment; I don't doubt there'll be a watch on it. If nothing untoward happens and she's sent down for the pistol and nothing else, she might serve a short sentence and be with us again sooner than you think.'

'I pray you are right. I'll join Etienne at the Chateau Mollet, then I'll be on hand when we hear from London.'

Chapter Twelve

The cell had no heating, and in spite of having an overcoat and scarf, Justine was so cold her fingers and toes were numb. She wrapped herself in the coat and the smelly blanket, but dare not shut her eyes in case she talked in her sleep. Sleep was difficult in any case because every hour during the night, the light, which had been turned off at six, was switched on again and the guard peered at her through the spyhole in the door. Nevertheless she must have dozed because she woke so stiff and cramped it was some time before she could get her limbs to work. She stood up and began running on the spot, banging her arms against her sides to warm herself. She could hear the sound of heavy boots and doors being opened along the corridor.

When they came to her she was breathless, but a little

warmer. The woman warder pointed to the slop bucket. 'Bring that.'

She was led to a drain where she was invited to empty the bucket, then taken back to her cell. 'I have no toiletries,' she said. 'How am I to wash?'

'Send home for things.' The woman laughed. 'Oh, I forgot, you are not allowed privileges.' And with that she left, locking the door behind her.

Justine broke the ice on her water jug, washed and dried herself on the rag that hung on a nail beside the basin; it made her feel fresher if not cleaner. Then it was back to jumping up and down to keep warm while she recited all the poetry she could remember. Tiring of that, she pulled the table under the fanlight, climbed on it and found herself looking out onto the street. There were people out there coming and going. Could she get a message out? But she had nothing with which to write and nothing to write it on. She tried shouting, but was ignored. No one wanted to know or help a prisoner for fear of being tainted.

She heard the heavy footsteps again and scrambled down so that she was facing the door when it was opened. She was handed an enamel plate containing a crust of bread. She ate it voraciously, washing it down with water from the jug.

Her head was full of questions she would have liked to ask: Did anyone know where she was? What was going to happen to her? How long was she going to be kept prisoner? When was her trial? Would she be allowed a defence lawyer? Could she have a book to read, pencil and paper? She would not give her gaolers the satisfaction of knowing they had worried and frightened her, so she kept silent.

At midday she was given a small cup of soup and half a small loaf of brown bread, and in the middle of the afternoon was taken to the rue des Saussaies again and confronted with the same Gestapo major who had questioned her before. There was a typewriter on his desk which she immediately recognised as her own. It took a monumental effort not to appear agitated by this.

The major stared at her long and hard before speaking. 'Is this machine yours?'

She hesitated. 'I don't know, I can't tell. There must be hundreds like it.'

'But not hundreds with a faulty letter E.' He stood up, came round the desk and poked his finger hard into her breast which made her gasp. 'It was used to type these lies.' He turned and picked up a copy of *France Vivra* and waved it under her nose. 'Do you deny it?'

'What is it?' She pretended to be curious.

'You know well what it is. Subversive literature, lies to undermine the morale of the population, to cause dissent and unrest.'

'It has nothing to do with me.'

The blow he dealt to her face rocked her head on her shoulders. Her arms were pinioned to her sides by her escorts and she could not lift a hand to touch her face, nor ward off the next blow. 'We know exactly what you

284

have been up to. We have your accomplices and they are prepared to talk.'

'Then you had better ask them how they came to borrow my typewriter,' she retorted, wondering if what he said was true. Had others been arrested? 'I am a schoolteacher, nothing more. All I want is to be allowed to get on with my job in peace.'

'You have had many visitors to your apartment, they come and go at all times of day and night.'

She wondered who had told him that and immediately thought of the concierge. She was old and they would have frightened her. 'Then perhaps one of those borrowed my typewriter.'

'Men visitors. I hardly think they came to learn to type.'

'So? Is there a law against that now?'

He snorted with laughter. 'Against the oldest profession in the world? No, I do not think so, but why do you not extend your favours to German soldiers? I am sure they would be very generous.'

'There are enough ladies of the night catering for their needs without me adding to them. I am fussy whom I entertain.'

It was unwise of her to say that and it earned her several more blows. He picked up another piece of paper and placed it on the desk nearest to her, then he dipped a pen into an inkwell and offered it to her. 'Sign this.'

'What is it?'

'A statement.'

She glanced down at it and realised it was more

285

confession than statement. 'Certainly not. It is in German. I will sign nothing I cannot understand.'

He shouted for a clerk and gave instructions for the document to be translated and then waved a hand in dismissal. 'Take her away. Let her reflect on her situation for a few more days.'

With her head reeling and her face stinging, she was taken back to Cherche-Midi and locked once more in her cell where she did, indeed, reflect on her situation. Now she was in more trouble than the possession of a pistol. What was going on outside? What was Max doing? And Giles and all the others? Had they gone to ground? Did they know where she was? Had the Germans discovered who had blown up the railway line? Had there been reprisals? Were her friends safe? Were they all going about their business as if nothing had happened? And her family? Thank God they were in the *Zone Libre*. But not Max. Max was out there somewhere, probably worrying himself sick about what had happened to her, perhaps in danger himself. How long before her captors put two and two together and realised she was implicated in blowing up the ammunition train? How long before everyone in the circuit was rounded up?

She stopped herself dwelling on the dreadful things that might happen and concentrated on recalling happier times. Spoilt by her parents and older brother and sister, her childhood in the mountains of Haute Savoie had been idyllic. The Great War, with its millions of casualties, had hardly touched the child she was. She remembered the little lamb she had hand fed when its mother rejected it and how dejected she had been when it was taken away from her; and being carried on the shoulders of her father when the whole family had attended the agricultural fair in Annecy. And there was Pierre's wedding to Jeanne and being a bridesmaid at Annelise's wedding. What a day for celebration that had been! Only nine years old, she had not understood the cloud that had hung over her sister, but which disappeared on the day she was married. Everyone liked Charles, though Jacques was wary of him and hid behind his mother's skirts whenever his new stepfather approached. Charles had simply laughed it off.

She hadn't realised at the time how important Charles was, not until she was old enough to accept his invitation to visit them in England in 1931 as a twenty-first birthday treat. He was a baron, something like a French count, and her sister was Lady de Lacey and they lived in a mansion of enormous proportions with dozens of servants. Jacques had become Jack and a proper little English boy. And there were three more children: Elizabeth, Amy and four-year-old Edmund, all adored by both parents. She was taken to see all the sights: the Tower of London, the Houses of Parliament and Buckingham Palace and they caught a glimpse of King George and Queen Mary as they left in a carriage. They went to Norwich and Cambridge where they punted on the river, and to Wells on the north Norfolk coast, where they gathered cockles which Mrs Baxter boiled up for tea to be eaten with brown bread and butter. She had returned home to Dransville full of happy memories.

Annelise had not been spoilt by her elevated status; she was still the same loving sister she had always been and had often brought her children to Dransville for holidays before the war, where they were allowed to run wild about the meadows and hills. They had all, except Edmund who hadn't been born until 1927, attended the Winter Olympics at Chamonix in 1924 and she had boasted she could ski as well as any of the contestants. There would be no more holidays like that until the war was won. How long would that be? She could see no end to it. Whenever her present situation threatened to intrude, she forced herself back onto a happier plane, but in the end even that did not work, and she was thrown into despair. Her relationship with Max could spoil other people's happiness; people, like Lisabette, who did not deserve to be made miserable, but how could she let him go? But then, she might have no choice; she would be shot and that would be the end of it. But she would have the memory to take with her to the grave.

She deliberately put her mind to recalling every detail of that long, lazy morning of lovemaking: his hands exploring her body, his lips caressing her, his murmured words of love and her own uninhibited response. They had forgotten all about the war, forgotten they had just blown up a train and taken soldiers' lives, enemy lives it was true, but lives just the same, forgotten everything in the joy of finding each other. They had even forgotten about Lisabette. Would she find out about her and Max through someone else? If only she could get out of this place . . .

Her last meal of the day, another cup of thin soup and some dry bread, came at four o'clock and then at six the light went out and she was left to endure a second night of misery. She had never felt so cold and so hungry. If she had not had her overcoat, she would surely have frozen to death. Perhaps that would be the easier death. Why was she thinking of death? That was defeatist and she wasn't beaten yet.

Charles, in the MI6 communications room, was one of the first to hear of Justine's arrest and the scattering of the circuit. It was news he had been dreading. He knew about the sabotage on the railway and coming so soon afterwards he could only assume it was not unconnected. What had happened? The radio message had necessarily been brief and left him wanting to know more. What had she been charged with? Would she be able to hold out against prolonged interrogation? What was Max doing? Was Lizzie implicated? After all, she had been taking men over the Swiss border to freedom. How many people knew about that? Oh, how he wished he had gone over to France as soon as war was declared and fetched her home. And what was he to say to Annelise? Should he tell her? She would want to know how he knew.

'There isn't anything we can do,' Buckmaster told him when the message was relayed to him. 'Until we learn more details, we'll carry on as usual.'

'I'm also worried about my daughter and my wife's parents.'

'They're not in Paris, are they?'

'Not to my knowledge. But if Justine is made to talk—'
He stopped unable to put his fear into words.

'We'll know more when Etienne comes on air again this evening. Try not to worry.'

Try not to worry! How could he not worry?

He did not go off duty that evening, preferring to stay to hear the transmission, due at seven o'clock. Everyone was there: Major Buckmaster, Miss Atkins and several others, standing about waiting and hoping. They waited half an hour past the scheduled time, but nothing happened. Etienne was silent. 'It doesn't mean anything,' Buckmaster said. 'He might have been delayed or had trouble with the wireless.' The major was an optimist and disinclined to believe anything had gone wrong unless faced with irrefutable evidence. 'We'll see if he comes up in the morning.'

They dispersed and Charles went back to his London flat where he lived while working in London. He rang Annelise as he did every evening, but said nothing of Justine's arrest. He kept the conversation light, asked about what was happening at home and was Edmund behaving himself.

'As far as I know,' she said. 'He's at school.'

'I forgot. Stupid of me.'

'Are you all right? You sound distracted.'

'Do I? I'm fine, darling, but missing you. I'll try and come home for a few days soon. Have you heard from Amy? How is she?'

'Swotting for exams.'

'And Jack?'

'I haven't seen him since the New Year, but he writes. He's on a course, learning to fly a different aeroplane. He's not very communicative.'

'Head full of Belinda, I shouldn't wonder.'

'Perhaps. Young Bernard is behaving very oddly, creeping about with a notebook and pencil and looking guilty.'

'Have you asked him about it?'

'No, I don't like to pry, it's probably some silly game he's playing. He doesn't seem to mix with the other children.'

'Well, if you are really worried, try and get a look at the notebook. I'll speak to him when I come home, if you like. The others are OK, are they?'

'Yes, no bother at all. Cecily is a poppet and Raymond and Martin have joined the Boy Scouts; they are having great fun learning the Morse code and communicating in dots and dashes. I shall miss them when they go home.'

He smiled to himself as he rang off. His wife loved children, all children, it didn't matter about their background. She would be worried sick if she knew what had happened to her little sister. Grown up or not, Justine would always be her little sister. He spent a sleepless night wondering if she ought to be told. If she found out later that he had known about it and said nothing, she would be more than a little miffed.

* * *

Bernard, who rarely let his notebook out of his presence, had left it on his bedside table. It was too good an opportunity to miss and Annelise, who had gone into his room to put away his clean laundry, sat on the bed to skim through it. What she read opened her eyes in astonishment. Here were the detailed movements of almost everyone in the village, where they went, whom they saw, even what they talked about. He seemed particularly interested in Albert Storey, and the transcription of the conversation between Frank Lambert and Mrs Storey was engrossing. Surely he had made it up? But why? She smiled to herself, catching sight of copies of *The Adventures of Sherlock Holmes* and *The Thirty-nine Steps* on his table. He had been reading too many detective stories, that was it. But she ought to warn him against intrusion. She could not imagine Albert Storey or Frank Lambert taking kindly to being followed.

She looked up as he burst into the room. He stopped when he saw her and what she had in her hand. She smiled. 'I should not have looked at this,' she said, holding it out to him. 'It was unforgivable.'

'S'alright,' he said, taking it from her.

'It made me wonder why you were doing it,' she went on. 'It is not very nice following people about and listening to their private conversations.'

'I like solving mysteries.'

'Perhaps, but that doesn't mean you should spy on people.'

'Not even if they break the law?'

'No one is breaking the law,' she said.

'Mrs Storey said Mr Storey was a bigamist. That's breaking the law, isn't it?'

'Yes, but they were only guessing.'

'And Mrs Storey did threaten to do away with her husband.'

'I am sure she didn't mean it. Ordinary people don't just do away with people, Bernard, that's the stuff of fiction. You are not to go on with this. If any of these people were to hear about it, we should both be in trouble.' She paused, watching his face; his expression gave nothing away. He was learning from his hero, the inscrutable Sherlock Holmes. 'Have I your word?'

'OK,' he said reluctantly. 'Can I go now?'

'Yes, off you go.'

He disappeared, taking the notebook with him, leaving her still sitting on his bed in contemplation. Would he keep his word? Perhaps she ought to have confiscated his notes. They were certainly intriguing. Who would have thought Mrs Storey would be cheating on her husband so soon after marrying him?

Charles came home a few days later. He looked tired; the war was taking the life out of everyone. He need not have become so involved; he was past conscription age and could have stayed at home doing exercises with the Home Guard and no one would have thought the worse of him, but no, he must do his bit. Worrying him over some silly nonsense of Bernard's would be unkind. Perhaps she would leave it until he was more rested.

She discovered what was on his mind after they had eaten their evening meal and were sitting together on the sofa in the drawing room, curled up in each other's arms. They had always been close, not afraid to show their love for each other, and often sat by the light of the fire in calm contentment. This evening she sensed the tension in him. 'Things not going well at work?' she queried, turning her face up to his.

'No.' He paused. 'Sweetheart, I've got some bad news . . .'

'Jack!' Her heart was in her mouth.

'No, not Jack. As far as I know he's fine. It's Justine.'

'Justine?' She squirmed round to face him. 'What about her?'

'She's been arrested.'

'Arrested, whatever for? And how do you know?'

He smiled. 'I do work in Intelligence, Annelise.'

'Oh, so the way you found out is a secret?'

'Yes, but I'm going to tell you as much as I dare, but you must say nothing to anyone. Promise me.'

'Of course I promise. In any case, I can guess. She's been working for the Resistance, hasn't she?'

'Yes.'

'What will they do to her?'

'I don't know. And we've lost our communication with the group so we don't know what's going on. I asked if I could be sent to find out, but they won't let me go . . .'

'I should think not! You mustn't even think of it.'

'We have been in touch with a neighbouring circuit to

see if they know anything, but so far they haven't come back to us with anything positive.'

'You will tell me if they do?'

'Yes, of course.'

'What about Lizzie and Maman and Papa?'

'They are not involved.'

'Thank God for that. Oh, this is all so worrying. Here we are safe and sound in Nayton and they are going through goodness knows what terrors. If only Lizzie had come home at the start of the war. Can these clever people in London not find a way of bringing her out?'

'Sweetheart, Lizzie and your parents are safe where they are. The powers that be have more urgent concerns at the moment. I am afraid we have to be patient and hope it will all turn out for the best. Justine is strong and clever, she will come through it, you'll see.'

'I pray you are right.'

They were silent for some time. He did not tell her how worried everyone in Baker Street was about the lack of communication. They could not be sure Etienne or Max or Anne had not already been arrested and the whole circuit blown. Hanging about waiting for something to happen was fraying everyone's nerves.

He put his arm about her and drew her back into his embrace. 'Now, tell me what you've been up to.'

'Nothing much, the usual Women's Institute stuff, entertaining the airmen on the base. There are Americans there now and they appreciate being invited into people's homes. Some of the village girls have been going out with them. I know this because it's all written down in Bernard's notebook.'

'So you managed a peek at it, did you?'

'Yes. It is extraordinary. I can't make up my mind whether to be angry with him or marvel at his dedication. It's well written too, no spelling mistakes that I could see and very graphic.'

'What's it in aid of?'

'He sees himself as another Sherlock Holmes, tracking down murderers and spies. There was an intriguing bit about Frank Lambert and the new Mrs Storey. It seems they are having an affair and he heard them discussing how Mr Storey got rid of his first wife and whether he was a bigamist.'

'Bernard's been reading too many detective novels.'

'That's what I thought.

'Anyway, he promised me he wouldn't do it anymore.'

'That's all right, then.'

'What is this war doing to everybody, Charles? No one behaves normally anymore.'

'These are not normal times, darling. I simply thank God you are the same as you've always been and home is the same.'

She laughed. 'Not quite. We've lost most of the servants, half the house is shut up and the flower beds are all growing vegetables. Jones has begun sowing seeds in the greenhouse, now we've seen the back of the winter. He grumbled because he couldn't get oil to heat it and everything would be late as a consequence.'

He was glad to change the subject, and the doings of the

inhabitants of Nayton occupied them until it was time to listen to the nine o'clock news.

1942 was not a good year for the Allies. There was heavy fighting in North Africa and in the Far East where Singapore fell to the Japanese and thousands of British soldiers were taken prisoner, including many from the Royal Norfolks; Malta had been under ceaseless aerial bombardment since the previous December and the King had awarded its people the George Cross for their bravery. In Russia Leningrad was under siege but holding out gamely. In April, air raids on British historic cities were resumed after a few weeks respite and Exeter, Bath, York and Norwich were targeted in retaliation, so they were told, for the RAF attacks on Rostock and Lübeck.

Lucy had just put Peter to bed and was making herself a little supper when the air-raid siren went. She turned off the gas and fetched the baby from his cot. She was not particularly afraid; there had been raids before and though there had been a lot of damage and some loss of life, they were nothing like as bad as those on London. Sometimes she did not even bother to go to the shelter, but sat in the cupboard under the stairs, which everyone had been told was the safest part of the house. She debated now whether to go there or to the shelter. Peter was still fast asleep and she knew the shelter would be noisy and airless and he would be unsettled and miserable. On the other hand, she could hear the drone of aircraft and there seemed to be an awful lot of them.

She picked up a small case containing what she deemed essential supplies: nappies, baby food and Peter's teddy bear because he wouldn't go to sleep without it, sandwiches for herself and a flask of tea, a book to read and some knitting. Peter was growing out of all his clothes and she had taken to pulling out jumpers of her own to knit new ones for him. Carrying Peter and the case she opened the front door. The bombers were overhead and even as she stood on the step she saw some of them releasing bombs. The explosions that followed shook the house and flung debris into the air. It was too close for comfort and she dare not risk running for the shelter. She went back inside and dived under the stairs, shutting the door behind her.

There, amid the clutter of vacuum cleaner, ironing board, spare coats and shoes, she sat on a low stool rocking Peter in her arms and crooning lullabies, in an effort to drown out the dreadful noise going on outside. The screaming sound the bombs made as they fell was terrifying in itself and that was followed by explosions which shook the house. She hugged Peter to her and flung herself over him every time there was a bigger than usual bang. It went on and on; she was sure all the windows had been blown out and all the pictures – her lovely portrait – must have come off the wall and been shattered.

She was trying to reach about in the dark for the torch to see what time it was by her wristwatch, when the biggest explosion yet was followed by the sound of walls collapsing. Dust flew in under the gap beneath the door, making it difficult to breathe; above her the stairs rocked and she cowered over Peter, afraid they would collapse on them. They held, but how long for she did not know. She tried to push the door open but it wouldn't budge. She was trapped in the ruins of her home and all she could do was pray.

The casualties had been coming into the hospital all night and Amy was so busy she did not have time to think about her own safety, though she was worried about Lucy. Every time the ambulance men brought in new patients, they brought horrendous stories of what was happening. Cushion's wood store, Bullen's paint shop, Morgan's Brewery and the Wincarnis factory were all on fire. The Mackintosh chocolate factory and shops like Curl's and Bond's had been hit. But the worst of it was that large parts of the old city centre with its Victorian terrace houses had been destroyed, among them a whole row along Waterloo Road. She searched every new intake, but there was no Lucy, no Peter, and she didn't know whether to be glad or more worried than ever.

'They're probably safe in a shelter somewhere,' one of the ambulance men soothed her when she told him of her fears.

All the same, she couldn't wait to go off duty and see for herself. Picking her way through the devastation after the all-clear, she found herself looking at the ruins of the row of houses which included Lucy's home. It was simply a heap of rubble with a chimney stack sticking out of it. The fires which had raged had been put out and rescuers were digging in the debris.

'Did they get out?' she asked one of them.

He paused with a lump of masonry in his hand and turned to her. 'Who?'

'Lucy and her baby.' She pointed. 'They lived in that one.'

'I haven't seen them. They may have gone to the shelter down the road or been taken to the reception centre at the school. Have you tried those?'

The air-raid shelter was empty now the all-clear had sounded, but the reception centre was crowded with people, mostly women, children and old men. Wrapped in blankets, some simply stared into space, numb with the shock and horror of it. Being handed mugs of hot tea they drank unthinkingly. Children dashed noisily up and down; they had been frightened, but now they were safe they were letting off steam. Lucy was not there. Amy returned to the wreckage of the house.

'I can't find her,' she said to the man she had first approached. 'She often used to shelter under the stairs.'

'Right.' He shouted to others who were digging. 'Give us a hand, will you? I think there might be someone under this lot.'

Amy watched as they began moving the rubble, brick by brick. Lumps of concrete and splintered wood and furniture were picked up carefully and thrown to one side. Every now and again they stopped to listen. They heard nothing.

'Keep going,' Amy begged. 'Please keep going, I'm sure she's there.'

They had been working for hours and were exhausted. Some left to be replaced by others. Amy, tired of watching and doing nothing, joined in. It was dawn when they heard the faint cry of a baby. 'Peter!' she shouted. 'Peter!'

They all found reserves of energy and renewed their digging, taking great care not to dislodge anything that might be protecting the child. Bit by bit, they excavated the ruins of the staircase until they had made a small hole through which they could see Lucy, sheltering her child in her arms. He was covered in dirt and whimpering heartbrokenly.

Everyone but the fire chief was sent away and he set about very slowly and very gently enlarging the hole. Amy gasped as a lump of wood shifted and a shower of dust enveloped the rescuer and those he was trying to rescue. Peter stopped crying and she feared the worst. When the dust settled, the careful excavation was resumed and the fireman reached downwards and the next minute brought Peter out. He handed him to Amy and went back to work.

The poor little chap was filthy and scratched and he certainly needed his nappy changing. She didn't care about that. She held him close and wrapped her nurse's cloak round him. 'You're safe now, sweetheart, you're safe.'

'Stretcher!' the fireman yelled.

Two ambulance men ran up with one and Lucy was placed on it, just as the last of the staircase gave way and the chimney came toppling down, making everyone run for their lives. Amy dashed over to where the stretcher was being loaded into the ambulance. 'Is she alive?'

'Yes. We'll get her to hospital. Better bring the baby and come too.'

Lucy regained consciousness in the ambulance. 'Amy, is that you?' she murmured.

'Yes, yes, it's me. I've got Peter safe and sound.'

'Look after him for me.'

'Of course I will.'

'If anything happens to me, you'll have him, won't you?'

'Of course, but nothing is going to happen to you. You've been badly shaken up and you look a mess, but that can soon be cured.' She looked at the ambulance man for confirmation. He smiled but said nothing.

'My chest hurts and I've got a headache.'

'Are you surprised considering you had the weight of a whole house on you?'

'The house is gone?'

'Afraid so. But houses don't matter, do they? They can be rebuilt. The important thing is that you are alive and Peter is alive and none the worse.'

'Jack . . .'

'I'll let Jack know. In the meantime, you concentrate on getting better.'

But Jack was nowhere to be found. 'Off on a course,' she was told when she tried to contact him at his base. She rang home.

'Mama, I've got a favour to ask,' she told her mother. 'I've a friend here who's been bombed out. She hasn't anywhere to go. Can you put her up?'

'Of course. Do I know her?'

'Yes, it's Lucy Storey.'

'Lucy! Doesn't she want to go home to her father?'

'No, she doesn't. And he wouldn't have her anyway. She's got a baby, a little boy.'

'Oh, I'd forgottten that. 'What about the child's father?'

'In the forces. I can't contact him. You're not going to say no because of the child, are you?'

'Heavens, no. But what do you think Mr Storey will say?'

'I don't imagine he'll care.'

'When shall I expect her?'

'I'll bring her at the end of the week, when she is discharged from hospital. She's under observation because of a bruised chest, but the hospital is so full, they will be glad to hand her over to someone else. All she needs is rest and quiet.'

'Tell her to come. Tell her she will be very welcome. Mr Storey will see her arrive at the station. I'll have Bennett drive over and pick you up. I think there's enough petrol in the Rolls. Her father needn't know she's here, not to begin with, anyway.'

'Mama, you're an angel. Tell Mr Bennett to come to the hospital on Saturday midday.'

* * *

The arrival of Lucy and Peter caused a stir among the remaining servants who were agog with curiosity, as was Bernard, who found himself staring at the baby, trying to see some likeness to Mr Lambert, but there was none. Frank Lambert's hair was dark as night and his eyes were almost black. The baby was round-faced and fair with blue eyes, more like Jack than anyone, which only confirmed what he had told Edmund, but he kept that theory very much to himself. He wondered what Mr Storey would say when he realised where his daughter was. He certainly would not tell him and nor would anyone else, he realised, when Lady de Lacey, fussing over the new arrivals, warned them not to.

Jack stood looking at the heap of rubble which had once been Lucy's home and was suddenly overwhelmed by a feeling of loss. Fighting back tears, he stood looking at the remains of what had once been a haven of tranquillity and saw only the loving face of Lucy and the cherubic face of Peter etched on the rubble. He suddenly realised, without a shadow of doubt, that there was no one and nothing he cared about more than Lucy and his son. They were everything to him, more than Belinda, more than ambition, more than his life. She had to have survived so he could tell her so, she simply had to.

He had returned to base after his successful conversion to Lysanders, looking forward to a spot of leave and after that his new role in the Special Operations Squadron. He had heard about the so-called Baedeker raids while he was up in the Lake District, but not until he arrived in Norwich did he realise how severe the raid on the city had been. And to come face-to-face with this, so suddenly, had hit him like a blow to the stomach. Why had no one warned him? Surely Amy could have picked up the phone? Was she one of the casualties herself? Then he remembered she had no way of contacting him; no one at the base would have told her over the phone where he was and what he was doing. He turned on his heel and went to the nearest warden's post.

'Mrs Storey?' the warden queried. 'Yes, they got her out.'

'Alive?'

'I think so.'

'Think so? You're not sure?'

'Well, there were a lot of casualties, Flight Lieutenant, some so badly injured they probably didn't survive.'

'And the little boy?'

'He was OK. Went off in the ambulance with his mother and the other young lady.'

'Other young lady?'

'Yes. A nurse who was passing by.'

Amy! It had to be. He thanked the man and went to the hospital. His sister was on duty and he had to wait over half an hour before she managed to snatch a few minutes to talk to him.

'Lucy's OK,' she said. 'So's Peter. They escaped with no more than cuts and bruises. They are at home.'

'How can they be? The house has been destroyed. I've seen it. No one could be living there.'

She smiled, understanding how distraught he was; the silly man had finally realised what a treasure he had in Lucy. 'I meant home at Nayton Manor. She had nowhere else to go. I took her there. She and Peter are being cosseted and spoilt by Mama.'

'Does Mama know . . . ?'

'Who Peter is? I didn't tell her. How long before she puts two and two together is anybody's guess.'

'How could you do that, Amy? You knew how I felt.'

'Yes, I did. The trouble is you didn't know yourself. And I couldn't let them be put in a hostel, could I? Not when they're family. I suggest you go home and set things right.'

'My God, Amy, you can be a real bully when you choose, can't you?'

She laughed. 'It makes a change. You used to bully me dreadfully when we were children.'

'I'll be off then.' He turned to leave and then stopped suddenly. 'Does Storey know where his daughter is?'

'He didn't when I was there, but you know the village, everyone knows everyone else's business. I doubt it can be kept secret for long.'

He grinned and kissed her cheek. 'See you.' And then he was gone, leaving Amy to smile in satisfaction. Her brother was not the indifferent man he would have everyone believe.

Annelise realised exactly how matters stood between her son and Lucy Storey when the girl ran into his arms as soon as he came through the door and Jack kissed her. It made Annelise look at Peter, who was in her arms and squirming to be put down. She set him on his feet and he toddled over to his parents and grabbed them both round the legs. Jack bent and picked him up and kissed him too.

Only then did he turn to his mother. 'Hallo, Maman. I see you have met this little fellow.'

'Yes. I think you have a bit of explaining to do.'

'I'm sorry, Lady de Lacey,' Lucy said. 'I wanted to tell you, but I didn't know what Jack would say about it.'

'Come into the morning room, both of you, we won't be disturbed there. Then you can tell me all about it.'

Chapter Thirteen

The search for the so-called terrorists continued unabated. Already two dozen innocent Frenchmen had been executed. The *resistants* had known it might happen, but in the face of reality, Max began to wonder if the destruction of a freight train and a few tons of guns and ammunition was worth the lost lives. The railway line had been repaired and trains were running along it again, bringing supplies to the occupying troops and sending Frenchmen to work in German factories and whole families of Jews to goodness knew where. Giles told him that it was, that every defiant act proved the country was not subdued, that it still kept its fighting spirit and would never be beaten. But it didn't help Max to come to terms with the arrest of Justine, that brave, wonderful girl, whom he had come to love. He wished he could visit her, to let her know she was not forgotten, but Giles advised very forcefully against even trying.

'I've tried to see her more than once and been turned away,' he said. They had met at the safe house they used in the suburbs. It was a small basement apartment, scantily furnished, but it did have a back yard from which it was possible to escape by clambering over a wall into a neighbouring garden. 'For you to go would be foolhardy. How can we be sure Justine hasn't given her captors your real name? Having you in prison isn't going to help Justine and it would endanger the whole circuit. You ought to be putting your mind to our next operation. It's the surest way to hasten the end of the war and have all the prisoners freed.'

'I know, I know.'

'Just to please you, I'll try again to see her. As her principal, they might allow me to talk to her about school matters. I'll say I need to know if she will be rejoining the staff again after the summer vacation.'

Max was obliged to concede he was right. He gave a wry grin. 'If you do see her, give her my love.'

Giles left first and a few minutes later Max followed and made his way to his rendezvous with Etienne and their scheduled contact with London. They were going to meet in an apartment over an abandoned shop, its owner having joined the exodus to the south at the beginning of the occupation. He hung about, pacing the room, keeping away from the cobweb-festooned window in case he was spotted, but Etienne failed to turn up. He was still there at curfew time and deemed it wise to stay where he was until the morning.

He dare not sleep and that gave him plenty of time to think. His thoughts went from thinking up ways of liberating Justine, each of which he discarded as impractical, to worrying about Etienne and wondering if he had been arrested. If Etienne had been picked up with his wireless set on him, there would be no way out for him. He would be shot, but not before he had been tortured. How strong would he be? How strong would any of them be? How much had been wrung out of Justine? Was Anne safe? He hadn't seen anything of her since the night of the attack on the railway line when she had been acting as a messenger. Her instructions were the same as for everyone else: when someone was arrested, go to ground.

And then there was Lizzie, whom he had once loved, or thought he had. He knew now he had been wrong. When all this was over, if they survived, he was going to have to tell her the truth. How would she take it? It seemed an age since he had spent his leave at Dransville and so much had happened that was bound to change people. As far as he knew she was still taking escapees over the border. Was she safe? Was Roger with her? How far could he be trusted? He had meant to ask Etienne to request more information about him, but without Etienne he had no way of communicating. The first thing he must do when daylight came and the curfew was lifted was to try and find out what had happened to his wireless operator.

The night wore on. The city, which in peacetime had

been awake twenty-four hours a day, was silent, its streets empty except for patrolling German troops and Vichy police. Now and again the silence was disturbed by the sound of a German truck and he held his breath, waiting for its engine to stop and to hear heavy boots climbing the stairs, and when it passed by he let out a sigh of relief. Not this time.

He must have dozed, because he dreamt. He dreamt of Justine. They were in Scotland, walking in the hills hand in hand. It was summer and she was wearing a cotton dress printed with small flowers. Her hair was loose on her shoulders. Every now and again the wind lifted it and let it fall again. She was laughing; there was nothing of the half-starved Justine fighting her own war in Paris. He woke to find it was day and he was smiling.

He heard a sound in the shop downstairs. Someone was creeping about down there. It must have been what had woken him. He went to the head of the stairs to listen. A door opened and a woman came into the hall at the bottom of the stairs and looked upwards. It was Anne.

'Thank goodness,' she said. 'I thought you might have gone.'

He leant over the banister 'Anyone with you?'

'No.' She joined him on the landing. 'Etienne's been arrested.'

'I was afraid of that. What happened?'

'That last transmission was a long one. The detector vans were only just round the corner. They caught him as he was packing up.'

'You were there?'

'Yes, waiting for instructions, but Etienne pushed me out of the window onto the roof of an outbuilding when we heard them on the stairs. I climbed down a drainpipe and ran off into the alley. I waited to see if Etienne followed me but when I saw them bundle him into a police van, I made myself scarce. I feel bad about leaving him.'

'It was the right thing to do, you know that. Etienne knows it too.'

'What are we going to do now?'

'I'll have to find some way of contacting London. We've got to get them out.'

'Them?'

'Justine too. They'll hold out for a bit but we can't rely on it for long. I'm going to the school. Giles was going to see if he could see Justine on school business, but if not, at least find out how she is. He'll have to be told about Etienne. It makes everything so much more difficult. Until we know what's happening, we must lie low. Where are you staying?'

'With the count. I'm his new secretary. He's got me papers and a new cover story.'

'Good. You'd better go back there. I'll let you know what our orders are.'

He watched her go down the stairs and through the shop to the back entrance, and a minute or two later, he saw her emerge on the street from the alley and walk away. As soon as he saw her blend in with the crowds going to work, he himself left.

* * *

Justine stood in the familiar office at rue des Saussaies facing the Gestapo major who had been her constant interrogator. Two months she had been incarcerated, two months in which she had become skeletal and try as she might she could not keep clean, nor free of vermin. Her hair, for want of a shampoo or even a brush and comb, was a tangled mass of curls whose colour appeared to be a dirty grey. Her clothes were shabby and smelly. There was nothing left of the chic Parisienne she had once been.

She knew the routine by now. She would be asked the same questions over and over again to which she would give the same answers. Even the blows she received would come as no surprise. She wondered whether they would ever set a date for her trial but concluded they did not have enough evidence. That gave her hope that the others were safe. It also bolstered her courage.

She wondered why the door of the office had been left open; she could see everyone who came and went along the corridor. 'I've told you until I'm sick of telling you,' she said, pretending not to look at the open door. 'I know nothing about any illegal newspaper. I am a teacher, nothing more.' It was like a mantra she repeated over and over again. 'It's in the statement I signed.' The statement had been translated and altered at her insistence but in the end it approximated to her story and she had put her name to it.

'Let's leave the matter of the newspaper on one side,' he said. 'I want to know about the Resistance.'

'I know nothing about that either.'

'I am sure you are lying.'

'I am telling the truth. If you have evidence to the contrary, then produce it and put me on trial, otherwise let me go. I want to get back to work.'

'Teaching English, in the forlorn hope that it will come in useful.'

'No, I am not allowed to teach English anymore. My lessons are in Italian. And French, of course.'

She heard footsteps outside and, through the open door, caught a glimpse of Etienne being roughly escorted by two German soldiers. He had obviously been savagely beaten and looked dreadful. His face was a mass of bruises and he walked with a limp. For one second their eyes met and held, but it was enough to warn her not to react.

The major left his desk to kick the door shut, but she was sure she was meant to see their prisoner. 'We have been lenient with you so far,' he said, returning to his desk. 'But that cannot go on in the face of your continued refusal to cooperate.' He waved to her escorts to take her away. 'Let's see if a few nights in a punishment cell will change your mind.'

The punishment cell, she discovered when she was pushed into it and the door locked, was even smaller and dirtier than the one she had been occupying, no bigger than a cupboard and it had no window. Now even the thin soup was denied her and there was no bed. She spent the night huddled on the floor, unable to sleep. Her head was full of questions. How had Etienne been taken? Did it mean the whole circuit had been blown? What about Max and Giles and the others? Had they been rounded up? If they had, then there was no hope for any of them. She had never felt so low.

Unable to see daylight, she lost track of time; it seemed an age before she was let out and taken back to rue des Saussaies. She braced herself for the usual blows when she refused to answer the questions put to her, but the major was in a jovial mood. She wondered why. Was this some new ploy to get her to talk? 'Well, Ma'amselle Clavier, I have some good news for you,' he said.

Unwilling to show the least curiosity, she stood and waited, though she was so weak from hunger, her legs were hardly able to support her.

'We have set a date for your trial,' he said. 'That is good news, don't you think?'

'Yes.'

He smiled and lit a cigarette, blowing the smoke towards her. 'You will be transferred to Fresnes for the hearing.'

Fresnes was a huge prison on the outskirts of Paris and known for its harsh conditions, worse, so she had been told, than Cherche-Midi. 'Will I be allowed a defence lawyer?'

'Of course. One will be appointed, but I should not set your hopes too high, we have all the evidence we need to convict you.' He paused. 'Not only you, but everyone involved in Oberon.'

It was a huge effort of will to appear indifferent. 'Oberon? Isn't that a character in one of Shakespeare's plays?'

'I believe it is, but it is also the name of a group of

315

terrorists. They are being rounded up even as we speak. But you know that, don't you?'

'No.'

'You are one of them. There is no point in denying it, we have irrefutable proof.'

Her thoughts flew immediately to Etienne; did that mean he had talked? Or was there a traitor in their midst? What had happened to Max and Giles and Jeanne and all the others? It was all she could do to maintain an expression of indifference, when her head was seething like a cauldron on the boil. 'I shall be interested to hear this so-called proof,' she said, steeling herself to sound unconcerned. 'When is the trial to be?'

'Soon. When we have everyone safely behind bars.' He signalled to her escort. 'Take her back to her cell and give her some food and wine. She may also have a pencil and postcards to write to her family and friends.'

She wolfed down the food brought to her when she was back in her old cell, and drank the wine which was a rough red, but was welcome all the same. She still felt hungry. As for the pencil and postcards, she sat looking at them, wondering if she dare use them. It would be unwise to contact anyone in the circuit, but they must know by now where she was. Maman would be worrying that she had not been in touch, but writing to her might endanger Lizzie and Roger, always supposing Roger had not been the one to betray them. She addressed a card to Giles and then, biting the end of the pencil, mused on what to say. There was only room for a couple of sentences. 'I am well and enjoying my little holiday, but I shall be glad to get back to work,' she wrote. 'Give my regards to my pupils and colleagues.' It said nothing at all, except that she was alive and still sticking to her story.

'They wouldn't let me see her,' Giles told Max. 'But they gave me this.' They were talking in his office at the school. It was after hours and there was no one else in the building. If the police came, they would have to be let in by Giles who would take his time walking along the corridors to the front door and that would allow Max time to escape through a door leading onto a backstreet. There were exercise books and papers on the desk which Giles would be in the middle of marking.

'Enjoying my little holiday,' Max read aloud from the card Giles had given him. 'What does that tell us?'

'Not a lot, but what did you expect? At least she still has her wits about her and fingers to hold a pencil.'

'Don't! It doesn't bear thinking about. Did you learn anything about Etienne?'

'No, but I did learn that Justine is to be put on trial at Fresnes and I could appoint a defence lawyer for her. He'd have to be approved by the Boche, of course.'

'Get the best you can. I've got money for contingencies. In the meanwhile we must think up ways of setting her free. Etienne too. In transit from one prison to another would be best. Did they tell you when that was to be?'

'No, but the lawyer will be told.' He paused. 'Have you managed to contact London?'

'No. I assume that they will know something has happened when they don't hear from Etienne.' He had thought of going to Prosper's circuit and asking them to send a message but had decided to leave them out of it. He could not be sure that circuit had not also been infiltrated. There were traitors everywhere. 'We are on our own over this.'

'Where shall we meet?'

'In Count Mollet's cellar. It's the only safe place left, but for how much longer is anyone's guess. Bring me news when you know it.'

'Right, but you take care.'

'And you.' They shook hands and Max let himself out of the back door which Giles locked behind him, then went back to his desk, wondering how long it would be before he was arrested. He had given Jeanne, who was the youngest and possibly the weakest of the group, sick leave and told her to take herself off to the unoccupied zone. All the others had been told to resume their ordinary lives and not attempt to communicate with each other, but if there were a traitor in their midst . . . He shuddered at the thought.

The slopes of the mountain were green again. The skiers had gone and the village was peaceful, or as peaceful as it was possible to be under the circumstances. Under the outward calm, the area was seething with clandestine activity. In the forest of the higher slopes, a secret army was being trained, an army led by Roger, whom everyone knew as Dirk. He was annoyed that London seemed to be ignoring his frequent requests for arms and ammunition and a wireless operator, requests he sent over the border into Switzerland by escapees who had found their way to Annecy and were sent on to Lizzie. They had no way of knowing if the messages ever arrived. 'How could they be so inefficient? Or perhaps they don't trust me.'

They were talking in the byre where they were scrubbing out the pails after finishing the milking. The cows were once more enjoying the fresh grass on the slopes and the yield was a little better than it had been. The extra was never declared, but hidden in Madame Clavier's dairy where she made cheese or butter which she sold, along with the skimmed milk, to local people she could trust. Now and again the Vichy authorities came on an inspection, but Hans usually forewarned them and nothing untoward had ever been found.

'I expect they have limited supplies and they are more urgently needed elsewhere,' Elizabeth said. 'You can train without weapons, can't you?'

'Not properly. How can men learn how to use a rifle if they've never handled one? Or set explosive charges.'

'You've got a few rifles, you'll just have to share them. And I don't think it's a good idea to play with explosives. You'll have the Vichy police down on us like a ton of bricks. We don't want to draw attention to ourselves or we won't be able to use the crossing.'

She and Roger worked together on the farm and in their undercover work and had, as a consequence, become close.

She knew how he felt about her because he often told her so and he didn't seem to mind when she told him to stop his nonsense because she wasn't listening. He did not know she was not Pierre's daughter, nor of her relationship with Max. Max seemed a distant figure now, someone she had once known but had half forgotten. Did that mean she had never really loved him?

'Are you expecting Justine with more escapees?' he asked.

'No. We haven't heard from her for ages. She usually manages to send us a postcard now and then to say she's OK but there's been nothing for weeks. Mamie is worried she might have been arrested.'

'Wouldn't Antoine let you know if that had happened?'

Antoine? Was that Max? If it was, he would know how worried they would be. Perhaps he was in trouble too. 'Perhaps he can't.'

'Right, that's made up my mind for me. I'm going to Paris to find out what's going on.'

'It's too risky.'

He laughed. 'I do believe you care, after all.'

'Of course I care.' Saying that was easy, but how profoundly did she mean it? You couldn't love someone you didn't trust with secrets, could you?

'Good.' He grabbed her and kissed her. 'I'll hold you to that when I come back.'

She could not dissuade him from his foolhardiness and the next morning he cycled into Annecy where he left the bicycle with Alphonse, donned the German uniform again and caught a train to Paris. In his pocket were false travel documents provided by Hans. Poor Hans, he was now in so deep, he dare not refuse to do as he was asked.

Elizabeth was left behind to wait and worry. He didn't seem to see danger, even when it was staring him in the face. He thought giving Hans money meant he could trust him, but you couldn't buy loyalty, could you? And supposing those German identity papers let him down? Supposing he was arrested? He would be shot. A future without Roger's cheerful countenance and unfailing optimism seemed bleak indeed. Was she beginning to fall in love with him? It was foolish if she was; she knew nothing about him. He never spoke of his family, his childhood and growing up, except in general terms that told her nothing.

Roger saw no point in being stealthy. He had to rely on his disguise to keep him safe and German soldiers in Paris did not skulk about. They were cocksure and arrogant. He had had plenty of practice at being cocksure and arrogant himself. It had been his defence against the harsh world of a dreadful boarding school where the older boys were still allowed to have fags. Seven years old when he first went there, torn from the arms of his mother by a stepfather who hated him, he had been terrified. The initiation into the duties of a fag had only exacerbated that. He was required to walk the length of a beam in the roof of the gymnasium watched by half the school; he wanted desperately to duck out of it. He wasn't sure what he feared most: falling off the beam to the floor twenty feet below him or the kicking he would have if he refused. He had decided a quick death was better than a slow one. He still held to that belief.

He had survived by being stubborn and doing everything asked of him, however dangerous or ill-conceived, until he had been privileged to have a fag himself, and, to his lasting shame, he had not spared him. He had become as high and mighty, as cruel as those who had once tormented him. His mother had died, he was convinced of a broken heart, and after that he never went home again. His home was wherever he happened to be: school, college and then the army.

Girls were a different matter; he was not sure how to handle them. He liked to think they were all like his mother, gentle, forgiving and vulnerable, so he was never knowingly cruel to any of his girlfriends. They didn't last long when he found out they were not all like his mother, that some of them were hard-hearted and grasping, though on reflection, he had come to the conclusion he attracted the wrong kind of girl. Until he met Lisabette and fell instantly and irrevocably in love with her.

But his upbringing had scarred him. Even with Lisabette he found he couldn't stop his bantering and though he was deeply sincere in what he said to her, it came out of his mouth like a joke, as if he were afraid to let go, to reveal his own vulnerability, his fear of being rejected. And so far she had rejected him. He didn't know how to overcome that, but perhaps going to Paris and finding out what had happened to her aunt, might put him in a more favourable light.

Without looking round or in any way betraying his nervousness, he went up the steps of Justine's apartment on the rue de la Pompe and banged on the door. After a minute it was answered by a little old woman in a black dress and a shawl. Seeing his uniform she seemed to shrink into herself. 'Fraulein Clavier?' he enquired.

'Not here.' She drew her shawl tighter about her. 'They took her away.'

'They?' He spoke in French but remembered to have a German accent.

'The police. German soldiers.'

'Where did they take her?'

'Don't know. Prison perhaps.'

'How long ago was this?'

She shrugged. 'Months. April I think.'

'Who lives in the apartment now?'

'No one.'

'Show me.'

'I don't know that I should.'

'Yes, you should, unless you want to be arrested yourself.'

Trembling, she led the way, hardly able to unlock the door of the apartment her hands were shaking so much. He followed her in. The place had obviously been thoroughly searched; drawers and cupboards had been left open, their contents strewn about the floor. He went from room to room; they were all the same.

'It will do,' he said. 'I am requisitioning it on behalf of

the occupying forces. I will move in immediately. Give me the key, madame.' He held out his hand and she put the key into his palm. 'You may go now.'

She scuttled away. He flung himself onto the sofa and let out a huge breath of relief and chuckled softly. Being arrogant had its compensations. But what now? Straight back to Dransville with the news or should he stay and try to find out what had happened? He was hungry; he would go out and try to find some food and then go over the flat himself to see if anything had been missed by the searchers, then he would decide. He turned and left, carefully locking the door behind him and pocketing the key.

Max made his way stealthily on foot, pausing every now and again to listen for the police patrols and the heavy sound of jackboots because anyone out and about during curfew was either a policeman, a German soldier or a doctor who was allowed to attend his patients. His way took him along the rue de la Pompe and past Justine's apartment. There was a German captain coming down the steps. It was too late to hide; his only hope was to walk on past.

'Antoine Descourt.'

Max started to run. The captain ran after him. He dodged down a side road and sprinted for all he was worth, straight into the arms of a couple of German troopers. They had obviously been out on a spree and were more than slightly tipsy, but sober enough to hold onto him. 'You want this fellow, Herr Hauptmann?' they called out to Roger as he joined them.

324

'Yes. I'll take charge of him now.'

Max recognised the voice and was unsure whether to be relieved or more worried than ever. He stopped struggling and felt Roger's heavy hand on his shoulder.

'Can you manage him on your own, sir?' one of the soldiers asked.

'Yes, there's a police van round the corner. On your way or you will be late reporting back. I will see you are commended.'

'Thank you, sir.' They left, arms round each other, weaving erratically.

'You don't make it easy for yourself, do you?' Roger said. He didn't loosen his grip on Max's shoulder for fear he'd make a break for it.

'What are you doing back in Paris?' Max spoke in French.

'Looking for you, since Justine appears to be behind bars.'

'Did you put her there?'

'Me? Whatever makes you think that?'

'You seem very comfortable in that uniform. And you came out of her house as if you owned it.'

'So I did. I was looking for her. Shall we walk? I think we should get off the street.'

They turned and started back the way they had come. 'Why were you looking for her, if you knew she was in prison?'

'I didn't know until the concierge told me. I came because her parents are very worried they haven't heard from her. I volunteered to find out what had happened to put their minds at rest and also to ask Justine to get in touch with London on behalf of the Annecy *resistants*. The powers that be have been very tardy sending us arms and ammunition.'

'I wouldn't know anything about that.'

'No?'

'No.'

'I think,' Roger said slowly, releasing him, 'you are going to have to learn to trust me.'

They had reached Justine's apartment. Roger turned and started up the steps. 'Come on,' he said, when Max hesitated. 'It's the safest place for you at the moment.'

Max followed him up to the apartment where Roger let them in with his key. 'You seem to have made yourself at home,' he said.

'As I said, it's the safest place for both of us. The concierge thinks I have requisitioned it on behalf of the Boche. I'm counting on her being too frightened to check up on that. There's no food in the place. I'm going down to ask her to provide a little coffee, sweetener and milk. She might find us a bit of bread too, until we can go out and find some food. Have you got a ration card?'

'Yes.'

Roger went out onto the landing and called down the stairwell. 'Madame Concierge.'

The old lady appeared at the bottom of the stairs. 'Coffee, Madame,' he ordered. 'Milk, sugar, bread and butter and a bottle of wine.'

She did not answer but went back into her own quarters and reappeared a little later with the items on a tray. He met her halfway down the stairs and took it from her. Returning to the apartment, he filled the kettle and put it on the gas stove, made coffee, buttered the bread, found some wine glasses and took the whole lot into the sitting room and put it on the coffee table.

'Now we'll talk,' he said in English to the silent Max.

Max didn't know what to make of Roger. Whose side was he on? What did he know? What didn't he know? 'What about?' he asked warily.

'Justine. That will do for a start. How long has she been in jail?'

'A couple of months.' He knew the exact date; it was the day after they blew up the train.

'Look, Descourt or whatever you name is, you have to trust me. I know Justine was helping escapees – goodness knows, I was one myself – and I don't believe that's all she was doing, but I'm guessing that if she has not been brought to trial and sentenced, they haven't got much on her yet. If you want to keep your secrets, you are going to have to get her out. And soon. Before they wear her down.'

'Do you think I haven't thought of that?'

'What have you done about it?'

Max was silent, debating within himself whether he could trust the man. He spoke English like an Englishman; he had answered London's earlier questions correctly, but that uniform and the self-assured way he wore it still left niggling doubts. 'If you really want to help, then you find out when she's being transferred. You seem to be able to move about quite freely.'

'It's only this uniform, but you better be thankful for it because it will help us in the end.'

'Where did you learn to be so bloody cocky,' Max demanded. 'Did they leave nerves out when they put you together?'

Roger laughed. 'I've learnt to hide them, my friend. Did you go to an upper-crust English public school?'

'No.'

'I did. I was sent at the age of seven. A boy of seven, an only child, spoilt by a doting mother and hated by his stepfather, is little more than a baby, but he learns, he learns quickly if he wants to survive. The best way to stop the bullies is to learn not to care. I've grown up not caring. It's taken a war and a lovely woman to change that.'

'Justine?'

'No, although I could become quite fond of Justine, fond enough not to want to see her in the hands of the Gestapo. So, do we cooperate?' He held out his hand.

Max hesitated and then shook it. 'She's in Cherche-Midi but being moved to Fresnes soon for her trial. We think the best time to try and free her is en route.'

'How many men can you muster?'

'A dozen, but we can't move until we know the date and time. Giles is trying to find out but no luck so far.'

'Are you all armed?'

'More or less, but I don't think a shooting match will serve, innocent people might be hurt. We'll have to rely on the element of surprise.'

'Right. Tomorrow, I'll recce the route.'

'You don't need to be involved.'

'Oh, yes I do. You need me and my uniform and my knowledge of German. Besides, I want to contact London for the Annecy *resistants*. We need help if we are going to be any use when the time comes.'

'I'm afraid that is going to be more difficult than you thought. Our pianist has been picked up.' If Roger knew what a pianist was, Max thought, it might go some way to convincing him he could be trusted.

'Damn! I'd counted on him. He's the one that relayed all those silly questions I had to answer, isn't he?'

'Yes.' Max laughed, relaxing for the first time since seeing him come down the steps of Justine's apartment.

'You planning to get him out too?'

'Yes. It's going to take a bit more organising, since the Boche are unlikely to send them to Fresnes together.'

'How long do you think he'll hold out?'

'It's already been several days and there have been no more arrests, so he must still be keeping them guessing.'

'We've no time to lose. I'll go to the prison tomorrow morning to see what I can find out about a move. You go and alert your troops, they're going to be needed.'

But for Etienne it was all too late. He had been executed by firing squad at dawn that same morning.

* * *

The MI6 communications room in London was at first relieved when Etienne's wireless came back on line. It sounded a little strange, Vera Atkins thought. The call sign was correct, but one of the secret codes had been omitted and it didn't sound quite like Etienne's touch. 'He's been off line so long, he's simply forgotten to include it,' someone said.

'Double-check,' Buckmaster said. There were always two codes in every transmission, one that could be given to an interrogator, if it became necessary, and a second that, if omitted, meant the operator had been arrested. 'Vera, you know him well, ask him some questions only he can answer.'

She and Charles devised some queries that sounded innocuous and would not alert the enemy if they were standing over Etienne while he transmitted. The answers came back correctly with the added request for a new drop of arms and ammunition on a site they had not used before. According to Etienne the usual ground was no longer safe.

'Do we send it or not?' Buckmaster was in the habit of asking Vera her opinion, and in her opinion, something was not right.

'We could pretend to go along with it, but delay sending anything until we've been able to check with neighbouring circuits.'

'Supposing they have been infiltrated too?' Charles said. He was concerned for Max and Justine and this wasn't helping. Every time he went home Annelise asked him if he had news of Justine and he could tell her nothing. It was building a wall between them because she thought he was deliberately withholding the truth. The only thing that was keeping her mind off it was her little grandson and preparations for a wedding when Jack managed some leave.

'If they have, we are in serious trouble,' the major said. 'Have we got anyone new we can send out?'

'There are one or two coming to the end of their training,' Vera said. 'I'll see how they are coming along.'

Chapter Fourteen

Lucy found it hard to believe the change in her circumstances. Here she was living in this enormous house, housed and fed and treated as one of the family, but she didn't feel like family and she suspected they were only being nice to her because of Peter. Everyone adored him, especially Lady de Lacey who would have spoilt him and given in to his every tantrum if Lucy had not remonstrated and made it clear that Peter would have to learn he could not always have his own way.

Lady de Lacey had accepted that with good grace, had even apologised which made Lucy feel awful. She mourned the loss of her little home and her independence and she missed Jack. He had only been home once since she had come to live at Nayton Manor, and though they had snatched a hug and a kiss now and again, they did not sleep together. It just would not do, not until they were married, which was laughable considering they had already done the deed and everyone knew it. He was soon gone again, and without him and Amy, she felt out of her depth.

Lady de Lacey had not condemned her for having Peter, but her ladyship had assumed she would marry Jack. It had been Lucy's girlish dream, that Jack would love her and marry her and they would live happily ever after, but that was all it was, castles in the air and, at the time, she hadn't known any better. Now she was having enormous doubts. If only that bomb had not dropped on her home. If only her life could have stayed as it was, bringing Peter up on her own, seeing Jack now and again and enjoying his sweet lovemaking, uncomplicated by things like weddings. Was Jack marrying her simply to make an honest woman of her and would he soon tire of her and find someone else, someone of his own class? How did she know there wasn't someone like that already?

She ought not to be here. The villagers stared at her when she wheeled Peter out in his pushchair and she could not always avoid her pa. He ignored her as if she were invisible, and Frank Lambert jeered at her, telling her she seemed to have fallen on her feet but they would soon find out she was a whore, daughter of another whore, and she would be back where she started.

She didn't want to believe that about her mother. She didn't want her memories of her mother to be tainted, but she could not get the words out of her head. Added to what Pa had told her the day he told her to leave, they festered inside her, making her doubt herself. She didn't tell anyone what Frank had said, couldn't talk about it, not even to Amy, who came home as frequently as she could. She did, however, tell her she had misgivings about marrying Jack, one Saturday when they were sitting in the garden after lunch, watching Peter play on the lawn with Cecily, who treated him like a live doll. He didn't seem to mind. Beside them on a garden table was a jug of orange juice made from the concentrate that Lucy was allowed for Peter and which she picked up at the doctor's surgery.

'Why?' Amy demanded. 'You do love him, don't you?'

'Of course I do, but no one knows a thing about me. I don't know myself. Perhaps there's something bad in my past . . .'

'Rubbish! How can you think such a thing? You should have more faith in yourself, Lucy. You are sweet and gentle and loving and you are a splendid mother. Jack loves you and he adores Peter. I love you. Mama and Papa love you.'

'I know.' It was said with a heavy sigh. 'But it doesn't stop me wondering about what happened to make my mother go off like that.'

'I've said all along you should try and trace her. She ought to be at your wedding.'

'You sound very confident.'

'And so should you be. The best way to start is through Mr Storey and his work as a railwayman. Do you think he's always worked for the railways?'

'As long as I can remember. He was certainly working for them at Eccles. Before that I don't know.'

Amy was thoughtful. Papa was one of the principal stakeholders in the railway and he would know where to find Mr Storey's work record, but her father was still in London, doing his mysterious war work. And when he came home he was often exhausted, so she couldn't bother him about it. 'Do you think Mr Storey served in the armed forces during the last war?'

'He did say something about being wounded in the war, that was when he told me I wasn't his daughter.'

'No pictures of him in uniform or anything like that?'

'Not that I ever saw.'

'I wish I could get into his house, there must be something there to give us a clue.'

'Amy, don't you dare!'

'No, I suppose it's not a good idea. I'm going to start by finding out where Eccles is. Can you remember anything about it at all?'

'No. I remember my first day at school and thinking my mother had abandoned me. I cried buckets and the teacher wasn't very sympathetic, but Mum came and fetched me in the afternoon and I never minded after that. We left soon afterwards and came to Nayton.'

'How big was the school?'

'Not very big. Two classes, infants and juniors and two teachers.'

'A village, then, not a town. If Mr Storey worked on the railways and you lived on station road, there must be a station there.' She stopped suddenly. 'I know. Come on.' She stood up and hurried indoors. Lucy made sure Peter was happy with Cecily and followed. She found Amy in her father's study, opening out a huge railway map. 'It's bound to be here, somewhere.' She turned the map over to look at the index. 'There's an Eccles near Manchester and another in Kent and an Eccles Road here in Norfolk. Do you think that could be it?'

'Could be. Pa has a Norfolk accent.'

'Right. I'm going to start from there, but it'll have to wait until I've got some more leave. Will you come with me? Mama will look after Peter while we're gone.'

But Lucy would not. She baulked at the idea, afraid to confront her past, and nothing Amy said could persuade her. 'You go on your own,' she said. 'But if you succeed and the news is bad, I shall leave here and you won't hear of me again.'

Amy returned to Norwich next day, leaving Lucy feeling so unsettled, she couldn't keep still. She helped in the house, though Annelise insisted she did not need to; she worked with the only remaining gardener weeding flower beds; she left Peter with Lady de Lacey and went for long walks, sometimes along the riverbank, sometimes through the woods, though she avoided the clearing where the old cottage was because it gave her the creeps. Occasionally she took Peter and his pushchair on the bus to Swaffham. But whatever she was doing, her brain was busy trying to recall something of the past. She was even tempted to call on Bert Storey and demand to be told the truth. It was not fear of him that put her off, but fear of what he might tell her. In any case, could she believe him?

'Lucy, are you unhappy here?' Lady de Lacey asked her one day. Lucy had got up from the breakfast table and run into the morning room in tears and her ladyship had followed, pulled up a chair beside her and put her arm about her shoulders.

'No. You are very good to me. It's . . . it's . . .'

'Come on, I am sure you can tell me.' She noticed the letter in Lucy's hand. 'You haven't quarrelled with Jack, have you?'

'No, he's the same as he always is. We've never quarrelled, at least, no more than a little tiff, soon got over. But I don't think it's right, tying him down to marrying me when perhaps he doesn't want to.'

'What makes you think he doesn't want to?'

'Perhaps he's only doing it for Peter's sake.'

'Has he said that?'

'No, but he wouldn't, would he? He's a gentleman.'

Annelise smiled. 'I asked him especially if he was sure about marrying you and he said he was. He said when he thought he had lost you in that raid, he knew there would never be anyone else for him, so you can put that idea right out of your head. As for being a gentleman, he is that – I certainly hope so – but not in the sense you mean it.' She paused. 'I was once like you. My parents have a small farm in France which was where I grew up, working on the farm. During the last war I fell in love with a soldier and bore his child, but he died before we could be married. It was a terrible disgrace and I was shunned by almost everyone and my family felt shamed, though they stuck by me. I met Lord de Lacey – he wasn't a lord then – and fell in love again. We married and came to England and Charles adopted Jack. I have been happy, very happy, so it can happen, my dear.'

Lucy stared at her. 'He never told me that. I knew he was a stepson but I assumed you were a widow. Does he know?'

'Yes, he knows, all my children know. And now you do too. You do love Jack, don't you?'

'Yes, oh, yes. I've loved him for ages, long before he even noticed me.'

'Then, how can you even think of refusing him?'

'I am thinking of what's best for him.'

'You are what's best for him. Now, let's have no more tears.'

Lucy sniffed and mopped her face. She hadn't told Lady de Lacey the real reason for her tears, that she was afraid her mother had been . . . No, she couldn't even think that. Jack's letter, so cheerful, so full of optimism, had triggered off her feelings of doubt all over again. 'Amy said she was going to try and find my mother,' she said.

Annelise smiled. 'That would put the cat among the pigeons, wouldn't it? I wonder how the law stands when someone who has been declared dead, suddenly reappears after her husband has married again.'

'I don't know. Pa told me it wouldn't make any difference.'

'Do you want her found?'

Lucy thought for a minute before answering. 'Yes, then at least I'd know why she left, but I think it'll be like looking for a needle in a haystack.'

No railway stations had their names displayed and you either had to know the route and the stations along the line or rely on other passengers or the guard to tell you when you had reached your destination. Amy wasn't even sure Eccles Road was her destination, but it was easily reached from Norwich by train and it was better to ask her questions in person. She did not think she would receive answers if she simply wrote a letter. Besides, the idea of sleuthing appealed to her. As soon as she arrived she went in search of the stationmaster.

He was a middle-aged man past call-up age and very wary of Amy and her questions, but her most winning smile and a five-pound note stilled his conscience. He confirmed that Mr Albert Storey had been a porter there. 'I remember he had a wife and baby,' he volunteered. 'Pretty little thing, she was.'

'Was the baby born here?'

'No, though the little one weren't above a week or two old when they arrived.'

'Was she called Lucy? The baby I mean.'

'Can't remember. Might have been. What do you want to know for?'

'I have a very dear friend called Lucy Storey, who is going to marry my brother but she has lost touch with her mother and I'd like to trace her, so that she can come to the wedding.'

'Can't help you there, I'm afraid.'

'How long were they here?'

'Can't say. A few years. He was a bombastic sod, beggin' your pardon, miss; liked his drink, liked to throw his money about in the pub. I never could understand why she married him; she was always smart, well spoken too – a cut above, if you get my meanin'.'

'Did he have money, if he was only a porter?'

'Seemed to. He liked a flutter on the gee-gees too, so he never had it for long.'

'Where did they come from, do you know?'

'No idea.' A train came in and he left to see to it. Amy watched him supervising the unloading of a trunk and a few parcels from the guard's van and sending the train on its way with a whistle and a wave of his green flag. Then he was back. 'Sorry, I can't help you anymore. You could ask the railway company. They are bound to have records, though this being wartime an' all they might not be willing to tell you.'

'No, perhaps not.'

'Why don't you try advertising for her? She might see it, or someone she knows might point it out to her.'

'I tried that but it didn't work, no one answered. I'm sorry to have troubled you. When is the next train to Norwich?'

He consulted the large clock on the wall above the door of the waiting room. 'Three-fifteen. You'll need to cross to the other line.'

She had just over an hour to wait. Amy thanked him again and set out to explore the village. There wasn't much to it; a scattering of houses, a farm or two and a tiny Victorian school surrounded by an asphalt playground. It was playtime and the children were out, skipping and playing hopscotch or simply standing about in groups talking. Next to it was the head teacher's house.

As she stood and watched, a teacher came out with a handbell which she rang vigorously. The children stopped whatever they were doing and ran to line up in three groups. One by one each group filed back into the school. When the last had gone, Amy went in by the gate and approached the teacher. 'Excuse me, may I ask you a question?'

The woman turned. She was past middle age, her grey hair was drawn into a bun and she wore a brown skirt, white blouse and brown cardigan. 'What do you want to know?'

'Have you been here long, long enough to remember a little girl called Lucy Storey?'

The woman's expression was wary. 'Why do you want to know?'

Amy repeated the reason she had given to the stationmaster. 'Lucy remembers coming to school.'

'Yes, she did, but she wasn't here above a year or two before they left. Her father moved for promotion, I believe.'

'Do you know where they came from?'

'No idea, I'm afraid.' She looked back at the school; all

341

the children had gone inside and the door was shut. 'I must go. Sorry I can't help you anymore.'

Amy thanked her and returned to the station. She really hadn't learnt anything at all, except that Bert Storey had been as unpleasant then as he was now.

That evening she rang her father from the nurse's home. 'Papa,' she said, after the usual greetings and exchange of news. 'You are still in touch with the railway people, aren't you?'

'Not really. The government has taken over the running of the railways. Why do you want to know?'

'I'm trying to trace Lucy's mother, so that she can come to the wedding, and I thought you would know where Bert Storey came from. I've found out he was at Eccles Road before Nayton, but where was he before that? The railways keep records of employees, don't they?'

'Yes, but how is that going to help find Mrs Storey? After all, she is supposed to be dead.'

'Well, it would be nice for Lucy to know one way or another. If I could find out where she came from originally, she might have family. She might have gone back to them or at least they might know where she is.'

'There are a lot of "mights", there, Amy.'

'Yes, but I have to start somewhere. You can find out for me, can't you?'

'Amy, do you think I have nothing better to do with my time than chase shadows? I have important work to do, and any spare time I have is spent at Nayton with your mother.'

'I know, I know, and I wouldn't ask, but how else am I to find out what I want to know? It's important for Lucy. Don't you see?'

'I'll think about it, but it might take a bit of time. You will just have to be patient.'

They talked a little more, then Charles rang off. Amy and Lucy lived in their own little world, concerned only for their own problems, and though they undoubtedly read the newspapers and listened to the BBC news, they had no idea of what was going on behind the scenes, the lies and deception, the risks and danger other people were taking, people close to them, if they only knew. He could not tell them, of course, could not even tell Annelise.

As far as the SOE knew, Justine was still in prison and so, they thought, was Etienne. It was not Etienne sending his messages, they were ninety-nine per cent sure of that, because although the call sign was correct, the secret code was still not there, but they continued to feed whoever it was with false information, but it left them all on edge, wondering what had happened to Max and the others on the circuit. If Etienne had given his interrogators his call sign, then he had probably also revealed the names of the others. Charles feared for them all.

And to add to his worries, and another secret to be kept from Annelise, was the fact that Jack was now in the Special Duties Squadron flying black-painted Lysanders and Whitleys in and out of France. Why he had to be so foolhardy, Charles could not imagine. He could understand if, having been taken off ops, he was content with a desk job, but to take on something even more perilous, just as he was about to be married, seemed the height of folly.

Jack himself could not have explained. He supposed it had something to do with being French-born and sympathetic to the plight of his countrymen and women who were trying to live under the yoke of the Nazis. It was also an empathy with Justine, who had been his friend and playmate when he was a toddler and, of course, his sister, stuck so far from home and unable to communicate. If they could fight the occupation with all the risks it entailed, then he ought to do something to help. In the back of his mind was also the idea that he might, one day, on one of his fleeting visits to France, learn something of how his family were coping, be able to bring a message back home, perhaps.

He had volunteered for the duty before Lucy had been bombed out. It had been a reckless gesture to help him forget his tangled love life, which, with the dropping of that bomb in Norwich, had suddenly become untangled.

He decided that it would be kinder to tell Belinda to face-to-face that their affair was at an end and so he arranged to meet her in London as usual at Marietta's restaurant. She was so busy grumbling about the deteriorating quality of the food, he could hardly get a word in. After an indifferent meal they went on to a nightclub at her insistence. It was crowded with servicemen, particularly Americans, and there was hardly room to move, let alone talk. Belinda, who had changed out of uniform into a long evening dress and high-heeled shoes, was in her element. She loved the noise and glitter, and though he was ready to leave soon after midnight, she wanted to stay and it was four o'clock in the morning before they found their way back to her father's flat.

She was, he realised, as she fumbled with the key, decidedly tipsy, and he wondered whether to put off saying anything. As soon as they were inside, she kicked off her shoes and flung herself on a sofa. He went into the kitchen and made a pot of strong coffee, noting she had no trouble finding things like coffee, sugar, booze or make-up; these things could always be had if you had money to pay for them. It was when he saw her well-stocked larder, he thought of Lucy, coping with the rationing and shortages in her little house, trying not to be extravagant with the money he had given her. It would never have occurred to her to go to the black market. He put the pot, some milk and sugar and two cups and saucers on a tray and carried it in to her.

'You are becoming very domesticated, Jack,' she said. 'I would never have believed it of you.'

'Yes, well, when needs must . . . You need sobering up.'

'I'm not drunk, Jack. I can still make it to bed.' She attempted to get to her feet but fell back again.

'Not now. Drink this.' He handed her a cup of coffee. 'I want to talk to you.'

'Talk away.'

He sat down opposite her. He hadn't drunk half as much as she had and was cold sober. Why he had ever felt like marrying her, he could not say. It was, he supposed, because as a very young man he had decided the sort of girl he wanted to marry and she had fitted the bill. Although it had not been many years before, he was no longer that young man. War aged people quickly, made men of boys. It made you appreciate the better things of life, the good and bad in people, sometimes where you least expected it.

He had rehearsed what he was going to say, but looking at her perfectly coiffured blond hair, perfectly manicured nails, bright-red lips and silk-clad legs, the words fled. Instead he simply, said, 'I'm going to be married.'

She laughed. 'That's a funny way to propose. Aren't you supposed to ask the girl first?'

'I did and she said yes.'

'She!' She sat bolt upright, spilling her coffee down her dress. She put the cup back on its saucer and began mopping her front with a handkerchief. 'It'll never come out. It's ruined and it cost the earth.'

'That's the trouble with you,' he said. 'All you care about are material things. I'm trying to tell you something.'

'You just did.'

'I'm glad you understood.'

'Oh, I understood all right. You've been two-timing me. Who is she?'

'You wouldn't know her.'

'What's she got that I haven't?'

He smiled. 'My son.'

'What?' she shrieked.

'My son. He's eighteen months old now. His name's Peter.'

'I don't want to know his bloody name. How long has this been going on? Ages, by the sound of it.' She gave a bitter laugh. 'I thought you were going off me a bit, but I thought it was the war and all that, made excuses for you . . .'

'I'm sorry, Belinda. I should have told you long ago.'

'So you bloody well should. And now you're going to say you're only doing it to make an honest woman of her for the sake of the child.'

'No, I'm not. I'm marrying her because I love her and it feels right.'

'OK, rub it in, why don't you?'

'I'm being honest with you.'

'It's a bit late for that, don't you think? I don't know what Mum and Dad will say. Mum's been talking of a wedding for ages, making plans.'

'Then she's been a bit premature, considering we were never engaged.'

'Now I know why. God, to think of the years I've wasted on you . . . You cad, you unbounded cad.'

'I'm sorry,' he said again.

'I don't want to hear it. Go away and leave me alone.'

He stood up to leave. 'You can still have your society wedding, Belinda,' he said softly. 'But not to me.'

It was a good thing she was too drunk to aim properly. The coffee pot crashed against the wall behind his head and hot coffee cascaded down the wall and onto the carpet. He heard another missile hit the door and shatter as he shut it behind him. It had been an uncomfortable hour or so, but Belinda's anger had been easier to cope with than tears, although she had probably been right to call him a cad. He consoled himself with the thought that she wasn't heartbroken and her pride would soon recover and she would find someone else. No doubt their mutual friends would be told that she had dumped him. She could say what she liked; no doubt he deserved it, but he felt as though a great weight had been lifted from his shoulders.

The war would end one day and then he and Lucy could look to the future. They would buy a house and he would find a job that excited and challenged him and they would have more children like Peter. He smiled, remembering his last leave. It had been frustrating to have to behave themselves, but Lucy had insisted and they had both laughed and said, 'After the wedding . . .' in unison.

It was five-thirty in the morning and broad daylight. There was no point in trying to find a hotel, so he took a taxi to Liverpool Street station to catch the first train to Cambridge where he could pick up a bus to his base near Newmarket.

He was no sooner back than his squadron leader sent for him. 'I've got a job for you, Flight Lieutenant de Lacey,' he said. 'You're to take a bod to France tonight. Briefing at eighteen hundred hours.'

He saluted and left to go back to his billet and catch up with the sleep he had missed the night before. He had learnt to sleep when and where he could and the normal daytime sounds of people walking about in the corridor, of loud voices calling to each other, of tannoys and aeroplanes coming and going, even the prospect of what was to come that night, did not impinge. He slept until woken by his servant at five o'clock. He dressed, went to the mess for a meal and then attended the briefing. Not that he was told any more about the mission than was necessary for him to know. He wasn't even told the names of the people he ferried, nor the contents of the canisters he dropped by parachute, though he could guess.

Vera Atkins was there with a young man dressed in an ill-fitting civilian suit. They sat to one side while the squadron leader explained the mission. As far as Jack was concerned it was fairly straightforward. There would only be two flares, he was told, and they would not be lit until the aircraft was heard. Jack's navigation had to be spot on.

He went back to his billet and changed into flying gear, checking he had everything he needed for the flight. He went out to the airfield, ready to do the pre-flight checks. Vera and the young man were walking towards him. He watched them speak to each other and shake hands, then his passenger, who was carrying a heavy case, continued alone and climbed the steps into the rear cockpit and was strapped in by the ground crew. The chocks were pulled away and they moved across the field and were soon airborne. All Jack had to guide him was a map and a compass. Everything else in his life went on hold until he came back.

He felt strangely calm, though his passenger was evidently nervous. 'Have you done this before?' he asked Jack over the intercom.

'Yes, lots of times, piece of cake. I'll tell you when we're nearly there.' The 'lots of times' was a bit of an exaggeration, but he said it, not to boast, but to reassure.

'Thank you.'

'Don't thank me. I'm only doing my job.'

Jack knew where the coastal guns were on both sides and managed to dodge them without being spotted; it wouldn't be the first time he had been fired on by his own side. They flew on, eerily alone in the moonlit sky. These operations were only undertaken when the moon was full, or almost full, and the shadow of their aircraft kept pace across the countryside below them.

'How visible are we?' the young man asked.

'Practically invisible,' Jack said cheerfully. 'Two minutes to go. Are you ready?'

'Yes.'

Jack checked his position and reduced height. His passenger was silent, but Jack could feel his tension. 'There's the beacon. Hold onto your hat.' He went down to treetop height, then passed over the first flare, touched down, bumped along and stopped only a few feet from the second.

Almost immediately a man in dark clothes appeared by the aircraft to take the case from the passenger and help him out. 'Gilbert?' he queried.

'Yes, and bloody glad to be on terra firma again. Who are you?'

'Antoine Descourt.'

'I shall have to ask you for a password, I'm afraid.'

Max laughed. 'Titania.' He tapped the side of the fuselage. 'On your way, pilot.'

Jack, who was preparing to turn the Lysander round ready for take-off, turned in his seat. 'Max,' he said.

'Good Lord! Jack de Lacey.'

'Justine?' Jack shouted above the noise of the engines he was revving for take-off. 'Lizzie?'

'We're going to get Justine out of jail and Lizzie is OK. No time to talk. Get a move on.'

Jack gave him a thumbs up, waited until the two men were clear and turned the aircraft. Seconds later he was airborne. He circled once, wiggled his wings in salute and made for home.

As soon as the aircraft was airborne, Max extinguished the flares and scattered the ashes with brushwood, then he went back to the newcomer. 'Let's get out of here,' he said.

Gilbert picked up his suitcase and followed Max through a copse of trees to a farm track where a small van was parked with its engine running. It had a gas container on its roof. A man emerged from the van. Gilbert, faced with a German in uniform, prepared to make a dash for it. Max detained him by grabbing his arm.

His look of terror made Roger laugh. 'It's all right, my friend. We come in many guises. 'I'm Dirk to my friends, Hauptmann Otto Bergman to my enemies.'

'He's one of us,' Max said, hoisting the suitcase into the back of the van. 'And as mad as a hatter.' Prosper, whose real name Max did not know, had tracked him down and told him to expect a new wireless operator, giving him the time and place and left it to him to arrange for his reception.

'I'm afraid I am going to have to tie your hands and feet together,' Roger told Gilbert. 'If we are stopped, you are my prisoner. Get that?'

'It's a fine way to greet a chap who's only come to help,' Gilbert grumbled, though he submitted.

Half an hour later they were in the barn of a farm, where Gilbert's bonds were untied so that he could unpack his radio and make his first transmission. It was necessarily short and simply established his safe arrival, that Justine was still in Cherche-Midi and Etienne had been executed, but Antoine was safe and trying to rebuild the circuit. Then the radio was packed up again and they were on their way once more. Now Max was back in communication with London again, he felt immeasurably relieved, but only when they were safely in the secret cellar at Chateau Mollet did they allow themselves to relax. Anne arrived with food and drink and while they ate they talked, at first warily, especially as Gilbert still felt uncomfortable with the German uniform, but increasingly openly. Gilbert told them of SOE's suspicions that it was not

Etienne transmitting and assumed it was a German operator who must have got the call sign out of him. 'But not his secret code,' he added. 'SOE have been feeding the new operator with false information about targets.'

Max laughed. 'So that's what all the coming and going has been about. The Germans have been making raids and putting extra guards on all sorts of weird places that we would never consider targeting. We thought it might have been Etienne leading them a dance, but then we heard he had been executed. And without him I couldn't contact London. I want you to ask for rifles, a couple of German pistols with ammunition and a cover and identity documents for Justine. She'll have to disappear when we get her out and I daren't risk trying to get them here. It's too easy for people to talk when they're frightened.'

'Do you think she has talked?' Gilbert asked.

'No,' Max said. 'If she had we should all have been rounded up and she would have been tried and sentenced before now, but they must be wearing her down gradually. She is due to go on trial in Fresnes next week. We mean to free her before she reaches there. Dirk is going to find out when and how she is being moved and if possible get a message to her. Until we know the exact route she'll take we can't finalise plans to intercept.'

'If we start a shooting match in the street, innocent people might be hurt,' Roger said. 'I've got a better idea . . .'

Justine had lost track of the days. At first she had counted them religiously, each day followed by a night, scratched in the dirty whitewash of the wall of her cell, but as the months had passed, she had realised it was a futile exercise, it didn't bring her any nearer to being released and only depressed her. Every few days she was taken for further interrogation, where she was asked the same questions over and over again, sometimes couched in a different way in order to confuse her. She pretended to be muddled and then to remember some little thing to add to her previous answers which meant nothing at all and served only to keep her brain active. It was important not to let her brain go the way of her body, which was rapidly succumbing to poor food and lack of exercise. There was no fat left on her and the muscles in her legs were weak. Her wrists were no bigger than a child's. She wondered if she might starve to death before they had a chance to execute her as they had Etienne. Her interrogator had taken great delight in telling her of his death and she had had to keep her expression passive and pretend indifference to the fate of a man she had supposedly never met. But it depressed her.

The day of her trial dawned. Her defence lawyer would have a few minutes with her at the court before proceedings began she was told when she enquired about her defence. He would, she had been told, be a German officer appointed by the court, so she had little cause to hope for an acquittal.

She was given a facecloth, some harsh soap, a scrap of towel and a comb that morning and told to clean herself up for her appearance. For two pins she wouldn't have bothered, but her pride and self-respect took over and she did her best with what she had been given. 'My dress is filthy and torn,' she told the woman jailer. 'What am I to do about that?'

She was given a pink cotton dress whose printed flowers had faded. It was much too big for her, but it was clean; she tried not to think of who had worn it before her. She dressed and sat down to wait. Her nerves were taut, her head trying to think of all the questions she might be asked and how she would answer them; no doubt they would try and catch her out. How much did they really know about Oberon? Or *France Vivra*?

At ten-thirty her cell was unlocked, her jailer marched her out to the lobby where a German captain and a private waited to escort her to a police van to take her to Fresnes. Her eyes lit up at the sight of them but she quickly looked down at her feet and shuffled forward. They took an arm each and almost dragged her out and bundled her into the van before climbing in beside her. Giles, wearing a peaked cap, was in the driving seat. 'We must hurry,' he said. 'When the real escort arrives and they realise what's happened, there'll be a hue and cry.'

He drove off with Justine holding tightly to Max's hand. Through the streets of Paris they went, weaving in and out of the traffic, along the rue du Cherche-Midi, down the avenue du Maine to Porte d'Orleans, going fast, but not too fast. After a few miles they turned off onto a country road and, half an hour later, arrived at the Chateau Mollet where they tumbled out and made for the cellar, all except Giles who was going to drive the stolen van as far away as possible and dump it before returning to school. He kissed Justine's cheek. 'Good luck,' he said.

They never saw him again; betrayed by one of his older pupils, he was picked up before he could dump the van.

As soon as they were safely inside, Max took Justine into his arms and hugged her. 'Thank God, it worked. Are you all right, sweetheart?'

She was crying. Tears were running down her face, unstoppable. She hadn't cried all the time she had been incarcerated, except the day she learnt Etienne had died, and that had not been for long. Tears, she believed, would weaken her. But now all the pent-up emotion of months came rushing to the surface and she sobbed. He held her close against his chest. 'It's all right, sweetheart,' he murmured, feeling the bones of her ribs under his hand. 'You are safe now. I've got you.'

Roger disappeared to tell Anne Justine had arrived and would need nourishing food and some decent clothes, leaving Max and Justine alone. He drew her down onto a bench. Racks of wine bottles reached from floor to ceiling behind them. 'Was it very awful?'

'Pretty bad. Etienne is dead. They shot him.'

'We know. The Germans have been using his radio to contact London. Thankfully, London realised what was happening.'

'I saw him, you know, only a glimpse but he was a terrible mess. They tortured him before they killed him. I kept thinking it would be my turn next.'

'What did you tell them?'

'Nothing, I swear. I stuck to my story. But I can understand people giving way, though. Solitary confinement eats away your brain, especially when you know the only time you'll see another soul is when you are taken for interrogation. The temptation to talk for talking's sake is hard to resist.'

'What do you think the Germans know about Oberon?'

'They know its name and they told me they had arrested everyone connected with it. I didn't know whether to believe them or not, but I pretended I hadn't a clue what they were talking about.' She paused. 'Was anyone else arrested?'

'No.'

'Then Etienne died a hero.'

'And you, my darling, are a heroine.' He kissed her tenderly, afraid of her fragility.

'What now?' she asked, when she was able to draw breath. 'They will be looking for me and my rescuers.'

'Yes, we know that. You are not safe in Paris and neither is Roger. It won't be long before the Boche realise there's no such person as Hauptmann Bergman, so he is going to take you to Dransville as your nursing attendant.'

'You have learnt to trust him, then?'

'Yes, I'm sorry I ever doubted him. We've got new identity documents for you. You are Marianne Raphael, the niece of Madame Clavier's long-dead sister. You have been seriously ill in a sanatorium after working in a munitions factory, which will account for your emaciated condition. You are being sent to Dransville to regain your strength. And that is true enough,' he said, leaning back to look at her. She was all skin and bone, her cheeks hollow, her lovely blond hair was the colour of dry dust with no life to it. There were sores on her face and her arms were covered in bruises. It made him boil with anger.

She reached up to touch his face. She had dreamt of doing that all the time she had been incarcerated, dreamt of feeling his skin, of tracing the outline of his dear face with her fingers, of putting her lips to his and learning to *feel* again. 'Aren't you coming too?'

'No. I must stay here. I've work to do getting the circuit going again. I've been sent a new pianist which is a great relief. He flew in two days ago.'

'Must you? Why not come to Dransville with me? You've done your bit and the longer you go on, the greater the risk. I don't want to lose you.'

'You won't lose me, sweetheart. I have every intention of surviving this war and living happily ever after with you. But to do that, I need to know you are safe. When you are strong enough, you and Lizzie must get over the border. I want to know you are both back in England.' He paused. 'Talking of England, you'll never guess who was piloting the plane that brought the new man in. It was Jack.'

'Jack?'

'Your nephew, large as life. I told him we were going to get you out and Lizzie was OK. We didn't have time to talk, every second on the ground is a risk.'

'Did he look well?'

'I couldn't tell in the dark and he had his flying helmet on, but he sounded OK.'

'Oh, Max, I am so tired, so very, very tired of it all.'

'I know, sweetheart, we all are. The count is going to give us a bed tonight, so when it gets dark we'll go up to the chateau. Tomorrow the new you will leave for Dransville.'

She could hardly believe she was free. There would be no trial, no imprisonment or execution, not this time anyway. She had been saved because three men, three very brave men, had put their lives on the line to save her. Lying beside Max that night after they had gently and tenderly made love, she cried herself to sleep. If Max knew she wept, he did not say anything.

Chapter Fifteen

Elizabeth was making her way from the cowshed to the house when she heard the sound of a horse coming up the hill towards the farm. She went to the gate to see who it could be; she hated being caught unawares, especially if she had escapees on the premises who needed to be hidden. It was, she realised with relief, only Alphonse Montbaun's pony and trap. He had passengers. More men to hide, she supposed, or perhaps young Frenchmen who would rather live rough in the forest than be sent to Germany to work. It was her job to take food and wine to them every other day. It was a great strain on the farm's resources, but with stolen ration cards, they managed.

She put up a hand to shield her face from the sun so that she could see them arrive and then she gave a squeak of excitement and ran indoors. 'Mamie, Papie, come and see who's here.'

Then she ran back to the gate, followed at a slower pace by her grandparents. 'Merciful heaven!' Marie Clavier stood and crossed herself. Then she ran forward to embrace Justine who had climbed from the vehicle.

Elizabeth stood, a little apprehensive, waiting for Roger to come to her. He was no longer in that dreaded uniform, but dressed in a white hospital coat over black trousers and a plain white shirt. 'Well, Lisabette,' he said, moving forward to take both her hands in his and hold her at arm's length. 'I said I'd be back, didn't I?'

'You did.' At first she thought he looked the same as he always had, but there was a subtle difference. She couldn't quite put her finger on it. He looked tired, but it was more than that. Whatever had happened in Paris had left its mark. His smile was the same and yet it had a tautness about it as if it were an effort, and his eyes, raking hers, had somehow lost their sparkle.

He pulled her towards him and she found herself enveloped in a bear hug. 'I've got a bone to pick with you,' he murmured in her ear.

'Why, what have I done?'

'It's what you didn't do that matters. It can wait until we are alone.'

The sound of her grandmother's voice stopped her asking what he meant and she drew away.

Released from her daughter's embrace, Marie had seen, for the first time, Justine's emaciated condition. 'What has happened to you? You are all skin and bone. Have you been ill?'

'Let's go inside,' Justine suggested. 'I'll tell you everything then.'

Elizabeth turned to Alphonse. 'Will you join us in a celebratory drink?'

'I would but I can't,' he said. 'I've got to get back for an inspection.' Inspections were the bane of his life; he was always afraid the inspectors might see something they weren't supposed to see. Luckily he had friends in the agricultural bureau who usually forewarned him.

'Good luck, then,' she said and, taking Roger's arm, followed her grandparents and Justine into the farmhouse.

In the kitchen, Justine sank into a chair at the table while her mother bustled about finding food. 'You must eat and rest,' the old lady said. Then as an afterthought, 'Are they after you, the Boche? Have we got to hide you?'

'I think, Madame Clavier,' Roger put in, 'she ought not to be seen while she looks so ill.'

'Oh, Justine, what have you been up to?' the old lady asked.

It took some time to tell a sanitised version of what had happened and by that time food and wine from their hidden store were on the table and they drank to their reunion and again to victory.

Later, when Elizabeth went out to do the evening milking, Roger followed her. He had discarded the white coat and was, once again, Dirk Vanveldt. He made no attempt to help her, but stood watching as she herded the cows into their stalls and began on the first one. 'Why didn't you tell me you were English?' he asked.

'Oh, is that the bone you want to pick with me?' Her head was in the cow's flank.

'Yes.'

'It seemed safer to stick to my cover story. After all, I didn't know . . .'

'Didn't know what? Whether to trust me or not?'

She turned to face him. 'All the escapees were told the same story, it was safer that way; what they didn't know, they couldn't tell. I didn't know you would decide to stay in France and we would . . .' She hesitated.

'We would what? Fall in love?'

'Do you? Love me I mean?'

'You flaming well know I do. I've told you often enough.'

'I didn't know whether you meant it. You always seemed to be joking.'

'I'm not joking now.'

'No. I'm sorry I didn't tell you.'

'Nor did you tell me you were as good as engaged to Antoine Descourt before the war. That's if it really is his name.'

'Did he tell you that?'

'No, Justine did, on the way down here. She didn't know it was all news to me.'

'We had known each other for years, all part of the same set. We just drifted into it. I was too young to know my own mind . . .'

He took her hands and drew her to her feet to face him. 'And do you know your own mind now?' The flippant young man who had first come to Dransville, who never

363

treated anything seriously, had disappeared and in his place was a man of substance, a man scarred perhaps, but all the stronger for that.

'Yes, I think so.'

'Only think so? Can't you be more definite than that?'

She laughed. 'What do you want me to say?'

'I want you to say you love me and will marry me.' He paused. 'But only if you mean it.'

She laughed. 'I wouldn't say it if I didn't mean it.'

He gave her a tiny shake. 'Well?'

'Oh, Roger, I think I'd die if anything happened to you. All the time you were gone I kept imagining all sorts of terrible things, that I might never see you again, and I knew then.'

He gave a whoop of joy, folded her in his arms and kissed her long and hard.

'What do we tell Max?' she asked when she was able to draw breath.

'So that's his name! Never mind. I don't think he'll be heartbroken, not after seeing him and Justine together. She is worrying how to tell you. That's how she came to mention it in the first place. It would be nice if you could put her mind at rest. She's got enough on her plate getting over being in prison. She was tortured, you know, but she never talked.'

'I guessed as much. She is very brave.'

'Yes, she is. I doubt she will ever tell us all she went through. She deserves to be happy.'

'Of course she does. I'll talk to her when I've finished

364

milking.' She looked back at the cow, swishing her tail behind her. 'Poor thing thinks I've abandoned her.' She laughed suddenly. 'What do you think our grandchildren will say when we tell them you proposed to me in a cowshed while I was milking?'

He grinned his old grin and pulled her to him to kiss her again. It went on rather a long time and would have gone on longer if the cow had not impatiently stepped sideways and nearly knocked them both over. 'Later,' he said, releasing her. 'When we don't have an audience.' Then he helped her finish her task.

'Justine has been freed,' Charles told Annelise when he went home for a few days soon after hearing of the successful operation. They had finished their evening meal, the children were all in bed and they were sitting in their favourite place side by side on the sofa with his arm round her. 'She's back at Dransville with your mother.'

'Oh, thank the Lord for that. Will she be safe there?'

'She should be. If there's any danger, she can easily slip into Switzerland.' It sounded simple said like that, but they both knew it wasn't.

'What about Lizzie?'

'As far as we know she is safe and well.'

'How much longer is this going on, Charles? I'm so tired of it all. I want Lizzie home. I want my parents to be safe and the world at peace. There doesn't seem to be any good news anywhere.' The war in North Africa didn't appear to be getting anywhere, the Germans were at the gates of Stalingrad and the Japanese were advancing in the Far East. Worst of all, a recent raid on the French port of Dieppe by a force of Canadians, British and Americans had been a dreadful failure and resulted in heavy loss of life and thousands of men taken prisoner.

'I know, sweetheart. We all are. But the tide will turn, you'll see. We'll win, we just have to be patient. You still have the wedding to look forward to, don't you?'

'Yes, but we can't arrange a date until we know when Jack will have enough leave to allow them a bit of a honeymoon. And Amy is determined to find Lucy's mother so that she can be here for the ceremony. It's become a sort of crusade with her.'

'Yes, I know. She asked me to find out where Mr Storey worked before Lucy was born.'

'Did you?'

'Yes. He came out of the army early in 1918 after being wounded in the thigh and subsequently went back to his job as a gardener on the estate of Sir Robert Manning at Waterbury. He joined the railway in 1920 and moved to Eccles Road. He was married by then and had a baby, presumably Lucy.'

'Where's Waterbury?'

'It's a village in the north Cambridgeshire fens.'

'So that's where Amy's gone today. She came home yesterday on a weekend's leave and left again this morning, saying she was going sleuthing. She said she'd be back this evening.' She paused. 'I can't help wondering if it's such a good idea, Charles, stirring up the past.

What is Bert Storey going to say if a wife he thought was dead turns up again? If Amy does manage to find her, we can't let her come back here, can we? There's the new Mrs Storey . . .'

'I think it will be up to Lucy and her mother to decide, but let's wait and see, shall we? It might never come to that.'

Seen from the windows of the train, the countryside was flat as a pancake. The sky was riven with clouds, pink on the edges, a deeper mauve in the centre. The farms and their buildings sat in isolation as if some giant hand had picked them up and dumped them where they stood. The surrounding fields, all but a few meadows where cattle grazed, had been ploughed up for arable crops. The rape, which had carpeted acres and acres of land in the early summer, had been harvested, but some of the seeds had drifted into the hedgerows and along the railway track making patches of golden yellow amidst the white of the all-pervading cow parsley. The barley had been harvested and soon it would be the turn of the wheat and potatoes. East Anglia was doing its bit to feed the nation.

Amy left the train at Waterbury station, which was almost a mirror image of the one at Nayton, and made her way the stationmaster's office, hoping someone might remember Bert Storey working there, but the only employee was past normal retirement age and had been brought in to replace the previous man who had left to join the army. He had only been there a few months and could tell her nothing.

She thanked him and went out onto the dusty road, wondering where to go first. Waterbury was a small village with nothing in particular to commend it to a tourist. There was a post office across the green with a letter box and a telephone box outside and a rusting sign advertising Lyons ice cream, though she doubted if there was any ice cream to be had. There was a butcher and a grocer on either side of it and, a little further along the village street, a blacksmith and a cobbler. There were two public houses, the Green Man, which stood at the crossroads, and a thatched one called the Lord Protector, which had a picture of Oliver Cromwell on its creaking sign. Dotted around the green and up and down the main village road were houses, some small and old and typically on the tilt due to the peat and clay subsoils doing battle with each other. Others had been built after the last war when there was a boom in house building. The rectory was a sturdy Victorian building of grey bricks. The church looked interesting, so she went inside.

It was a typical country church with wooden pews and whitewashed walls on which some plaques commemorated noteworthy parishioners. 'To the memory of Sir Robert Manning, Bart, 27th January 1873–21st November 1920,' she read on one which had an ornately carved heraldic shield at the top. Underneath that was 'Alicia Geraldine Manning, his wife, born 10th May 1878, died 6th January 1921.' She did not long outlive her husband, Amy noted. But there was more. On another, smaller memorial beside it, was the inscription: 'To the memory of Lieutenant Graham Manning MC, only son and heir of Sir Robert Manning, who left this life for eternal glory on 10th May 1920, aged twenty-two, as a result of being gassed in the War to end all Wars. May he rest in peace'.

Amy moved on, feeling as if she had intruded on another family's grief. Who had been left, she wondered? Had Sir Robert had daughters? Had Lieutenant Manning been married? Other plaques commemorated more of the Manning family but they were all older. On the opposite wall was a list of the villagers who had died serving their country, headed by the lieutenant. She went outside and wandered among the gravestones, reading the inscriptions, but some were so worn they were indecipherable. The Manning family, as befitted their station, had an enormous vault surrounded by posts and chains. She moved on, looking for the name of Storey, but couldn't find it. She wished she knew Lucy's mother's maiden name, but Lucy hadn't known it.

A middle-aged man in clerical garb came up the path from the vicarage. She noticed he had a pronounced limp. 'Good afternoon, Rector,' she greeted him. 'I've been looking round the church.'

'You are very welcome, miss.' He was thin, his dog collar seemed too big for his neck. He had light sandy hair and a friendly smile. 'Any particular reason?'

Amy introduced herself and repeated the reason she had given everyone else and why she thought Waterbury was the place to start.

'I don't know the name,' he said. 'There's certainly no one called Storey living in the village now. Do you know the lady's maiden name?'

'No, I wish I did. I think Mr and Mrs Storey would have been married between 1918 and 1919, perhaps earlier.'

'I wasn't here then. Would you like to look at the marriage register?'

'Yes, please. That might help.'

He led the way into the church and through to the vestry, where he unlocked a cupboard and brought out the register. 'I'll leave you to it,' he said, putting it on a table. 'Come and find me when you've finished. I shan't be far away.' He left with a faint swish of his black skirt.

Amy pulled up a chair and opened the book, turning the pages until she came to 1918. It was a year for weddings, she discovered, and supposed that those soldiers and sailors who had survived the war had wanted to settle down with their sweethearts. Her fingers followed the names down the page. There was no Storey in 1918. She began on 1919, page after page. She was almost giving up when she spotted what she was looking for. She read it again, just to make sure. Albert John Storey had married Margaret Lucilla Falconer in July 1920. Lucy had been born in November, so Margaret must have been pregnant when she married. In a small village like Waterbury that would have caused a stir.

She shut the book and went to find the incumbent. He was talking to a lady who was arranging flowers on the altar. She waited until he had finished before approaching him. 'Any luck?' he asked.

'Yes. Lucy's mother's name was Falconer and her father was James Falconer.'

'Falconer?' He sounded surprised. 'Are you sure?'

'Yes. Do you know the family?'

'The Reverend James Falconer was my predecessor. He died in 1937. I didn't realise he had had children. None came to the funeral which I conducted.'

It didn't sound as if Lucy's mother had returned home, after all. 'I'm sure Lucy didn't know about it. Her mother told her she had no living relatives. I believe they may have been estranged.'

'Mrs Falconer still lives in the village.'

'Does she?' Amy's hopes, which had plummeted, rose again. 'Do you think she would see me?'

'I don't see why not, but if you are doubtful, I'll ask her first. Are you staying in the village?'

'I hadn't planned to, I'm on leave, you see, but I could stay one night if she can't see me today.'

'Let's go now, then. It's only across the green.'

He led the way, talking as he went. 'This is a close-knit community,' he said. 'Until the war, most of the inhabitants depended on the estate for a living.'

'You mean Sir Robert Manning?'

'Yes. Both he and his wife died soon after the war, from influenza, I was told, though the epidemic was really over by then. They were unlucky to catch the tail end of it. Their only son, who came home from the war suffering from the effects of gas, predeceased them. A cousin inherited but he sold up a year or two later. The upkeep was crippling. The land was sold piecemeal to local farmers and the house is now a convalescent home for servicemen. Some of them come to the services and I go up there and visit those that can't make it.'

He stopped outside the gate of a thatched cottage. The small front garden was a riot of colour; roses, clematis and poppies vied with delphiniums, lupins, hollyhocks and tall regal lilies. Standing on the path, clippers in one hand and a trug on the other arm, was a woman in her early sixties. She was neatly dressed in a dark-grey skirt and white blouse. 'Good morning, Daniel,' she called. 'Isn't it a glorious day? Too nice to be indoors.'

'It certainly is. I've brought you a visitor.' He turned to Amy. 'Wait here a minute, will you? I'll talk to her first.'

Amy watched as he opened the gate and went up the path and spoke to Mrs Falconer. She saw her brush a wisp of grey hair away from her face and look up at the young man as he talked. Suddenly she started back and put a hand to her mouth, her eyes wide in shock. He put a hand on her shoulder to reassure her, and went on talking. She nodded and then they went indoors. It looked as though there would be no interview, after all. Amy was unsure whether to stay or leave, but out of courtesy, decided to stay and hear what the rector had to say. He rejoined her after a few minutes.

'I told her what you told me,' he said. 'She was so shocked I had to take her indoors and settle her in a chair with a glass of water.'

'I'm sorry, I didn't mean to upset her.'

'I am sure you didn't, but she has recovered sufficiently to speak to you. She wants to know more.'

Amy thanked him, walked up to the door, knocked gently and went in.

She found herself in a comfortable sitting room.

Flowers filled a bowl in the empty hearth and their scent filled the room. There were ornaments and framed photographs dotted about. Mrs Falconer was sitting in an armchair with a glass of water on a small table by her side, which also held a folded newspaper, a book and a pair of spectacles. She looked up as Amy entered. Her blue eyes were bright but wary. 'I understand you are Lord de Lacey's daughter.'

'Yes. My name is Amy.'

'Sit down, please.'

Amy sat facing her. 'I'm sorry if my coming has shocked you. The reverend explained why I am here, did he?'

'You have news of my daughter?'

'No, I'm sorry. I was hoping to trace her myself. You see, she left the marital home around 1928 without saying a word to Lucy. Lucy is her daughter.'

'Lucilla, after me? My name is Lucilla.'

'Possibly, but she has always been known as Lucy to us. She told us her mother had always been loving and caring and she couldn't understand why she just walked out. I suspect the marriage wasn't a happy one and she couldn't bear it any longer, but Lucy has always wondered why she didn't take her with her. She was only eight years old at the time.'

Mrs Falconer was silent for a long time, then she took a sip of water and spoke again, so softly Amy had to listen carefully to hear her. 'We should never have made her marry him. I said all along it was wrong. I pleaded with them not to do it, but I was overruled.'

'By whom?'

'Everyone. My husband, Sir Robert and Lady Manning.'

'Sir Robert?'

'Everyone obeyed Sir Robert in those days, even my husband – especially my husband. And Margaret would never have dared defy her father.'

'Why Albert Storey? He wasn't Lucy's real father, was he?'

'No. He worked on the estate. He had been wounded and, according to Sir Robert, wasn't up to the heavy work. He was a bit of a rebel too, making the others discontented. I never liked him . . .'

'Couldn't you have defied your husband?'

'I had sworn to love, honour and obey. It is not a vow to be taken lightly.'

Amy let that pass. 'Lucy had a rough time with Mr Storey after her mother left until he threw her out just before the war. He told her she wasn't his daughter and he wanted to marry again.'

'Margaret's dead? But you said—'

'We don't know, Mrs Falconer. That's what I'm trying to find out.'

'I haven't seen her since the day she married. Sir Robert paid for her to go into a nursing home to have her child and found a job for Albert Storey on the railways. They never came back here. My husband washed his hands of her, you see. He said he had no daughter. He was as hard and unforgiving as Sir Robert and him a clergyman! Whenever anyone asked me how Margaret was getting on, I pretended I had heard from her and she was well.'

'Didn't she write?'

'Yes, but I didn't know it at the time. I found the letters after my husband died two years back. He had kept them from me unopened, but for some reason hadn't seen fit to destroy them. I have often wondered if he meant me to find them after he'd gone. She must have thought I didn't care.'

'How did you persuade Bert Storey to marry her? He knew the child was not his.'

'With money. Sir Robert paid him a lump sum to get them started and my husband settled a generous monthly allowance on him which was to end when the child turned sixteen. It was all done through the bank, he said. He didn't want to know where they were living, so I never knew. After he died, I thought of trying to find her, but . . .' She shrugged her shoulders. 'The letters stopped when they left Eccles Road. I hadn't replied to any of them and she must have given up. The trail had gone cold. I told myself it was meant to be. But I grieved, I really did, and I felt ashamed that I had done nothing to help my own child. I doubted I would be forgiven.'

'I'm sure that's not true.' The mystery was clearer now, but there were still unanswered questions; where did Mrs Storey go when she left Nayton, if not home to her mother? 'Did Mrs Storey have other relatives or friends she could have gone to stay with?'

'I have a sister who lives in Lancashire, but I'm sure if Margaret went there, Barbara would have told me. As for friends, I don't know. Only people in the village and old school friends. Goodness knows where they are now.' She picked up her glass, saw it was empty and put it down again. 'This has been such a shock after all these years. I can't get over it.'

'Would you like me to make you a cup of tea?'

'Do you mind? I'm feeling decidedly wobbly. The kitchen is through there.' She nodded towards a door. 'You'll find the tea caddy in a cupboard beside the gas stove and the milk on the floor of the larder. Cups and saucers on the dresser. I don't take sugar but it you want some there's a bowl on the shelf in the larder.'

Amy easily found everything and was soon back in the sitting room with two cups of tea on a tray which she put on the dining table. 'I hope it's to your liking,' she said, handing one to Mrs Falconer.

She took a sip. 'Just right, thank you. Sit down and drink yours and tell me all about Lucy. Is she like her mother?'

'I was only a child when Mrs Storey disappeared, so I don't remember her very well, but everyone says Lucy has the same gentle personality. She is beautiful in a serene kind of way, with dark honey-coloured hair and lovely expressive eyes. We always said she was a cut above Bert Storey, which must have been down to her mother's influence.'

'If my maths serves me, Lucy was sixteen in 1936,' Mrs Falconer said thoughtfully. 'But you say Bert Storey didn't throw her out until 1939. I wonder why?'

'I suppose it was because she worked hard for her keep, looking after him and manning the crossing gates,' Amy said. 'Then when he met his new lady friend, he didn't need her anymore. Or maybe the lady objected to having her around.'

'Poor child. If only I'd known . . .'

'She is going to marry my half-brother, Jack. He adores her, we all do, they have a little son.'

'Oh, not again!'

'The difference is, Mrs Falconer, that my brother has not abrogated his responsibilities; he is going to marry her as soon as he has leave.'

'Graham would have married Margaret.'

'Graham?'

'Graham Manning, Sir Robert's son. He was Lucy's real father, but he died that summer. He was gassed, you see, and never properly recovered. It didn't make any difference to Margaret. She had loved him ever since they were children and played together with his cousins and she was convinced he would get better, if only they could get away from his father's dominance. She told me they had been planning how to do it . . .' She stopped to take several gulps of tea. 'Sir Robert said that at least with his son's death, he was saved the disgrace of a bastard in the family. Hard-hearted man, all he could think of was the good name of the family. And look what happened to it – he died and so did his wife and there were no other offspring. We are all turned to dust in the end, both high and low.'

'Yes. I am thankful my father isn't a bit like that.'

'It's funny how things turn out, isn't it? Margaret wasn't considered good enough to be a Manning and now her daughter is going to be a de Lacey and that's far more exalted.'

Amy smiled. 'My mother is going to arrange the wedding. If we can't find Lucy's mother, then I'm sure she would love to have her grandmother there. Would you come?'

'I don't know. I'm not sure. It's been so long since Margaret left and . . .' Her voice trailed off.

'I understand. Would you like Lucy to come and visit you first, to make your acquaintance? You must have a lot to talk about.'

Mrs Falconer took a long time considering this, while Amy waited. 'Would she come?' she asked at last.

'I'm sure she would.'

'Then, yes, bring her.'

Amy set off back to Nayton elated. She hadn't found the long-lost Margaret, but she had found a grandmother for Lucy.

Frank pulled the switch to set the signals at go and looked out of the box for the approaching train. He was disgruntled and had half a mind to enlist. He didn't have to, being in a reserved occupation, but life in Nayton was boring, especially since his ma had died the year before. He missed her more than he would have expected. He missed her constant complaining and her nagging him to find a wife. 'I'll need someone to look after me soon,' she had said over and over again. 'I can't see you bathing and feeding your old mother.'

He couldn't see it either, but in the end, it hadn't been

necessary. She had had a stroke from which she never recovered. He was left to fend for himself. Molly was still married to Bert Storey and hadn't done a thing about leaving him. She wasn't half as much fun as she had been in the beginning. She only used him to satisfy her lust, which had been great at first, but was beginning to pall. And she was forever grumbling about her husband and the things he said and did. It was as if grumbling was her lifeblood and she couldn't do without it; recently she had started grumbling at him, nearly as bad as his mother, she was. And seeing the delectable Lucy about the village again inflamed him. She was no better than she should be, what with wheeling that sprog about in that posh pushchair just as if she owned the place. She had fallen on her feet and no mistake. One day, if and when Jack succeeded his father, she might become Lady de Lacey and look down her nose at him. It made him see red. Yes, he'd join up. He might find a wife to his liking somewhere else. He might become a hero. He liked the idea of that.

He heard the distant train. It was a military freight train, loaded with guns and ammunition, he knew that because everyone along the line was forewarned because of the danger. He'd seen dozens go through and had become quite blasé about them. The more the merrier, he told himself, let the Hun have it. Yes, tomorrow he'd go into Swaffham and join up.

The train came into view around the bend. It was a long one and he couldn't see the end of it. And then he noticed the first wagon was on fire. Flames licked at the tarpaulin that covered it. Frank didn't stop to think. He slammed the points shut to prevent it entering the station and waved to the driver to stop, then he grabbed a fire extinguisher and skittled down the steps to the engine. 'You're on fire,' he shouted, climbing up and squirting the extinguisher into the burning truck; it hissed but made no difference. 'Reverse down the siding.'

The driver looked back and saw the flames. He jumped down and fled in the direction of the station, passing Bert on the way, who had come to see what was going on. 'Get back!' Frank yelled at him, while putting the engine into reverse. 'Go and alert everyone. I'll try and get it down the siding before it blows the whole village up.'

Slowly the train began to move. The flames were higher now, the tarpaulin gone. 'I reckon it caught a spark from the engine,' Frank said to the fireman as they worked. 'You'd think they'd have more sense . . .' He paused as the train hit the buffers at the end of the siding. 'Better bale out.'

The explosion shook the village. The ground heaved and all the windows at the station, and those in every house within half a mile, were shattered. Tiles slid off roofs and crashed on the ground. Trees lost their leaves which swirled upwards and were carried away on the blast. It was followed by more bangs, one after the other.

At Nayton Manor they heard it and felt it. 'What was that?' Lucy asked, grabbing Peter and hugging him to her, remembering the bomb that had nearly killed them.

The children, who had been playing in the garden, ran indoors and rushed up to Annelise, who gathered them round her, trying to calm them, though she was shaking herself and worried about Charles who was outside somewhere.

'Was it a bomb?' Bernard asked her.

'It might have been.' She put her arms round Cecily, who was crying. 'It certainly sounded like it.'

'Or a plane crash,' Raymond suggested.

But they had heard no aeroplanes, either friend or foe. The explosion seemed to come from nowhere.

Bernard, the most intrepid of them, went upstairs to look out of his bedroom window. He was soon back. 'There's a huge fire,' he said, eyes alight with excitement. 'You can see it above the trees. The flames are shooting into the sky. It looks as though the whole wood is burning.'

They trooped upstairs to see for themselves. Huge clouds of black smoke, licked by orange flames, reached skywards above the trees. And every now and again they heard another smaller explosion. They heard the sound of fire-engine bells as they stood there. Lucy took Peter downstairs and sat on the bottom step hugging him. It reminded her too much of being bombed out. She had nearly died, might have done, if Amy had not insisted she was under the rubble and might still be alive. Were there people buried in ruins in Nayton? Was anyone trying to get them out?

Charles came in the front door. He looked dishevelled but not hurt. 'Is everyone safe?' he asked her.

'Yes, they are upstairs watching from Bernard's bedroom window. Was it a bomb?'

'No, an ammunition train.' He ran upstairs to join his wife. Lucy followed to hear what he had to say.

'Oh, Charles,' Annelise said, disengaging herself from Cecily and going to touch his arm. 'Are you all right? I've been so worried. I didn't know where you were.'

'I was in the church talking to the rector. I'm supposed to be reading the lesson tomorrow.'

'Do you know what happened?'

'An ammunition train approached the station with one of its trucks on fire, the engine driver told us. Frank Lambert switched the points so it couldn't get into the station and then tried putting it out. He backed it down the old siding. There were a few people on the platform who witnessed it but they dived for cover when the first truck went up. It's as well they did because that was a small one compared to the one that followed. The whole train blew up.'

'How many casualties?' Annelise asked.

'Frank Lambert and the fireman. Bert Storey has been badly injured and not expected to live. I'm sorry, Lucy. I know you didn't get on but . . .' He paused. 'A few people have cuts and bruises from flying glass and bits of wood, but no other deaths. Lambert must take the credit for that. But for him the whole village would have become an inferno. As it is, I don't think there will be much left of the wood. At least it sheltered the Manor from the blast.'

'Can I do anything to help?'

'No, best stay indoors, all of you, and keep the windows shut, until the fire is put out and the smoke stops drifting.'

'I wonder where Amy is,' Annelise said. 'She won't be able to get home.'

* * *

The train had stopped soon after they left Swaffham and the passengers had been sitting in it for hours. No one knew why it had come to a halt; rumours abounded. There had been an air raid and the line had been bombed, there were those who swore they had heard an explosion; someone had been killed crossing the line; the train had run out of coal; there was a spy on board and the train was being searched for him, but there was no sign of any searchers, no sign of any railway employees either. Had they been deserted? No trains passed going in the opposite direction which was held to be significant. Several of the passengers had jumped out and were walking up and down the line.

Amy had been looking forward to being back home and telling Lucy and her parents her exciting news, but here she was stuck less than ten miles from home. Nayton was the next station along the line and if something had happened there to keep a train motionless for hours, then it must be something bad. It worried her. If only there was a habitation with a telephone nearby she could ring home and find out, and though there were telephone lines strung along the line as far as the eye could see, there was no way of making use of them. She was debating whether to try and walk when the guard made his way from carriage to carriage.

He had walked back to Swaffham, he told everyone, and tried to telephone Nayton station to find out why the signals were against them, but the lines were down. He had been instructed to escort the passengers back along the line to the road bridge where buses were being sent to pick them up and take them back to Swaffham.

There was a hue and cry over this, especially from two American airmen who were due back on their base at Nayton that evening and would be in trouble if they didn't arrive on time. 'I reckon we could make it across the fields,' one of them said. 'Count us out.'

'Me too,' Amy said. 'I live in Nayton. I know the way.'

'Then we'll follow you,' the airman said, hoisting his rucksack on his shoulder.

All three clambered down and set off along the track in the direction of Nayton, leaving everyone else to go in the opposite direction.

'I'm John Housman,' the taller of the two said. He had dark hair, soft amber eyes and a ready smile. He wore a sergeant's stripes on his arm. 'This is Gerry Bartrum.'

'My name is Amy de Lacey.'

'Nice name,' Gerry commented. He was shorter and broader than John and he had a crooked nose.

'Isn't that the name of the family at Nayton Manor?' John asked.

'Yes, that's where I live. My father is Lord de Lacey.'

'Oh, my, a real live aristocrat.'

She laughed. ''Fraid so.'

They had come to an unmanned level crossing. With Lucy leading the way, they left the line and struck off up a narrow country road, hardly wide enough for a single car. On either side were tall hedges, enclosing fields. They kept up a lively conversation as they walked and the miles didn't seem too long. It was only when they reached the airbase they found out what had happened. Nayton station was closed while the line was checked and the damage at the station cleared up. The telephone lines were down and there had been a tremendous fire in the woods surrounding the Manor which still smouldered. They weren't sure how many casualties there had been. Amy, more anxious than ever, was offered a lift home in a jeep and that was how she finally arrived. It was nearly midnight. Everyone had gone to bed. Amy let herself in and crept upstairs.

'Amy is that you?' Her mother came out on the landing in a dressing gown. She had evidently been listening for her.

'Yes, Mama. Safe and sound. Is everyone all right?'

'We are, but Frank Lambert is dead and Bert Storey not expected to live.'

'No? Oh, my goodness. Was it the explosion?'

'Yes. I'll tell you about it in the morning. Do you want a hot drink?'

'No thanks, I had one at the American base.'

'What were you doing there?'

'They brought me home after we were stranded.'

'Go to bed, then.' Annelise kissed Amy's cheek. 'Goodnight, darling. We'll talk in the morning.'

Chapter Sixteen

Bernard was first up the next morning and was out of the house before anyone else was awake. He wanted to see the damage for himself. He went down through the kitchen garden where the greenhouses had lost all their glass, crossed the paddock, kicking at charred remnants of he knew not what as he went, then down the estate road and into the wood. There was an acrid smell that caught in his throat and made him want to cough. The belt of trees came to an end and now all around him were blackened stumps and the ground was covered in wet black ash. The old cottage, the tryst of lovers, had gone, there was nothing left of it, not even one brick standing on another. He stood and stared, his mouth open in amazement. He had seen pictures of bomb damage in the newspapers, but it had given him no idea what devastation really looked like.

A few yards on he came to what had once been the railway siding. Blackened twisted metal pointed skywards. Everywhere were the scattered remains of what had once been a train, some of it huge lumps, some only tiny fragments. The trees closest to the line had been torn up, their roots exposed. Someone, the police or the army perhaps, had enclosed the site with posts and a rope and a sign saying, 'Danger. Keep out.' He ducked under the rope and walked warily forward. There was a hole in the ground filled with rubble as if the earth had heaved itself upwards and then subsided in on itself. He was awestruck.

And then he saw something else. A bony hand sticking out of the soil; a skeleton's hand. He took a stick and prodded at it. A skull came to light; it seemed to be grinning at him. He turned and fled and he didn't stop running until he reached the house and burst into the kitchen where Mrs Baxter was busy preparing breakfast.

'Where've you been?' she demanded. 'You're making black marks all over my clean floor.'

'There's a skeleton,' he said, gasping for breath. 'The other side of the wood, where the train blew up. I saw its hand and its head and its teeth.'

He didn't wait to hear her reply, but dashed through the kitchen in search of Lord de Lacey.

Charles, who had always been an early riser, was coming down the stairs for his breakfast. Bernard repeated what he had told Mrs Baxter.

'Calm down,' Charles said, taking the boy by the shoulders. 'Tell me slowly.'

Bernard said it again. 'It was buried in the earth by the hole,' he said.

'Perhaps someone was walking in the woods when the train blew up. I hadn't thought of that. We must find out who it was. Will you take me and show me?'

Bernard had regained some of his courage, and with Lord de Lacey beside him, led the way.

It was immediately apparent to Charles that the skeleton was not new. Whoever it was had not died as a result of the explosion; he or she had been dead long before that. 'Run and tell Mr Bennett to call the police,' he said. 'And ask Mr Jones to come here at once. We'll have to put a guard on it, until it's taken away.'

It was impossible to keep a find like that secret and the discovery of the skeleton was the talking point of the village and there was much speculation as to who it could be. No one appeared to be missing. A post-mortem established that the body was that of a woman in her late twenties or early thirties and that she had died as a result of a blow to the head with a blunt instrument. It had become a murder investigation and everyone in the village was being questioned.

'She need not necessarily have come from the village,' Charles said, after the police sergeant had left them. They were all reeling from the revelation. 'She could have been killed elsewhere and brought to the wood because it was a good place to hide a body. If it hadn't been for the explosion, it never would have been found.'

'How long had it been there?' Lucy asked. She had been

overjoyed when Amy told her that her grandmother was alive and wanted to see her, but disappointed that no one knew anything of her mother.

'Years, so I was told,' he said. 'Too long for the body to be identified.'

'I think,' Lucy said thoughtfully. 'It might be my mother.'

'Oh, my dear girl,' Annelise said, putting her arms round her. 'Do you really think so?'

'Pa often lost his temper and hit her. Perhaps . . .' Her voice trailed off as she pictured the scene. It didn't need much imagination.

'I'd better go after the sergeant and see what he has to say,' Charles said and left the room.

Two days later they were told that Bert Storey, at death's door, had confessed to killing his wife with a poker in a fit of temper and getting Frank Lambert to help him carry the body into the wood and bury it. The news was broken to Lucy by Lord de Lacey.

'I'm sorry, Lucy,' he said gently. 'This must be a terrible blow to you.'

'It is and it isn't,' she said. She was quiet, but not distraught so much as numb. 'When I think back, it becomes obvious. No one ever saw my mother alive after Pa said she left and he refused to have her searched for. She was a loving mother. She didn't take me with her because she never left.'

'What do you want to do about it? Do you want a funeral? We could arrange one, if you like. That way you can say goodbye to her properly.'

'Yes, please. I wonder how this will affect my grandmother? I was going to see her the day after tomorrow, it's all been arranged. I had hoped it would be a happy time, but now . . . Do you think I ought to postpone it?'

'No, she will have to be told and it would be better coming from you. And you will have such a lot to tell each other.'

'I must write to Jack. Do you think he could get some leave for the funeral?'

'I'm sure he'll try.'

Jack, whose squadron had moved from Newmarket to Tempsford, knew about the explosion and the loss of life; it was in all the newspapers. Frank Lambert was a hero, saving the village of Nayton from total destruction, and everyone said he deserved a medal. It just went to show, Jack thought on reading it, that even the most unpleasant character could have some good in him. But there were also reports of a murder. Funny that, Bernard had been right about Bert Storey, though he had the victim wrong. Poor Lucy, it was hard to imagine how she must be feeling. He had always said she was of gentle stock and he had been proved right. Not that it made a blind bit of difference to him; Lucy was Lucy and that was all that mattered. At least now she knew the truth, not only about what happened to her mother, but what had gone before.

He had had a long letter from her, telling him about the explosion and the discovery of the body and meeting her grandmother for the first time. 'She is exactly how I remember my mother,' she had written. 'We got on like a house on fire and she adores Peter. We are going to have a funeral for my mother and Lady de Lacey has invited her to come and stay. I hope the press leave us alone for that. Darling Jack, I love you dearly and always will, but I can't help wondering if all this nastiness will make a difference to how you feel about me . . .'

He started to write a reply, but screwed it up and instead applied for leave on compassionate grounds and it was granted.

The arrival of Jack seemed to open the dam behind Lucy's eyes and she flew into his arms and burst into tears. He held her close, letting her cry. 'Shush, sweetheart,' he said, kissing the top of her head. 'It's all right. Everything is going to be all right. Come and sit down in the drawing room and tell me all about it.' He put his arm about her and took her to sit beside him on the sofa. He gave her his handkerchief. 'Talk when you're ready.'

She stopped crying, mopped her eyes and gave him a watery smile. 'Silly me.'

'No, you are not silly. You are you and I wouldn't have you any other way.'

'The funeral is tomorrow. You will come, won't you?'

'Of course. That's why I'm here, to be beside you.'

'Pa has already been buried in Swaffham. I couldn't bring myself to go.'

'That's hardly surprising after what he did.'

'He nearly got away with it.'

'Don't think about it. Think about the good things. You have a grandmother, and perhaps there are other relatives you never knew about. And there's our wedding. You are looking forward to that, aren't you?'

'Oh, Jack, need you ask? It's all I've ever dreamt of. We'll have to wait for all the fuss to die down, though. I don't want it spoilt by gossip and nosy newspaper reporters. They've hardly left me alone. I've been doing my best to protect Peter, and your father kept the press at bay while he was here, but he had to go back to London.'

'You hold your head up, sweetheart, and don't mind them. The gossip and the press interest will soon die down and it will be yesterday's news. There's a war to be won, after all.'

Lucy wanted the funeral to be a private affair, but the newspapers had other ideas. Their reporters and cameramen were there in force. If Jack had not been beside her on one side and her new-found grandmother on the other, Lady de Lacey in front and Amy behind shielding her, she didn't know how she would have coped. All the children had been left at the Manor under the watchful eye of Annie – even Bernard, who had been rather subdued since finding the body.

The service followed the prayer book order. There was no eulogy; it didn't seem appropriate and no one would have known what to say. Margaret Storey was laid to rest, the congregation dispersed and the press departed, disappointed that there had been no story, nothing worth reporting. They went back to dispensing news of the war, or such of it as they were allowed to print.

Justine recovered slowly and by early autumn was strong enough to help on the farm and take over some of Elizabeth's tasks. She knew the mountains and the forest even better than Elizabeth and would often make her way up there with provisions for the secret army. She was known in the village but no one thought it strange that she should prefer to live with her parents in the unoccupied zone rather than under the yoke of the Nazis in Paris. They knew nothing of her forged identity and would not have turned a hair if they had. Fortunately, there were few German sympathisers in the village and they were mostly those, like the hoteliers, who depended on German soldiers on leave to provide them with a living. But things were about to change.

The Allies invaded French North Africa, intending to clear the continent of German and Vichy troops. They needed to make the Mediterranean safe for Allied shipping and prepare for the invasion of southern France. It was something the Resistance forces on the mainland fully expected to happen the following year and they stepped up their preparations. Roger had a strong fighting force in the forests above Dransville, made up, for the most part, of men taking to the mountain forests to avoid *service du travail obligatoire*, dreamt up by Vichy to send workers to Germany to help with their war effort. They had become known as *refracteurs*. They had been sent some arms and ammunition from London, though to Roger's mind, not nearly enough.

The Vichy forces in North Africa were overcome by Free French forces and changed sides, which would have been good news indeed, if it had not alarmed the German command who, sensing the danger from the south, decided to occupy the whole of France. Vichy put up no resistance and the *Zone Libre* was no more.

The effect on Dransville was a little slower in making itself felt, but they all knew life was going to become even more difficult. Rules and regulations, which might have become lax, were reinforced and new ones issued every day. The population grumbled but defiance was cruelly punished and many more men were expected to register for forced labour and fled to join those in the mountain forests. It would not be long before the Germans decided to flush them out and Elizabeth was hardly surprised when Hans warned her that a force of German troops and Vichy Milice were on their way.

Roger had been up there with the men for the last two days and Justine had left that morning loaded with a heavy rucksack of food and warm clothing for them. Winter was on its way and there had been snow on the higher ground, but none yet in Dransville itself. In a week or so, there would be more and then they would need skis or snowshoes to get about. The Germans knew this and, realising they were no match for mountain men under those conditions, were determined to put an end to that particular resistance while the weather was in their favour.

'I'll have to go and warn them,' she told her grandparents.

They were worried to death. Not only was Justine up there, but so were Henri and Philippe and now Lisabette seemed determined to join them. The war had well and truly come to Haute Savoie. 'Wrap up warm,' was all Grandmère could find to say, giving her a hug.

It was a long walk but Elizabeth knew the short cuts to where the men were hiding in the deepest, most impenetrable part of the forest. She was spotted by a lookout who came forward to greet her. It was her cousin Philippe. He was roughly dressed and was carrying a rifle, one of those dropped by the SOE.

'Lisabette, what are you doing here?'

She was breathless from her hasty climb and could hardly get the words out. He took her into the camp where Roger was supervising training. He hugged her. 'Is something wrong at the farm?'

'No, everyone is OK. Hans came to warn me, there are hundreds of German and Vichy troops on their way here.'

'They have to find us first.'

'I believe someone betrayed your whereabouts. In any case, with so many of you up here, it wouldn't be difficult to find you.'

'We'll be ready.' He turned and issued orders. Everyone scrambled to obey.

'You're going to fight it out?'

'Of course.'

Philippe, who had gone back to his lookout post, returned half an hour later. 'The mountain is swarming with troops.'

'Right. We're ready for them.' Then to Elizabeth, 'You stay here with Justine.' And then he was gone, along with his men. The two women were left in the deserted camp.

It was not long before they heard firing. 'I wish there was something I could do to help,' Elizabeth said.

'There will be casualties,' Justine said. 'The best we can do is to be prepared for them. There are first-aid supplies somewhere here.' She went into a sort of cave left from old mine workings, where food and ammunition were stored. The ammunition was gone and most of the food, but Justine found a large box marked with a red cross. 'Let's see what we've got here.'

'You are very calm.'

'I've learnt to be. It's what the Boche most hate, someone who can't be ruffled.'

'You never said much about the time you were in prison.'

'I didn't want to upset Papa and Maman. Besides, it's not something I want to remember. Trouble is, it's hard to forget; it's etched on your soul and becomes part of you. I don't know how much longer I would have lasted if Max and Roger, and Giles too, hadn't rescued me. Poor Giles, he was executed, you know, someone betrayed him. We found out just before we left. I worry about Max, it could so easily happen to him.'

The firing was getting nearer and more intense; it sounded as if the enemy were closing in. There were shouts and groans, not too far away. The girls wondered whether to stay or leave. They could climb higher into the mountains, find somewhere else to hide but were reluctant to desert the men who might need them.

Henri staggered into the camp. 'Philippe is dead. The snow is littered with dead and wounded . . .'

'Roger?' Elizabeth asked.

'Don't know. He was in the thick of it. We've got to get out of here. I'm for the Swiss border. You ought to come too.'

'No,' Elizabeth said. 'Not while I don't know what's happened to Roger.'

'He might have been taken prisoner. The Germans are herding them back to the town. They're jubilant.'

'What happened?'

'We were outnumbered and outgunned. If we had had machine guns and mortars we would have won the day.' He hugged both girls. 'I'll be back. Come the spring, I'll be back. Give my love to my mother and father and Mamie and Papie.'

They watched him set off, wondering if he would make it safely across the border. 'I've got to look for Roger,' Elizabeth said.

'Later. We don't know if all the Germans have left.'

They stayed hidden all night, huddled together for warmth, not sleeping, not talking either. A few survivors drifted into the camp and followed in the wake of Henri but they suspected that others who had escaped the round-up had scattered, perhaps gone back to their homes.

At dawn, they stirred their cramped limbs and set off through the trees in the direction of the valley. It was snowing and the bodies that lay scattered were being slowly covered. Elizabeth ran from one to the next. Some of them were young men she had known, some were strangers. Roger was not among them.

'He may have got away,' Justine said. 'You know his luck.'

'Luck runs out,' Elizabeth said.

'We'd better get a move on. The Boche will be back to collect the bodies as soon as the light strengthens.'

Elizabeth was reluctant to abandon the search, but as nothing was moving on the slopes, she followed Justine.

They dare not go direct to the farm but took a route to Annecy, relying on Alphonse to give them a lift home. If anyone questioned them, they had been visiting friends and stayed the night when they heard the firing. Elizabeth was subdued. There was nothing in her head but Roger. She imagined him wounded and lying in the snow, unable to move, freezing to death; every step was taking her away from him. If he didn't turn up, she would have to go back and search for him.

The slaughterhouse was living up to its name. It was crowded with wounded men who had been brought down the mountain by their comrades. Alphonse was risking his life to shelter them. He had fetched a trustworthy doctor, so they could be treated and, if not too badly hurt, dispersed to their homes or safe houses. He was glad to see Justine and Elizabeth.

'Thank God you are safe,' he said. 'Dirk is out of his wits worrying about you.'

'You mean he's here?' Elizabeth queried.

'Yes. He's taken a bullet in the leg. His comrades carried him here. You'll find him over there.' He jerked his head in the direction of the injured men who were lying, wrapped in blankets on the concrete floor.

Elizabeth ran to Roger and fell on her knees beside him. 'Thank God, you are alive,' she said, taking his hand. 'How badly are you hurt?'

'I'll mend. That is, if the Hun doesn't get me first.'

'Don't say that.' She tried to rub some warmth into his hands which were icy cold. 'We'll get you home and look after you.'

'It was a disaster, Lizzie, a total disaster. It's my fault. All those men dead, all these . . .' he waved a hand at his wounded comrades '. . . and dozens more taken prisoner. I doubt they will be treated fairly.'

'You mustn't blame yourself. The men wanted to be there.'

'I endangered you too. If I'd gone home that first time, you would not have become involved. I'll never forgive myself.'

'I was already involved, you know that. I would have done what I did even if you had not been around, so no more of that. Has the doctor said you can be moved?'

'Yes, but I can't go under my own steam, I'm afraid.'

She found Alphonse, who had arranged a herd of cows in the front of the abattoir, pretending he was going to be busy slaughtering them. They were milling about, blocking the entrance. 'May I borrow your pony and trap to take Dirk home?'

'Yes, but bring it straight back. I'm going to need it.'

They were going to put him on the floor of the trap and cover him with a blanket but there were so many troops and police searching everything that moved, they decided it would be better if he sat beside them openly. If they were stopped he had his false identity papers on him and a ready reason why they had been to Annecy. They just had to pray no one would look under the blanket that covered his legs. It was a painful journey for him and he winced whenever the trap went over a bump, but he bore it stoically.

But their troubles were far from over. As soon as they stopped outside the farmhouse, they knew something was wrong. The doctor's pony was tethered outside and all the curtains were drawn. Justine scrambled down almost before they stopped and dashed into the house. Elizabeth was torn between following her and helping Roger. But she couldn't get him out on her own.

'Go on,' he said. 'I'll be OK here for a few minutes.'

She found Justine comforting her mother in the kitchen. 'It's Papa,' she said. 'He's had another stroke.'

'Oh, no, and he was so much better.'

'It was all that shooting,' Marie said between sobs. 'Germans all over the place and everyone gone into the hills, the boys and you too. He was frightened. And then they came and told us Philippe was dead and Henri had disappeared, probably dead too. He couldn't take it.'

The doctor came into the room. All three women looked at him expectantly. 'I'm sorry,' he said. 'I couldn't save him.'

Elizabeth couldn't take it in. Her loving Papie gone, gone for ever. It was so unfair. He had never done anyone any harm, not even the hated Boche, but because of them he had died. It wasn't in her nature to hate, but she hated now. And she was angry, too angry to cry. She stood looking at Mamie who was being comforted by a tearful Justine. How would she cope without the man who had been by her side for fifty years and more?

A cry of fury and pain and the sound of a horse neighing suddenly reminded her of Roger and she dashed outside to find him lying on the ground. He had obviously tried to get down by himself. 'You idiot,' she said. 'What on earth did you think you were playing at?' It was easier to be cross than give way to the emotion that threatened to overwhelm her.

'Thought I could make it,' he murmured and promptly passed out.

The doctor helped her to carry him indoors and put him to bed, where he examined the wound and dug out the bullet. 'I won't ask how he got it,' he said, putting a dressing and bandage on the leg. 'But I should find a good hiding place for him if I were you.'

'You won't betray us?'

'No, I won't betray you. Keep the wound clean and change the dressing every day.' He snapped his bag shut and went to take his leave of Madame Clavier. 'I'll send the undertaker up,' he said.

The three women were left to cope as best they could.

* * *

The official French newspapers and Radio Paris were full of the German success. Dransville had suddenly hit the headlines. Max read the details with horror. How much of it was true he could not tell, but even if only half of it was, it must have been terrifying for the civilian population, and that included Justine and Lizzie and Monsieur and Madame Clavier. According to the official report, the terrorists, as they were being called, had sustained heavy casualties, and some sons of the Fatherland had laid down their lives, but they would be avenged. Some of the rebels had escaped into hiding but the population need have no doubt they would be searched out and punished. Anyone found sheltering them would be shot on sight. It did not make happy reading.

'Ask London for instructions,' he told Gilbert when they met as arranged in one of the several safe houses scattered about the city. His network had been responsible for several acts of sabotage recently and his own situation was becoming more precarious. 'They may know more than we do.'

But the SOE in London, who naturally listened to Radio Paris, knew only the official version. Roger's wireless was silent. Max and Gilbert were ordered to make their way to Dransville and report back. This was no more than Max had hoped for and he made rapid preparations to leave.

Travel was harder than ever. Identity papers, travel permits and tickets were scrutinised at every station. Everyone travelling by road, either in gas-fuelled vehicles or on bicycles, was stopped. He arranged a convoluted itinerary, using buses, trains and taxis, each journey of short duration and not in a direct line, the sort a paint and wallpaper salesman might make. He only hoped his credentials would stand up to the scrutiny. Gilbert would follow a little way behind with his case disguised as a doctor's medical equipment.

Roger was recovering slowly, nursed by the patient Elizabeth. The dead had been buried and there had been trials of those captured which had been travesties of justice. The sentences ranged from execution to deportation to Germany for forced labour. Justine had discovered that a few of the *refracteurs* had regrouped and were back in the mountains, including Henri, who could not bring himself to desert his comrades and had come back to die with them if necessary. They were determined to stay hidden until they could be re-formed and rearmed and in the meantime they had to be fed. She was often away for days at a time. Elizabeth went about her tasks on the farm, trying to pretend everything was normal, but nothing was normal.

The little town was swarming with German troops, either billeted there or come to enjoy the skiing. She was in constant fear that one of them would come to the farm and start sniffing around. Roger was in the attic, hidden behind all the junk that her grandparents had hoarded over the years because they didn't like to throw it away, but a determined searcher would soon find him. He was becoming impatient to be out and about, to be doing something positive. 'Have patience,' she told him. 'You are still weak.'

'And so I will be while I lie here doing nothing,' he told her. 'I need exercise to get my muscles working again. We can think up a reason why I limp, can't we? At least I won't look as though I have been dodging my STO.' He reached for her hand and drew her down to sit on the side of his narrow camp bed. 'Lizzie, sweetheart, you are looking tired, and is it any wonder, having to nurse me as well as your grandmother? Not to mention keeping the farm running. I could help.'

Elizabeth was feeling more than tired, she was exhausted. It was not only the physical side of running around after two invalids, the milking, the butter and cheese making, the coping with shortages of food for themselves and winter fodder for the animals, but the mental and emotional strain. She was worried about her grandmother too. The death of her husband and grandson had hit her hard and after the funerals she had seemed to fold in on herself. She hardly spoke and had to be coaxed to eat at all and then she only pecked at her food.

'Very well, if you think you can get down the stairs.'

He grinned. 'Dirk Vanveldt rides again.'

The fact that he was up and about did make a difference and he was always so cheerful and buoyed everyone up, even her grandmother who managed a wan smile for his jokes. But Elizabeth was beginning to wonder how it was all going to end. Would they ever get back to England and home? How she longed for it. Sometimes she dreamt of Nayton and her parents. Had they changed? She couldn't imagine that ever happening. Was the village the same as it always had been, a haven of peace, or had that been caught up in the war like everything else? And Jack and Amy, what were they doing? Since that short radio message over a year before, there had been no news of them, though she listened to the BBC whenever she could.

One Sunday in November they heard the church bells of Westminster Abbey pealing out over the air waves. They were celebrating the Allied victory at El Alamein and Churchill's words were relayed to them. 'This is not the end. It is not even the beginning of the end. But it is, perhaps, the end of the beginning.' It gave hope to those struggling under the occupation.

The arrival of Max sent them all into a flap. He came at dead of night. At first she thought it was the Gestapo come to search the place and, throwing on a dressing gown, went to wake Roger. 'There's someone at the door.'

'Then go and let them in, but take your time. Don't rush.' His coolness calmed her. She left him throwing on some clothes and went to open the door.

'It's ruddy cold out here,' Max said.

'Max!' She took his arm and pulled him inside. He was followed by another man she had not seen before.

'This is Gilbert,' Max said. 'Gilbert, this is Elizabeth and this—' He didn't finish. Justine had come into the kitchen and thrown herself into his arms. She was followed by Roger and for a moment there was pandemonium as everyone started talking at once.

They calmed down eventually and sat round the kitchen table, nursing mugs of hot cocoa while their tales were told, and by the time they finished it was nearly dawn. Justine took Max off somewhere to be alone with him, Elizabeth and Roger went to milk the cows and Gilbert went up to the attic to set up his wireless.

In London, Charles attended a meeting where they discussed the situation. They were all concerned that Antoine had been on the ground too long and ought to be replaced. They were even more sure when Gilbert came on air and gave them a graphic and necessarily brief account of the situation in Dransville. It was not good.

'Fetch them out,' Buckmaster said. 'All of them. Can we get a plane in?'

Vera volunteered to find out and the meeting dispersed. With nothing he could do, Charles went home for the weekend, but he dare not tell Annelise what he had learnt. The deception lay heavily on his conscience. He consoled himself with the pleasure he would have telling her when everyone was safely back on home soil. Annelise was in a happy mood. The gossip had died down, Lucy was delighted with her grandmother, who had gone home to Waterbury but would return for the wedding. Peter was toddling about everywhere and getting into mischief but everyone adored the little scrap. And Bernard had said he didn't want to be a detective after all, not if he was going to have to deal with gruesome remains.

When Charles went back to Baker Street on Monday, he learnt that Vera had confirmed there was a field they could use which was big enough to land a Lysander, but that could only take one passenger, two at a squeeze, and the weather was against them at the moment. Heavy snow in Haute Savoie would make a landing on a makeshift runway extremely hazardous. Charles's heart sank.

'Can they get into Spain?' Buckmaster asked.

'I suppose they could, but it would be risky,' one of the others said. 'Best to wait until the weather clears and we can get an aircraft in.'

'Then what?'

'Take two out at a time.'

'Which two?'

'We'll leave it for them to decide.'

'Well, I'm not going,' Elizabeth said. They were sitting round the kitchen table after supper after hearing the latest transmission. 'Mamie is very frail and needs me. You others go if you want.'

'I'm not leaving without you,' Roger said. 'So you can count me out too.'

'And me,' Justine said. 'I can't leave Maman.'

'And if you think I'm going to leave you three here to cope, you had better think again.' This from Max.

'If you are ordered to, then you won't have any choice, will you?' Roger said.

'And the same goes for you,' Max countered. 'We are not free to do as we like.'

They had expected to be stuck in Dransville until the snow melted, but Pierre, miserable and angry over the loss of his son, was itching to do something, anything which might hurt the Boche and he had solved the problem for them. He had a friend who had vineyards between Mâcon and Lyon where there was no snow and he was prepared to let a plane land on a piece of ground which was lying fallow. He could call on men to prepare the ground, once the date was decided. London had been informed and everything was being arranged for the next full moon. All they had to do was get themselves there. How had yet to be decided.

They had two weeks to wait. But before that could happen, Elizabeth had more heartbreak. Her beloved Mamie caught a chill which turned to pneumonia. She nursed her devotedly, taking turns with Justine. At first they thought she would pull through, but she was old and weakened by all she had been through and the doctor could not obtain the medication she needed. She was slowly slipping away from them and there was nothing they could do.

'I don't mind,' she told them, fighting for breath to speak. 'I'll be with Albert and Philippe where there's no hunger, no cold, no fear. Bless me, child, and let me go.'

In tears, Elizabeth sent for Pierre and Jeanne and the good Father, who gave the old lady the last rites. They watched over her all night, whispering quietly among themselves, taking it in turns to sit and hold her hand, while one or other of the others crept away to make hot drinks, laced with cognac brought out of hiding. Towards dawn, with the sky over the mountains turning to pale pink, Marie Clavier took her last breath.

No one moved. Then Pierre and Justine crossed

themselves and Elizabeth fell on her knees beside the bed and sobbed her heart out. Roger's gentle hand on her shoulder comforted her. 'She is at peace now, darling.'

'I can't believe she's gone. It isn't fair, it really isn't fair. She was so good and brave.'

'Yes, she was, and you must be good and brave too, my love. Come away and let others say their goodbyes.' He helped her to her feet and guided her downstairs where she sat at the kitchen table, too numb to think what to do next. He made her a mug of ersatz coffee, added a good slug of cognac and made her drink it. Then he sat beside her and took her hand and waited while she drank it. 'Better now?'

'Yes.' She gave him a watery smile and got to her feet. 'We had better go and do the milking.'

'That's my brave girl,' he said as he followed her.

Saturday, 12th December, dawned bright but cold. Everything was ready. Mrs Baxter, with the help of nearly everyone in the village who had contributed a little something, had produced a sumptuous buffet for the guests, though she insisted it was nowhere near the standard of pre-war spreads she had put on. There was a cake, of sorts, which contained a lot of carrot and apple, but Mrs Baxter still had a few raisins and sultanas in her store cupboard and they had gone in too. It was impossible to buy icing sugar, so it was not decorated except with white card and flowers, but Lucy assured her it looked lovely. There were flowers too, mostly chrysanthemums, hellebores, a few late roses and lilies

Jones had been nurturing, which was nothing short of miraculous, considering every pane of glass had had to be replaced in the greenhouses.

The order of service and the music had been decided on, Bernard and Edmund had been told not to go away because they must be dressed in their best suits ready to act as ushers and show everyone to their seats in the church. Apart from the villagers, there would not be many guests; it was too difficult for people to leave wartime commitments, and besides, Lucy didn't want a crowd of witnesses to what amounted to the legalising of a union which had already taken place. She sat in front of the mirror in her bedroom in her underclothes and felt sick with worry. Only three hours to go, everything was ready, but there was no bridegroom.

Her pale blue costume hung on a hanger on the door of her wardrobe and beside it on another hanger was a white blouse made of parachute silk. Both had been made by Lady de Lacey's dressmaker. There had been silk enough to make a long dress, but Lucy refused to be married in white. 'It's not right,' she had said. 'And, in any case, Jack will be in uniform.'

But there was no Jack, in uniform or out of it. Lord de Lacey was missing too. What had happened? Her imagination ran the gamut of every possible disaster and then shifted to wondering if Jack had changed his mind and didn't want to marry her after all. How was she going to hold her head up in the village, the silly girl who thought someone like Jack de Lacey would deign to marry her, poor deluded cow. She would have to leave, go away where no one knew her. Tears bubbled in her eyes. She blinked hard, but they wouldn't go away.

'Lucy, what's the matter?' Amy had come into the room. She was to be a bridesmaid and was wearing a light wool dress in a kind of amber colour which should have clashed with her hair, but didn't. Annie was looking after Cecily, who was going to be the other bridesmaid; she was so excited at the prospect they were afraid she would make herself sick. 'Why aren't you dressed?'

'I can't. I really can't.'

'Last-minute nerves.'

'It's not my nerve that has gone.' She rounded on Amy. 'It's Jack's. He's not here, is he?'

'He did say it might be tight. If the train is late . . .'

'If he really wanted to marry me, he'd have been here last night.'

'Bride and groom under the same roof the night before the wedding, dear me, that would never do.'

'It's all very well for you to joke about it.'

'Oh, come on, Lucy, cheer up. If he's missed the train, he's missed the train. Papa isn't here either. I imagine they planned to come down together. The guests will just have to amuse themselves until they arrive.'

'He could have phoned.'

'The lines are still down, or had you forgotten?' The line had been restored to the station, but not as far as the Manor which wasn't considered a priority.

'Oh.'

Annelise, in a deep-rose dress and jacket, joined them; she, too, was concerned. 'I'm going to ask the Reverend to put off the ceremony for an hour or two,' she said. 'The guests can come up here and wait. We'll go back to the church when the men arrive.'

'Do you know what's happened to them?' Amy asked.

'No.'

'If it had been anything bad, we would have heard, wouldn't we?' Lucy asked, groping for reassurance.

'Yes, of course we would. Lucy, please dress and come downstairs. Your grandmother is waiting for you. I've dressed Peter and he needs amusing so he doesn't get dirty again.'

They were all in the drawing room, family, guests and the Reverend Royston, all speculating on the delay, when two taxis drew up on the gravel outside the front door. Out tumbled Lord de Lacey, Jack, Justine, Elizabeth, Max and Roger.

With screams of excitement, everyone ran out to meet them. Lucy flew to Jack who hugged her and kissed her. Annelise rushed to Elizabeth and enveloped her in a bear hug, while tears ran down both faces. Then she turned to Justine and hugged her. 'I can't believe it. Where have you all come from? Why didn't you let us know?'

'We couldn't,' Charles said. 'Besides, I wanted it to be a surprise. I'm sorry we're late. The weather held us up.'

'The weather?' Amy queried.

'Strong winds over France,' Jack said. 'Let's go inside. It's cold out here.'

The rector was waiting in the hall. 'The wedding, My Lord . . .'

'Yes, of course, the wedding. Give us an hour, Rector, will you?'

While Jack dashed upstairs to change, Charles went into the drawing room to apologise to the guests and to invite them to drink champagne to toast the safe return of the prodigals before making their way back to the church. 'The wedding will go ahead as planned,' he told them. He took Annelise by the hand and led her to their bedroom, where he broke the news of her parents' deaths. She wept a little, but pulled herself together so as not to spoil everyone else's enjoyment. Her mourning would come later when she had a chance to talk properly to Justine and Elizabeth.

The ceremony was not the ordeal Lucy expected it to be. Calmed by the presence of Jack at her side, she made her vows in a clear, untroubled voice. All was well in her world. It was not until the last guest had left that the story of the rescue was told. It had been an extraordinarily risky operation, landing two Lysanders on French soil on the same landing field on the same night. Jack had been piloting the second one which brought out Elizabeth and Roger. By that time, their presence was known to the enemy and they had taken off with gunfire on their tail. The rest of the journey home had been plagued by anti-aircraft fire.

'I got such a shock when I realised it was Jack,' Elizabeth said. 'What he did was so brave.'

'Brave, who's talking about brave?' Jack said. He was sitting on a sofa beside Lucy with his arm about her and her head on his shoulder. Secure in his embrace, she was almost asleep. 'You are the brave ones, all four of you. I only had to brace myself for a few hours, you had years of it.'

'I hope Pierre and his helpers managed to get away,' Justine said.

'And Gilbert,' Max added. 'He had to stay behind. He was going into the forest with the secret army. Someone else will be sent out to reorganise the *resistants*.'

'But not you,' Justine said.

'Nor you, Roger.' Elizabeth added.

The two men smiled at each other and said nothing. The war was not over yet and who knew where they would end up?

'Two more weddings to arrange,' Annelise said. She was subdued but no longer tearful. She had accepted that her parents, at least, were at peace. 'Give me a little time, won't you?'

'Yes, but not too long,' Elizabeth said, amid laughter.

ALSO BY MARY NICHOLS

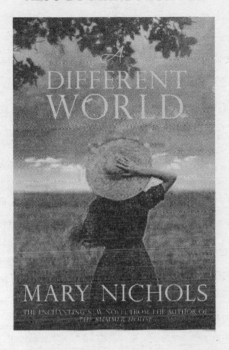

1939. Warsaw, Poland. Pilot Jan Grabowski receives orders that take him to the heart of the escalating conflict. He leaves behind his wife, Rulka, who sees Poland overcome by the Nazis. In constant danger and amid cruel reprisals, she joins the Resistance.

Norfolk. Louise Fairhurst's war is very different. Evacuated with her class of ten-year-olds from London she finds herself acting mother as well as teacher to the children. She has much to do settling city children down in the countryside, and she wonders whether she should have stayed in London until a chance meeting with Jan alters her path...

To discover more great books and to
place an order visit our website at
www.allisonandbusby.com

Don't forget to sign up to our free newsletter at
www. allisonandbusby.com/newsletter
for latest releases, events and exclusive offers

Allison & Busby Books
@AllisonandBusby

You can also call us on
020 7580 1080
for orders, queries
and reading recommendations